D0096885

The zombie apocalypse is unleashed in Z.A. Recht's
PLAGUE OF THE DEAD

"An awesome zombie novel . . . a literal, intelligent thriller."
—David Moody, author of *Hater* and the acclaimed Autumn series

"Hypnotically readable."
—R. Thomas Riley, author of *Through the Glass Darkly*

"The perfect combination of viral thriller and zombie nightmare. . . . Z. A. Recht pulls out all the stops in this action-packed zombie extravaganza."
—Ryan C. Thomas, author of *The Summer I Died*

"One of the most believable zombie stories I've read. . . . There's hardly a moment to catch your breath as Recht deftly moves the narrative in directions that seem quite plausible in today's post-9/11 age."
—R. Thomas Riley

"Fantastic . . . a zombie-fied *Out of the Ashes,* a blend of *28 Days Later* zombies and Romero zombies, with a climax so intense it literally had me shaking."
—Travis Adkins, author of *After Twilight: Walking with the Dead*

"Zombies . . . military . . . global devastation. . . . Z.A. Recht has engineered a virus so infectious even die-hard zombie critics will get down with the sickness."
—D. L. Snell, author of *Roses of Blood on Barbwire Vines*

Survivors is also available as an ebook

"Well-written. . . . Scary. . . . *Plague of the Dead* actually makes you believe that something like this could really happen. . . . I could not put this book down."

—*Read Reviews*

"Every character is believable, the zombies are both hideous and understated, and the action is mile-a-minute fast. . . . Recommended for post-apocalyptic fiction fans, action-adventure lovers, and zombie phreaks from all shambling walks of life."

—*The Alternative*

"Intense and action-packed! Recht aims for the head with this one!"

—Geoff Bough, *Revenant Magazine*

The global zombie takeover grows more terrifying in Z.A. Recht's
THUNDER AND ASHES

"Shamblers, sprinters, and a generous helping of guts, brains, and heart— for those who believe sequels never outshine the original, *Thunder and Ashes* is just the cure."

—D. L. Snell

"Plenty of blood and guts . . . an enjoyable read for zombie fans."

—*Fatally Yours*

"Just when you thought that *Plague of the Dead* could not be bested, along comes the sequel. . . . *Thunder and Ashes* will once again make you turn your lights on."

—J. L. Bourne, author of *Day by Day Armageddon*

"A compelling story told in a captivating voice. . . . Recht writes a raw, brutal style perfect for the story's raw brutality, and it's impossible to read the novel and not get caught up in its characters and their seemingly futile quest. . . . This is no ordinary post-apocalyptic odyssey."

—*Booklist*

"The action is unrelenting, the character interaction is believable, the world-building is intriguing and impressive. . . . Excellent pacing. . . . Tight and engaging. . . . Fans should definitely add *Thunder and Ashes* to their collection."

—*Flames Rising*

"[A] post-apocalyptic zombie treat. . . . Recht's style is cinematic . . . fast paced and thoroughly convincing. . . . Some of the book's finest moments of both theme and action come from shades of both *Seven Samurai* and *The Road Warrior*."

—*Quiet Earth*

"Every bit as good as *Plague of the Dead*. . . . A very entertaining read."
—*The Alternative*

Also by Z.A. Recht

Plague of the Dead

Thunder and Ashes

SURVIVORS

THE MORNINGSTAR PLAGUE

Z.A. RECHT

with Thom Brannan

Gallery Books

New York   London   Toronto   Sydney   New Delhi

Gallery Books
A Division of Simon & Schuster, Inc.
1230 Avenue of the Americas
New York, NY 10020

This book is a work of fiction. Names, characters, places, and incidents either are products of the author's imagination or are used fictitiously. Any resemblance to actual events or locales or persons, living or dead, is entirely coincidental.

Copyright © 2012 by Z.A. Recht

All rights reserved, including the right to reproduce this book or portions thereof in any form whatsoever. For information address Gallery Books Subsidiary Rights Department, 1230 Avenue of the Americas, New York, NY 10020.

First Gallery Books trade paperback edition June 2012

GALLERY BOOKS and colophon are registered trademarks of Simon & Schuster, Inc.

For information about special discounts for bulk purchases, please contact Simon & Schuster Special Sales at 1-866-506-1949 or business@simonandschuster.com.

The Simon & Schuster Speakers Bureau can bring authors to your live event. For more information or to book an event contact the Simon & Schuster Speakers Bureau at 1-866-248-3049 or visit our website at www.simonspeakers.com.

Manufactured in the United States of America

10 9 8 7 6 5 4 3 2 1

Library of Congress Cataloging-in-Publication Data

Recht, Z. A. (Zachary Allan), 1983–2009.
    Survivors : the morningstar strain / Z.A. Recht ; with Thom Brannan.—
1st Gallery Books trade paperback ed.
        p.   cm.
    ISBN 978-1-4516-2882-1 (trade pbk. : alk. paper)—ISBN 978-1-4516-2883-8 (e-book)
    1. Virus diseases—Fiction. 2. Zombies—Fiction. I. Brannan, Thom. II. Title.
    PS3618.E4234S87 2012
    813'.6—dc23   2012000604

ISBN 978-1-4516-2882-1
ISBN 978-1-4516-2883-8 (ebook)

To Z . . . may his memory always be a blessing!

PROLOGUE

Mount Weather
15 June 2007
0930 hrs_

A STIFF BREEZE CAUGHT a smartly flapping American flag flying high above the active compound. Far below the forested ridge of this Appalachian mountain, soldiers and civilians bustled about, performing their duties as though their lives depended on them—as they very well did.

The world as the living had known it was gone. No longer were there jobs to go to, no commutes or taxes or law enforcement. Bills, parent-teacher conferences, concerts, trips to the mall, all a memory.

In peacetime, before the Morningstar pandemic, the secure facility at Mount Weather was meant to serve as a civilian command center in the event of emergency. Just such an emergency had occurred as the Morningstar strain swept the globe. Major cities had long since been abandoned or completely overrun. Now only small, rural towns and isolated, protected bases like Mount Weather persevered. The rest of the planet belonged to the infected; the meek would have to wait their turn for the inheritance.

The human race was now an endangered species.

The infected weren't just sick—they were rabid, openly hostile. They attacked on sight. They hunted in packs, and they were lethal.

And infectious. Anyone bitten or scratched, and the cycle of infection began anew, with the unfortunate victim a walking, talking, sweating, and crying incubation chamber.

But that wasn't the worst of it. Since no antiviruses had any effect, and no one had known about Morningstar long enough to develop a comprehensive defense, the only way to deal with an infected victim was to kill it.

The next stage was a bit more macabre. The corpses of the fallen infected would reanimate, stumbling to their feet and continuing the virus's mission to spread the infection to new hosts. Only a blow to the head by any means necessary would put one down permanently.

The very idea of the dead returning to some semblance of life had sent spasms rippling through the political—not to mention the religious—world. As if the disorder caused by the virus wasn't enough, this new discovery had caused an unknowable number of riots and all-pervasive panic.

Still, some carried on, despite the odds. The fences of Mount Weather had been reinforced, and men and women took turns defending them, toting rifles along in perimeter patrols. When an infected wandered too close, the volunteer marksmen did their duty by putting a round through its head. Often early on, then dwindling to once or twice a day, a shot would ring out, echoing across the compound.

Corpse details wearing full hazmat suits were sent out to collect and dispose of the fallen infected. Several small, ashen, and still smoldering trenches marred the view outside the fences. This was where the bodies were burned. The perimeter guards pulled the collars of their shirts as far as they could over the lower halves of their faces to protect themselves from the stench as they passed.

Armed guards, on duty 24/7, wore down under their grueling

schedules and the tension of being on high alert. The ravenous infected were not the only threats they had to be vigilant against.

What was left of the United States government was at war with itself. Remnants had found figures of authority to gather around, and began to plot and plan against former allies. Old feuds and petty grudges informed most of the movements, but there was one imperative above all: find a cure, and keep it for yourself.

It was a sad, strange cycle of hostility where man fights virus, virus fights man, and man fights man so that he might better fight the virus.

Just like in any war, knowledge, intelligence, and espionage often tipped the scales.

Special Agent Sawyer was in the business of all of these, at the apex.

Tall, broad-chested, and with short brown hair, Sawyer had the look of a classic all-American about him. He carried himself well, with perfect posture and a no-nonsense set to his face. He kept his eyes hidden behind mirrored sunglasses. Months earlier, he would have been wearing a business suit, but in these uncertain times, he took a more pragmatic approach to his clothing. Black BDU pants were bloused over steel-toed boots, and a vest hung over a long-sleeved olive drab T-shirt. He marched more than walked, hands swinging nine to the front, six to the rear.

His destination was an administration center near the heart of the compound. Inside the building was the one man who had the ability to make Sawyer nervous: the Chairman of the Joint Chiefs of Staff.

The Chairman was, for all intents and purposes, the president of the United States. Technically, the real president was still in power, hiding in a bunker farther north. The Joint Chiefs knew his exact location, but found it was better to leave an impotent figurehead in charge than remove him and risk someone more effective taking over.

This encampment followed the Chairman and his promises of a grand future. Specifically, his rallying cry had been to locate a cure for the Morningstar strain.

Sawyer remembered the Chairman's rousing speech on the floor of Congress during an emergency session. It was just charismatic enough to not seem as transparent as it was. That had been in the early days, when the first infections on American soil were still being reported and hardly believed. It all seemed so very long ago.

"Now is not the time to bicker about sealing our borders or deporting the sick," the Chairman had said, pounding his fist on the lectern to enunciate his words. "Now is not the time to play politics, or to discuss the failing of our health care systems. Now is most *certainly* not the time to be talking about terrorist threats or future attacks on our home soil. The problem is *real,* the problem is *growing,* and *we must deal with it now*!"

That had earned the man a standing ovation from half the people in attendance, generally along party lines. The other half hadn't seemed so impressed.

"The damage has already been done. When Pearl Harbor was smothered in smoke and shrapnel, did we discuss fleeing, or closing our borders? No! We acted! We attacked the problem, resolved it, and rebuilt what had been lost. When the British, overwhelmed by the Luftwaffe, cried out to us for assistance, did we shirk our duty and shy away from conflict? Did we turn tail and run in the face of war? No! We acted! We attacked, we routed, we *won*! When thousands were dying of malaria along the Panama Canal, did we ignore their pleas for help? No! We acted! We created a cure! And we can do so again! We need to act swiftly—we need to act *now*—we need to find a cure for this devilish virus and prevent any more death and suffering on the part of the *people of this great nation*!"

The ovation had reached a fever pitch, and grew even louder in intensity when the Chairman was escorted offstage by a pair of Secret Service agents.

Sawyer, who had been watching from the rear of the chamber, felt the Chairman's theory was sound, even if his words rang hollow. He was right. Morningstar wasn't the kind of issue that would be solved with half-assed containment measures or postmortem vaccines. The world needed a *cure.*

That was what the subjective side of his brain told him, anyway. But Sawyer had never had much use for that area of gray matter.

His objective side saw a new power rising, and Sawyer, ever conscious of his own position, threw himself behind it. It was a gamble, but if the Chairman ended up winning this dogfight, Sawyer could very well become one of the true movers and shakers of this brave new world. It certainly wasn't because of the Chairman himself. Sawyer found the man overbearing, pretentious, and entirely too timid when it came to deploying expendable assets. Sawyer no longer had the manpower, equipment, or leeway to act as he needed.

Still, despite the burdensome restrictions laid upon him, Sawyer was doing very well. Months after the initial plague and with the conflict far from over, Sawyer found himself among the highest-ranked operatives of the Second American Civil War.

One side, led by portions of Congress, the Senate, and the president of the United States, was trying feverishly to distribute supplies and reinforcements to those towns that still struggled against the virus. They sent out antiviral medications in the futile hope of slowing the spread of the disease. Sawyer watched in disgust as their efforts crumbled.

Their hearts are in the right place, but their brains certainly aren't. One doesn't change the world with heart. One changes it with force.

The other side, championed by the Chairman of the Joint Chiefs and backed by the remainder of Congress and the Senate, sought a cure for the virus, and were willing to stop at nothing to find it. That sort of ruthless determination was something else Sawyer could identify with. It was someplace he could call home.

They had already staged several successful operations. The Reunited States of America, as they had taken to calling themselves, had sent troops to raid both USAMRIID at Fort Detrick and the laboratories at the Centers for Disease Control in Atlanta for information and specialists. Those researchers who had at first balked at the idea of working for a rebel faction were soon made to see the error of their ways, thanks largely to Sawyer's unique methods of persuasion. The assembled plunder and personnel had been brought together here, at Mount Weather.

All of them were working around the clock in makeshift labs constructed out of ammunition bunkers—and all of them were failing miserably. Day after day, one after another, disappointing and negative reports came through the system. The search for a cure for Morningstar was stillborn.

And that, Sawyer reasoned, was likely the reason he was being called in for an audience with the Chairman.

Mount Weather's buildings were modern, aboveground structures nestled among lush summer trees. They weren't of the sort of architecture one expected to see in a government installation. Mount Weather could pass for a business park, all gleaming steel and glass set in monochromatic facades. Sawyer strode up the paved path and past the whitewashed walls into the largest of the buildings, which had been appropriated for executive offices.

A young woman sat at a receptionist's desk, dressed in neatly ironed clothing and looking prim and proper enough to pass for a librarian; she glanced up as Sawyer approached. She said nothing, but reached to a hands-free module set in her ear and pressed a button. After a moment, she spoke into the receiver. "He's here."

Sawyer expected to hear no response; the woman nodded, clicked off her headset, and pushed herself away from her desk. "The Chairman will see you now. Follow me, please."

Sawyer pulled off his sunglasses and prepared himself. He'd been through this song and dance before. The Chairman got a kick out of acting important. He loved to have people presented to him, as if they were supplicants. It didn't matter. Every man was allowed a vice or two, in Sawyer's opinion. His own personal favorite of the Seven Deadly Sins was Wrath, but if Pride was what got the Chairman off, then more power to him.

The woman escorted Sawyer through a doorway and into the Chairman's private office. It was simple and businesslike, speaking to the character of the man who sat behind the desk. A small table had been set off to one side with a coffee brewer and a pair of used, stained mugs. The one bookshelf was half-empty, but what papers were on display were all on the subject of government and health care. Sawyer's naturally observant nature picked up an open volume on the Chairman's desk. It was too far away to read, but from the two small black-

and-white pictures he saw, Sawyer guessed it was a treatise on epidemics. The Chairman had been doing his homework.

The man himself was almost sickeningly charming; a natural politician. Somehow his graying hair looked as though it were tended to by a full-time staff. How he managed that feat alone given the current state of things was a mystery to Sawyer. He didn't get up from behind his desk, and addressed Sawyer with his hands folded in front of him.

"Sawyer! It's good to see you. I've heard you've been helping out quite a bit lately."

"I do my part."

"Organizing local reconnaissance, assisting patrols, taking up perimeter shifts—that's a lot. And it's very much appreciated. We need good men like you with us."

Sawyer waited until he heard the door behind click shut as the receptionist left. "Please, sir. You know I don't like politics. Just tell me why I'm here."

The Chairman chuckled. "All right, then. Down to business. What can you tell me?"

"Derrick missed his check-in. I ordered the OP to displace and put some eyes on the scene," Sawyer said. He remained standing, feet shoulder-width apart and arms tucked behind his back, but as he spoke his eyes continually roved the room. He never seemed to inspect the Chairman himself, seemingly much more interested in his surroundings—but that was just how Sawyer functioned. His attention was very much centered on the man behind the desk; Sawyer just didn't allow it to show.

"And?"

"Derrick failed. It seems Mason got some unexpected backup while our men were in the process of extracting Dr. Demilio. OP squad said it looked like they'd fortified the entrances. They also reported at least one friendly body on the roof. They didn't risk getting close enough to learn more, but it's reasonable to assume that Derrick and his squad are KIA," Sawyer said. No inflection slipped through into his speech. He delivered the bad news with characteristic remote detachment.

"Goddammit," hissed the Chairman, leaning forward and frowning with his eyes at Sawyer. The change in the Chairman's mood was like flipping a switch. "What is this? First you say you can't cut them off because of this or that, bad luck, or the weather—but I was all right with that, because you had your precious little ace in the hole. You had them heading to Omaha."

"Granted," Sawyer said, noting the Chairman's thinly veiled insults and feeling his stomach twist in response. "I—"

"Fuck your excuses," scowled the Chairman. "I'm sick of them. I want Dr. Anna Demilio *here,* in this *compound,* working in this *lab,* finding us the goddamn *cure* we need to *fix our fucking country!*"

"I've always been able to bring her back, sir," said Sawyer, narrowing his eyes. "There have been obstacles."

"What obstacles? You have complete jurisdiction! You asked for the goddamn assignment! You said it *meant* something to you," said the Chairman, stabbing a chubby finger into the top of his desk to punctuate each sentence.

"I don't have *complete* jurisdiction, sir," said Sawyer.

The Chairman looked puzzled a moment, then leaned back in his chair, an appreciative grin spreading across his face.

"You're gunning for rights to the First Guard again, aren't you? You should have been a politician, Sawyer. You know how to manipulate a situation until it seems like it's the right choice to go your way—and then you twist it back to your advantage," said the Chairman. The grin vanished. "You can forget about it."

Sawyer drew in a slow breath, preparing himself for the inevitable debate.

When the government had fractured into its current state, one of the most chaotic splinterings had been among the military. Infighting was common and units found that the only way to maintain cohesion—and therefore, control over themselves and their bases—would be to make their ultimate responsibility to civilians. Either the individual units disbanded due to the infighting, or they began to disregard orders from higher up. The military units that did *not* disband soon became cohesive and functional but completely neutral entities, who spent their days acting as guards at refugee camps or in surviving towns. They answered to no one but themselves and refused to acknowledge the authority of either the Federal Government or the Reunited States of America.

There was active fighting, although carried out mainly by civilians—or self-deputized paramilitary units. And even then, the fighting was usually over medical supplies or rumors about advances in research from one side or the other.

There were, however, hard-core faction members with military experience. These were formed into fully functional units, and their main purpose remained to seek and destroy, not to act as police or to guard objectives. They were the marauders, the vanguard. The Chairman's Reunited States of America had three such units, with nearly a hundred men apiece. Two were currently engaged in operations along the East Coast. The First Guard, however, was on station at Mount Weather, serving as the Chairman's personal security force. They were well armed, well trained, and, thanks to the several nearby Army depots, well equipped. The Chairman maintained direct command over the First Guard. The Second and Third units took their orders from a democratic roundtable-style provisional government the Chairman had come up with. It was a strong political move on his part. It kept whispered accusations of dictatorship from floating around.

Sawyer found the entire concept preposterous.

"No, sir, I don't want to take the First Guard from you," he said. "That's not my aim."

"You're not getting a single man. Not a single rifle! You created this problem when you let Demilio go, and it was your own partner who helped her get out! You've been sitting in a pile of your own shit for months now, Sawyer. I recommend you start digging yourself out."

Sawyer frowned slightly. The man was beginning to annoy him. He opened his mouth to speak, but before he could offer up a protest or defense the Chairman picked up his phone and stabbed a call button. "Guard!"

The guard, a Marine in full webgear bearing a sidearm, was quick to enter. He came in noiselessly, using a second entrance in the rear of the office. The Chairman fixed Sawyer with a stare as the Marine came to parade rest behind him.

"Mr. Sawyer is no longer welcome at the Mount Weather Facility. He is not to be allowed to return unless he has Dr. Anna Demilio with him, alive. Do you understand?"

Sawyer and the Marine both knew the Chairman's words were mostly grandstanding. The soldier nodded anyway. "Yes, sir." The Marine stepped over toward Sawyer and placed a hand on his elbow. "Sir, if you will follow m—"

· The Marine's next words came out as an inarticulate gasp of pain. Sawyer, moving like greased lightning, looped his arm around the Marine's, putting pressure on the soldier's wrist and sending him flipping to the floor. He hit heavily, the air whoofing out of his lungs. The Chairman, startled, reached for the telephone. Sawyer's other hand was already at the Marine's holster, pulling the pistol free and whipping it about. A laser sight danced on the Chairman's forehead.

For a moment, the three occupants of the office did absolutely nothing.

The Chairman sat motionless, phone dangling from his hand. The red-faced Marine gasped for breath on the floor, and Sawyer, his knee planted firmly on the Marine's back, kept careful control of his aim.

"Are you going to shoot me now? Is that the plan?" the Chairman finally asked, regaining his self-control. He was frightened, but he hid it well. "Take over this little operation for yourself?"

"No, you idiot," Sawyer growled. He was angry now. "You're not Caesar, and I am not your Brutus. And you sure as hell don't have a job I'm interested in. What you do have are the men and the gear I need to get Demilio and kill Mason. Let me ask you: have I *ever* been unclear on that point?"

The Chairman licked his lips and thought for a moment.

"I repeat," said Sawyer, finger tightening on the trigger, "have I *ever* been unclear about wanting to kill Mason and bring Demilio back here?"

"No, not once," said the Chairman. "You've been clear."

"I'm doing this to make a point," said Sawyer, still pinning the Marine to the floor with his knee and a twisted wrist. "Do you see this man on the floor here? He could probably kill you ten times a day without breaking a sweat. Me? Hell, I could kill you before I realized I'd decided to. But neither one of us does it. We've got better things to do. But in order for me to do what I need to, I need *some* of your precious 'First Guard.' I need *fighters*. I can't take on Mason and all of his friends out there in Omaha by myself, but I know for damn sure I can take care of *you* right here."

"So," said the Chairman, taking a slow breath. They were into the bargaining phase now, and he was beginning to realize he wasn't going to be shot. "What kind of . . . concessions are you asking for this time, specifically?"

Sawyer knew his answer. He'd given it careful consideration well before he'd even been summoned to the Chairman's office.

"Fifty men. Rifles, pistols, ammunition, grenades, and provisions for said personnel. Access to ammo cache eight."

"Stop," said the Chairman, holding up a hand. "Cache eight is—"

"Heavy weapons and explosives, I know. Are we back to questioning my methods?" Sawyer asked, twisting the Marine's wrist enough to elicit an audible gasp of pain.

"All right, all right, you've got access to number eight. What else?"

"Access to the motor pool. And two Huey gunships."

"What?" gaped the Chairman. "The risk aside, the limited amount of fuel we have right now just can't be used in those flying boulders—"

"Do you want the job done right or don't you? It's a hostile world out there, and they have adapted to it. They'll be dug in. It's an urban environment. We *must* have air support. It just won't work otherwise. Stop thinking like a bean counter and try to think like me for half a second. Besides, when we've wiped them out and have Demilio in custody, the Hueys will make the ride back that much shorter."

The Chairman finally, reluctantly nodded. "Done."

"Good. Glad that we're able to come to an understanding here. You give me those things, I'll give you the Doctor."

"And she'll give us our cure," said the Chairman. "We'll go down in history for this. We'll be immortal."

"Until then, sir, we're just meat," said Sawyer, finally releasing the Marine, who collapsed, tenderly nursing his wrist and fixing Sawyer with a hateful glare. "I'm going to go get my men ready. We'll move out tomorrow. I'll bring you your Doctor. And I'll leave all the *important* things"—Sawyer gestured to the papers, treatises, and books—"to you. I'll be back soon."

He put on his sunglasses and walked out.

CHAPTER 1
CATCHING UP

Abraham, KS
25 June 2007
0823 hrs_

A BLACK PLUME OF smoke rose up from what had once been Abraham's modest medical clinic. The fire that had started it had begun in the early hours, when the skeleton crew staffing the place was on rounds and the half-dozen patients were asleep.

Gunshots had alerted the townsfolk to the danger, and, like the survivors they were, they quickly banded together. There were two sources of water in Abraham: a modest water tower that stood in the center of town, and various hand pumps scattered here and there, mostly on private property. Bucket brigades were formed, and the townsfolk ran as fast as they could from pump to pump, tower to blaze. Bit by bit, they were containing the fire, limiting damage to only the clinic.

Sheriff Keaton Wallace paused in his mad dash for a fresh bucket of water, unable to continue. He'd lost count of the number of times he'd made the run back and forth, and now he hunched over on his knees, gasping for breath.

One of his deputies, a man named Wes, paused by the Sheriff's side. "You all right, Keaton?"

Keaton waved him off. "I'm fine, I'm fine. Don't worry about me! Keep going! Keep going!"

With a last, pained look, Wes took off in the direction of the nearest hand pump, an empty bucket dangling from each hand.

Keaton glanced up at the smoldering ruins of the clinic and gritted his teeth.

"God damn you, Lutz," he muttered. "I should have killed you when I had the chance."

The moment the words left Keaton's mouth, he regretted them. Murder was the mark of the raiders. He was better than that. So were the good people of Abraham. He couldn't allow himself to sink to the level of the Lutz brothers and their marauders.

"Hey!" came a voice. Keaton looked up at the face of one of Abraham's newest residents.

"Ron," said Keaton, still resting on his knees. "Where's your girl?"

"Katie's looking after the burn victims," Ron said. "The fire's burned itself out, though. Shouldn't be much longer. Love to talk more, Sheriff, but I've gotta get some more water!"

Ron turned and ran off in the same direction as Wes, buckets clanging together as he ran.

Abraham had been through a lot since Morningstar had visited their town months before. When the first infected had appeared, the present-minded among them had risen up and contained the outbreak, then set themselves to fortifying their town. They'd put up chain-link fencing, constructed guard towers, and patrolled along the city's edge. At first, the battles had been intense, with infected coming at them a dozen at a time. As time went on, their numbers had begun to dwindle, and the citizens of Abraham had begun to feel safer. Areas had been fenced off and crops planted.

That was when the Lutzes made their appearance.

Recruiting followers from the dregs of society—many of whom

Keaton had had previous run-ins with—Herman and George had set themselves up as the uncontested warlords of the area, taking over a nearby distribution center that held enough resources to keep their murderous rampages well supplied for the time being.

Their first raids were meant to do little more than shock and awe the townsfolk into acquiescing to their demands of food and supplies.

When Abraham had taken a stand and refused to surrender, the raiders had stepped things up a notch, burning the crops outside the protective fences and depriving the town of their most abundant sources of food. Then they had taken to lying in ambush outside the town, waiting for citizens to venture forth in hunting and scavenging parties.

The men they encountered were killed, and stripped of their gear.

The women were taken away, back to the raider's base, and Keaton shuddered as he thought of what they had been put through at the hands of the criminals who held them as slaves.

Then, right when Keaton had begun to despair that the raiders were there to stay, Abraham had received some unexpected visitors. Their leader, who called himself Francis Sherman, was in dire need of repairs, saying he and his companions needed to get to Omaha and couldn't very well do so with broken-down vehicles. Abraham's mechanic, Jose Arctura, had volunteered to fix up their vehicles, on one condition: rescue his daughter from the ravages of the raiders, or kill as many of them as possible.

The soldiers had not only managed to rescue most of the captured women, including Jose's young daughter, but had also set fire to the distribution center. George Lutz had been killed in the action. The other had lain wounded after a firefight with Abraham's ardent defenders, and had been taken to the clinic to recover before being hauled off to a jail cell.

Unfortunately, as Keaton remembered a touch too late, Lutz was possessed of a canny intelligence. Over the days he'd spent in the clinic, he must have slowly cobbled together a makeshift bomb, and had used it to great effect in the still morning air before the town was up and about. From the damage to the structure, it looked to Keaton that Lutz had blown out a window and part of a wall, setting the building aflame.

Herman Lutz had escaped in the confusion.

"Next time," promised Sheriff Keaton. "Next time, you're a dead man."

⭐ ⭐ ⭐ ⭐ ⭐

A low rumble and the sudden storm cloud of billowing black smoke rising above the trees did not bode well for the group of men taking a hard trail east. It smelled of oil, burning rubber, and death—and it was right in their path.

Hal Dorne, a man with graying hair and a slight paunch, the eldest of the group and the one most prone to a good session of griping, was the first to notice the plume of smoke, and he pointed it out to the rest of the group. It was yet another obstacle in what had become a veritable gauntlet of challenges and battles for them. Their attrition rate was staggering. Out of the nearly thirty seamen from the USS *Ramage* that had started the trek, just under a dozen now remained. One crippled Army private named Mark Stiles limped along beside Hal, using his rifle as a crutch. He had a badly wounded leg that was refusing to heal properly, and he cringed in pain with each step he took.

"Looks like we'll have to go around again," Hal murmured to Commander Harris, grimacing, with his hands planted on his hips. "If there's trouble down the road, we better do what we can to avoid it."

Stiles shook his head and leaned hard against a rusting signpost, sliding down to a sitting position. "Not again, guys. I can't take this. My leg feels like it's on fire. Can't we at least get close enough to see what the problem is? Maybe it's nothing . . . just natural."

"What, and lose two more of us, like last time?" asked a sailor named Rico. He was a Hispanic man in his young twenties, wearing faded jeans and a patched brown button-up shirt. Months earlier, he would have been decked out in white: a proper sailor's uniform. "To hell with that. I say we go around."

"Not to mention that where there's a town, and a line of carriers waiting to chow down on us," added Hillyard, another sailor who still wore much of his military gear. The clothing had been abandoned along the way, replaced by practical civilian wear, but he still wore the wide olive drab pistol belt, plastic canteen, and standard-issue holster and pistol about his waist.

"That'd be our luck," said Wendell, a petty officer first class and the second-highest-ranking military man in the group. He was small in stature, with the look of a person who smiled often, and short brown hair still growing in from his military buzz.

"You Navy bastards," muttered Stiles, wincing as he moved his leg to keep it from stiffening up. "If this was an Army gig, we'd have that town cleared in half an hour."

"If this was an Army gig, we'd all be reading our maps upside down," said Rico, earning chuckles.

Quartermaster Third Class Allen, who read maps for a living, started in on Stiles. "You bet your ass! I saw an Army grunt last year, holding a map on its side and wondering what the Z meant on the compass rose . . ."

Hal listened to the banter and scratched at his stubbly chin. It had been days since he'd found the time or inclination to shave. He shifted on his feet, and the light weight of his pack struck him with a new thought.

"—and then he rolled it into a tube, and—"

"You know what, though?" Hal said, interrupting Allen's diatribe. "We only have enough food to make it another week, tops, on foot. Sooner or later we'll have to hit a town and see if there's anything we can scavenge. Until things settle down some more, looting's our best bet of staying alive. Shit, I can't believe I'm even saying all this. Do you all realize that a few months ago I was in the South Pacific, lying in a hammock and drinking cold beer? I'm fucking retired. A guy can't even enjoy his old age in all of this wanton, nasty . . ."

The men in the retinue tuned out the rest of Hal's rant. He had a tendency to go on for hours about his would've-could'ves. No one minded hearing his stories about beautiful half-naked island girls or his tales of fresh, highly alcoholic fruit punches, but they knew better than to interrupt him when he started off on a negative tangent.

Commander Harris, until recently the executive officer of the USS

Ramage, now the de facto leader of the group of survivors around him, took a chance and cut Hal off.

"Hal's right. We need to resupply. We're most of the way to Omaha, and I'll be damned if we don't make it because we were too hungry to keep hoofing it. We'll scout the town, and if it looks right, we'll see what we can get."

This left dour faces all around, save for Stiles, who seemed pleased that he would at least be able to walk on even pavement a while longer. He grunted as he lifted himself from his sitting position, jostling the signpost he'd leaned his back against. The top came loose and swung down, hanging by a single hinge.

Harris cocked his head to the side to read the gently swinging sign.

"Abraham," he read. "Two miles. Well, Abraham, ready or not, here we come. All right, shipmates, check your weapons and ammo. We don't know what we're in for, but we're going to damn well be ready for it."

The nine remaining crewmen of the USS *Ramage* wearily went about their business, checking bootlaces, tucking in religious medallions that might jingle, one or two saying a quick, silent prayer.

"All right, Harris," Hal said, folding his arms and keeping a bit of distance between himself and the military men. "This is your show. What's our angle?"

He looked on as Harris considered the landscape. They had passed a bridge about a mile back where the concrete had been pocked by ricochets, and found two abandoned vehicles. Near those were a few scattered bodies. They looked to have been shot to death rather than killed by infection (or the infected). Hal knew that made Harris nervous. He was learning to deal with the infected, but there was no defense from an enemy sniper. A sharpshooter at range could kill a man before his companions even heard the shot.

Ahead of the group lay a gently curving road, sloping slightly downward and flanked on both sides by evergreens. Even this far inland, the foliage of the Rockies could take root. Harris drew his binoculars up to his eyes and scanned the distance. After a minute of this, he passed the binocs to Hal.

SURVIVORS

The pines filtered out after about a quarter of a mile. Beyond that, open fields. A pile of chalky debris littered one of them. Harris wondered about it, making a note to check it carefully as they passed, and panned onward. At the far end of the fields, he spotted the town.

Even at this distance, he could see the medieval-looking gates that served as a main entrance. Harris quirked a grin behind the binoculars. The townsfolk were apparently a resourceful bunch. They'd used upended shipping containers as guard towers, improving them with roofs, ladders, and barbed wire. The gates themselves seemed to be made out of wrought iron, welded in spots to further strengthen it.

The front of the town was not, however, where the smoke was coming from. The black funnel issued forth from the rear of the town, and through the binoculars Harris could dimly make out ant-sized people forming an ant-sized bucket brigade. He couldn't be sure, but he also thought he saw a few men standing by with rifles.

"They're in trouble," Harris said, speaking when Hal lowered the binoculars. The others looked over at him expectantly. "I don't know what to make of it, though. I saw some armed men down there. They might all be hostile, for all we know. They might shoot us on sight. Opinions?"

"They might also be friendly and in need of a few extra hands to handle the fire, sir," said Allen.

"Either way, we still need food," chimed Hal.

"Let's go for it," said Stiles, leaning heavily on his good leg.

Harris considered. The group had been on foot most of the way eastward. Finding working vehicles was becoming harder and harder. Occasionally they'd get lucky and find one that would take them a few dozen miles before running out of gas or giving in to damage. Consequently, they had become quite adept at road marching, but there was no way they'd make it much farther without replenishing their supplies.

With a nod, he waved the men forward, and they put all that hard march experience to work, making good time from the hill to the open fields in front of the town.

✯ ✯ ✯ ✯ ✯

It didn't take Harris's binoculars to make out the figures on the guard towers staring at the ragtag group upon its approach. That caused hackles to rise, but when no rifles came out, Harris and the others did their best to relax and remain placid, not making any threatening movements. As they drew nearer, they could make out more details.

The town's defenses were still under construction, Hal noted. Or, perhaps, they were being repaired. He couldn't tell. Either way, it was impressive. They'd found a use for their now-useless cars, adding them to the barriers flanking the main gates. On the roofs of these cars stood riflemen, though each with his weapon shouldered. The men in the guard towers were similarly armed, but inactive. The threat was implicit, however; one hostile move, and the new arrivals would come under a hail of fire.

"Afternoon," Hal said, stepping past Harris and waving up at the guard towers, ignoring the annoyed look Harris shot at him. "My friends and I were heading east and noticed you were having a little trouble with fire. Anything we can do?"

"Not unless you brought a fire engine and some hoses with you," said one of the men in the guard tower. He had a strong look about him, and wore, half-hidden under an open button-down shirt, a bronze badge of office. "We've got it under control. Just a little excitement at the town clinic. Look, if you folks are after food or shelter, we'll do what we can, but we can't afford to be too trusting these days. You understand."

"Well, we are running a little low on vittles ourselves," said Hal, thumbing his hat back to get a better look up at the man. "We'd be willing to trade for 'em, of course. Wouldn't be asking for freebies. Though I *have* to get a discount. I'm a retired serviceman, see. Some things shouldn't change, plague or no plague," Hal said, flashing a grin.

The man in the guard tower chuckled. "Name's Keaton. Sheriff of Abraham."

"I'm Hal Dorne. Retired mechanic, professional ne'er-do-well, and sort of between careers at the moment," Hal said, nodding. "I should be sitting on an island getting drunk and sunburned right now, but it looks like things got a little twisted."

"Well, Hal, like I said, we're open to doing what we can for folks, but we've learned a few tough lessons about trust—so if I let you in, you'll have to surrender your weapons at the police station," Keaton said.

The man in the tower next to Keaton leaned over and whispered something frantically.

"I know that, but it doesn't mean they'll be anything like Sherman, does it?" Keaton said back, at normal volume.

Hal caught Sherman's name, but brushed it off, certain he'd misheard the Sheriff, or thinking perhaps that he was referring to another individual.

Harris spoke up, drawing the group's attention.

"How about it, men? It's a risk. If we give up our weapons, we're all theirs," Harris said.

"Nah," said Rico, shaking his head. "Nah, man. Nah, check it out— if these boys were going to wreck on us, they would have done it by now. I think we can trust them, man."

Allen and the deckhands nodded in agreement.

"Yeah," nodded Stiles, wiping sweat from his forehead. "I say we trust them."

Harris pursed his lips, sighed, and turned to the guard towers. "All right. We agree! We'll surrender our weapons."

"Good to hear it!" Keaton shouted down. He turned, speaking to someone out of sight behind the barricades. "Wes, get the gates open! We've got visitors!" Keaton turned back to the road-weary men. "Welcome to Abraham. Enjoy your stay."

The gates opened outward with a series of mighty creaks, so heavy was their construction that no amount of grease could ever really ease them up. One civilian appeared behind each gate, ratcheting them outward until they stood wide. They were latched open, and the civilians retreated inside their town. Hal noted the mechanism they'd installed on the gate, which only allowed it to swing one way without a release on the inside being held in.

Hal and Stiles approached warily as the gate swung shut behind them, closing with a clang. Keaton had climbed down from the guard tower and met them with another man; this one was shorter, thinner, with a long, hooked nose and the appearance of a sharp-eyed hawk.

"Gentlemen, this is my deputy, Wes," Keaton said, introducing the newcomer.

"True pleasure, gents," said Hal, shaking both men's hands. "These are my friends—I guess you could call most of them that—right here. This is Harris. Rico, Hillyard, and Allen and the four behind them are Navy working men—not like Harris, the pencil-pusher," said Hal, earning an eye-roll from Harris, "and this is Mark Stiles, formerly of the Army."

Keaton and Wes exchanged unreadable glances.

"What was that for?" asked Allen, picking up on the civilians' brief exchange. "You got something to say about the Navy?"

"Or the Army?" chimed in Stiles, grinning.

"Nah," said Wes, "we've just been getting more soldiers through these parts than we're used to, that's all. Before Morningstar, all we ever got were farmers. Now we've got sailors and mechanics and generals—"

"Generals?" asked Hal and Harris simultaneously. Stiles perked up as well, looking intently at the Sheriff's deputy.

"What do you mean, generals?" pressed Harris, speaking quickly. "Who'd you see?"

"Whoa, it's nothing," said Wes, backing up a few steps, misreading Harris's sudden curiosity as hostility. "It's just that we had a few guys come through here a while back. One of them said he was a general, that's all."

"What did he say his name was?" asked Hal.

"Uh, Sherman. General Sherman," Wes said.

The little group of survivors let up a whoop. "They're alive!" Hal said. "I can't believe they made it this far! Hell, they pulled it off!"

The exclamations were forthcoming for several long moments, with speculation about the well-being of Sherman's group flying back and forth. When the excited chatter began to die down, Keaton seized a chance and spoke up.

"How do you fellows know Sherman? He didn't mention he had anyone on the way behind him," Keaton said.

"Oh, he wouldn't have known we were coming," Hal said, waving it off as he unholstered his sidearm and passed it to Wes, who had warily begun the collection of firearms from the newcomers. "It's a long story."

"I'll have to hear it," said Keaton, "but now that you're in and we're sure you're not here for trouble, I have to go make sure the clinic gets taken care of. Most of the fire's out, but it's still smoldering in parts."

"Someone knock a lantern over?" asked Allen, ducking the sling of his MP-5 as he handed it to Wes.

"No, someone left a few common household cleaning supplies near one smart asshole, who seized the opportunity," Keaton shrugged. "Just like you, it's a long story. Anyway, I'll catch up with you later. You mentioned you needed food. The only place we have that does that kind of bartering is Eileen's. It's a pub just down the street, on the right, before you get to the town green. They have some stock up for trade."

"A pub? Does it have beer?" Rico called out to Keaton's swiftly retreating back.

"It sure does—if you want to call it that," replied Keaton, speaking over his shoulder.

"What about pussy?" Allen sang out to no response. Wendell slapped the back of his head.

But that decided matters for the survivors. The sailors quickly volunteered to go and barter for food—and whatever passed for beer in Abraham. Harris followed behind them, muttering about keeping them in line. The truth of the matter was that he likely didn't mind the idea of a brew himself.

This left Hal and Stiles standing with Wes near Abraham's main gate. The poor deputy looked half-buried under confiscated firearms. He stumbled over to a nearby lawn cart and carefully dumped the weapons into the rear end, tucking the barrel of an errant rifle into the compartment.

Wes turned with a slowly reddening face and, looking at Stiles, stumbled over his words.

"Uh, I kind of need to—ah, your rifle—I need to bring it to the station," he managed, pointing at the Winchester that Stiles was using for a crutch.

Stiles looked down at it, blinked, and stared back at the deputy. "I kind of depend on it. Got something else I can use in the meantime?"

"Well, not on me. But wait," Wes said, snapping his fingers. "We'll get you an actual crutch at the clinic. I was going to go by there after I took care of the weapons anyway. You can ride with me in the cart until then."

"Works for me," Stiles said, limping over to the cart. He slid into the passenger seat and tucked his rifle in with the other weapons, giving it a tender pat as he did so. He had become quite attached to it over the past several weeks—almost literally.

"Don't think you're leaving me here," Hal said, pushing Stiles over. "Make room—I'm coming, too."

"Aren't you the one who's always bitching about how you should be lounging around and drinking?" Stiles pointed out. "I would have thought you'd be the first to run off to the pub. Never know when we'll see another one."

"Oh, I can, and I will, I assure you," Hal said with an easy grin. "But I'd kind of like to see this operation Abraham's running first. Seems like a good opportunity for a tour."

Wes took the driver's seat. The cart was slow but ran with a quiet electric whine, moving efficiently along the mostly deserted streets. The citizens, it seemed, were congregated near the other end of town, distracted by or helping with the clinic fire.

"So," said Wes, glancing at Stiles, "if you don't mind my asking, how'd you hurt your leg? Get shot?"

Stiles had been attacked in Hyattsburg by a carrier of Morningstar, and had been badly bitten. The wound never seemed to heal up properly, but Stiles never became ill. He was a true rarity: a human being with a natural immunity to the Morningstar strain.

Stiles began to explain. "Well, actually, I was—"

Hal shoved Stiles hard on the shoulder. "Yeah . . . he was shot. Friendly fire. Went out to take a piss one night and Rico drilled him by accident."

Stiles looked confused for the barest of moments, then took the hint, nodding and laughing. "It was my own fault. I should've stayed inside the perimeter."

"Ouch." Wes chuckled and turned the cart into the parking lot of a small, single-story brick building. The landscaping had gone to pot and was overgrown, but the lot itself was still holding up strong, a pool of black in a cradle of green. The deputy pulled the cart to a stop in front of the entrance, and began to pull weapons out of the rear compartment.

Hal took the opportunity to lean in close to Stiles. He lowered his voice. "Look, I know this is the first time we've been around anybody, and for all we know they'll understand you're lucky enough to be immune. But until we know for sure, don't let a damn soul know you've been bitten. They'd kill you the second they figured it out, no matter if you haven't turned. *I* would. Hell, we almost *did* kill you. In fact, if we get to this clinic and they want to look at your wound, don't show it to them. Tell them you're fine, it's just sore. Stick to the bullet wound story. I'll let Rico and the others in on it."

"I get you," whispered Stiles. "No problem. It's probably better if we kept this to ourselves."

"Yeah," breathed Hal.

Wes had vanished, laden with weapons, into the building, which Hal and Stiles saw now was marked as the Sheriff's office by a bronze-and-concrete plaque half-hidden in the tall grass.

"At least there's still a little law and order here," said Stiles, nodding toward the plaque.

"Yep. A little bit of civilization goes a long way these days," agreed Hal. "Not that I've ever been a fan of it. That's why I left it in the first place."

Wes reappeared, kicking open the swinging doors to the Sheriff's office, arms empty. "All right, gentlemen, your gear is secured. Don't worry," he added, "we put them in the evidence locker. No one but

Keaton and I have the keys to get in there. Your things are safe and sound."

"Good," said Stiles, nodding slightly. "If there's a single ding on my Winchester, there'll be hell to pay."

"I was meaning to ask you about that," Wes said, taking over the driver's seat and sending the cart whirring along on its way. "One hell of a piece you got there. Where'd you find it?"

"Some gun nut's private storeroom back in Oregon," Stiles said. "It's an original. An antique."

"I could have guessed as much," said Wes. "I'm something of a weapons enthusiast myself. You don't find pieces like that anymore—or if you do, they're way out of my price range. At least, they used to be when money was an issue."

"Yeah. I almost regret having to use it as a crutch, but I don't really have a choice."

Wes banked the cart around a corner. The smoke from the smoldering clinic was growing closer. "Don't worry. I stuck it in a locker by itself. A piece like that needs some tender loving care."

"Thanks," said Stiles, holding on to the rollbars as the cart made the turn. "That weapon and I have saved each other's lives a dozen times over."

The electric cart turned a second corner, and the burning clinic came into full view.

It wasn't completely destroyed. A corner had burned out and collapsed, but the bucket brigades had managed to keep the flames from spreading to the rest of the building. Sheriff Keaton was on the scene, running around, making sure that everything was going smoothly, directing application of water like an experienced fire chief. Wes leapt out of the cart to join him, and Hal followed suit. Stiles remained seated in the cart, nursing his wounded leg.

"What's it look like, Sheriff?" Wes asked.

"The worst's over, Wes," replied the Sheriff. "We're down to ashes and an occasional flare-up. Gonna have to overhaul the insulation in the walls, make sure all the smoldering is out. God damn that idiot who left those cleaning supplies by Herman."

"Herman?" asked Hal, managing to bite back a laugh. "The guy who did this is named *Herman*?"

"Don't laugh," Keaton said, narrowing his eyes. "Herman Lutz is a complete sociopath, and a goddamn smart one, too. Sherman helped us bring him down, but we got him alive and were keeping him here, at the clinic. He was pretty badly hurt, but he was improving. As far as we can tell, he got a hold of some chemicals and built himself a bomb. Blew the goddamned wall right off the back end of the clinic. His bed's empty. All in all, he managed a great escape. We tracked him a little. Looks like he headed east."

"Aren't you going to go after him?"

"Why? He's only one person, and now we're watching for him. It'd be suicide for him to try and come back here. Good riddance to him— wherever he is, I hope he rots there."

The sounds of crackling wood and the smell of scorched tiling were all that filled the air for a long moment. No one spoke. Hal looked off to the east, where Herman Lutz had disappeared, and sighed.

A voice broke the silence. From the passenger side of the cart, Stiles raised a hand. "Say, uh, hate to interrupt . . . but would now be a good time to ask for that crutch?"

CHAPTER 2
DAILY GRIND

Omaha, NE
26 June 2007
1120 hrs_

IT TURNED OUT TO be a beautiful day, with the temperature pleasant, and a soft breeze serving to whisk away what little sweat those enjoying the outdoors might have felt. Missing, however, were the hallmarks of any major city. Not a single engine could be heard for miles. Abandoned vehicles lay about, some parked neatly, others smashed against telephone poles or turned up on their sides in ditches, sitting cockeyed in storefront windows or blocking intersections, silent and still.

Glass shards littered overgrown lawns, and halfway-boarded-up windows hinted at last stands. Even the birds seemed loath to venture into the city, their chirps distant and muted, almost apprehensive. Only two figures still lived and breathed in the streets of Omaha, but they were as still as the tomblike buildings around them.

Ewan Brewster and Trevor Westscott might as well have been statues.

The pair of survivors were kneeling behind a concrete stoop on the outskirts of the city, hugging their weapons close. Brewster's double-barreled shotgun hung across his lap, and Trev's snap-out baton was held close to his chest. He tapped it rhythmically against his shoulder in perfect time to the sound of the infected's breathing.

Both men wore rugged hiking packs stuffed to the brim with recently scavenged food and several bottles of prescription medications. They were trying to get back to their home base, but trouble had come their way in the form of an older man with bloodshot eyes who had burst out of his apartment building as the two began to walk past. Brewster and Trev had immediately dived for cover, and, owing to luck more than anything else, the man hadn't seen them.

That was only half a blessing, however. The man definitely knew they were there. He just didn't seem to know where. He grunted, flicking his head this way and that, drooled blood and spittle pooling at his feet on the top step of his building. His body twitched spasmodically as he stood there, motions seemingly beyond conscious control. In fact, they seemed to annoy him: every time a shoulder or arm twitched, he would glance at the offending limb with the same predatory flash in his eyes that a young, curious housecat gets when it spots its own tail.

The man was a living infected, and the first one of that kind that Brewster and Trev had spotted in nearly two weeks. Through his veins coursed the Morningstar strain—by now the virus had erased anything human that remained in his wrecked shell. He now existed only to spread the infection. He was, body and soul, the Enemy.

Though Brewster and Trev were well armed and able to finish him off if they wished, they remained behind cover. A shot would bring more infected out of hiding to their location—possibly even other sprinters.

"Sprinters" were what the survivors had taken to calling the living infected. They were still human, physiologically speaking, with all the advantages and disadvantages that entailed. One of those advantages was their namesake. They could run down a clean, uninfected human with little trouble . . . they didn't know pain, or fatigue, or fear. Escaping a group of them was one of the most harrowing experiences the postpandemic world offered. They also drew breath, and had working vocal cords, which made their howling a much larger threat than a mere gunshot. When an infected managed to spot a survivor, it would let out an unearthly, angry wail, bringing any other infected that were within earshot down on the survivors' heads.

It was that howling that was worrying Brewster and Trev more than anything else.

"Plan?" whispered Trev, pulling a lock of grown-out brown hair away from his eyes and glancing around the corner of the stoop at the infected.

"I don't know, man," Brewster said, an unlit cigarette clamped between his teeth. "How far is the Fac?"

"We're about five blocks out," Trev replied in the same low whisper. "Too far to run if there are any other sprinters around."

Brewster thought on this a moment, then reached up a hand to the battered and chipped radio that was clipped to the collar of his shirt. He turned the volume down to a nearly imperceptible level and switched it on.

"Krueger, come in," Brewster whispered into the radio. "Krueger! Wake the fuck up and answer your radio."

Across the way, the infected turned its head in the direction of the hidden survivors and took a quick step forward, studying the stoop they were kneeling behind. Trev spotted the movement, pushed himself tighter against the concrete, and slapped Brewster's shoulder, his eyes alone speaking volumes. Brewster slowly released his hold on the radio and grasped his rifle. If the infected discovered them, they would be forced to run and gun.

Suddenly, Brewster's radio squawked softly. *"Brewster, Krueger. Go ahead."*

"Shit!" Brewster was quick to reply. "Krueger! We're pinned four blocks out on Meadows Parkway. Think you can work some magic?"

"Give me a minute," came Krueger's response.

"I don't know if we have a minute," said Trev, peeking around the stoop once more to check on the infected.

It had left the steps entirely, and was now standing on the street, much closer than it had been just moments earlier.

"I think it can hear us," added Trev, furrowing his brow.

"That would be our luck," said Brewster. "Krueger? Come on, man."

"Almost in position, over," came Krueger's disembodied voice. Brewster and Trev could hear the sound of footsteps ringing on metal rungs and Krueger's heavy breathing through the radio. He was climbing.

"Tell me why, again, we don't have headsets?" Brewster moaned softly. "Next time we hit the streets, I'm raiding a goddamn Radio Shack."

The infected took a few more quick, lurching steps toward the survivors' hiding spot, head tilted to the side like a dog, still rasping with every fast, shallow breath. Its mouth drifted farther open, saliva slipping between rotted teeth faster with each step.

"All right. In position. Where on Meadows are you, over?" came Krueger's voice again.

"The apartment buildings adjacent to the highway, far side from your location," Brewster said. He felt a trickle of sweat break out on his forehead and meander slowly toward his eye. It would be a matter of seconds before the infected located them. "Hurry up, man. He's almost on us."

For a long moment, silence. Brewster glanced down at his radio and wondered if it had died on him. The quick shuffle of infected footsteps toward Brewster and Trev was the loudest thing they'd heard.

A whine cut through the air, little more than a high-pitched zip, and the infected sprouted a blossom of blood and tissue, center mass.

The infected let out a sigh, fell limply to his knees, and pitched over onto the pavement. Blood began to pool around the corpse. A moment after that, the crack of an echoing gunshot reached Brewster's ears.

"Nice shooting," Brewster said into the radio, breathing a shuddering sigh of relief.

"Gracias," Krueger replied. *"That's a new record for me, by the way. Range finder said just over half a mile."*

"Congratu-fuckin-lations," Brewster laughed. "We'll see if we can double that within the next couple of months."

"If it's you that Sherman keeps sending out on these scrounging treks, I have no doubt of that," said Krueger. *"You're always screwing up."*

"Oh, fuck you," replied Brewster.

"Hey, now," said Krueger. *"I'm looking at you through the scope of a high-powered rifle. People in that situation don't usually tell me 'fuck you.'"*

Brewster held up a hand with an extended middle finger by way of reply. A wry chuckle escaped from the radio.

Krueger had taken over a tower in an industrial park next door to the research facility the group had occupied several weeks earlier, and lived there almost exclusively these days. None of the infected could seem to master climbing, so Krueger was well protected at the top of his bare-steel castle, to say nothing of the commanding view of the landscape it gave the sniper. In the last month, Krueger had gone through nearly a thousand hard-won rounds of supersonic ammo. As far as his accuracy went, Krueger only ever made one boast: that he didn't keep track of his hits, only his misses. ("It's much simpler that way.")

"All right, head on back. I'll keep an eye on you. My shot might've dredged up a couple infected closer to the Fac. Better stay on guard as you pass the tower."

Trev and Brewster picked themselves up and dusted off, carefully avoiding the spreading pool of blood from the dead sprinter. It was "hot" blood, teeming with the Morningstar strain. One false move and they could find themselves infected as well.

Almost as an afterthought, as he walked by, Trev swung down with his snap-out baton and smashed in the side of the dead man's head, making sure the figure would stay down forever.

★ ★ ★ ★ ★

Finding supplies for their group of survivors was getting harder.

At first it was easy enough—scavenging teams would only have to venture a block or two away to find a half-empty store to loot. After several weeks, though, the nearby larders had run dry, and they were forced to move farther into the infected city.

Trev found the excursions exhilarating, while Brewster despised them. To Brewster, each foraging expedition was another chance he'd get infected and die, and he had no wish to try either of those things before he reached the age of fifty. Trev, on the other hand, saw it as his civic duty to remove each and every one of the infected he came across. That, Sherman said, was why the pair made a good team. Brewster provided a sense of caution, and Trevor the enthusiasm.

Trev and Brewster began the trek back to their makeshift base, walking a bit apart, overlapping the areas they scanned while they traveled. Brewster's forehead was furrowed in thought. All the time he'd spent with Trev over the last couple of weeks had him a bit out of sorts. He shook his head . . . that Trev chose an ASP baton, or sometimes two, as his weapon of choice was beyond the soldier.

What kind of man chooses a slender rod of flexible metal over solid firepower?

Still . . . Brewster had to admit that he admired the way Trev became an engine of destruction when facing down the infected. He sincerely doubted that he would ever be able to become like that. In any case, he'd be glad to be off the streets and back at the facility.

It was a rather Spartan complex of single-story office buildings flanked by an industrial processing plant. The whole compound was on the far western edge of Omaha, so they were out of auditory range of downtown. A good thing, too, considering that there must have been thousands—hundreds of thousands—of infected lurking in there. To add to their luck, the area was encircled by a chain-link fence, creating a safe zone wherein the survivors could move about freely without having to worry about ambush.

Mbutu Ngasy, well-known among the survivors for his laconic but uncannily intuitive nature, had dubbed the facility "Sherman's Freehold."

"I should probably ditch the Cipro," Trevor remarked, looking over his shoulder at his pack.

Brewster stumbled over a crack in the pavement, cursed, then glanced at his companion. "Why?"

"It's marked expired. April of oh-six."

Brewster shrugged. "Bring it anyway. You never know what the medicos could use. Maybe it'll be all right." He shot a sideways glance at Trev. "Look, I've been meaning to ask you some things."

The other man blinked. "Fire away."

"I hear people talking. I don't mean any offense, or anything, but is it true what they say? That you think the infected are demons?" Brewster asked, casting another sidelong glance at Trevor.

"No offense taken. And yes, that's true. They *are* demons," Trev said, laughing, "but it's all semantics, anyway, isn't it? Call them infected, call them demons, call them little green plastic army men for all I care. They're out to get us, and we're out to get them, and that's what really matters."

"Okay," said Brewster. "But don't you think you'd be better off sticking with a firearm like the rest of us? I mean, if you get any of that blood on you, Rebecca and Anna will have you in a restraining jacket down in BL4 before the night's out."

Trev nodded slowly. "That makes sense. I . . . I really can't explain it properly. All I know is, when I came across my first infected, this baton was, ah, presented to me. It was a gift—like I was supposed to use it. I sort of saw it as a sign. It's worked out well for me so far. Besides, I carry a backup pistol." Trev tapped a revolver holstered on his belt.

"So, you see this as a sort of mission from God, to—"

"Whoa, whoa," Trevor interrupted. "I never said anything about God."

Brewster raised his eyebrows and reconsidered. "Sorry, man. I didn't mean to upset you."

Trevor sighed and kicked a loose piece of pavement out of his way. Sherman's Freehold was growing closer. They could see Jack the Welder on the rooftop, waving at them.

"Truth be told, I'm agnostic. I've never been sure of God or the Devil or any of that stuff. But this? This pandemic, this *plague*? Demons, man."

Brewster grinned. "That's kind of ironic."

Trevor chuckled. "Tell me about it. But now I have a purpose—I suppose I'm still *technically* the crazy bastard I was last year, but look around. Everything's dead. Or dying. Almost everybody. Those of us who are left have seen death, seen pain, and seen loss—we've seen those bloody-eyed bastards up close. Ask yourself this question, Ewan: Who's crazy anymore, huh? No one? Or everyone? Me? *You?*"

Brewster was silent as he considered Trevor's words.

The pair crossed the bullet-pocked street that led to Sherman's Freehold. Jack the Welder (who, despite having been with the group since the fall of Suez in January, refused to give his last name) unlocked the main gates for them. They entered, shut the swinging doors behind them, and secured them well.

This building had become their home, their fortress, and most important, their last, best hope at defeating the Morningstar strain. Over the past several weeks the survivors had settled in. The main entryway, once open and inviting with wide windows and double doors, had been completely reworked. Two-by-fours had been bolted neatly across the window frames, sealing them completely shut. The doors themselves had been reinforced with chain mesh and a folding steel bar to lock them firmly in place.

The result was a much dimmer but safer entryway. Candles weren't hard to come by. No one had used them much before the pandemic, and yet almost every house or place of business had a bundle hidden away somewhere. They were now being put to good use. Here and there a pillar of wax sat burning away, giving the entryway a flickering, shadowy ambience.

Originally meant as a reception area, it still bore the marks of its previous incarnation. A few inspirational posters hung on the walls, and a long-dead office plant sat neglected in a corner next to a smaller and green plastic one. Chairs and couches meant for clients had been dragged into a rough circle off to the side, leaving a clear aisle between the exit and the hall that led deeper into the facility.

A stack of old magazines and tabloids was scattered across the only coffee table in the room. Lounging near the unruly pile with her feet propped up on the table was a slight Japanese girl, thumbing her way through a copy of *The Week*. She wore her hair short, and had bright, intelligent eyes. She spared Trev and Brewster a glance. "How'd you make out?" she asked.

"I see you're making good use of your time, Juni," said Trev, nodding at the magazines. "As for the run—mostly medicines," Trevor said, shrugging his pack higher on his shoulders. "I'm not sure about some of them, though."

"They're expired," Brewster added.

"Hmm," shrugged Juni, flipping a page. "Becky'll be happy about that."

"What's Becky's personal weather forecast looking like today, Juni?" Brewster asked. "Sunny? Stormy?"

Juni peered at him from behind the pages of her magazine. "Partly cloudy."

"Great," said Brewster, sighing. Rebecca, a young woman who was pretty as a picture, but one that had become rather volatile, was something of a mystery to the group. One moment she was enthusiastic and helpful, and the next, taciturn and short-tempered.

"I'd get those supplies to her, though," Juni said, dropping the magazine on her lap. "She's probably on her way down to meet the Doc right now."

"We're on it," Trevor said, slapping Brewster on the shoulder. "Let's go, bud."

"See you around, beautiful," said Brewster, grinning at Juni. She rolled her eyes and returned her attention to the stack of magazines in front of her. Then, just as quickly, she called out: "When do you think Sherman'll let me go out with you two? I hate just *sitting* here."

Trev and Brewster exchanged glances and kept on moving deeper into the facility. Juni was becoming a broken record about going on scavenging runs.

A long hallway ran away from reception and led to a four-way intersection. Three of the halls were flanked by offices, most of which had been taken over as personal living spaces and personalized in one way or another. It would help with the group's morale, Sherman had said, if they were allowed a little leeway. Brewster had noted that the survivors had taken a kind of pride in adding their own touches to their rooms.

A door with a welded Celtic knot design emblazoned on it marked Jack the Welder's room. He'd found quite a treasure trove in the industrial park next door. He was forever sculpting this or that out of spare bits of metal, owing to his profession and, he said, his aspirations as an artist.

The next room was Mitsui's, the Japanese contractor, and the room beyond his was Juni's. They were both Japanese, but only Juni spoke English these days, and the pair had formed a friendship because of it. It wasn't anything romantic. Mitsui was far too old for Juni's interest, and he would have considered it an improper relationship. Still, the pair stuck together, with Juni translating anything Mitsui needed to say. The door to Juni's room was wide open and the walls were covered in brightly colored murals of trees, flowers, and steep mountainsides, mostly inspired by ads in the magazines she read, the pages carefully unstapled and reassembled for the pictures. Only the far wall remained unfinished, in black-and-white outlines.

General Francis Sherman's room was at the far end of the hall. The door was shut and locked, and besides the General, only Sergeant Major Thomas had ever been inside. No one knew what Sherman kept in there, but it was a frequent topic of conversation during downtime.

Thomas refused to keep a room of his own. When he needed rest, he often slept on the couch in the facility's entryway. He said that, should they be attacked in the night, he would hear the commotion first and raise the alarm.

Mbutu Ngasy, the air traffic controller formerly of Mombasa, Kenya, and witness to the first human attacks on record, made himself at home on the building's roof. He'd constructed a tent out of tarp and stakes, and had found a telescope in one of the nearby abandoned stores. It was a common sight for Brewster to see the tall, wide-shouldered man crouched on the edge of the roof, watching the stars at night and plotting their courses. He said it reminded him of his old job, and made him feel at peace. Of all the survivors, Mbutu was the most mysterious. He said little unless pressed, but what he did say invariably came true. Trevor called him a psychic. Brewster didn't think so, but he and Trev had to agree that Mbutu was definitely intuitive. He had a sixth sense when it came to danger. The group loved him for it, and when Mbutu spoke, they listened well.

Brewster was proud of his own room, and never hesitated to joke about his digs. He'd found and liberated a number of old posters—mostly of B movies, some of bands now long dead—and plastered them on the walls. Those walls he couldn't cover were spray-painted in a dizzying array of colors. He called it his art, and jokingly claimed that once the pandemic was over and done with, his room would be a stop on a museum tour.

Whenever he had to poke his head in there, Brewster saw how Rebecca Hall's room reflected her dual personality. She'd shoved the desk the previous occupant had used against a far wall, and laid out her medical gear on the surface in a neat, orderly fashion. Everything was perfectly arranged. A map of the United States was pinned to the wall, with red thumbtacks stuck through many of the major cities—those infected beyond hope. Yellow tacks pockmarked the map as well, denoting areas where infection was likely. Two lonely green tacks adorned the map: one stuck on the western edge of Omaha, and one over Abraham, Kansas—the two bastions of humanity that Brewster was aware of, places devoid of the virus. The other end of the room reflected her second, unpredictable side. Clothing lay scattered around the floor in heaps, some dirty, some clean, all wrinkled. Her bed—more of a cot than anything else—was up against the far wall, unmade. The covers lay half-on, half-off the mattress, and her pillow had fallen to the floor.

Trevor, like Mbutu, didn't keep residence in the main complex. He barely slept, for that matter. He'd settled for wandering the halls at night, after most of the group had gone to sleep. He once told Brewster that when he did feel the need to rest, he would pull a chair to a window and doze with one eye open, always on the lookout for a demon to hunt.

Krueger was safe and sound in his watchtower, outside the main complex. Of all the survivors, he had chosen the safest spot—though not for that reason. The forty-foot tower he lived in gave him a 360-degree view of the area, and, combined with his .30-06 rifle, made him the group's first and finest line of defense. Brewster never felt anxious when Krueger was awake and in his tower—he was confident that any threat that approached would be dealt with before he even knew they were in peril.

Brewster and Trev walked calmly past these rooms. They'd become quite comfortable in their lives here, and usually kept their minds occupied with thoughts of scavenging food and supplies, and the hope of developing a vaccine.

Trev and Brewster came to the four-way intersection and moved straight on through, heading for the wide stairwell that led to the true reason behind the building's existence: a biosafety level four laboratory.

Only two were officially recognized in the United States. One was at Fort Detrick, in Maryland: the U.S. Army Medical Research Institute of Infectious Diseases, or USAMRIID for short. The second was in Atlanta, run by the Centers for Disease Control.

This other lab was off the books and privately funded, the survivors camped above humanity's last, best hope of developing a vaccine.

Before they reached the stairwell, however, they passed a locked office door on their left. From inside, Brewster could hear the sound of rhythmic pounding. *Thump-thump. Thump-thump. Thump-thump.*

Inside the room were two soldiers, prisoners of Sherman's survivors. They'd surrendered when Sherman's group had caught them unaware, and were now relegated to the small, featureless room that was serving as their prison cell. The only entertainment they were allowed was a ragged copy of *National Geographic* and a moldy tennis ball. They almost didn't even get that much, but Sherman, who had an empathetic streak in him, couldn't bear the thought of leaving the enemy soldiers alone with nothing at all to do. Even convicted felons were allowed some form of entertainment.

Thump-thump. Thump-thump.

Brewster paused, turned to the door, and slammed his palm against it. "Hey! Knock it off! We didn't give you that damn tennis ball so you could annoy the shit out of us with it!"

A moment passed in silence before a surly voice answered back. "Yeah? Why don't you come in here and get it?"

"Don't tempt me," Brewster said, and turned away, catching up with Trev.

"Why do we even keep those two in there?" Trevor asked.

"Collateral, I guess. Hostages, maybe. What do you want us to do with 'em? It's not like we have a lot of options."

"We have plenty of options," Trev said, pulling open the stairwell door and holding it as Brewster stepped through. "In case you've forgotten, those bastards tried to kill us. They had us dead to rights when we first got here. And they killed Matt! They *shot* him right in front of Juni!"

"Hell, we've all done our share of killing—"

"In self-defense," Trev said, voice rising slightly. "They're murderers. And now they're costing us food, water, shelter—I say we just take them out back and shoot them."

Brewster raised his eyebrows. For a "crazy man," Trev was normally very rational. He'd never heard him advocate execution before. "That's a little drastic, the whole eye-for-an-eye thing. I'm sure Sherman knows what he's doing. If he thought they were a threat, or if he thought we couldn't handle them, we would have gotten rid of them by now. They did dig the slit trench. And they're still in the process."

"Maybe," Trev said, but he didn't sound convinced. His boots rang out on the stairs as the pair descended. The slit trench was something that none of the survivors wanted to work on . . . while the Fac had light and water they brought in, the restrooms didn't work so well, so Denton and Thomas had rescued a couple of porta-potties from a construction site and brought them in. The prisoners had dug the trench from the toilets to the runoff behind the Fac and had to work on it from time to time to keep things flowing.

Brewster tapped Trev on the shoulder in a conciliatory gesture. "Look, I see where you're coming from. But they'll get what's coming to them in the end. Hell, maybe Sherman's keeping them around just to have a couple of guinea pigs for Dr. Demilio to test on."

Trev chuckled and shook his head. "All right. You've got me there."

The pair circled the wide landing and headed down the last set of stairs into the basement, nearly running directly into Rebecca Hall, the short young woman with dirty-blond hair who had been with the group since before Suez. Her naturally trim form had grown even thinner over the past few months. She ate little, spoke less, and when she did open her mouth it was usually with a biting comment. It wasn't that she was unpleasant. Unlike the rest of the group, Brewster knew that she held little to no hope for the future. She managed to paint a grim enough expression on her face to discourage any flirtatious advances from the male survivors. She was backing out of a medical supply closet toting a cart behind her when she almost collided with Brewster and Trevor.

"Hey!" she exclaimed, narrowing her eyes. "Watch where you're going!"

"Hiya, sunshine," Brewster said, grinning. "We've got some presents for you."

"Oh, goody," Rebecca said acidly, and pointed an outstretched finger at the cart. "Just dump them there. I'm heading to the lab now, anyway."

Brewster, a literalist when it suited him, opened his rucksack and upended the contents onto the cart. Rebecca cast him an agonized glance and began sorting through the boxes and bottles. Trevor took his time, unloading his findings by hand while engaging Rebecca in conversation. "Tell the Doc that some of this stuff is beyond its expiration date," he said, holding up one of the bottles of Cipro to illustrate his point. "It might still be good, but she should know. How're things coming in there?"

"How do you think?" Rebecca snapped, then looked guilty for doing so. She took a deep breath and softened up. "I'm sorry. It's just not going so well. Every day it's the same tests, the same negative results. I'm not sure what we're missing. Hell, I don't understand most of what we're doing in there. I'm no help at all."

"Don't worry," Trevor said, handing her the last bottle of medicine. "I'm sure you two will figure it out sooner or later."

"And maybe once you do we'll get to see you smile," Brewster said, still grinning. "I mean, come on. Just once. It won't break your face. I swear."

Rebecca held up her middle finger. "Get back upstairs. If you stick around down here, I might break *your* face. I'll get the cart."

Brewster chuckled. After Thomas, Rebecca seemed to dislike Brewster the most. Irrepressible as always, he favored Rebecca with a wry smile, returning her gesture with one of his own.

"See you, Becky," said Trev, waving.

✶ ✶ ✶ ✶ ✶

Rebecca watched the men walk back up the stairs, chatting back and forth, until the doors swung shut behind them. Once they were gone, she grabbed the wheeled cart and began the walk toward the biosafety level four laboratory. A second set of double doors, directly opposite those leading to the stairs, confronted her. A simple keypad sat in place of a handle. Normally she would have had to enter a six-digit access code to enter, but Mitsui, handy with electronics, had disabled it. There was no need for security at this particular checkpoint any longer. Rebecca backed into the doors, pushing them open for the cart, which she pulled in after herself.

A long, dim hallway stretched out before her. It was as Spartan as the rest of the facility: white walls, white tiled floor, white ceiling panels. The lighting was only half-on. Every other bulb sat dark to conserve what little power reserves they had. The cart's wheels squeaked with each rotation. That and Rebecca's footsteps were the only sounds in the corridor, echoing dully off the walls.

Rebecca glanced to her left as she passed a side room with a wide observation window set into the wall. The room was dark and devoid of life, but the light from the hallway was just enough to give her a look at several rows of lab stations. Freezers lined the far wall, and surgical gowns and masks hung near the door. A sign beside the entryway warned passersby that the room was a biological hazard area, complete with a red-on-white painting of the international biohazard symbol. Beneath that, in smaller, precise lettering, was the simple code: "BL1." Within, she could make out the still form of Gregory Mason, still recovering from the wounds he had received in his fight with Derrick, another National Security Agency employee, upon their taking of the Fac.

She continued on down the hallway, passing another doorway with a similar warning etched beside it, and the lettering "BL2." The door to that room, unlike the first, was solid steel, and had the look of a submarine hatch, minus the wheel. Rebecca knew it would seal airtight when pulled shut. In addition to the gowns, Rebecca saw a rack of hanging gas masks with a shelf of replacement filters inside. The scientists who had worked in there before the pandemic would have to wear them: several of the diseases they would have been looking into were airborne and highly contagious.

Rebecca came up short against yet another pair of thick, swinging doors with a small black plastic keypad in place of a knob. This was the second security checkpoint, still active. She entered a code into the keypad, and the locks retracted. Before the pandemic, there would have been an armed security guard there to check her paperwork as well.

Rebecca backed through the door towing the cart behind her. The doors swung shut quietly, and she heard the locks click back into place.

There were only two doorways in this section of hallway, and no offices. The closest portal was off to her left, and had the same submarine-like hatch as the BL2 lab. Instead of a simple entryway, however, it had a small, one-man decontamination area added into the design, a control point. Outside the portal hung full plastic face shields and hoods alongside a number of hazmat suits. They weren't completely airtight, but close enough. The researchers working in that room would have to go through several stages of preparation before they could clock in or out, and for good reason: the diseases stored inside could easily kill, and were highly infectious. A small screwed-in sign on the hatch read "BL3."

The only other door in the hallway sat at the far end of a narrow catwalk, separated by an open, empty space from the rest of the building.

Unlike the other labs, the sign on this one was much larger, and printed in bright red ink, reading "BL4." A sign below that, in smaller lettering, read: WARNING: EXTREME BIOLOGICAL HAZARD.

The entryway always gave her pause. It seemed to be out of place, as if it belonged on the set of a science-fiction movie, not in a research laboratory.

SURVIVORS

It was a room within a room: a self-contained environment, held separate from the rest of the facility by several clever safeguards. Getting in, even with proper authorization, took a lot of doing. A lit-up keypad sat silently blinking next to the portal. That was Rebecca's first obstacle.

She sighed and pursed her lips. The whole lab seemed ominous, somehow, in the dim light. Maybe it was just the knowledge that specimens of the deadliest diseases mankind had ever known were on the other side of those steel walls—including Morningstar.

Rebecca shook her head and wheeled the squeaking cart up to the hatch, punched in a nine-digit combination on the keypad. The LED embedded in the top of the device winked green, and the hatch's dead bolts slid back with the sound of scraping metal, and in her mind she heard blunt swords drawn from stainless steel sheaths. She pulled the door open and pushed the cart inside ahead of her. She stepped through and watched the door shut firmly behind her. The dead bolts slid back into place automatically.

The small ready room she found herself in was much brighter than the corridor outside. The lab got preferential treatment when it came to using their energy stores.

Along one wall hung a rack of space suits, as Anna occasionally called them. Becky knew it was a misnomer. The things weren't designed to handle a vacuum, but they *were* airtight. They were old, but still serviceable. Rebecca let go of the cart and walked over to them. She pulled one of the Chemturions free, rubbing down the corner of a strip of duct tape on the breast that had "Hall" written on it in permanent marker.

Rebecca sealed the suit, pulled a nozzle down from the ceiling, and attached it to the waist of the Chemturion. With a hiss of released air, the suit swelled up and held. Rebecca detached the hose and inspected the blown-up suit for any recent tears or leaks. Carefully, she ran a paper towel over the entirety of the suit, holding it millimeters from the surface, looking for a telltale flutter of leaking air. Seeing none, and hearing no hiss of escaping air, she unsealed the suit. It went limp in her hands as the air rushed out.

That was good. Even the tiniest rip could mean certain death.

Rebecca self-consciously glanced around the room as if looking for observers, then rebuked herself silently. She was alone—and a good thing, too, because you couldn't wear a Chemturion with street clothes on underneath it. Any protruding buttons or zippers might cause a tear in the material.

She pulled her shirt off over her head, tossed it onto a narrow bench, then removed her shoes, socks, pants, and undergarments. All of these were similarly tossed onto the bench. She noted a similar pile of clothing on the far end of the bench—this one, by contrast, neatly folded and stacked—which meant Dr. Demilio was hard at work in the lab already. Naked and shivering in the slightly chill air, Becky retrieved her Chemturion from its rack and prepared to enter it.

"Chemical centurion," she said, holding it at arm's length. Rebecca unzipped the suit the rest of the way and stepped inside. Next, she pulled on a triple layer of latex gloves and used duct tape to seal the cuffs of the suit around her wrists. Finally, she adjusted her helmet and checked her seals by reattaching the air hose. Inside the suit, normal sounds were drowned out by the sounds of rushing air and her own breathing, captured and amplified by the helmet.

Rebecca grabbed the cart and pushed it over to the only other door in the ready room. She pulled it open and stepped inside.

This room was smaller and narrower than the ready room, with several nozzles protruding from the ceiling and walls, and one final door at the far end. Rebecca shook open a piece of thin plastic sheeting and laid it over her boxes, then pressed a small red button next to the door. The nozzles opened up, drenching Rebecca's suit and the cart in disinfectant spray. The shower lasted for nearly a minute before it finally tapered off.

Rebecca pulled open the last door and stepped forward into BL4. The other rooms—the one with the Chemturions and the disinfectant shower—had merely served to prepare her for entry. She would have to go through the exact same routine in reverse when she wanted to leave. She wheeled the cart up against a table and pulled a nearby air hose down from the ceiling. As she attached it to her suit, she looked around the lab for Dr. Anna Demilio.

SURVIVORS

Anna was at the far end of the lab, facing away from Rebecca. She was hunched over a tray holding several dozen samples of Morningstar, dropping a possible vaccine into each sample to watch for a reaction. From the way her hooded head shook subtly with each drop, it wasn't going well.

"Bad day?" Rebecca asked. Anna didn't respond. Rebecca raised her voice over the hiss of the air hoses. "Doctor?"

Anna raised her head and looked over her shoulder at Rebecca.

"Good morning," Anna said.

"Afternoon," Rebecca said.

"Already? Jesus." Anna pointed at an empty spot along one of the lab's far walls. "You can put that cart over there. I won't be needing any of that stuff until later this afternoon. My cultures aren't ready yet."

"Any progress?" Rebecca asked as she wheeled the cart over to the designated spot.

"I wish," said Anna, leaning over her samples once again and dropping another possible vaccine into one of the test tubes. "Damn it. Another negative. I must be missing something."

"Don't worry about it," Rebecca said, shrugging. "We've only been here a month and a half."

"I know, I know," Anna replied. "Most of these vaccines take years to develop. And eggs to grow them in, which we are conspicuously short of."

"Don't sell yourself short. You just haven't had enough time."

"Well, maybe, but I was hoping to at least have gotten *some* idea of what direction I should head in by now," Anna said, frowning behind her faceplate. "Instead, I'm just waltzing in a slow circle. And in the meantime, God knows how many more people are dying from the infection."

"I wish I knew more about what you were doing," Rebecca said over the hiss of the forced air. "I might be able to help you out better."

"Thanks, but even with two of us, we might never find what we're looking for," Anna sighed.

"Well, let's start small, then," Rebecca said, leaning her faceplate closer to Anna's workspace. The Doctor was using a dropper to place samples of light green liquid into test tubes filled with a red, viscous substance. "What are you doing right now, with that thing?"

"Killing time, mostly," Anna said, then noted Rebecca's serious interest and changed her tone. "I had the thought that if I can't figure out where to start looking for a vaccine, I may as well start looking for a better way to kill the virus."

"Like a cure—"

"No!" Anna said, cutting Becky off. "That's not what I mean. What I'm working on today is a virucide. If I can't figure out a vaccine, maybe I can make a weapon. A drug to treat an infected person with after they've been bitten, but before they've turned feral."

"Ah," Becky mused, leaning closer. "So what's in the test tubes?"

"The red ones are Morningstar samples. The green ones are my virucides. So far, I haven't had shit for luck. Morningstar is one resilient little bastard. It lives through just about anything I throw at it," Anna explained, using her dropper as a pointer. "Except for the usual killers, like bleach, or ultraviolet light. But those are a little tough to inject and expect a healthy response."

Becky furrowed her brow behind her faceplate and exhaled slowly, considering. Her breath formed a mist on the faceplate, which was quickly whisked away by the cool air flow in the suit.

"Mind if I ask one more question?" Becky said.

"As long as you ask it without blocking my light," replied Anna, pointing up at the fluorescent lamp that Rebecca was standing under.

Becky took a step back. "Where are you getting all these samples of Morningstar? I know for a fact Sherman said no to the idea of capturing test subjects when Thomas brought it up."

"It's easy enough," Anna said, setting down her dropper and turning to face Becky. She leaned against the countertop and folded her arms, looking intently at the pretty young woman. "I have the help of an old friend."

"What do you mean?"

"He's been with us since the very beginning. One of the very first victims of Morningstar, as a matter of fact. We had him shipped here once we'd finished our tests at USAMRIID so the Deucalion folks could take a look at him. He's just in the other room, there. Want to meet him?"

Anna pointed at a small, windowless metal door in the corner of the laboratory. Becky frowned. The thought of one of the infected in the same building in which she lived, worked, and slept disturbed her. At the same time, curiosity was rearing its ugly head.

"Yeah," Becky said, somewhat reluctantly. "If you're sure it's safe."

"Oh, it's safe enough," Anna said, moving off toward the door. "He's strapped down tight. And he's been very helpful so far."

Anna unhooked her air hose, which let off a puff of pressurized atmosphere, and reattached herself to a hose closer to the door. Rebecca followed suit.

"Remember," Anna said, staring at Rebecca, "he can't get at you, so don't freak out or try to run. You'll rip your suit and then you'll be in a world of shit."

Rebecca didn't need the reminder. "I'm ready. Let's see this volunteer of yours."

Anna unlatched the door and pulled it open. It didn't squeak or groan, turning on well-oiled and maintained hinges. Within was a small space reserved for the observation of viral victims. A single gurney was inside, flanked by banks of monitoring equipment. Most of it was dark. There was no need for a heart monitor.

Strapped down on the gurney was a graying husk of a carrier. He appeared to have been in his early thirties, and was wearing a straitjacket. Further restraints crisscrossed his body, strapping him down to the gurney and rendering him nearly motionless. His head was free, however, and when the door opened, he turned to investigate the noise.

His cracked, dry eyes widened slightly at the sight of Anna and Rebecca, and he let out a low, mournful moan. He opened his mouth and snapped at them over and over, in an almost hypnotic, rhythmic motion.

"Rebecca, may I introduce you to Dr. Klaus Mayer, formerly of Antwerp, late of Mombasa, and the closest thing the world has to a Patient Zero. How are we doing today, Doctor?"

Mayer moaned and rocked his head back and forth by way of reply, jaws still snapping uselessly.

"I'll be back in an hour for some more samples, Dr. Mayer," Anna said, speaking as though he were just another patient. "In the meantime, get some rest. You look a little feverish."

She let the door swing shut as she moved away, affording Rebecca one last slack-jawed stare at the long-undead infected, before her view was cut off by the cold steel of the door.

CHAPTER 3
BITE MARKS
AND DOG FOOD

Abraham, KS
27 June 2007
0900 hrs_

A ROUNDTABLE DISCUSSION WAS taking place at Eileen's Pub in Abraham. The fire had been dealt with, the town had calmed down, and the citizenry had returned to whatever their normal routines were these days—all except for Keaton, Wes, Hal, Stiles, and the ragged group of sailors. They had sat around the candlelit interior of the pub through the night, nursing lukewarm, bitter beer and discussing their options.

"Omaha, Omaha, Omaha," said Keaton, repeating the word like a Buddhist mantra, emphasizing by thumping a mug on the table. "Feels like the new Jerusalem. Or Mecca. Everyone seems to want to get there."

"And for good reason," said Commander Harris, sipping at his pint.

The bitter taste didn't seem to bother him a bit. "If we're ever going to get rid of the Morningstar strain, we need what's there."

"Dr. Demilio, you mean," said Wes. His beer was untouched. "I don't understand what all the fuss is about. We've got a good thing going here in Abraham. We can ride out the storm here."

"Yeah," agreed Hillyard, brushing his hair out of his eyes. "But what's a town to do, surrounded by nothing but the dead and the infected? Just sit here and wait to die yourself?"

"At least we won't get infected. We're pretty well protected," Wes said, a touch defensively.

"Yeah, but for how long?" Allen said. "You've already got a bombed-up clinic, and from what Keaton said, you had yourself some problems with bandits in the past. Who's to say another group won't be along in the future? Infection might not get you—but a bullet does the job just as well."

"Well, I, for one, am not going anywhere," Keaton said. "I can't leave. These people are my responsibility."

"Me, neither," said Wes. "I'm sticking it out here."

Hal Dorne sighed. The conversation had been going on for the better part of an hour, and was leading nowhere. He tipped his glass back and drained it, slammed it upside down on the tabletop, and folded his arms in front of him. "Well, I'm definitely going to Omaha."

His statement drew a few looks of surprise.

"Do you even think you can make it alone?" Keaton asked. "It's a two-hundred-mile no-man's-land between here and there, at least."

"Oh, he won't be going alone," said Stiles, staring at the floor. His new crutch was leaning against his chair. "I have to go, too."

"Why? It's safer here."

"I know, I know," Stiles said. "I didn't say I *wanted* to go. I said I *have* to go."

Hal shot Stiles a warning look. *Don't tell them,* it said. *Don't say a word.* Conversation around the table died down as the sailors saw what was coming next. Allen was shaking his head slowly.

"They're looking for a vaccine for Morningstar there," Stiles said. "I could help. You see, I—"

Stiles was interrupted as the door to Eileen's creaked open and two people entered. One was a toughly built young man with a bum leg; it looked as though it had sustained an injury that was still healing. The other was a perky, pretty young woman who wore her hair tied up in a topknot. The pair seemed to be together, as they never moved more than a few feet away from one another.

The male spoke first. "Eileen! It's Miller time. Katie and I are thirsty."

Eileen, a heavyset woman and the proprietor of the establishment that bore her name, looked up from behind the bar. "I've told you already. No tabs."

"Relax," said the man. "I come bearing gifts." The pair approached the bar and heaved a thick plastic bag onto the polished oak surface. "See? Katie and I found a patch of potatoes when we were out scouting. Figured you could make a stew out of them. Or maybe brew some vodka."

"Well, well," said Eileen, eyeing the sack. "Maybe I misjudged you, Ron. All right . . . a pint per pound."

Ron shook his head. "Two pints per pound."

"One and a half."

"Done," Ron said, and shook Eileen's hand on it.

The roundtable discussion continued as Ron and Katie bartered with Eileen—except for Stiles. He stared, slack-jawed, at the newcomers.

"It can't be," Stiles said after a long moment, his gaze locked on the couple at the bar. The conversation at the table ceased again, and all eyes turned to him.

"What can't be?" asked Commander Harris.

"It can't be," repeated Stiles, still staring at Ron and Katie. "It's not possible."

The newcomers, meanwhile, had noticed the silence at the large table and turned away from the bar to see what the fuss was about.

They did a double take when they spotted Stiles.

"Mark? Mark Stiles?" asked Ron.

"Ron! Katie!" Stiles shouted, leaping up out of his chair and stumbling a bit on his bad wheel. "I can't believe it!"

"A lot of that going around," murmured Harris, taking another swig of his beer.

Ron's look of elation quickly faded. He backed up against the bar, holding an arm across Katie's chest to prevent her from getting any closer to Stiles. His expression became unreadable. "You're supposed to be dead. We saw you die."

Stiles sighed. "No, you didn't. You saw me lead the crowd of infected off on a side street so you could get away clean."

"But you were—" Ron began.

"Yeah. I was bitten."

At this, every occupant of the pub backed away, some knocking over chairs in their haste. Only the sailors, Hal, and Harris remained seated.

Stiles caught the patrons' reaction and let out a bitter laugh. "Yeah. That's right. I'm *infected*. I'm a carrier of Morningstar. But keep those weapons holstered. I might be contagious, but I'm not going to turn on you."

"I don't understand," Katie said, a confused look on her face. "How . . . ?"

"I guess I'm immune," Stiles said, speaking slowly and clearly. "I don't know why. Or how. But I never turned."

"What happened to you?" Ron asked, reaching behind himself for the pint glass of beer Eileen had offered him. He downed it quickly.

"That," said Stiles, "is a long story. After I led the infected away from you—which was not easy, let me tell you—I found an old shop and barricaded myself inside. And I waited to die."

The pub was silent, intent on Stiles's story.

"For a while I thought about suicide. I didn't want to turn. I found an infected in the building with me and I thought, *That's not going to be me. I'd do anything for that to not be me.* But I couldn't do it. I sat there and put the barrel in my mouth and almost pulled the trigger, but I just couldn't. Over and over, like it was some kind of ritual. But something wouldn't let me. So I sat and waited. After the first week passed, I realized I wasn't getting sick. Then I thought that maybe it would just take longer for it to affect me, so I sat and waited some more. Can you imagine . . . can you even *imagine* what it's like to sit and *know* that you're going to die? That it's only a matter of time before you become what you've been fighting for months?"

The pub patrons couldn't meet Stiles's roving gaze. They fixed their looks on their beers and pub food and pretended they didn't hear what the soldier was saying, but they were listening intently to every word.

"No fever. No delirium. Nothing. Just a nasty bite that wouldn't heal up properly," Stiles said, gesturing at his bandaged leg. "So I barricaded myself inside the store, hoarded some food, and hunkered down. Then I realized something just as depressing . . . when I thought I was going to turn, I was just waiting to die. And then, once I didn't," Stiles said with a sad laugh, "I realized that I was in the *exact same situation*. Just sitting, and waiting to die."

"How did you get here, then?" Ron asked.

Stiles hooked a finger in Harris's direction. "The cavalry found me. We had a little bit of a shoot-out, but once we realized neither of us was infected, we sort of joined up."

Hal cleared his throat, and the patrons looked in his direction. "That's why Stiles needs to go to Omaha. The rest of us can stay here, if we wanted to—but not him. He's the only one we know of who's naturally immune to the Morningstar strain. His blood is the key. This could save us from extinction. And I'm going with him. I may be retired, but I ain't dead. Not by a long shot."

"Shit, I'm with you," said Rico, standing up from the table. "You know it."

"Me, too," said Hillyard. "From here to hell and back." Allen thumped him on the shoulder in agreement.

Wendell said nothing, but folded his arms across his chest and nodded his assent. His crew of deckhands did the same.

"I'm on to Omaha, too," said Harris. "Never planned otherwise. You've got my sub and all the ammo I can carry."

Ron and Katie exchanged glances. They looked over at the round table and its occupants. "We're in. Abraham gave us a breather. We love it here. But we can't let this chance slip away. Keaton?"

The Sheriff looked over at Ron, an inquisitive expression on his face. "Yeah?"

"Better unlock the evidence locker," Ron said. "I'm going to need my weapon back."

Keaton sighed. "I still can't come with you. As narcissistic as it sounds, Abraham needs me."

"Don't worry, Sheriff. We don't think any less of you because of it," Harris said, slapping Keaton's shoulder. "You're doing a damn fine job here. Keep your people safe. With a little luck, we'll be back with a weapon the infected can't do a damn thing about—a vaccine."

"Luck be with you, guys," said Wes. "I'm staying here, too. But I'll be praying for you. Now let's go. You've got a long road ahead of you."

✫ ✫ ✫ ✫

Keaton's evidence locker was a veritable arms cache. Stiles was impressed—the Sheriff could field a small army with the gear he'd stockpiled. Confiscated weapons from bandits, standard-issue police firearms, homeland security gear—all of it sorted and stacked and labeled on stainless steel shelves. Gas masks, riot armor, tear gas, rifles, pistols, and even an M-249 Squad Automatic Weapon adorned the interior of the locker.

Stiles whistled. "Where'd you get *that* big fucker?" he asked, lightly touching the SAW.

"Got it off a dead raider. There were two of them, but your buddy Sherman has the other," Keaton said. "Now, let's see . . . where'd Wes put your gear? Wes. *Wes!*"

A distant reply echoed from outside the locker. "Yeah? What is it?"

"Where'd you put the gear you took from these guys?"

"Storage locker three. Most of it, anyway. Stiles's Winchester is in the rifle case on top of the fourth shelf. Didn't want to damage it."

As the rest of the sailors and Hal rummaged through the locker for their weapons and gear, Stiles reached up to retrieve the weapons case on the shelf top. He unlatched it and withdrew the Winchester, inspecting it carefully.

"Look good?" asked Keaton.

"Beautiful," said Stiles, nodding.

He leaned on his rifle and watched the others gather their gear. PO1 Wendell pulled back the bolt on his MP-5, checking to make sure the chamber was clear, then locked and loaded it with a fresh magazine. He glanced at Harris. "Good to go, sir."

Ron and Katie were busy pulling their own gear from a separate locker. Ron checked his revolver carefully, frowning at the bit of rust that had accumulated on it during its weeks in storage. "I'm going to need some gun oil for this," he muttered.

"Easily done," said Keaton, pointing to a shelf in the corner. Bottles of solvent and oil lined the shelf. Ron helped himself to a few of the bottles and set about cleaning his weapon as the rest of the group finished re-equipping themselves.

"Look," Keaton said, "I know you don't want to hear it, but I've got to say it anyway: be careful."

"Don't worry," said Hal. "We'll get Stiles to Omaha in one piece. Everything depends on it. You just worry about Abraham."

Stiles's cheeks flushed. "You make it sound like I'm more important than I am. I'm just a guy."

"In this case, my friend, you *are* important," Hal replied.

"All right," said Keaton, folding his arms across his chest, "you're all set. We're sorry to see you go—we could use the extra rifles—but if you pull this off, maybe, just maybe, we won't need any rifles anymore."

Harris grinned. "Shit. Once we wipe out the Morningstar, there'll still be rifles, and riflemen to use 'em. People will always be people."

"Thanks, Sheriff," said Harris. "We're indebted to you for your hospitality."

"And to Eileen for the beer," Allen said wistfully.

Wes's voice came echoing through the locker once more. "Aren't you forgetting something, Keaton?"

The Sheriff cast a confused glance in the direction of Wes's voice, then brightened. "Ah! That's right! We've been saving something for a rainy day. There's a man we'd like you to meet. I'm sure he'll be happy to see you once we tell him you're friends with General Sherman."

"Who?"

"You'll see. Wes! Bring that cart around front! We're going to Jose's!"

"Yes, sir, oh-mighty-Sheriff, sir!" came Wes's reply.

"Knock it off and bring the damn cart around already."

★ ★ ★ ★ ★

There was only enough room in the electric cart for four. Wes and Keaton took the front seats, and Harris and Hal took the rear. As they cruised along Abraham's streets, Hal's thoughts turned to the home he'd left behind.

There, his only worry had been keeping up his supply of alcohol and working on his next invention. Things had turned upside down for him when he'd found himself cast out of his island paradise. Here, though, he got a taste of what life could be like if the Morningstar strain ceased to be.

The town of Abraham was well maintained. Aside from the tall, unkempt grass, ancient oaks lined the streets and the town green had been turned into a finely manicured garden. Hal spotted herb plots, perfect lines of amber grain, cornstalks, and low-lying vines with what he could only assume were unripe watermelons growing on them. This was a town that could survive, thick and thin, due not only to good leadership but a solid work ethic. The people he saw, though doubtless bereaved by those lost in the pandemic, were all smiles. Disaster had brought them closer together. It had actually had a positive effect on them. Hal grinned at the thought.

They passed a playground, and Hal watched as a pair of children on a swing set competed to see who could swing higher. He was always afraid he'd go too high and flip over when he was a kid. The thought made him grin even more. Simpler times.

The cart turned onto a narrow side street, slowed, and stopped, breaking Hal's reverie.

"We're here," announced Keaton, sliding out of the driver's seat and pointing at a hand-painted sign on a steel-shuttered door. It read ARC-TURA'S BODY SHOP—OPEN FOR BUSINESS.

"A mechanic? What do we need a mechanic for?" wondered Harris.

"You'll see. Call it a parting gift." Keaton pounded on the steel shutters. "Jose! Customers!"

It took a moment before a response was forthcoming.

"Customers? Ai, no customers for weeks. What do you want now? Got another truck you need fixed?"

"Not quite," said Keaton, raising his voice to be heard through the shutters. "We need that jalopy of yours."

"What?" came the incredulous reply. "And what makes you think I'm going to hand it over to you, eh? *Americanos estúpidos, siempre incomodándome para esto o ése. ¿Cuáles son yo, un servicio del coche de alquiler?*"

"Oh, knock it off, Jose. It only works on cute women, anyway. *Sprechen sie* English, *pendejo,*" Keaton shot back. "Besides, I think you'll want to meet these guys. They're friends of Francis Sherman."

"Sherman? General Sherman? *Mierda,* that's all you had to say! One minute—I have to unlock the shutters."

The sound of rattling chains and clinking steel sounded from behind the shutters, and after a moment, they rolled up with a loud clatter, folding into the ceiling. Revealed was a large garage, lined with tool benches and heavy equipment. In front of them stood a darkly tanned man, short, with close-cropped black hair and a thin mustache. He was wearing oil-stained coveralls and had a wrench hung from a tool belt. Behind him, bent over an ancient-looking Ford sedan, was a young woman in similar dress. She turned to face the newcomers, wiping her face clean with a rag she had stuck in the waistband of her pants.

"How can I help you? We do it all here. Transmissions, rotations— we can even roll back the odometer for the right price."

"I like her," Hal said.

Jose put his arm around the young woman's shoulders and brought her forward. The girl was pretty, with long dark hair pulled back in a braid. She shared the same tan complexion as her father, and had an exotic, enticing look about her. She carried herself confidently. "This is my daughter, Adelina. She's the smartest thing this side of the Mississippi—and a better mechanic than I ever could hope to be."

Keaton waved at the visiting duo. "Adelina, these men are friends of Sherman's. The older one is Hal—the younger's Harris, from the Navy."

"Sherman? He's the one who rescued me from—" Adelina broke off her sentence, overcome, and rushed to hug Hal and Harris, who both flushed and backed away at the girl's sudden outburst of emotion. She sniffled. "He rescued me from those—those pigs!"

Jose wrapped his arms around her and patted her on the head. *"Es bien, amor, son ahora ida. Ellos no pueda le lastimó más,"* he said. He turned to Hal and Harris. "Those raiders—the ones under the Lutz brothers—they did . . . *things* to her."

"I just wish I could have killed some of them myself," muttered Adelina.

Jose frowned. "You're not like them, *mijitia.*"

Keaton cleared his throat. "Jose, I hate to interrupt, but . . ."

Jose looked over at the Sheriff. "Right. The jalopy. I was saving it in case we were overrun and needed to make a break for it, but—for friends of Sherman, no problemo. I'm afraid it's not in the best of shape, though."

Jose and Adelina led the little group over to a corner of the garage. A car, covered by a tan tarp, sat gathering dust in the shadows. The pair of mechanics yanked back the cover, revealing an old pickup truck. Dings and dents covered the exterior, and rust was everywhere. The windshield was opaque from the amount of grime that had gathered on it, and the seat coverings were ripped and torn.

Jose noticed the looks of disbelief on the faces of Hal and Harris, and laughed out loud. "Don't let her looks fool you. She runs—mostly. The keys are in the glove compartment."

Harris frowned, a bit confused. "Wait a minute—are you just giving us this car?"

Jose nodded, still smiling. "Of course. Like I said, for friends of Sherman, I'll do anything. He gave me back my daughter. The least

I can do is give you this piece of shit. It's the best I have, but it's still a piece of shit." He seesawed his hand. "Not much of a contingency plan, right? It'll get you to Omaha a bit quicker, though."

"How'd you know we were going to Omaha?" Harris asked, narrowing his eyes. He was the suspicious type. Hal supposed it came from being a ranking officer. One always needed to keep his ears open for loose lips.

"That's where Sherman was headed," Jose said, opening the passenger door of the jalopy and retrieving the key from the glove compartment. "Doesn't take a rocket scientist to figure out that's where you're going, too."

"This'll help us out tremendously, Mr. Arctura," said Harris, accepting the key ring from the mechanic.

"There's a catch," said Jose, raising a finger. "Gasoline."

"What about it?" Harris asked, furrowing his brow.

"Not much left here. We siphoned off what we could, but we're down to dregs," Jose explained. "You've got about a half a tank in that truck. It'll get you—maybe—a hundred miles closer to Omaha. From there you'll have to hoof it, unless you can scrounge up some more fuel somewhere."

"That's good enough for us, Jose," said Harris. "You're very generous."

"No, no," said Jose, waving off the thanks. "You're welcome to anything in my shop."

Harris nodded curtly. "We'll just make do with the truck, Jose. And you have my thanks nonetheless. Well, Hal—shall we?"

"Let's," agreed Hal, slipping into the passenger seat of the truck. "We'll make good time in this thing."

Commander Harris took the driver's seat, turning over the engine. It whined a bit, screeched, and caught, purring contentedly.

"A word of warning," said Jose, raising his voice above the sound of the engine. "If she starts to make a coughing noise on the road, shift into neutral or you'll blow the transmission. Oh, and she pulls to the left, so keep an eye out for that."

"Thanks for the heads-up," said Hal, leaning out the passenger window. "If we make it to Omaha in one piece, we'll make sure to bring her back to you."

"Keep it. It's yours. Once you find that vaccine you're looking for, I'm going to go find myself an abandoned Lamborghini."

Adelina chuckled and shook her head. "Just be safe."

"Yes, ma'am," said Harris, and shifted into drive.

✯ ✯ ✯ ✯ ✯

Rico and Hillyard sat, watching Wendell and the deckhands play a round of Spades at another table. Allen was drunk, teetering on the back two legs of a bar stool and doing a surprisingly good job of it. Stiles sat behind him on the floor, his legs out in front of him, watching the balancing act. The crew sat in a pretty wide circle of townsfolk . . . not exactly hostile, and not exactly unwelcoming, but the news of Stiles's condition had definitely changed the tone of the pub when the group returned. Ron and Katie were making the rounds, saying their good-byes.

"I think I can take four," said Jones, looking intently, if a little drunkenly, at his hand of thirteen cards.

"Five more," said Wendell, his eyes closed and looking up at the ceiling. He'd played more hands of Spades than any other sailor on the *Ramage,* definitely more than all of the deckhands put together.

"All right!" shouted Allen from his stool. "Nine for Wendell and Jooones!"

"Three," whispered Stiles from the floor.

"Three," said Smith, who had made the same bid for the last ten games. His partner Brown groaned and Jones laughed.

"Goddammit," Brown said. "Do you even know how to play this game? Every fucking time, three tricks, you sandbagging motherfucker. After this hand"—he slammed his cards on the table, facedown—"we are swapping partners."

"Your bid?" asked Wendell.

Brown pursed his lips and sank into his chair. "Nil."

Allen let loose with a gigantic burp. "Three for Brith. Smown. Fuck . . . those two."

The door to the pub eased open and Harris walked in, followed by Hal and the Sheriff.

"Oh, thank God," Brown said, throwing his cards into the air. "Tell me I don't have to finish this round."

"You don't. Mount up, men," Harris said over Brown's cheer. "We're headed out. And we've got a ride."

Omaha, NE
27 June 2007
0915 hrs_

Ewan Brewster was getting very tired of scavenging duty. He knew it was necessary. Without a regular supply of food and medicines, the Fac wouldn't have lasted as long as it had. Still, he reasoned, why did *he* have to do it? He'd much rather let Juni have his spot, and take up residence behind the nice, thick front doors of the Fac, safe and sound. He was sure she'd jump at the chance.

Ewan doubted Trevor felt the same way. As a matter of fact, he had a sneaking suspicion that Trev might even be happier at the prospect of heading out solo, without anything or anyone restraining him.

Their expedition the day before had yielded a pack full of expired medical supplies, but, as Trevor had predicted, Dr. Demilio had thrown the majority of them out. Brewster groaned and made a scene, but he knew it wouldn't do him any good. The next scavenging run was set. To remove some of the sting, Sherman had decreed that it would be a full run, and not just Trev and Ewan.

Before their first run, months earlier, Trevor and Brewster had spent an hour going over a map of western Omaha until they spotted a free clinic, more than a mile from the Fac. It would be the farthest they had ever ventured from the safety of their compound, and Brewster had been nervous at the prospect. Still, the clinic would likely have everything they needed. It had been worth a shot. The risk had paid off, loading them up with enough basic supplies to keep Anna happy for several weeks. As time went on and they picked the shelves clean, Ewan knew they'd either have to leave Omaha entirely to find a new clinic or hospital worth searching, or head deeper into Omaha itself, which was, at best, a chancy proposition. At worst, it was suicide.

The city teemed with infected. Doc Demilio had told him the pre-Morningstar population of Omaha proper was almost a half-million souls. He had no idea how many of them had made it out, and no inclination to find out.

Junko Koji lazily watched from one of the lobby's comfortable chairs as Brewster and Trev prepared to go out. She sat next to Denton, arms folded across her slight chest, with the barest hint of a smile on her face.

Brewster noticed the look.

"What is it now, Juni?" Brewster asked, snapping a pistol belt around his waist. "Don't look so fuckin' smug. Just because you're the forever door guard now doesn't mean this won't be you at some point."

"That's not it. I just like watching you squirm," she replied, her smile widening.

"You're a contrary little minx if ever I saw one," said Brewster. "Still don't know what to make of you."

Trev slapped him hard on the shoulder. "Leave her be. She's all right."

"Hey, I have talents," Juni said, spreading her arms wide. "Want to know how to say 'fuck you' in Russian? How about in French? Japanese? German? Oh, I know. How about Farsi?"

"What in the fuck is a Farsi?" Brewster asked, strapping Kevlar body armor across his chest and checking to make sure the fit was right. It wasn't as useful against infected as it was against armed opponents, but it would still stop a bite or keep the soldier from being raked by a shambler's fingernails.

"See?" Juni grinned. "You can't even see me, I'm so far up." She twirled a lock of hair around her finger. "It's not my fault Sherman wants the brains to stay here, while you two go out and be the brawn."

"Now you're just being mean," Brewster said, but favored her with a smile anyway. Juni was growing on him. He liked her light sense of humor. He pulled a K-pot from the stack of gear set near the doorway, but decided against wearing it, tossing it back into the container. Instead, he fished a faded black baseball cap, sweat-stained and well worn, from one of the cargo pockets in his trousers and fitted it snugly over his head.

"You know," Trev said, "you don't have to keep trying so hard. No one knows you're knockin' boots."

Brewster, for once at a loss for words, said nothing.

Equipped, the pair lifted the wooden and metal bars that locked the main doors, waited as Denton threw back the dead bolt with a twist of his key, and pulled open the doors. They shaded their eyes from the sunlight that cut into the room.

Their excursions into the streets of Omaha were always done during the day. The sunlight invigorated them, was their best friend on these runs. The old wisdom of using darkness as cover had gone away with the advent of the Morningstar strain. The infected, for reasons unknown, always preferred darkness. They would only come out into the light if they spotted prey. Otherwise, they would find a darkened room or shady alleyway and wait until the light faded. They waited until nightfall before they resumed their plodding patrol of the streets that had once held bustling pedestrians and the rumbling of delivery trucks making their rounds.

That made midday the safest time to scavenge.

Trevor and Brewster exited the Fac, closed the door behind them, and heard the heavy thunk of Juni sliding the bars back into place. The rest of the group would be out in another minute or two. Trev and Brewster had farther to travel, so they'd decided to move out earlier.

"Man, it's a beautiful day," remarked Trevor, taking a moment to lean his head back and let the sunlight warm his face. "Not a cloud in the sky."

"Yeah," agreed Brewster, scanning slowly with his double-barreled street-sweeper for any signs of life, or unlife. "I just wish we didn't have to do this. Definitely *nothing* beautiful in most of those buildings."

"I have to appreciate a nice thing while I still can. Well—want to get to it?"

"Yeah, sure," Brewster said, shouldering his shotgun. He knew that Mitsui and Jack, stationed on the rooftop above, were keeping an eye on their progress in between rounds of chess. He could afford to relax for the first couple blocks of their journey, but he'd have to fall back on guard when the Fac was no longer in sight.

It's not a city anymore, Ewan Brewster reminded himself. Now it's just a goddamn graveyard.

Resting on one knee, he covered the street to the right. Trevor, who usually eschewed firearms, held his revolver and was crouched across from Brewster, scanning left. They moved forward.

$$\star \quad \star \quad \star \quad \star \quad \star$$

They stuck to the middle of the street, which went against every instinct for Brewster. In another time and place, his brain would be shouting at him to hug the buildings, watch the opposite roofs and windows for snipers, and cover his buddies. Experience and training both screamed at him to get the hell out of the center of the road.

Brewster knew that if he listened to that voice now, he stood a good chance of being tackled from the side by an infected lounging in the shadows cast by the structures. This brave new world meant new rules, new tactics. He'd had to unlearn a lot over the past few months.

As always, aside from their own footsteps, everything was dead quiet. Brewster kicked at a bramble that, like thousands of others, had spent the spring growing out of a crack in the pavement.

"Hey, hey, hey," chastised Trev, keeping his voice low. "The weed wants to live, just like you."

"Just reminds me that all of this is going to be gone in a few years," Brewster murmured.

"What?"

"All this," Brewster said, gesturing around at the buildings that surrounded them. "Stuff growing up through the cracks is just the start. Fast-forward ten years, this place will be a big, overgrown jungle."

Trev squinted up at the structures. "Well, it's going to take a while," he said. "I'd say you still have a few years to do some sightseeing once Anna figures out the vaccine. And, you know, I don't think there ever was a jungle in Nebraska."

"You know what I mean." Brewster stopped and grimaced.

"What *now*?" pressed Trev.

"It's just that—" started Brewster, but shook his head. "Never mind. Let's go."

"Whatever you say."

For a moment, Brewster saw a flash of emotion on Trev's face, worry that he was beginning to sulk. He knew he was no fun when he got in one of those moods, and Trev never liked his outing spoiled by griping.

It's not my fault. Whining's one of my greatest talents.

The two moved through a distant intersection beneath traffic lights that hadn't worked in months, turned left, and vanished from sight.

★ ★ ★ ★ ★

Behind Brewster and Trevor, the front door to the Fac swung silently open once more, and the rest of the scavengers filtered out. General Sherman was first, looking left and right to clear the street before beckoning the others after him. Thomas was the second to appear, like Sherman, scanning the streets suspiciously. Mbutu, the solidly built man who might, in better times, have been mistaken for a linebacker, followed slowly as Sherman surveyed the Fac's front yard. It had been a parking lot, but with only enough room for a single row of cars to pull up in front of the building, the sidewalk and street just beyond. Opposite was a two-story row of storefronts with apartments in the upper floor and angled, shingled roofs.

They stood within the perimeter of the fence for a few moments. Though it made Sherman feel like a prisoner, the fenced-in backyard gave him a place to jog in the mornings without having to worry about a gruesome death-by-infected. Others among the survivors had their own uses for the yard, which they had extended to include part of the neighboring industrial plant. All of the exterior windows were neatly bolted shut with two-by-four metal slats, thanks to Jack the Welder and Mitsui. They'd left narrow, reinforced slits in each, so the occupants could still see outside and, if need be, fire at any attackers.

So far, Sherman consoled himself, the roughest opposition they had run up against had been the odd curious shambler or sprinter.

And it eased his heart to know that, if things got hot on their scavenging run, they would all have a safe place to fall back to. The thing that weighed on him heavily was the two men locked in that side office. Sooner or later, someone would come for them, and they wouldn't be polite about it. These scavenging runs had more than just one purpose . . . Sherman wanted to keep his men on-point and sharp for when that day did come.

Well, Sherman thought, *no point in procrastinating.*

"All right, ladies, we know the drill. Move fast, move quiet. If you engage contacts, fall back to the Fac, and we'll cover your retreat." Sherman double-checked the radio clipped to his front shirt pocket. Satisfied it was running on a full charge, he nodded and gestured toward the barren, trash-swept streets of Omaha. "Let's get to it."

"The Radio Shack is five klicks, north by northeast," Thomas said, indicating direction with his jaw. "We can skirt the outlying section of Omaha proper and return on the same arc. Mitsui will be happy when we get back."

Sherman grunted. "Hell, *I'll* be happy when we get back."

He looked to Mbutu Ngasy, whom he half-jokingly considered his human dowsing rod. The man had a knack for diagnosing a situation and gauging the safety of it. The former air traffic controller had kept them out of more than one potential tomb, and they listened to him when he felt a tingle in his Mbutu-sense. The large man favored Sherman with a wide smile.

"Once more into the breach, is that right, General?"

Sherman raised his eyebrows. "Not you, too. I'm not in the Army anymore, remember? I hold no rank."

Thomas cleared his throat. "We'd best be moving along, sir. We don't have that far to go, but inside the dark of the buildings, the infected will be active."

Sherman hefted his pack. "Quite right, Thomas. Let's go."

★ ★ ★ ★ ★

Brewster and Trev crouched in a large parking lot, eyeing the quiet front of a store and debating whether to go in.

"I say, it'll be better than whatever they're going to whip up at the Fac," Trevor said calmly, but Brewster was clearly wearing on him.

"We'll never hear the fuckin' end of it, man. I promise you. If even one of them barks at me, I won't be held responsible—"

Trev held up his hands. "One package. We'll be real quiet about it when we get it in, and no one will know for sure which team it was."

Brewster looked the storefront. "Fine. But I don't want to go in the front. This isn't even really on our route. You planned this shit, didn't you?"

Snorting a laugh, Trev rolled his eyes and pointed at the side of the large building, indicating they should follow that wall to find a loading dock or utility entrance. They moved that way, eyes roving for shadows within shadows that would indicate an infected, watching for shards of glass on the asphalt that might give away their position if stepped on, or empty cans that would do the same.

The roll-up door at the back of the building was padlocked shut. Brewster checked the side strap of his bag and swore softly.

"Pinch bar," he said. "I forgot the fucking—"

"Right here," Trev said, cutting him off. "You left it sitting next to the entryway when you picked up your body armor."

Taking the bar, he grimaced. "Gonna need a checklist. Damn it, I'm too young to be senile."

Sliding the bar between the wall and the hasp of the lock, he pulled down with steady pressure. Trev waited for the first telltale sound that the screws were giving. At the first creak, he tapped Ewan, and they went dead still, listening with everything they had. Pursing his lips, Trev nodded and Brewster continued working on the lock. More steady pressure, and with a sudden wrench the hasp slipped free of its moorings.

Pumping his fist in the air, Brewster put the lock on the ground and rolled up the door. He and Trev slipped inside and rolled the door shut.

"Big store to clear," Trev said.

"Better get started, then," Brewster said, and tossed the lock clattering on the concrete backroom floor. Immediately, the noise drew a groan from somewhere among the shelves.

Trev shook his head, snapping out the ASP. "Lucky there's only one."

Brewster gestured with a "go ahead," and Trev stepped forward, what little amusement there was from Ewan's antics fading away. Taking over was the cold satisfaction he knew that soon, very soon, there would be one less demon in the world. He stalked forward, checking side aisles for the dead person that was in there.

The sound of a step was all the warning Trevor got, and he ducked under the outstretched arms of the male shambler as it reached for him from the right side. He took a shuffle step forward and spun that way, the ASP whistling through the air in a quick arc and slamming into the side of the dead thing's neck.

Though it felt no pain, the force of the impact threw the shambler off balance and it staggered away. It wore a store uniform and apron, stained with gore from its own death wound, some bit of entrails slipping out of a hole in its middle. Single-minded, the dead man turned toward Trev again, jaws widening and black bile slipping out over its chin. It swiped filthy arms at Trev and he danced easily out of its reach.

The thing stepped forward and Trev stepped back, matching its pace.

"Come on," Brewster said. "Quit playing and let's get on with it."

Trev stood up straight and swung the baton, catching the dead man in the temple with a crunch. It collapsed, falling to his booted feet, one filthy and emaciated claw scrambling for purchase on the scuffed leather there.

"Buzzkill," Trev said, stomping on the dead man's neck.

✫ ✫ ✫ ✫

Thomas and Sherman swept the inside of the Radio Shack for the things on Mitsui's wish list, while Mbutu Ngasy stood sentinel at the door.

"DC-to-DC converter," Sherman said, reading from the piece of paper, "variable settings, two each."

"Check," Thomas responded, looking in a pack on the counter of the store. It looked to him as if a giant robot had thrown up in the canvas vessel, but Mitsui was adamant that everything there would be needed.

"Signal generator."

"Check."

"Fluke multimeter."

"Check."

"Card read/write device."

"Check. General," Thomas said, interrupting the reading. "Sir, we're not going to make the rest of the run in the allotted time if we go through the list again."

Sherman raised an eyebrow at the man. "You never forgo a second check."

Muscles bunched and relaxed in the grizzled sergeant major's jaw. "Sir, instead of fucking around with whatever it is Mitsui is doing to the security systems of the Fac, we should be working on shoring up the defenses."

Not meeting Thomas's gaze, Sherman looked down at the list. "We're next to impervious from the infected there."

"I don't mean the infected, sir. Don't tell me you haven't thought that there will be more of those government men coming."

Sherman heaved a sigh. "It's a damn shame, isn't it? I thought that our problems with our fellow man might have been over with the raiders outside Abraham."

"Yes, sir. It is a shame. But it is what it is, sir."

Sherman cast a glance at the former sergeant major in the gloom. "You have an idea, or you wouldn't have piped up."

Thomas allowed himself a rare grin. "That I do, sir. Mason."

He let that name sink in for a minute. The former government agent was an untapped resource. Gutshot, it would be quite a while until the man was back on his feet, but there was nothing wrong with his mind. Any other time, Thomas would be surprised that General Sherman would overlook such a valuable commodity that Mason carried around in his head, but these days being what they were, with the General worried about keeping his handful of survivors fed and clothed, not to mention the critical research going on beneath their feet, Thomas was unfazed.

He has taken so much on his shoulders. Perhaps too much.

"And I think it would be better if we talked about it on the move."

A quick nod showed Sherman's assent. "Right again. Let's hit the next place on the list. Walk with me, talk with me."

Thomas shouldered the pack and turned toward the door. "It's my understanding, sir, that Mason was on a team with the agents that we expelled from the Fac when we arrived."

"Yes. From my own conversations with him, they were sent by a rogue faction of the government, convinced that Anna was carrying a cure around with her. It's nonsense."

"We know that, sir. But if that's what they think, they'll be back, and if a member of Mason's team is in charge of the assault . . ."

"Then Mason will know the tactics he's likely to deploy. Good thinking, Thomas. Remind me to put you in for an award. Pick one."

Thomas nodded. "As soon as we get back, sir."

They left the Radio Shack only when Mbutu had given them the all-clear and headed farther north. The last place on their list was an old-time army/navy surplus store Denton had found a listing for in an aging phone book. Thomas was looking forward to it, as the survivors were using a hodgepodge of gear and the surplus store represented a chance to fix all that. He hated disorganization.

Thomas held all this in mind as they hoofed it to the store. Although he and the general had retired from service when they went AWOL, if the government ever got around to it, he'd be branded a deserter. But he also knew that the discipline that came with being part of a unit was a major component of the glue that was holding their band together. They wouldn't force anything on the men, but Thomas would provide the opportunity for them to get back to what was familiar before Morningstar.

With three blocks to go, Mbutu went still, a frown creasing his normally impassive face.

Thomas noticed this and immediately fell silent, bringing his arms to bear. Sherman did the same.

Mbutu turned to face a storefront that had been painted over in black, windows and all, from top to bottom. The only nonblack portion was a splash of red that was the name of the store, Kathedral.

"In there?" Thomas asked, gesturing with his shotgun. "Shouldn't be a big deal. The windows are painted black, so it's not like they can see—"

He was cut off by a meaty thud. The scavenging team went silent again, and the sound repeated itself, this time more insistently.

It was joined by others.

"Bug out," Sherman said.

The trio set off at a quick jog, sticking to the center of the wide and empty shopping center parking lot. A sharp *crack* urged them to greater speed, running carefully and placing their feet deliberately, doing their best to avoid the concrete blocks set in the middle of rows. Thomas, his gray head always swiveling from left to right and searching for threats, saw a single and lonely delivery truck sitting near the end of the shopping center building.

With an overwhelming crash, the storefront window came out of its frame and shattered on the asphalt. Unable to help himself, Mbutu stopped running to look back at what was coming out after them. From the look on his face, he wasn't quite sure what to make of them.

Five former teens, now blind and drooling monsters, all stepped or fell out of the broken window, looking as if they were a part of the same unorthodox army: black shirts over black, baggy pants, festooned with silver chains and armbands. Heavy piercings fell from rotted flesh, the weight tearing through after a long period of inactivity.

"What are those?" he asked.

Thomas turned to look and almost laughed. "Punks. Just punks. In the days before Morningstar, I may or may not have prayed to Providence for an opportunity to show these emo losers what real pain was."

"They know now," Sherman said. "Come on, they're in no shape to track us down."

He and Mbutu turned and continued their jog. Thomas stood in the parking lot for a minute longer, looking back at the quintet of shamblers.

"I don't even have the words," he said, shaking his head and turning to catch up with his team.

✯ ✯ ✯ ✯ ✯

Brewster shifted the heavy pack around on his shoulders and made a face. Trevor remembered a time when Ewan had said that typically, in Africa, his MOLLE pack weighed up to seventy-five pounds, but it had been different, then. The pack now only weighed forty pounds, but circumstances changed everything.

"I know you said only one, but this is a big goddamn bag. How come we couldn't make this stop on the way back?"

"You know how it gets," Trev said as he adjusted the straps on Brewster's pack. "Sometimes we get milk runs, sometimes we have to lead a chase back. So far, this has been a milk run, and it would be a shame to waste this opportunity."

"Meanwhile," Brewster said as they walked back to the big roll-up door, "I carry an extra forty pounds of stuff we probably won't need. I never thought I'd say this, but I miss IEDs and terrorists. Take them over these shambling fuckheads any day."

Trev got down on the ground and pushed the door up an inch, looking around. It had only been seven months since the outbreak began, and Trev had seen all stages of the virus. He was no longer surprised by it, but every day that they ran across a sprinter made him wonder just what those things were living on, how they could survive. He knew that the demons were impervious to most forms of injury, and even if you did kill them they'd come back, but even with their unnatural, virus-fed vitality, the demons were still wearing human skins. How long could they live for?

Shaking his head, Trev dismissed that train of thought. It was enough that they existed, and he was there to kill them.

He was putting up with the former private's bitching pretty easily today, and not only because he'd had the opportunity to dispatch a demon; in spite of his bitching, Brewster had gone along with Trev's idea. It gave him hope for their future, immediate and long-term.

"All clear," Trev said, pushing the gate the rest of the way open. "It's not much farther to the next pharmacy."

"You're not the one carrying forty pounds of—"

Brewster's comment as he stepped outside was cut off by the snarling impact of a sprinter, almost two hundred pounds of rabid, subhuman creature bowling him over. The thing's lips were pulled back inhumanly far, revealing most of its teeth, and it made hungry, almost mewling sounds as it reached out for Brewster's unprotected neck. In all its clawing, it hooked fingertips in the loops and straps of his body armor.

Frustrated, it pulled back its head and opened its mouth to howl, which would surely bring more of its kind.

The howl was cut off by the end of Trev's ASP as he forced the head of the baton down the foul thing's throat.

It backed off Brewster immediately, yanking the ASP out of Trev's hand as it stood. The sprinter's head was forced back at an unnatural angle by the sudden sword-swallowing act it had become a part of. Strangled screams coughed out of the sprinter's mouth as it tried to force a howl around the protrusion.

"Foreign object," Brewster muttered as he got to his feet. Trev helped him check himself. They found no rips or tears in his clothing or skin, and Ewan looked up at the feverish sprinter and, for just a moment, his face reddened.

Trev knew the feeling, when the mad rage overcame him.

A low rumble started in Ewan's gut and he threw himself at the creature.

Grabbing the handle of the ASP, Brewster yanked down and drew his knee up, shattering the thing's teeth on the metal tube lodged in its throat. The sprinter fell, and Brewster stomped on its hands, breaking bones with each footfall, until they were little more than sacks of meat.

He fell back, spitting and wiping his mouth. "Foul fucking thing," he finally had the breath to say.

Trev, who had been watching all this with curious detachment, retrieved his ASP and finished off the creature.

"Now you see how I see them."

★ ★ ★ ★ ★

The scavenging teams filtered in back at the base, disgorging the contents of their packs onto the table in the executive meeting room, the largest flat surface in the entirety of the Fac. Brewster had a flush to his face and neck as he emptied his pack.

"What is this?" Juni asked, pulling at one corner of the generic wrapping of the large sack. "And why is it so heavy?" With a grunt, she put her weight into it and flipped the forty-pound bag.

Denton snorted a laugh at her expression.

"Dog food, Brewster? You brought *dog food*? What I look like to you? *Scheissekopf!*"

"Fine, fine," Brewster said, his blush deepening as he looked over at Trev, who was clearly enjoying the entire exchange. "We'll get rid of it. Whatever. Feed it to the captive assholes or something."

He snatched the bag up and headed out of the room, almost running headlong into Thomas.

"Slow your roll, asshat," Thomas growled at Brewster in the hallway. "What's that? Dog food?"

"Yes," Brewster sighed.

A glint came into Thomas's eyes. "Well, shit on me. I thought you'd never do anything right, Brewster. Let me guess, they didn't like it?" He indicated the group in the conference room.

Brewster nodded.

"Well, in times like this, there's an old saying that always comforts me," Thomas said, laying a hand on Brewster's shoulder. "And that's 'Fuck 'em.' Put it in the back, where the civvies don't look. When the food runs low, we'll feed it to 'em on the sly. Good thinking, PFC."

Ewan Brewster watched Thomas's retreating back as he legged his own pack into the conference room, a smile growing on his face.

CHAPTER 4
FIGHT OR FLIGHT

Lexington, NE
28 June 2007
1643 hrs_

"I do not like this," said Rico. "I do not like this one bit."

Stiles nodded in agreement.

They were standing in front of a gently sloping road. Abandoned cars littered the pavement, some with windows broken out. Several had smashed into one another, as if the drivers were frantically attempting to get away from quickly approaching doom. Hoods and trunks were smashed in, and stains marred the pavement, old oil mixed with old blood.

Yet it wasn't the vehicles that made Stiles nervous. It was the bridge that lay beyond them. It was a congested swarm of smashed auto bodies and several freight trucks, one of which was tipped up on its side, blocking nearly all of the bridge. It had probably started the trouble, trapping the vehicles fleeing Lexington behind it. Everyone would have had to run for it on foot. Five months before, when sprinters were everywhere, it would have been a hellish scene. Even from the bank looking out, the small group could see dried blood-stains in the windows of the wrecked cars, and a similar dark rivulet had stained the side of the bridge a rusty color where it had run out to drip into the Platte River.

"If there were any other way around, man—" started Allen, but he was cut off by Harris.

"There isn't. We went over this with Keaton while you lot were drinking. This is the only way across the river for miles. Unless you want to try to swim across in full clothing with sixty pounds of gear on your back, of course."

Hillyard scowled, but said nothing. The commander was right. The bridge was the only choice.

"We either go across, or we spend a week trying to find another crossing," said Wendell. The petty officer looked resigned. "And we might not even find one. Bridges could be out, like I-80's. Even if we did find one, it might be too late to get Stiles to Omaha. The infected could've overrun the Doc and her friends by then, for all we know."

"Across it is," said Harris, holding his MP-5 at the ready. "Stay sharp. It might be bright and sunny out here, but some of those trucks look nice and shady. Lots of places to hide."

The thought made the group shuffle. They started out, glancing back at the truck they would have to leave behind; there was no way they'd get it through the snarl of bent and burned cars that were block-ing most of the lanes on the bridge.

Hal and Stiles stuck close to Rico and Wendell. Hal held out his pistol defensively, and Stiles was glad for the crutch in his armpit, even still grimacing at the pain in his leg. He levered a round into the Win-chester and held the rifle out in front of himself, ready for anything.

"All right, gentlemen, here we go," said Harris.

The group wound through the wreckage of the cars and onto the baking tan surface of the concrete bridge.

"Maybe we should just run for it," whispered Brown. "The infected hate the sun, right? It's hot as hell out here. If there are any still around, maybe they'd rather just stay put."

"They'll follow us," said Stiles. "You and I both know that. They only stay in the dark if they can't find us."

"Shut up!" whispered Wendell. "Keep quiet! And stay close together. Watch each other's backs!"

The group moved farther onto the bridge.

The long, narrow span was jammed full of vehicles, bumper to bumper. Here and there a trail of blood led away from the cars, and a splash of gore on the guardrails spoke of violence long since past. Several corpses were scattered about. A few lay on the pavement, some still sat in their cars. Most were missing limbs and had large caverns in their midsections where they'd been gutted and eaten.

The backup of trucks was near the middle of the bridge. The one that had tipped over had blocked all but a few feet of open space. Several corpses lay in the space, stacked atop one another, and scores of bullet holes pockmarked the hood of the overturned truck and the pavement around the open space. Stiles had the scene all worked out in his head, now: The truck had lost control, blocking the highway. Behind it, thousands of people had all been trying to flee Lexington at once, and, finding traffic halted, had all come running across. The first few dozen probably made it through with time to spare. .

But then the infected would have caught up. It appeared as if a few intrepid folks had made a stand near the overturned truck, holding the small pass with whatever weapons they had, until at last they were overrun themselves. The corpses they had already passed must have been the last defenders. With a little luck, their lives had bought enough time for their fellow refugees to flee to safety.

"Up and over, people," said Harris, pointing at the overturned truck. The group gave the corpses a wide berth. Chances were good the virus was as dead as they were, but there was no use in risking contact with anything potentially infected. They climbed, one by one, over the truck's engine block and cab.

On the other side, more bodies greeted them. They all, Stiles noted, lay facing the tiny gap between the truck and the bridge's edge. Infected, then, gunned down as they tried to get through.

They continued along silently, more than halfway across now.

"Something big went down here," whispered Allen, leaning in close to the side of a maroon Chevrolet, a corpse still buckled into the front seat. A rusting revolver lay on its lap, exposed for months to the elements by the sedan's shattered windows. "Wonder how this guy checked out."

"Shut up!" Harris said.

Rico turned, and his boot caught a slick of oil that had run out from under a battered Ford pickup. He slipped, falling hard on his rear. His weapon discharged once, making the group jump. The surrounding vehicles bounced the sound back and forth and amplified it, and the trees along the riverbank caught it and sent it back, echoing for what seemed like forever.

"Oh, fuck me," whispered a wide-eyed Rico, looking up from the ground.

The response was immediate: from out of one of the trucks behind them came the sound of a dozen low-pitched moans.

"Shamblers!" cried Harris. "Back to back! Keep moving toward the far end! Move, people, move!"

The sailors formed up, each scanning a field of fire.

An infected corpse loomed up from the shade behind a wrecked SUV, a rotting hand grasping at the trunk. It pulled itself up to a standing position. Wendell took aim and fired. The round caught the shambler in the forehead, and it dropped back down to the ground, unmoving.

"They're coming from behind!" Jones called out. Undead things had begun to emerge from their hiding places under the wrecked trucks, lured by the sounds of gunfire and the macabre moans of their shambling brethren.

Rico's MP-5 chattered on semiauto, but many of his rounds missed, striking the creatures in the chest and neck. Two more went down, but the odds were swiftly turning in the shamblers' favor. More were coming.

The large, empty trailers behind the trucks were as inviting to the infected as a bed was to an exhausted soldier. They didn't seem to mind the heat. It was the darkness that comforted them.

Their figures, merely silhouettes in the back of the open trucks at first, became more distinct as they stumbled into the light. Most appeared to be from the vehicle wrecks, and they sported open and dry wounds to the head. Two were missing limbs, and one had blood caked around its mouth, dried into a grotesque beard.

"We're surrounded!" said Smith.

Stiles's eyebrows shot up, and he looked from the imminent threat toward the far end of the bridge. Shamblers were now approaching from both directions. From the Lexington side of the bridge, infected were pulling themselves from piled wrecks. The survivors moved closer together, firing at will. Shamblers dropped left and right, but for each one that fell, a pair seemed to appear and take its place, the virus's version of a stumbling Hydra.

Worse, from what Stiles could see, there were small neighborhoods on either side of their destination. He could see even more doddering figures emerging from side streets to reinforce their undead companions.

"This is very, very bad," said Rico in a trembling voice.

"Thank you!" Stiles shouted, not having to keep quiet anymore. He levered another round into his Winchester and dropped a shambler with a well-aimed shot. "It's always nice to know when things have gotten somehow worse. I swear to God"—he shot another dead thing dead again—"if we get out of this, I'm going to feed you that fucking gun."

A scream cut through the gunfire. A shambler, crawling under a car, had grabbed Brown by the leg and was pulling him down. He fell hard and his breath was knocked out of him in a whoof of pain. Brown twisted his weapon around and fired at the prone shambler. The shot might have worked—but Brown's own foot was in the way. The round tore through his boot, ripped through his flesh, and exited the sole of his boot. The sailor screamed in pain and reached out his free hand to Jones and Smith.

Smith grabbed at Brown's arm, trying to pull him free, but the shambler had a firm grip.

"Don't let go, man!" Brown cried. "Don't let go!"

"I've got you, I've got you!" Smith yelled. "Hold on!"

Brown's reply was cut off as the shambler sank its teeth into the sailor's leg. Blood poured from the wound.

"Brown!" Smith shouted. "Don't let go!"

Despite his strong grip, Smith felt Brown's hands slipping away. With a final effort, Smith attempted to pull the wounded sailor free as Jones opened fire on the dead man. His hands came loose, and Brown, screaming in agony, vanished under the car, dragged violently by the shambler. Wet, sloshing noises drowned out the sailor's wails. Smith recoiled, horrified. Brown, out of sight under the vehicle, was being eaten alive. Brown's screams abated, and fell away into silence.

"He's gone! Focus fire on the shamblers!" Harris said, all business. There would be time to mourn for Brown later. "Rico! Hillyard! Cover our backs! Everyone else, focus fire front! Clear us a goddamn path!"

The shamblers were looming up as if by magic, appearing from behind the remnants of cars and pulling themselves up from the shady confines of half-open trunks. What had once been a half-dozen were now well into the twenties, drawn by the gunfire and frantic shouts of the survivors.

"Gangway, motherfuckers!" Allen shouted, flipping the selector switch of his MP-5 to three-round burst.

Stiles watched Harris follow suit, sending rounds downrange as fast as he could manage. He didn't even seem to be trying for head shots anymore. The inertia of the lead was enough to cause the shamblers to stumble and fall, giving the survivors a chance to move past them without fear of being grappled and bitten.

"Move! Move!" Harris shouted. "Get to the exit! Go!"

The group double-timed it, firing as they went. Most of their rounds went astray, but a few struck home. Here and there a shambler fell, pegged through the head or neck. The majority, however, absorbed the fire and continued their advance, arms held out in front of them, moaning incessantly.

Hal leapt up onto the roof of a wrecked car and scanned the scene.

Shamblers had cut off their retreat, and even more were between them and the far end of the bridge. One, with a bloody stump for a hand, tried to climb up on the car, but Stiles took careful aim with his weapon and fired. The round tore through the infected's head, and it slumped against the hood, slowly sliding off to the pavement, leaving a trail of brackish, congealed blood in its wake.

"We can't win this!" Hal said.

"Fuck winning this!" Allen shouted, firing into the shambling hoard. "I just wanna live!"

Stiles took stock of the situation, and realized Hal was right. They were vastly outnumbered, and on the confines of the bridge, they had no room to maneuver. Another shout from Hal, atop the car, solved the problem for them:

"Jump for it!" he yelled, gesturing wildly at the edge of the bridge. "It's only a few feet!"

"They'll just follow along the bank!" Smith protested.

"They're shamblers! We swim fast enough, we live!" said Hal. "You do what you want. I'm out of here!"

Turning and saying the quickest prayer he ever had, Hal leapt from the bridge and hit the water, sinking down under his splash, the heavy pack he was wearing pulling him under. Stiles followed shortly after.

"Come on, you assholes!" Allen shouted. "Basic water survival! Find something that floats and follow it into the drink!"

He pulled a five-gallon bucket from the back of a nearby pickup truck and emptied it onto the tarmac before throwing it over the side and throwing himself after. Stiles smiled at this, even as he fired round after round at the approaching death.

Navy training, God love it.

Rico and Hillyard each grabbed ice chests and followed them over the handrail, and Wendell had found a basketball somewhere.

A hard hat came sailing over to Harris, and he stopped his barrage of bullets to catch it.

"One for you, skipp—" Jones's yell was cut off by the sudden appearance of a hand from the bed of the utility truck he'd liberated the hard hat from. It sat up out of the back, a desiccated and dry bundle of infected sticks, and ate a chunk out of Jones's shoulder.

Smith dove at the dead thing, knocking it away from his shipmate with screams of rage before emptying his clip into the infected's skull.

The mass of hungry dead gathered and Stiles could wait no longer to see how the deckhands' tragedy would resolve itself.

He could swear, as he hit the water, that he heard a pair of gunshots ring out.

✭ ✭ ✭ ✭ ✭

Hal Dorne kicked in the water, cursing himself for an idiot while his chest burned.

Out of the frying pan, into the river.

A strong hand closed over his and pulled him up. As he burst from the depths, he caught a glimpse of his rescuer. Quartermaster Third Class Allen, grinning from ear to ear, held the retiree up with one hand, the other wrapped around a yellow five-gallon bucket.

"Come on, old man," he chided. "Plenty of buoyancy in this here piece of plastic for the both of us. Good idea, using the river. Bad idea, not taking anything with you but your heavy-ass pack."

Hal shook the water from his eyes. "Whatever, punk. Where's Stiles?"

"Right here," Stiles said from four feet away. He floated on his back, the bottoms of his boots tucked in his underarms, helping him stay up. "I think I lost my crutch."

"Enough chatter," Harris said on the way past, holding a gray construction hard hat to his chest. "We have to get to the opposite bank and outrun this group of infected if we want to make it."

The group turned and linked arms where they could, kicking together as a team and working to the bank of the river. The whole way, Wendell kept coughing, spitting up water.

"Fucking monsters," he said, finally loud enough for Hal to hear. "Goddamn abominations. Shit-sucking *assholes*!"

This last was screamed out, causing most heads to turn his way, those of the sailors and the infected on dry land.

"That's torn it," Stiles said, looking at the shambling mass of undead idiots trying to wade in for a hot mouthful. The unliving, unthinking bastards were walking out into the water, arms out and oblivious to the current. One by one, they stepped in, and as they got about waist-high in the water, the river swept them away.

"Holy shit," Allen said. "I think we got one of them, whaddaya call? Strategies?"

Harris's face was grim set, and he nodded. "Good job, Wendell. Take up the call, men, and keep kicking!"

Again working as a team, the group turned into the current to maintain their relative position to the shore and started yelling obscenities at the infected still on the muddy bank. What started as a game for most turned sour quickly, as the cathartic shouts began to release some of the pent-up frustrations of the past six months. Throats that were calling out witticisms were rapidly going hoarse as real emotions brought out the agonies each of the men was carrying with him. For a full five minutes, until all of the slow-moving infected had stepped into the water, the seamen (and Hal, Stiles, Katie, and Ron) shouted and raged into the uncaring blue sky.

Panting, crying, half-sick with swallowed river water, Wendell turned to the nearest sailor, Rico, and smiled.

"Well. *I* feel better."

The loss of Smith, Jones, and Brown weighed heavily on the group, but Hal knew it was more so on Wendell, as he was their Sea Dad on the USS *Ramage*; in doing their indoc and teaching them the ship's damage control systems, he'd gotten to know the trio of deckhands. Of the almost three hundred men that the *Ramage* carried, the deckhands were all that was left of Wendell's seafaring family. Hal knew he didn't really feel better, but he got it out, and that would have to be enough until they reached Omaha.

Harris, as was befitting the group's leader, was the first to reach shore and start the mad scramble up the muddy slope. One by one, the survivors helped each other out of the water.

"Fuck," Rico said, slumping down against a tree stump. "What now? Our shit's all wet, our ammo might be ruined, and we're out our truck. We still got, what, two hundred miles to go?"

"Stow that bilge, sailor," Harris said, looking out thoughtfully. "US 283. We follow this to get to 80, then . . ." The Commander trailed off.

Hal tried to remember something, a detail that was just mentioned in passing. "What's over here?"

"Besides Lexington?" Katie asked. "I think Wes said there was a military—"

"Museum!" Harris finished with a laugh. "The Heartland Museum of Military Vehicles."

"Very nice," Hal said. "Boys, we have a little more hiking in front of us, but pretty soon we'll be riding in style."

Stiles nudged Hillyard. "'In style,' he says. Like a six-by-six is the lap of luxury."

"The museum is just on the other side of I-80," Harris said. "Not too far from here. And then we have, yes, two hundred miles to go. So get up, wring your socks out, and let's get a move on."

"Yeah, you bunch of Navy sissies," Stiles said, hopping on his one good foot. "This is no time for a sit-down, or sit-in, or whatever you hippies call it."

✯ ✯ ✯ ✯

True to Harris's memory, the Heartland Museum of Military Vehicles was just across I-80, less than a mile from where the group came up out of the water.

They lay on their bellies, taking turns looking through the binoculars and feeling the wind go out of their sails.

"Have I already mentioned that I do not like this?" asked Rico.

"Man, shut the fuck up," Wendell said. "We're about to get us some wheels and get off our goddamn feet, all right?"

"Whatever you say, Pollyanna. What I want to know is, how are we going to get in there and back out in one piece?"

Wendell sighed, dropping his chin to his chest.

Harris knew Rico had a good question; directly across US-283 from the museum stood a giant Wal-Mart whose parking lot looked like a war zone. Cars were crashed into each other, burned out and overturned metal husks littering the black pavement, and the sun was on its way down. In the utter still of post-Morningstar Nebraska, the group could hear the stirrings of infected in the wreckage of the parking lot.

"I don't care how good the prices are," Allen said from the back. "I don't want to go to Wal-Mart today."

"Bet your ass," Stiles said. "How many people do you think bought it in there?"

Harris looked west at the sky. "However many are in there, or in the parking lot, we've either got to backtrack and find someplace safe to bed down for the night, or try to slip past."

Hal shook his head. "Why are we even using the freeway? If we cut across there"—he pointed at a parking lot full of tractors and backhoes—"we should come out in the museum's lot. Shouldn't we?"

"No room to move," Stiles said. "If there are any infected in that lot, we'll be hemmed in on all sides. At least on the asphalt, we'll have someplace to run. Or, limp, in my case. Lots of shadows, too . . . plenty of places for an infected to lie in wait."

Ron got a light in his eyes. "Well, what if we sent a runner around the back of the Wal-Mart? Someone that could make a lot of noise—"

"I tried that once, remember?" Stiles said, pointing at his wounded leg. "Look what it got me."

"It got you bit, but it bought us the time we needed to escape Hyattsburg," Ron said.

"No," Harris said, shaking his head. "There are no heroes here today. We've already lost three people. I don't want any more blood on my hands before the sun sets."

That subdued the talk for a couple of minutes, but every second that passed brought the sun that much closer to the horizon, and everybody knew it.

"We go," Harris finally said. "We'll go quietly and in single file. Rico, you have the best eyes at night, so you head us out. I'll follow you, then Hal. Katie, Ron, Stiles, Wendell, Allen. Hillyard, bring up the rear. Watch where you put your feet, and keep one hand on the shoulder of the person in front of you. If there are any sudden stops, we don't want a train wreck. Ron, you keep a hand on Katie and one on Stiles, since he's got his hands full. Any questions?"

"Like how come we don't have any night-vision gear?" Allen muttered to himself.

"I heard that. Now line up, and let's get the hell over there."

Everyone linked themselves up according to plan, and they headed out to cross I-80. The overpass was almost as badly jammed as the Platte River bridge, and the group stuck close.

"Where are they?" Allen asked in a whisper.

Wendell, immediately in front of him, shot back a dirty look. "They're back on the bridge, eating my deckhands. But shut up anyway."

Allen bit his lip. He nodded, and they continued across the overpass.

Rico stepped off the shoulder and into the deep grass on the eastern side of the highway, across from the large parking lot. He held his MP-5 at the ready but kept the safety on; Harris knew the incident at the bridge had carried its lesson to him. Stepping carefully, he moved the group ahead, first bringing his back foot up to the heel of his front foot, and then advancing the front foot again. Walking that way, the group made slow, torturous progress toward Heartland Road.

"Holy shit, we're gonna make it," Allen breathed at Wendell, who turned back again.

"I told you, shut the fu—*argh!*"

Wendell lurched back, almost pulling Stiles and Allen to the ground with him as he flailed his rifle butt at his right boot. Attached there, teeth sunk deep into leather, was a quarter of an infected. Besides the head, which was busily gnawing at Wendell's foot, there was part of a torso and half an arm, which spun circles in the air, slapping a stump on the calf muscle in front of it.

Its mouth full of government-issue leather, the infected couldn't moan its findings to all its brethren, so the group relaxed. Except for Wendell, who was still stabbing down with his rifle at the head, which refused to let go. Allen did fall then, both hands clamped over his mouth suppressing a mad giggle.

"Stop it," Stiles said, moving over to poke Allen with his Winchester. "Quit that laughing right now. You think you're the only one that wants to get ahead?"

At that, Allen turned a dark red and rolled onto his face, coughing into the grass, and Stiles started giggling, too. Rico looked back, a smile creasing his face, and soon Allen's laughing fit had spread to everyone in the group.

Except Wendell, who was unable to dislodge the tenacious infected from his shoe.

"Come on, you motherfuckers," he bit out. "Will someone give me a hand here?"

Allen fell into another fit. "He, he's already got a head, n-now he wants a hand!"

"Oh, fuck you," Wendell grunted out, lunging and swinging his rifle butt at Allen instead of the infected.

"All right, all right," Allen said, getting to his feet. "But just this once. I don't want you to become too dependent on—"

"Will you just fucking do it?"

Allen reared his left leg back to boot the side of the infected's head.

"Not again," Rico said, catching his boot. He tilted his head in the direction the head might have gone, and Harris saw in the brush a square of metal. Laughter died down quickly, replaced with somber expressions. Rico let go of Allen's leg and, from the ditch next to the fence of the farming equipment yard, pulled a speed limit sign.

He handed it to Hillyard, who gripped the sign and twirled it in his hands. Measuring, he laid the end of the 55 on the infected's neck and stood on the other end of the sign. With a squelching sound the metal sign bit into the dead man's flesh. Right away it met resistance, and Rico had to stand on the sign with Hillyard to get it to go through the spine. Breaking past, it went through with a rush. Satisfied, Rico laid the sign down and held up the unanimated head by the hair for Allen to see.

"We quiet now, fool."

✯ ✯ ✯ ✯ ✯

The sliding gate in front of the Heartland Museum of Military Vehicles was closed and locked. Razor wire, newer than the rest of the fence, was looped along the top of the gate and all along the front. The metal and the asphalt in front of the gate were all burned and greasy, and Hal knew what had been happening there, remembering the mound of cremated dead in Abraham.

"Might be trouble here," Wendell said. "This gate is still closed, and there ain't any dead around, littering up the place."

Harris tightened his jaw. "If there are people here, then maybe they'll help us."

Allen turned to the Commander with a look on his face. "How do you figure?"

A grim smile grew on Hal's face. "It's a military museum, right? People who put these things together are known for supporting the troops, kid. And if they know we're toting along a possible cure for all this mess . . ."

"Hoo-ah," Stiles said. "I love being a bargaining chip."

"Hey," Hal said, abashed, "that's not—"

"I know, I know," Stiles said, waving the retiree off. "It's just a bit more responsibility than I'm used to, is all. You people act like I'm the second coming or something."

"Might be," Hillyard said quietly. "Back from the dead . . ."

"All right, all right," Harris said. "Stow it for later. Right now, we need a way into this place that won't get any of us cut up." He reflected for a moment. "Or shot up. Any ideas? I'm open to suggestion."

"You don't want to get shot," a new voice rasped from the encroaching darkness, "you keep your hands away from those guns."

The sudden stillness in the group was as if each of them had been turned to statues. Slowly, very slowly, Allen let his MP-5 hang by its belt around his neck. Just as slowly, he put his hands up.

"We come in peace," he said.

A soft click answered him.

"You better."

Soundlessly, the razor-wired gate began to pull back. Hal, looking down, saw that it ran in a well-greased track instead of on wheels. He nodded in appreciation. "That's a good idea, right there," he said. "Keep it quiet on the way in and out."

"Right," the voice said. "Everybody in, and put your hands up like the smart boy there. Nice and quiet, and real slow."

"I can't keep my hands off my rifle," Stiles said, one hand in the air. "I'm kind of using it."

"Hop."

Grumbling, Mark Stiles slipped the strap of his rifle over his head and hopped toward the gate, hands up in the air. As soon as they had all filed in, the gate began to slide closed again.

"Well," Hal asked, annoyed. "Where to now?"

Silence greeted him. Then the returning sound of crickets.

"How do you like that?" Allen said. "We let one guy get the drop on all of us, and then he doesn't even stick around to gloat."

"Shut up," Harris said. "He's still there."

"Too right," the voice said, this time from the shadows inside the perimeter of the fence.

"And who says he's alone?" said another, from behind the group.

A pair of men, dressed in matching khaki fatigues, came out of the shadows on either side of the gate, each brandishing an assault rifle. The man on the left of the gate looked to be in his mid-forties, square of shoulder and slim. His military haircut was showing streaks of gray on the sides of his head, and there was some gray showing in his neatly trimmed beard. He held an M-16 on the group. From the other side was an older man, a mane of shaggy white hair barely held back into a ponytail that draped over one meaty shoulder. In his hands was an AK-47.

They approached the group on tangents to each other, overlapping their potential fields of fire without stepping into each other's way. The easy method by which they corralled the group of survivors showed that they had done this before and were supremely confident in their ability to deal with threats.

"Everyone thataway," the younger man said, gesturing deeper into the museum grounds. They started moving, and the two men followed at an easy pace, tracking each of the survivors in turn with the ends of their rifles.

"There's no need for this," Harris said as they marched forward. "All we came for—"

"Shut up," rasped the younger man. "It'll keep until we get inside. We try to keep it quiet out here, you understand?"

Lips tight, Harris nodded and continued forward.

They came to a roll-up door. The older man clicked the radio he wore on his lapel twice, and there was a metal sound on the other side. Quickly and quietly, the door came up on a dark interior and the survivors were ushered inside.

Upon seeing the yawning gulf of shadows, Rico gulped and lowered his hands. "No way, *vato*. No more dark and scary places for me."

The younger man stepped up behind Rico and placed the barrel of his rifle in his back. "Hands up and inside, Jack, or I drop you."

"Nah-ah," said Rico. "You already said you guys like it quiet."

The older man grinned and unsheathed a kukri knife from his back, the wicked and curving blade gleaming in the dying light of the day.

"Come on in, Rico," Allen said. "Show 'em how we play nice."

Raising his hands again, Rico entered the building.

☆ ☆ ☆ ☆ ☆

Once the door slid all the way shut, lights came on, filling the long warehouse with blazing fluorescence, and the survivors got their first good look at the men that had captured them.

The younger man, Stone by the name on his shirt, was powerfully built. The old-style BDU shirt he wore was tight at the shoulders and loose at the waist, and when he moved, he did it with the grace of a jungle cat. Under the harsh fluorescent light the gray in his beard and high-and-tight haircut stood out, more so than under the fading light of day. Strapped to his side was a sheathed machete on the left, a black .44 revolver on the right. As he watched the group, muscle bunched at his jaw.

The older man, Gravy by the tattoo scrawled across the back of his fist, was a study in contrast to Stone. While still a powerful man, judging by the size of his hammy forearms, he was also slovenly and didn't care about it. As he watched Stone evaluate the survivors, he itched at his beard and hitched up his ill-fitting trousers. Finally, after long moments of watching, he spoke.

"Come on, Stony. We ain't got all night to figure this out. Supply run is tonight, and you know how he gets when we fuck up his timetable."

"If there's anyone fucking up the timetable," Stone said in his gravelly voice, "it's these people here."

While they talked, Hal took in the interior of the museum. At the sight of a beautifully preserved (or restored) M2 half-track, Hal whistled.

"This place, was it yours? Before . . ."

"Shut up, old man," Gravy said, and Stone waved him off.

"Take it easy. I'll watch them. You go and get the Chief."

Grumbling and staring daggers at the group as a whole, Gravy lumbered off deeper into the museum building. Watching his retreating back, Hal imagined crosshairs at the base of the man's back.

"To answer your question, no. The owners of this place were long gone by the time we got here. They're probably safe and secure in a mountain retreat with a tank parked in their driveway. So this place is ours now."

"So, you don't have any need for, say, that half-track there. Or the APC. I saw an armored personnel carrier in the yard," Hal said, his tone conversational. However, there was a tightness in him, a need he could feel deep in his gut to try and jump this man and get out of there.

But he held back. Something about the way the man moved, the way he held himself, even in the face of eight captives who were still armed with assault rifles . . . he was dangerous, and Hal could feel it. But he was also earnest.

"I can't make that call, sir. I can't even say if you'll be leaving here on your feet or feet-first. The Chief will decide that when he gets here."

"I'm here now," a voice rang out at the group. It came from a short man, compact in the same way a bullet is and just as tough. He was fast approaching the group, with the older man in tow. "Gravy says you found these guys trying to sneak in?"

"Not quite," Harris said, speaking to the man. "We were sneaking around, yes, but the sun is setting and you have an army of the dead on your front porch. Would you recommend we march through, calling out cadence as we went?"

The Chief walked right up to Harris, stopping three inches from him. He looked up with a grin.

"Cadence. Nice. You the leader here?"

"I am. Commander Harris of the USS *Ramage,* at your service. These are my men. And woman."

"And retiree," said Hal.

Eyebrows shot up on the Chief's face. "The *Ramage,* oh. How nice for you. That's a ship, right? Floats on the water?"

The naïveté of the question took Harris off his guard for a second. "Er, yes. What—"

"You're in *Nebraska*. You didn't sail here. I think perhaps you introduced yourself as a commander and used your ship name to try and evoke some kind of solicitude on my part. After all, the men call me Chief, which is another naval rank."

A thin smile rose on Harris's face. "Guilty."

"Well," the diminutive man said, producing a Glock 9mm and aiming it up at Harris's face, "I don't appreciate it. If I had the time, I would question each of you separately until someone gave me a wrong answer and then execute the lot of you as spies and thieves. And imposters.

"But I don't have time. And now I'm a man short for my scavenging run, which perhaps throws off my timetables. That, Commander Harris, puts a bee in my bonnet. Stone!"

"Yes, Chief," he answered.

"Take these people and relieve them of their firearms. Put them in the trailer. You will be their watch for the evening while we conduct the run."

With that, the Chief turned sharply and walked away, Gravy staying behind to help.

"This has been a horrible trip," Allen said. "Remind me to fire my travel agent."

★ ★ ★ ★ ★

One by one, Stone took the survivors out of the museum proper and escorted them to the trailer in the yard. Gravy stayed inside, cradling his AK-47 and watching the remaining members of the group as if he hoped one of them (or all of them) would step out of line and he would finally get to shoot somebody.

"Come with me," Stone said to Stiles, who was next in line, ushering him out a side door. The yard of the museum compound was a silent graveyard of old military vehicles. A half-track, twin to the one Hal had noticed earlier, sat next to a pair of German boat/cars with deflated tires. Past that stood an APC, loaded down with some sort of rocket system mounted on its back. Each of the heavy vehicles out there (at least a dozen of them) was slowly settling into the dirt. The former hardpack was suffering from a lack of maintenance; Stiles put that together in his head.

They're not using these vehicles for anything.

On the way out to the improvised stockade, Stiles could feel Stone's eyes on him, watching the way he moved.

"You're going to have to give up that rifle when we get there."

"Well," Stiles said, "do you have anything else I can use? A crutch would be nice. Maybe a long two-by-four? I'm not picky."

Stone was shaking his head. "No, no. I don't think you'll get your hands on anything you can use as a weapon. Besides, there will be no place for you to walk to. The Chief is going to keep you good and locked up until he gets back and decides what to do with the lot of you."

They arrived at the trailer and Stone twirled the tumblers on the combination lock fastened to the door. He stepped back and swung it wide, M-16 at the ready for an attack from within. When none came, he smiled and waved to Stiles.

"In you go. Leave the rifle."

With a sigh, Stiles leaned the Winchester against the side of the trailer and hopped inside. The door thunked shut behind him and he could hear the lock being set back in place. Illumination inside was thrown weakly from a single Coleman lantern hanging from the ceiling.

Hal Dorne sat in the trailer home, peering through the gloom at Stiles.

"Well, that went well."

Stiles barked a laugh. "You're telling me. I wonder how they get to wherever it is they run off to? They sure don't make use of the vehicles they have here."

"You noticed that, too. It just breaks my heart to see those machines out there, wasting away. Just two of them would be plenty. Did you see the wrecker? Five-ton beauty."

Stiles leaned against the wall and let himself down so he could sit. "Fuel. Got to be fuel."

"There's a whole parking lot full of fuel out there!"

"Yeah, and it's being watched over by guard dogs that don't sleep. Be real, Hal. How would you get past all those infected?"

Hal Dorne pursed his lips and shut up, dejected.

Stiles took the place in, eyes roaming over the newly installed walls that severely cut the twelve-by-sixty of the mobile home into a much smaller space. There was a small kitchenette and sofa where they were, as well as a table that had been ripped from its moorings and lay on its side.

Just then, the lock rattled against the door and the air in the trailer home moved around a bit as it opened. Rico came in, propelled roughly by unseen hands, and the door slammed shut.

His eyes met Stiles's and a small smile bloomed on his face. "I made a little bit of a scene about having to go out in the dark. Gravy volunteered to 'escort' me. That fat *hijo de puta* can move, man." He sat up, rubbing his shoulder where he'd landed on it, looking around the trailer. "Nice digs. Really wonderful accommodations, as Allen would say. What the fuck are we in for now?"

Hal remained silent, eyes hooded and thoughtful. Stiles just shook his head and gestured at the entirety of the mobile home.

"If we were with the Army group, they wouldn't have taken us so easy."

"Nah, man. They would have. You saw how many dead fuckers there were in the parking lot," Rico said. "Maybe there might have been a fight once we were inside, but not before. Not even you dumb shit grunts would want to bring that whole horde down on us."

Mark Stiles blew out some air and leaned his head on the wall. "Yeah, maybe. Still. I can't believe how fast that short Chief shut Harris down."

Hal's sharp reply was cut off by the door opening again. In stumbled Katie and Ron together, a thin trickle of blood coming from Ron's nose matching a red mark on the side of Katie's face.

"What happened to you two?" Hal asked as the door slammed shut. "That fucking Gravy—"

"It wasn't him," Katie said, helping Rico get Ron to the ground. "It was the other one, Stone. He wanted me to go next, and R-Ron wouldn't let me go without him. He tried to push Stone, and the next thing I knew—"

"Whoo, yeah," Ron said, his voice sounding muffled. "Tone has one hell of a short jab. I think my node id broken."

Katie sat next to him, rubbing his back in circles and crying silent tears.

"Allen and Wendell came to their feet pretty quick, but by then Gravy had his AK-47 out and was practically drooling," she said. "We got to watch him. He seems like he'd fit right in with the raiders."

Ron reached up with his free hand and patted the hand that Katie had on his shoulder. "It'd okay. Jut my node."

The door opened again, this time with Harris calmly entering the mobile home.

"They're speeding up," Stiles said.

"Yes, they've worked out a system to get us in here faster. The fat one, Gravy, he was harping on it, about how upset the Chief would be if they didn't get their asses in gear. You okay, Ron?"

Ron, with his eyes still shut, nodded an answer to the question. Stiles knew he and Katie had been a couple since before Morningstar hit their little town, spent a couple of weeks holed up together in a theater there until Sherman and his band had come through, and then stayed behind together in Abraham when they'd continued on to Omaha. There was no way a puissant band of squatters was going to separate them now.

Harris nodded, seeming to understand this, almost as well as Stiles, who had been there for the daring rescue from the theater. "Well, we can't predict what they are going to do. And we can't plan anything ourselves, really. We have to—"

"What do you mean, we can't plan?" Rico said, interrupting. "Once we're all in here, what's to stop us from putting our heads together and coming up with something?"

From the floor, Stiles said, "No plan survives contact with the enemy."

"No pla—that's right, Stiles," Harris said, glancing down at the tired soldier with admiration evident in his face. "We don't know how many of them there are, or what they're like. We've only seen the Chief, Stone, and Gravy. If they're like Gravy, then we're sunk no matter what. If they're like Stone, well . . ."

The door opened and Allen came stumbling in, followed shortly by Wendell and Hillyard. Allen looked back with a grin and shot the middle finger at whoever closed the door behind him. Taking a halting step into the mobile home, he looked around and took it all in, the grin fading.

"Wonderful accommodations."

"Hah!" Rico barked out. "I coulda just won a bet."

"Well, I'm glad you're enjoying your tour through the postapocalypse Hilton chain," Wendell said, "because it looks like we're going to be in here for quite a while. That short shit Chief came back and snatched Gravy away, complaining that Stone was taking too long. He said the 'raid' was going to take all night."

"Good," Stiles said. "I'm getting some shut-eye."

"You can sleep in a situation like this?" asked Wendell.

Stiles smiled with his eyes closed.

"As long as you keep it down."

29 June 2007
0927 hrs_

Hal was asleep on the floor of the mobile home when the door was yanked open with a loud clatter, bright light streaming in to sear his eyes. The doorway was darkened momentarily as Gravy's bulk filled it, then again by the Chief. He strode into the small space, thunderclouds on his brow.

"You bastards. You owe me one. Him," he said, pointing at Ron, sitting up on the couch with Katie. "Drag him out."

Gravy started forward, a sadistic grin on his face as he reached for Ron. Katie screamed, jumping in his path.

"You leave him alone! Leave him be!"

She balled up her fists and swung at Gravy, who took the punch on his shoulder and backhanded her with a meaty slap. She fell and Ron erupted from the sofa, driving at Gravy with fists and feet.

Gravy was more than a match for the tired traveler, though, and quickly caught Ron's arm, twisting it behind him in a hammerlock.

"Leave him alone!" Katie cried again, leaping at Gravy.

"Fine," the Chief said from the doorway. "They don't want to be separated? We'll see to that."

Laughing, Gravy dragged Ron and carried Katie to the door.

During the time it took for that to happen, the group was on their collective feet and shouting. The Chief walked back into the trailer and leveled his black Glock at Harris's nose.

"Enough. Calm your people."

Harris put his arms in front of him, palms out. "We're calm, we're calm. What is this?"

The Chief thumbed back the hammer on the automatic in his hand, a black matte 9mm. "My plans were upset last night. I was a man short on my raid, and—"

"There was no need to lock us—"

"Shut the fuck up!" the Chief bellowed at Harris. "I was a man short last night, and as a result, one of us died. So now we even up."

The Chief backed to the door quickly, keeping a bead on Harris, and stepped out.

As soon as he was over the threshold, Wendell, the closest, launched himself at the door to keep it open, Hal and Allen right behind him. What Hal saw in the yard in front of the trailer made him sick, because he knew what was coming next.

Ron was on his knees in front of Gravy and another, larger man, Katie next to him, and they held each other as they looked down a pair of gun barrels.

The Chief continued to back away from the mobile home, his gun trained on the doorway. Harris and Hal looked out over the sailors and both shouted.

"You might wanna look away," the Chief said, and passed his gun to the larger man, who turned it on Katie. "Now."

The nine-mil and AK roared as one and Katie and Ron both jumped from their knees, slumping together to the mud. Their blood, immediately slowing to a trickle, ran from the still-smoking holes in their heads and mingled in the cold morning.

"Lock 'em back up, Stone."

With that, the Chief turned and walked away. Gravy stood in the mud, looking down at the bodies and cradling his AK-47 as if it were his child and he was very proud of it.

He looked up into the stunned faces framed by the doorway and raised his rifle.

"Hold on," Stone said, crossing in front of him. "The Chief said to lock them up. All right? No need to lock them up if they're dead, right? *Right?*"

Slowly, Gravy lowered the rifle, still staring wide-eyed and crazy at the group in the doorway.

Stone walked over and closed the door.

"Be ready," he whispered before it shut.

★ ★ ★ ★ ★

Wendell kicked the inside of the door.

"I cannot believe this *shit!*"

"Come on, man," Hillyard said, approaching Wendell from behind. He reached out for him and was stopped by Stiles.

"No, he's right. Let him get it out of his system, because we all need our heads on straight." He turned to Harris, whose face was as ashen as Wendell's; he never got used to losing people and he never would.

"With due respect to Clausewitz, Commander Harris, we need us a plan."

"Yes," Harris said, still shaken. He looked around the trailer and saw all sets of eyes on him. Stiles's none-too-subtle reminder of his former rank worked in him. These were his people. He needed to take care of them. As his resolve hardened, so too did his face.

"Right. First off, did anyone hear what Stone said as the door closed?"

"He said, 'Be ready,'" said Hal. "What do you think it means?"

Harris was already nodding. "I think, gentlemen, that a good man is about to shed his indifference. What do we have available?"

Allen picked his head up. "Pipes," he said. He went to the small kitchen area and pointed. "Under here, PVC. We got a sink." He rapped on it with his knuckles. "Stainless steel. And if the water heater is still in here . . ."

His voice trailed off as he opened panels, rummaging.

"Fuck yeah. Two feet of copper whip right here. We just need to get it loose."

Hal stood, stretching. "Finally. I can contribute something." He bent down and reached into his boot, removing a six-inch Crescent wrench.

"What?" he responded to the looks aimed at him. "Mechanic, remember? Let me in there."

Two very tense hours passed as the survivors waited in the mobile home, coming to grips with their new weapons. Allen, who at one time had lived in a mobile home, had come alive, finding something for everyone to use. He and Wendell had taken turns whacking short lengths of PVC piping on the remains of the steel table to break and serrate the ends of them, making shivs. Rico then rubbed them against a piece of cinder block that had sat forgotten under the sofa, sharpening the ends and handing them back to Allen and Wendell. Stiles took a heater element out of the water heater, courtesy of Hal Dorne, and bent the metal until it snapped in the middle, making a wicked stabbing weapon.

Hal got the flexible length of copper heating coupling (as well as his short wrench) and Harris found a piece of rope that he wound around the piece of cinder block (when the shivs were done) to create a formidable monkey's fist with an eighteen-inch handle.

"What?" he asked Hal, who looked at the monkey's fist and then back to Harris. "Sailor, remember?" He turned and swung the monkey's fist with all his might, smashing a panel in the kitchen.

"All right," he said. "Let's give these sons of bitches what for."

☆ ☆ ☆ ☆ ☆

A violent impact on the door of the mobile home grabbed Stiles's attention. They all came to their feet, gripping their makeshift weapons and ready for a fight. Seconds later, the door opened and Stone came through, holding his M-16 at the ready.

"All right, it's time to . . . Jesus. What are you, the Warriors? Follow me."

Rico pulled the door shut, getting between it and Stone. "Follow you? Fuck you, *puto*. How do we know—"

"Rico," Harris said, "stand down. Didn't I tell you that Stone was one of the good guys? So what is it? Do you let us out of here and pretend that you don't know what happened?"

Stone straightened. "No, sir. I go with you. Kind of have to, now.

The Chief won't stand for any kind of insubordination, and I think knocking out the guard and letting you folks out would get me something harsh." He held up two sets of keys. "These are for the APC and the wrecker."

"Thank God," Hal Dorne said. "I call wrecker. Stiles rides shotgun with me."

Stiles nodded. "Speaking of, where's my Winchester?" He missed the gun.

Stone shook his head. "No can do. Your weapons, all of them, are inside the museum. Gravy's brother is there with them, cataloging them into our collection."

"Well, what are we waiting for?"

"It's too dangerous," Stone said. "Say we don't get past him quietly? He sounds an alarm, the entire compound will be down on our heads."

"It's what we talked about, men," Harris said. "Except now we don't have to try hot-wiring anything. Is there gas in those vehicles?"

"Yes," Stone said. "I filled them up earlier. We have to go. Shift change is in an hour and a half, so half of us . . . half of *them* are still asleep. The engines will wake them, but we should be able to make it out of here before they can dress and try to stop us."

The group looked around at each other. Finally, Rico said, "Fine," and the other sailors nodded.

"Well let's go, then."

Stone opened the door and looked out, scanning the yard for wandering ex-compatriots. Seeing none, he stepped nimbly down and over the unconscious guard, Simon, whom he'd knocked out with the butt of his rifle. Stone's face betrayed a slight twinge. Stiles knew Stone had possibly signed this man's death order for letting them escape on his watch.

The group of survivors filed out after him and headed for the vehicles. All except for Stiles, who began to limp determinedly toward the museum.

"What are you doing?" asked Stone.

"I'm going to get my rifle. All due respect, but I didn't come through undead hell with the Winchester all this time to just give it up."

A slow smile spread across Allen's face. "Oh, I like him." He started after Stiles, and Wendell followed after. Rico, after a moment's deliberation, followed as well. Stone looked from them to Harris, who was also smiling.

"Boys and their toys. Come on, Hal."

Stiles turned back, seeing the Commander walk after his men, hurrying to catch up, with Hal jogging after.

Cursing, Stone kicked at a rock, looking after the group.

"Well, Stone?" Harris asked over his shoulder. "In for a penny."

Stone heaved a sigh and ran to catch up with Stiles.

"Fine," he said, "but let me get us in. I want to put off dying as long as I can, thank you very much."

Stone opened the door and went in, scanning the immediate area for men. Seeing none, he waved the survivors in and stalked forward, leading them to the weapons cache. "It's right before shift change. There shouldn't be anybody around. The Chief is still sour, and he tends to operate on a line-of-sight style of management when he's in a mood, so everybody's going to stay away."

Before long, they came to the room where Gravy's brother stood, cataloging the weapons and ammo they'd stripped from the survivors. He went shirtless under a black leather jacket over jeans. Stiles stole a glance through the rectangular window and spun away quickly.

"Good God," he said. "He's bigger than his brother."

"Tiny," Stone said. "His name is Bronson, but we call him Tiny. Him and Gravy used to be professional wrestlers. Did you see your rifle?"

Stiles nodded. "Yeah. Right behind him. He's one of the guys from this morning, isn't he?"

"He is. Go get him," Stone said, opening the door.

Stiles gripped his metal stab and limped into the room. Tiny looked up, his face full of confusion.

"Hey! You're supposed to be locked up!"

Lurching, Stiles ran at the bigger man, screaming as his weight came down on his bad leg, and then he was there, stabbing at Tiny with his piece of heater. The first jab met flesh and Tiny bellowed, lashing out.

The back of his fist caught Stiles in the rib cage, lifting him from his feet and moving his entire body to the side. Stiles lost his grip on the suddenly blood-slicked heater element and swung his empty hands at Tiny.

The bigger man took the hits on his forearms and shoulders, bulling in to grab Stiles around the waist. He lifted up, squeezing and crushing the military man. Stiles kicked at the length of metal sticking out from the man's side, but that wasn't enough to make him let go.

"Fuck this," Allen said, and he ran into the room, stabbing his broken and sharpened PVC at the big man's unprotected side, but it failed to penetrate the leather of the jacket.

"Move!" Harris said, hefting the monkey's fist as he stepped into the room. Allen cleared away and Harris swung the flail, catching Tiny in the side of the head, right behind his ear. He faltered, his grip on Stiles weakening.

Wendell and Rico forced their way in, stabbing down at Tiny's thighs, the PVC pipe making short work of the jean material there. The big man grunted and went down to his knees, letting Stiles go, who fell back onto the table.

"Grab the guns," he said to Hal, who stood in the hallway with Stone.

Rico, Allen, and Wendell punched and stabbed down at Tiny until his large form stopped moving. Hillyard made his way around to stomp on the large head. Harris stood over the man, his face hardening again as he looked down at Katie's executioner. He bent over and snatched the metal heating element out of the man's side. He waved the quartet of sailors away.

"You had no right," he said, and stabbed it with a twisting motion into the man's inner thigh. A bright red jet of blood shot out of the wound, Tiny's life pulsing out onto the floor. They stood there for about a minute, watching the large man go pale as the pulses out of his leg got slower, less forceful.

"You had no right," Harris repeated, and turned to go.

"Everybody strapped?" Rico said. "There's more in there."

"More than we need," Allen said, and Stiles laughed. "What?"

"The world is over. There will never be more bullets than we need. But maybe there's more than we can carry."

"We should go," Stone said from the hallway. "Gravy will be along presently, and he won't like this."

"Fuck what he likes," Allen said, checking his MP-5. "We're armed and dangerous now."

"Come on."

Stone led the group back out, fully armed and ready for action.

When they hit the yard, there were two men standing over the still form of the sentry. One of them looked up at Stone as the survivors filed out behind him. He hit his partner and pointed, yelling something.

"Not good," Allen said.

The pair of sentries raised their weapons and the survivors answered in kind. The man on the left let off a three-round burst from his rifle before he was cut down by Rico's chattering MP-5, and Hal's revolver boomed out once, taking the other sentry in the middle, the force of the blast folding him in half.

"Not good at all," he said. "Come on, we have to move!"

Stone set out at a run, leaping for the door of the APC and yanking it open. Hal was close behind, into the cab of the five-ton wrecker and cranking the engine. The APC and wrecker roared to life as the survivors piled in and on the vehicles.

A red light began to flash on the roof of the museum proper, and Stone grimaced. "Someone's tripped the alarm!" he yelled. "They'll be coming!"

Harris whacked the roof of the APC cab and waved to Allen and Wendell, who rode the back of the wrecker. Their attention grabbed, he pointed at the light and then to the door, making a gun out of his hand. Wendell and Allen nodded and took firing positions as the vehicles began to move. Hillyard did the same from the back of the APC.

Men poured from the doors of the museum only to be pounded back by a hail of bullets from the *Ramage* sailors. Hal turned the wheel to swing the nose of the wrecker close to the building, knocking one man back and crushing another.

SURVIVORS

"Bye-bye fence," he muttered as the front end of the wrecker met with the gate in a cacophony of rending metal and screaming men. Stone steered the APC out the same way, his eyes glued to the mass of infected in the Wal-Mart parking lot, the mass of infected drawn by the sudden noises, who now held their gummy, blank stares on the open gate of the compound. Ignoring the vehicles speeding away, they began to descend on the museum and the morsels waiting within.

CHAPTER 5
ARCHITECTURE OF AGGRESSION

Abraham, KS
29 June 2007
1327 hrs_

A PAIR OF MEN stood on a small rise overlooking the outskirts of a small town. One of them stood with his arms folded behind his back, a blank expression on his face. He wore black combat boots and similarly colored coveralls, a utility belt covered in ammunition pouches and a holstered pistol at his waist. A radio was clipped to an epaulette. A small neck knife on a chain nestled inside the thin body armor over his torso.

The other man was not nearly as well dressed. His clothes were scorched and torn, and the growth of several days of beard stubble covered his face. He shifted nervously from foot to foot, eyeing the man in front of him. He could feel the difference between them.

After a long moment, the man in black spoke.

"You said these people were just townsfolk with pitchforks and hunting rifles," snarled Agent Sawyer. "You said you could keep them under control."

"I could have," said the ragged man. "But they had help. Soldiers. They killed my men—they killed my brother! My brother's dead!" His voice took on a steely edge.

Sawyer turned and backhanded the man across the face.

Ordinarily, Herman Lutz would have killed a man who dared to show him such disrespect. He knew better than to try and fight it out with Agent Sawyer. The man would kill him without breaking a sweat, and he knew it. Instead, he reached up a hand and wiped the trickle of blood flowing from his lower lip away, spitting into the grass at his feet.

"Control yourself," said Sawyer. "You want revenge?"

Herman Lutz nodded.

"You'll get it. More than just setting fire to a building or two. Though I don't know why I'm bothering. I supplied you with everything you needed to keep that area under control. Look around. Chaos everywhere. I got you machine guns. I got you Semtex. I sent you men and supplies. And here you are, alone, your job unfinished. There's not much use in this new world for a scum-sucker such as yourself who can't even keep a hick town from rebelling. I was counting on you to keep order, and you failed."

"Like I said, they had help—"

Sawyer looked as though he was about to launch another attack, and Herman Lutz allowed his voice to trail off to silence.

"What was that?" growled Sawyer.

"Nothing," mumbled Lutz.

"I said, 'What was that?'"

"Nothing, Sawyer. Nothing. Just give me another chance to show you what I can do."

Sawyer flashed Lutz a grim smile. "You'll get that chance. Do you have any men left, besides yourself?"

Lutz shrugged. "Maybe half a dozen, a couple miles behind me. They're the only other ones who got away."

"Then we have the advantage of numbers, and surprise," mused

Sawyer. "They'll be well dug in, but they're expecting infected, not live opponents. We'll take them fast. And then the cure will be ours."

Lutz said nothing, simply stood behind his superior, staring at the ground, his teeth clenched. "And I'll be able to avenge my brother. I can't wait to kill these bastards."

He saw a smile play across Sawyer's hard-etched features. "Mason, Mason . . . I know you're out there. And I'm coming for you."

Apparently, he had a bone to pick, too.

Lutz followed Sawyer back to a clearing where his team was hastily erecting a command tent. Black-clad troops moved quickly and efficiently through the forest, bringing supplies from the trucks and HMVs that couldn't make it past the trees that fenced the clearing. Aerial reconnaissance had picked out the area and the several trails through the woodlands that led close to it.

The raider looked at the activity in front of him and had to give at least that to the man in black: when he had asked for resources, whoever was behind him had pulled out all the stops.

"Go and get your men," Sawyer said. "Bring them here and stand by until we're settled in. We won't move on Abraham until well past sunset, so that will give us plenty of time to plan our assault. You know things about the town, yes? Numbers, weapons, et cetera?"

Lutz nodded. Sawyer answered with a grim smile.

"Good. Now get your people. And Lutz?"

He stopped and looked back. He'd already turned away to do as he was told, as much as it galled him to be ordered around.

"Try to stay out of the way, all right?"

Biting back his reply, the pack leader went away to fetch his men. He knew Sawyer couldn't have cared less. The raider felt inept under the government man's stare. If Sawyer considered him to be good at things, he'd feel like an asset, but from the way Sawyer had talked to him . . .

Lutz squared his shoulders. He'd show Sawyer how he had misjudged his usefulness. Even without his brother, who'd been killed by a small army contingent passing through this area, Herman Lutz was more than just a bad-tempered man with some men and guns.

✯ ✯ ✯ ✯ ✯

Agent Sawyer found his own team leader. "Huck! Sitrep."

Lieutenant Finnegan, whose new nickname was "Huck," now that he'd been placed under Agent Sawyer's command, always grimaced when he heard it. This scant evidence of the agent's sense of humor was perhaps the only scrap he ever showed, and the LT could do without it.

"Sir. Supplies are in place and the drivers are preparing to refuel the vehicles. The generator is set up and should be ready for you. Vasquez got a message from Command that the intel you requested has been sent, whenever you can retrieve it. Setting the watch and bunking the men down until the recon team returns."

Sawyer dismissed the LT and turned to the command tent. Huck followed him. The briefcase was there, set up near a compact communications stack that would connect the camp to the outside world. A nearby cell transmission tower was serving as their broadcast antenna; the RSA satellites had taken control of most others in geosynchronous orbit and the skies belonged to them. There were a few exceptions, of course: remnants of the old government hiding out at installations around the continental forty-eight that didn't know when they'd been beat; one or two persistent hackers in northern California.

Sawyer's smile turned chilly, and Huck knew he was thinking about something violent. The LT turned on the laptop and saw the information he'd requested already in his inbox. He gestured to it, and as Sawyer paged through the files, the smile on his face grew wider and colder.

✯ ✯ ✯ ✯ ✯

Lutz trudged along, thinking black thoughts about Sawyer and how to best handle things. A straight-up fight was out of the question; the agent was highly trained and merciless. He would, as the kids put it, eat Lutz's lunch. At the thought of shooting the government man in the back, a savage kind of glee passed through him, but then he would have the RSA soldiers to contend with. No, it would have to be something subtle, and Herman Lutz knew he was not good at subtle.

He had, however, a man in his ranks who was. George Lutz had warned his brother to keep an eye on this man more than once, and it was only Herman's ruthlessness when it came to keeping his men in check that held off any attempted coup. His name was Patton, and he was a thorn in Herman's paw. In contrast to Herman's own brash ways or George's constant menace, Patton was pleasant. Funny. A really nice guy to hang around with. He had a way about him, though . . . Herman could only talk to him for so long before he got the feeling that Patton was making fun, but never in a way that Herman could identify and take righteous offense.

He had his uses, and this would be one of them. Patton probably already had his approach all thought out.

An hour's walk after he left Agent Sawyer, Lutz was in sight of his camp. He whistled three notes to let them know he was coming, so none of his trigger-happy men would ventilate his head. He'd been shot at more than once in the preceding month, ever since they were burned out of their stronghold, and Herman suspected that these instances were not cases of mistaken identity. In fact, he suspected Jenkins was the one, but he had no proof, and if he wanted to stay in charge, he couldn't just off one of his own without something concrete.

Still. He threw Jenkins a beating one night, just to make sure he knew that Lutz was still the man. Through bloody lips and cracked teeth, Jenkins had assured him that, yes, he understood his place now.

But Lutz whistled anyway.

Five men stood in the encampment, all eyeing Lutz with varying degrees of either servility or hostility. That was how he liked it, but things were harder to manage now that his brother was out of the picture. George had a way with people, and Herman missed that about him.

All of the men there were dressed more or less the same way: denim jeans under dark T-shirts. It was hot, especially now that they weren't in an air-conditioned space anymore. Of all the things that Lutz had to hear about, that was the thing that popped up most often: the oppressive July heat.

The remains of the raiders had been mollified by the news of Sawyer's imminent arrival and the promise of swift and angry revenge against the people of Abraham. And so they waited, grumbling. The five men there (Patton, Jenkins, Coke, Charlie, and Blue) were standing around the remains of a wild hog and carving off bits to eat. Herman walked up to the ring and smelled the gamey pork.

"Where's Ritter?"

Coke pointed back over his shoulder with a white rib bone. "Out there, with a rifle. Dumb shit thinks he saw Bigfoot."

Herman barked out a laugh and pulled a large hunting knife from his belt. He began to cut a large piece of pig for himself. "Well, one of you can fill him in when he gets back. We're in business, boys. Sawyer and his RSA goons are setting up to torch the town. It'll be tonight. Only, I don't know how things are going to work out for us."

"They don't seem to hold us in the highest esteem?" Patton asked from behind a piece of pork. His eyes flicked from Coke's next to him to Herman. "We did kind of screw the pooch."

"Whatever. Sawyer says we can help burn Abraham to the ground, and then maybe come along with him after. He's got some other person he's chasing, and I get the feeling that Abraham is only a test run. But like I said, I don't really trust our G-man. So we need a backup . . . Patton, what's the word I'm looking for?"

"Contingency."

"That. Contingency plan. Now, who's been up to the compound?"

"Right here," Jenkins said through split lips. "Day before yesterday."

Herman's face split into an ugly grin.

"How many infected were still penned up in there?"

☆ ☆ ☆ ☆ ☆

Later that day, Lutz led Coke, Blue, Jenkins, Patton, and Ritter to Sawyer's encampment. The sentry there gave them a once-over and indicated a spot for them to wait . . . but not before confiscating their weapons, including Herman's big knife. The group stood, humiliated, while the troops bustled around them. Lutz could feel his men's stares on the back of his neck, and he did not relish the sensation.

An hour later, Agent Sawyer sauntered over to where the raiders stood.

"Good, you're here. I know, you got the impression that you'd be participating in the sack of Abraham, but I thought it would be best if you sat this one out and watched instead." He held up a hand, forestalling any of the other man's complaints.

"You'll have a front-row seat. Think of us as the instruments of your revenge," he said with a half smile that Lutz felt was deprecating; it seemed the same to him as some of the smiles he'd gotten from Patton. "Someone will come and get you when it's time."

Sawyer turned and walked away.

"What are we gonna do, Herman? Charlie's got the truck and he's on his way," Coke said at his back.

Herman looked at the sentry and saw that the man was paying them no attention. He turned to Coke and said, "Tell 'em you got to piss. Take a powder once you get out of sight and tear ass to catch up with Charlie. Hold him off, or it's our asses."

"Right," Coke said.

"Hey, soldier boy! I need to take a mean piss, man. My back teeth are floatin'."

The sentry rolled his eyes at Coke. "Find yourself a tree, redneck. You should be able to figure out the rest."

Coke gave the man a big smile. "Thankee kind, shithead," he muttered before disappearing into the trees. He drifted slowly away until he was out of sight, discovering once he got there that he really did have to piss. He was nervous . . . they'd done some crazy shit in the past, but the raiders had never been in a straight, stand-up fight with anyone. To their way of thinking, there was no need for that kind of John Wayne bullshit. Bushwhacking and sniping was the way to go; guerrilla hit-and-run tactics were king.

He faded back silently until he was sure the sentries wouldn't see him break away, and then loped off into the woods, hoping that he'd catch Charlie in time; catching backlash from Sawyer and company for the little stunt they had in mind would likely spell slow death for all of them.

Coke knew Herman had sent him because he was "soft." He wouldn't leave his fellows to Sawyer's tender mercies. Coke wasn't so sure about Patton or Jenkins. Ritter, maybe . . . he'd shown he was hard enough to be with the raiders, but the sadistic streak they all possessed never really surfaced in Ritter. Oh, he'd taken his turns with the girls, all right, and he'd sniped more than one homesteader from Abraham, but that mean side was pretty subdued.

Coke ran.

✵ ✵ ✵ ✵ ✵

On the other side of the camp, Agent Sawyer was getting the assault brief straight in his head. He liked to conduct these things without notes; it made him feel more in control, and he felt the men respected him more for it. The topographical maps he'd requested sat on the lighted desk in front of him, as well as satellite imagery of the town itself. Weather conditions for the evening were favorable: cloudy, with a storm brewing. Even though the storm kinked the plan to torch the town, explosives would do the job anyway, even in the hardest rains. And much faster, too . . . he didn't want to stick around to make sure everything burned.

Sawyer glanced at his watch and grinned. "The time is nigh," he said.

"What's that, sir?" Sergeant Dick said to the side of him. The agent turned his head, catching the enlisted man in his icy gaze.

"I said, the time is nigh. Do you know what *nigh* means, soldier?"

The Sergeant scowled. "Yes, sir."

"I'm sure you do. Tell Lieutenant Huck that I'm ready to conduct the brief."

"Yes, sir," the sergeant said and turned away, walking to the weapons cache at a brisk pace.

Grunts, thought Sawyer. *If I had my own men, I'd . . .*

The thought of all the things he might do stuck in the agent's brain.

For starters, he'd have that fucking doctor and her cure. And Mason. He would have Mason hung up by his goddamn balls and—

"Agent Sawyer?"

Pulling out of his happy place, Sawyer looked up to see another of the grunts standing in front of him. A sentry, this one was.

"What is it, soldier?"

He pointed over Sawyer's shoulder at the group of raiders standing alone at the edge of the camp. "I just got relieved, sir, and I noticed that there are only four of the civilians now."

Sawyer's head whipped around. "What?"

"One of them went off to piss, and I guess—"

"You guess?" The agent's gaze was back on the sentry, cold eyes glaring into the man's soul. "You fucking *guess*. What's your name?"

"Corporal Sims, sir."

"All right. *PFC* Sims. Dump your fucking pack somewhere and load up with ammo. Come find me when you're ready to go hunting."

Agent Sawyer turned his back on the soldier and cut a brisk swath toward Lutz and his men.

"Jesus!" Patton cried out. "Thank you! I've been telling Herman that we should go look for him, but he kept saying you'd fucking kill us!"

Agent Sawyer's gaze ripped into Lutz. "What is he saying?"

"Ah, he's saying, Agent, that he doesn't . . . uh—"

"I'm saying that Coke might not be coming back, man! He was scared shitless from the start, okay? Kept saying we should just vamoose out of here and, and . . ."

"And what?"

"Well," Patton stammered, looking down at his shoes. "Well, not get mixed up with you bad motherfuckers. Coke kept saying it, how we couldn't hang with you guys."

Some of the tension left Sawyer's shoulders. "Is that so?"

Patton wouldn't look up; he just nodded.

"He was right," Sawyer said. "And you better remember that. Anyone else want to scram out of here before the bullets fly?"

There was no answer from the raiders. He turned and walked back the way he came, intercepting the soldier running their way and turning him back toward the briefing.

"Hot damn," Ritter said.

✶ ✶ ✶ ✶ ✶

Coke ran through the forest as if the Hounds of Hell were on his trail.

A small part of his brain screamed at him to just keep on running. Screw Lutz, screw the RSA, screw the whole damn mess. He'd never been that nice a guy, and he wanted to hurt the Abraham townsfolk so bad he could taste it . . . but that Sawyer left a cold ball in his gut. And Patton's idea for shafting him was just as bad. No, the mix was just too much for Coke.

Almost.

Mean-spirited asshole that he was, he just couldn't see double-crossing the other raiders, or leaving Charlie to drive in there blind. If Lutz and the others were sidelined for the raid on Abraham, then they'd have no way to create the necessary diversion for Charlie to make it in safe and get away in the same condition. The raiders were a bad bunch, but they were his bad bunch. He'd been with them through some pretty sick times, and like it or not, he was one of them.

He stamped down on the screaming voice in his brain and ran faster.

Lutz had been right to send Coke. Of all the raiders, he and Charlie were the only ones that kept up a real exercise regimen. The others lifted weights and had pretty muscles to prove it, but Coke and Charlie were *fit*. Their compact frames spoke of long runs on the treadmills back at the compound, hours of calisthenics and isometric exercises. Coke snorted a laugh.

Ritter would have done laid down and died by now.

The running man was glad of another thing: the townspeople of Abraham had been more proactive at clearing the infected out of the surrounding woods than the raiders had given them credit for. There was no doubt in Coke's mind, if Sheriff Keaton hadn't been on top of that business, there was no way that Coke would have made it half this far without having to stop and gun down some infected. And that was something he did not want to do. That was one of the reasons he ran so obsessively: you end up out in the woods with a sprinter on you, you better be able to shag ass for as long as necessary.

Coke slowed for a minute to get his bearings, then turned west. The setting sun was low on the horizon, and he still had a mile to go before he hit pavement. Charlie would be in the dump truck at a point in the hills that overlooked Abraham, standing by for the start of festivities.

I just hope I make it in—

He yelped as a shambler stepped out from behind a tree, directly into his path. A moan issued from the throat of the thing for the half second it took for Coke to transition from a run to a flying elbow. The impact drove the infected back against a different tree, its skull compressing with a dry cracking sound between bone and wood.

Coke caught his balance and stomped out at the infected's hip, throwing it off balance, and the shambler fell to the forest floor. A quick boot put an end to the thing's existence, but the damage had been done.

Another moan sounded in the woods.

Coke looked forward to the sunset and started running again, cursing with every footstep.

✯ ✯ ✯ ✯ ✯

Herman Lutz and his small band of three stood at the back of the clearing, listening to the brief with some wonder. He'd had his own ideas about revenge on Abraham, but Sawyer . . . well, he had to hand it to the sick son of a bitch.

"Each incursion team point man will carry a set of bolt cutters. The entry points are here, here, and here," Agent Sawyer said, pointing to three spots on the map: the edge of town closest to the forest, the clearing where the people of Abraham burned the dead, and the opposite end of town from the formidable gates.

"Fat chance," Lutz said loud at this last. "We tried getting in that way, and they cut us to pieces. There's no way in hell—"

Sawyer turned and put up his hand. "Herman, shut the fuck up and try to use the three pounds of gray matter you've got holding your ears apart. This is where you attacked."

"Yes."

"And this is where they ran you to ground. And your man carrying the explosives, which I will assume is now in the capable hands of the Sheriff."

"Yes." A growl this time.

"Right. Try to follow me. If this is where they defeated you so soundly, Lutz, if this is where the tide was turned, so to speak, then this is the last place they think someone would try again. They've defended this port of entry, and defended it well. They will be overconfident in their ability to do it again, and on short notice.

"Now, back to business. Each team will surge in and plant their explosives in the sequence they are labeled. God help you if you fuck this part up. Point men and demolitions will then exit the area, leaving fire teams to start the loud portion of the assault. Strategic targets are here and here," he said, smacking the jailhouse and hospital, "and are not to be blown. Everything else gets razed. Fire teams will then start their retreat, drawing the townspeople after you. Make it look good, we want them to follow. Radio when you reach these positions, and we will take care of the rest."

Sawyer grinned at the mass of black-clad men in front of him.

"Any questions? Platoon leader, break your squads up and go over separate assignments. Fire Team Alpha, report to me in five minutes for your briefing. We head out at midnight."

Lutz saw Sawyer walking back to him.

"Look, I didn't mean—"

A fast and straight jab to Herman's solar plexus cut off his air and his words. He dropped to his knees, trying to gasp for breath and failing, badly. Agent Sawyer bent down to speak in the man's ear.

"Herman, you want to really consider what you're doing here. What I'm doing here. How these two things interconnect. Has it crossed your mind, Herman, that with all this intel I have on the town and out-lying areas, I don't fucking need you anymore? For anything?"

Herman coughed.

"I didn't think so. I'm keeping you and your boys around, Herman, because there is going to be some really dirty work coming up, and I don't want to soil these fine soldiers' hands with it. But keep pushing my buttons. Three can do the job as well as four."

Sawyer straightened up and walked away, adjusting his light body armor. Herman coughed again on the ground, finally getting his wind back.

"When the time comes, boys," he said, "I'm the one that knifes him in the back."

☆ ☆ ☆ ☆ ☆

Across the clearing, Sawyer was as gleeful as he'd ever been. Not as happy as the day he would bring in Dr. Demilio and take Mason's head, no, but chipper anyway. It had been a long time since the former NSA agent had been on a field op with so many men. (He'd worn body armor in his own camp then, too.) A full platoon of RSA soldiers scurried around the small camp, ready and willing to do the agent's bidding, and all that did was fan the fires that burned in him for bigger and better things.

The NCO in charge of Fire Team Alpha, Sergeant Helltree, reported to Agent Sawyer, his men arranged behind him at attention. "Sir, Fire Team Alpha is present and accounted for, awaiting orders."

The agent held up one finger. "Be a minute," he said, and walked behind his tent. He came right back with a pair of cases, each about four feet long. He put them down and opened one, looking up at the young Army man.

"This, Sergeant, is SIMON. Say hello."

CHAPTER 6
REVEILLE

Omaha, NE
30 June 2007
0712 hrs_

DAWN BROKE RELUCTANTLY OVER the silent city, revealing empty avenues and abandoned highways. Weeds, growing freely out of cracks in the pavement and peeking out from behind the flattened tires of swiftly rusting cars, glistened with midsummer dew. The buildings and storefronts were stark and empty, their windows broken out, or boarded up. A large flatbed truck sat blocking one street, its front end crumpled against the corner of a redbrick building. The interior was charred and burned out beyond recognition.

A black-capped chickadee, newly awakened, settled on the hood of the truck. It sang a few notes, then stopped, glanced about, and began to preen its feathers.

Behind the chickadee sat a narrow alleyway, as yet untouched by the breaking sun. Its entrance was clogged with collapsed cardboard boxes and empty bottles, and beyond lay nothing but brick and shadow.

Something moved within the darkness, drawn forth by the little speck of life perched on the hood of the burned-out truck.

With a shuddering moan, a bloated face loomed out of the alleyway, and a pair of sore-covered arms grabbed at the bird.

The chickadee was gone in a flash, flying around the corner with a surprised chirp.

Behind it, the infected stood in place, shoulders slumped forward. Once, it had been a human being. It was no longer. It stared in the direction the bird had gone, a bit of putrid, virus-laden drool slipping from the corner of its mouth. Frustrated at the escape of its prey, the infected flailed its arm once, batting at a nearby weed, and shuffled forward a few steps, scattering cardboard and trash underfoot.

A fine silk tie, now wrinkled and crusted with bits of dried flesh, hung loosely around its neck. A once-white button-up shirt was marred by a tear near the shoulder and a dark brown bloodstain. A similar stain coated both sleeves nearly to the elbows, hinting at a feast long since past. His dress pants had kept remarkably well, save for two holes worn at the knees, where the infected had knelt during the daytime hours in the shade. His leather shoes were in desperate need of a shine.

He might have had ambitions, once. He might have had dreams.

Now, he had only instinct.

The infected looked up, in the direction of the morning sun, groaned, and flailed its arm again before turning its back on the brightness. It spotted another patch of shadow in the distance, felt drawn toward it, and began to march slowly in its direction. It stumbled when it hit the curb, but caught itself on the corner of the truck, and continued onward.

The infected plodded along the middle of the street like a macabre marionette. Its legs jerked, its shoulders swayed, its head seemed barely connected to the body, so freely it rolled, but it never once deviated from its path. It thought only of its destination. There wasn't enough mind left for anything else.

Lack of attentiveness was certainly why the dead thing didn't bother to look around as it plodded along. If it had, it might have seen the two men with rifles, crouched low on a nearby rooftop.

One of them settled the barrel of his rifle on the lip of the roof, and took careful aim.

The crack of a gunshot echoed off the buildings, shattering the still morning air.

A block away, the black-capped chickadee was again startled, and took off from its new perch, silently resolving to find quieter territory.

The infected's head smacked off the pavement, a neat hole drilled through its temple. The skull, six months rotten, split open. Brackish blood and brain matter leaked out, forming a small pool around the figure. It lay still, spilling infected vitae on the ground.

On the rooftop, the shooter stood, worked the rifle bolt, and ejected the spent round over the edge. It pinwheeled through the air and tinkled off the sidewalk, joining an ever-growing scattering of empty brass casings. The shooter worked a fresh round into the chamber, his eyes on the freshly dispatched shambler.

"Nice shot, Krueger!" said the second man, peering at the infected through a pair of pocket-sized binoculars. "That does it for him."

"Thank you," said the sharpshooter, squatting low and resting the barrel of his weapon on the raised edge of the roof. "Poor schmuck walked right past us. That's getting pretty rare. First one in a week to come within fifty yards."

"Well, we've cleared out most of the buildings in these blocks, so I guess there aren't many left in the neighborhood. It might be a different story downtown," said the spotter, reaching down to rummage through a faded olive drab knapsack at his feet. He pulled out a battered Nikon camera, checked it over, and snapped a shot of the fresh kill with the sunrise in the background. "That'll make a good one, if I ever get it developed."

Krueger watched him as he worked. "Ever thought about building a dark room, Denton?" asked the soldier, holding back a yawn. The pair had been on guard duty all night, and their shift was nearly over. "It's not like we have a lack of materials. Or room."

"True." Denton nodded, putting the camera back in the knapsack. "Maybe I'll get around to it, after we're done with the perimeter."

The roof the two men were sitting on was spacious and flat, providing them with a 360-degree view of the surrounding neighborhood. Other than the stairwell door, the only other occupants of the roof were four long banks of angled solar panels. Their original purpose was to serve as a backup for the Fac, but they were now pulling duty as the primary generators. With the return of the sun, a security lamp over the stairwell door had begun to glow faintly, signaling that a charge was once again flowing. There were banks of batteries below, recharging a bit every day, but they were reserved solely for the biosafety level four laboratory.

The perimeter Denton referred to surrounded the entire building, which the group had taken to calling "the Fac" more than anything else. The fence also circled the Fac's narrow yard, and part of a nearby industrial complex. Chain-link fence had been the original deterrent, enclosing an area of a little over two acres, but over weeks the resident survivors had improved their defenses, not wanting to be caught off guard by a wave of infected with little more than metal mesh between them and certain death. They had dug a deep, narrow trench outside the fence, using the earth they moved to fill sacks liberated from the neighboring factory. The makeshift sandbags were stacked ten high and three deep on the inside of the fence, forming a heavy buttress that supported the fence and, hopefully, would keep it from being pushed over by dozens of angry infected.

The group hoped to create a safe outdoor environment where they could relax or grow their own food. No one was comfortable outdoors anymore. Not without a good, sturdy wall between them and the Morningstar strain, at least.

"You could put it in the basement," said Krueger, still on about the dark room. "In one of the labs Anna and Becky aren't using. There are four of 'em down there and they're only using one. Well, two, if you count Mason's room. There are no windows. It's perfect. You could get all those developed in your downtime. Hell, I'd like to see some of them. You've been taking them since Suez, right?"

"Before," corrected Denton. "I was attached to Alpha, covering Iraq, before they were redeployed to the canal. I have some shots of them there, too."

"Well, I wouldn't know about that. I'm an Echo. Or I was. How many rolls you got in there?" Krueger asked, leaning forward to peer in the top of Denton's loose, faded knapsack.

Denton flipped the cover shut. "Thirty or so."

Krueger whistled in appreciation and rested his head against the edge of the roof. He closed his eyes and let the sun warm his face for a moment. He sat up as a new thought struck him.

"Hey, you know, you might just be the only photographer left who saw all this go down, and took pictures to prove it," Krueger said, raising his eyebrows and grinning. "You could end up famous."

"Yeah," laughed Denton, "I can see the awards hanging on my living room wall right now. If anybody ever gives 'em out again."

That thought quieted the pair, and they sat in silence.

The sun rose higher in the sky.

✫ ✫ ✫ ✫ ✫

Directly below the watchmen, other survivors were beginning to stir. Thomas was the first to emerge from the rec room, where he bunked on the couch. Though he was of average height, his perfect posture and confident, purposeful way of moving made him seem inches taller. A perpetual scowl was etched on his face. He was dressed in a neatly ironed pair of jeans and a tucked-in, button-up shirt. He wore a pair of scuffed, well-used combat boots, and as he strode down the hall toward the Fac's makeshift kitchen they clomped and clicked and echoed off the concrete walls. No one ever dared tell him to his face, but Command Sergeant Major Thomas and his boots were the group's collective alarm clock.

If they had told him, however, they might have learned that Thomas was well aware of what he was doing. A smug smile threatened to ease the scowl as he marched along. The sound of muffled groans reached his ears. The veteran could imagine the sleepy survivors pulling pillows over their heads and retreating farther under their blankets. As for the sergeant major, Thomas just wasn't the type that enjoyed lounging in the sack. Sleep was a chore to be taken care of once a day. Then it was back to business.

Even so, there were some luxuries Thomas allowed himself to indulge in. One of the few was his morning cup of coffee. He had gotten into the habit of brewing a pot first thing every day, extra strong. The Fac had a break room just past the lobby, and the group had turned it into a functional, if Spartan, kitchen. A line of cabinets ran along the far wall. The only appliance had been a microwave oven, but it had been deemed a waste of electricity. The only electric appliances the survivors used now were a double-burner hot plate and a coffeepot. Jack and Mitsui had just finished installing a cast-iron woodstove against the outer wall, but no one in the group had yet mastered the art of cooking on it. Three round folding tables filled the center of the room, surrounded by metal chairs. A chalkboard on rollers was pushed up against the nearest wall and was covered with a hand-drawn map of the Fac and the surrounding blocks, with every building and alleyway marked. An X was drawn through each building that had been searched and subsequently secured. Only a few, out near the edges of the board, farthest from the Fac, stood unmarked.

When Thomas entered the room, the first thing he noticed was an already-full coffee pot on the counter. The second was a woman slumped over the nearest table, her head resting on folded arms. A Styrofoam cup of the brew sat unfinished next to her. She did not stir as Thomas crossed the room to the counter to check the coffee. He sniffed at it, grimaced, and upended the pot into the sink. The coffee was cold and stale.

There was no fresh coffee left to be had in Omaha, but Thomas had no quarrel with the instant stuff. In fact, he preferred it. They didn't pack gourmet blends in MREs, after all. Thomas reached into the cabinet above him and grabbed a fresh packet. He tore open the foil wrapper, poured in the grounds, and turned on the pot. The hard part done, he leaned back against the countertop to wait. In the meantime, he studied the room's other occupant.

The woman at the table still hadn't moved. If her back hadn't been slowly rising and falling with each breath, Thomas might have mistaken her for a corpse. He considered waking her, but decided against it. She was probably exhausted. Anna Demilio spent most of every day, not to mention many of her nights, working in the laboratories in the Fac's sublevel. She deserved her rest.

Thomas's ears pricked up as he heard a soft padding in the hall. A moment later, a disheveled, bleary-eyed young Japanese woman appeared in the doorway. She wore plain white pajamas and a ridiculous pair of pink bunny slippers, complete with little yellow whiskers and button eyes. She stretched her arms above her head and sighed.

"Good morning!" Juni said, and only then noticed the sleeping doctor. She clapped a hand over her mouth. Dr. Demilio shifted and murmured in her sleep, but didn't awaken. The girl slowly and silently wound her way across the kitchen to Thomas. In a much lower voice, she repeated: "Good morning!"

"I heard you the first time," said Thomas. He didn't bother whispering.

Thomas's brusque manner was only off-putting to strangers. Junko Koji, cooped up in the same building with the man for months, wasn't daunted in the least. "Do you know if we're still going out today?" she asked in the same low voice.

Thomas shrugged.

"Did Frank tell you if he's going to let me go this time?" Juni pressed.

Thomas shrugged again and glanced at the coffeepot. Only half-full. *Or half-empty,* he thought, *depending on how your philosophy bends itself.*

"I'd really like to go," said Juni.

Thomas relented. "General Sherman doesn't like sending untrained people into dangerous situations when he has other, better options," Thomas said.

"I survived for months out there!" protested Juni. "I'm as tough as any of you."

"You wear pink bunny slippers," deadpanned Thomas, glancing at the girl's footwear.

"That has nothing to do with it!" Juni said, her voice rising, forgetting about Anna as she stamped her foot on the ground in protest.

A groan diverted their attention to Anna. She had awoken during the brief conversation, and was rubbing the back of her neck, head still on the tabletop. "Oh, God, I did it again," she lamented. "My neck feels like concrete."

"Sleeping on a table will do that," said Thomas. Behind him, the coffeepot burbled and clicked, cycle complete. He turned to fetch a cup from an overhead cabinet. "You have a bed. Sack out like the rest of us. You push too hard, you start getting sloppy. We need you sharp."

As Thomas set about pouring himself a cup, Juni walked over to Anna and plopped down in the chair beside her. She rested her elbows on the table and her head in her hands, smiling at the Doctor. "He's no fun. Another late night?"

Anna repeated her groan. "I came up at five to get something to drink, but I must have fallen asleep after I sat down. What time is it now?"

Juni glanced at a clock on the wall. "Seven-fifteen."

Doctor Demilio gave an exaggerated shrug. "Two hours of sleep sounds about right. Guess I'd better get back downstairs." She picked up the cup sitting next to her, took a swig, and quickly spat it back with a sound of disgust. "Ugh. Thomas, I'm going to steal some of your coffee, if you don't mind. Mine's gone stale."

Thomas didn't reply. He was staring out the kitchen's only window, feet set shoulder width apart, one hand tucked behind his back while the other swirled around the steaming contents of his mug.

More sounds from the hall—a slamming door, rattling drawers, and muffled conversations—meant that other survivors were up and about. Today was another big day for the group. Dwindling supplies in their pantry meant yet another supply run was in order. Sherman had already told everyone to prepare for it. Every foray took them deeper into the city, and they'd been coming more often. The Fac now stood in the center of a four-block radius that had been picked clean of nonperishable food items and infected. The worst part, in Thomas's mind, was the frequency of the trips. If they had a truck to load up, it wouldn't have been so bad, but loading up with food one backpack at a time was hardly enough to feed fifteen mouths for very long.

But the same nagging worry tugged at the back of everyone's mind:

that sooner or later, they'd kick in the wrong door and stir up a hornet's nest.

On scavenging days, everyone was on high alert, even the ones who stayed behind to hold the fort.

Anna Demilio poured herself a cup from the fresh pot and spooned in a heap of sugar, paused a moment, and added a second spoonful.

"You're just asking for a crash," grumbled Thomas, looking sideways at Anna.

"Preaching to the choir, Thomas," was Anna's riposte. She blew on the coffee to cool it as she took her leave, patting Juni on the shoulder as she passed. "Good luck today."

"Oh, I'm just guarding the kitchen again," pouted Juni, frowning at Thomas's back. "Apparently people with pink bunny slippers can't shoot straight."

"Either way, you know where I'll be," Anna tossed over her shoulder. She headed for the rear of the building, to the stairwell that would take her to the basement. In a lower voice, she murmured to herself, "Back down in the dungeon with a laconic Austrian, a curious medic, and about fifty million bugs that want to kill me. I should have been a pediatrician."

"A pedia-*whatthefuck*?" came a sudden outburst from the room to Anna's left.

Without slowing, Anna shot back: "A *pediatrician*, Brewster. Greek. For a kid doctor. You know. The kind you'd go see if *you* got sick."

A face framed by a shock of tangled brown hair poked out from the side room, looking indignant. "Yeah? Well, you're . . . you've got *poor fashion sense!*"

Thomas caught laughter from across the hall as another pair of survivors left their respective rooms. He turned to see a man wearing a dirt-stained pair of coveralls shake his head. "First round of the day to Dr. Anna Demilio. She shoots, she scores!" he joked in a passable impression of a sports announcer. The other, a short, paper-thin Asian man, chuckled at the disappointed look on Brewster's face.

"What do you want from me?" demanded Brewster as the pair passed by. He threw his arms wide. "I just woke up. I'm not on my game, yet! Hey!" Brewster struggled after them, stumbling and trying to pull on his boots as he went. "Come on, guys! Jack? Mitsui? Wait up! Give me a chance, here! What if I said something like, uh, she needed to go to a proctologist because she's—"

"Too late," interrupted Jack. When he noticed the soldier was following them, he added: "Mitsui and I are going to the roof to take over for Krueger and Denton. You should head to the kitchen. Frank said he wanted to get started early today."

Brewster grumbled, but assented. By the time he had settled into one of the kitchen's folding metal chairs and finished double-knotting his bootlaces, everyone had assembled. Several conversations kept the room humming.

At the table farthest from the door sat Mbutu Ngasy. Across from him sat Gregory Mason, late of the U.S. National Security Agency, or "No Such Agency," as it was often jokingly referred to by the other branches. Every now and then, Mason would wince and unconsciously put a hand to his chest. He was still recovering from a serious wound received when the group had seized the Fac from its former hostile owners. A pistol round had punctured his lung and shattered a rib, and it was only through intense effort on the part of Anna Demilio, and continual observation by Rebecca Hall, that he had lived.

A virologist was no substitute for a trauma surgeon, Thomas thought. Anna had given Mason strict orders to take things slowly. She was unwilling to put her patchwork repairs through any stress tests.

Mason and the Kenyan were talking security, with Mbutu describing how the Mombasa airport had run things, and Mason pointing out where they could have made improvements.

Krueger and Denton wandered in a few minutes after Brewster, helped themselves to the last of the coffee, and leaned back in their chairs, looking drowsy. Thomas couldn't blame them. They had been up all night, and they would have to stay up a while longer, at least until the foraging party returned. It was safest to have every rifle on the battlements in case things went south. In a city the size of Omaha, trouble was always just around the corner. All it would take to spark an engagement would be a single mistake—opening a strange door too hastily, or even speaking out at the wrong time in the wrong place could bring dozens of infected down on the survivors.

Brewster sat with Junko to his right and Trevor Westscott to his left. The pair were engrossed in an animated discussion about the etymology of names. Juni was a prodigy with languages. She spoke several fluently, and enjoyed learning new words and new phrases. She actively collected colloquialisms in each of the languages she spoke, worked hard to master accents, and made a hobby out of understanding names. It had taken Brewster three weeks to figure out she wasn't American. No one would let him forget it, either. She had been using a student visa when Morningstar struck, stranding her in the United States.

"What about Mason?" asked Brewster, pointing over at the NSA agent. "Where's his name come from?"

"Jeez Louise, Brewster," sighed Juni, using one of the colloquialisms of which she was so fond. "That's the least interesting one in the room. Mason comes from mason—you know, a stonemason. An ancestor of his was one, probably. Just like Smith, or Baker. Those are common names for you guys, right? No big mystery."

"So what was their last name before they were a smith or a baker?"

"Well, a lot of the time Europeans just used their first name plus where you were from, if it wasn't your profession—but only if you were somewhere else," Juni said.

Trev and Brewster glanced at one another in confusion.

"You're following me, right?" Juni asked. Both men shook their heads. Juni looked exasperated. "Okay. Take Leonardo da Vinci. What's his last name?"

Trev and Brewster answered as one: "da Vinci."

"No! He had no last name. He was a bastard," Juni exclaimed, looking positively scandalized. "How can you two not know this stuff?"

"Well, uh, I volunteered for the infantry. I don't know what Trev's excuse is," Brewster said with a grin.

"Go on," prompted Trev, ignoring the soldier.

"He was a bastard, so he couldn't take his father's name. So he was called 'da Vinci,' which means, 'from Vinci.' So his name is actually

'Leonardo, from Vinci,'" Juni finished. She sat back in her chair and crossed her arms, an impish grin on her face.

"I wonder what mine means," mused Brewster.

"I don't even know why I try," said Juni, throwing her arms up in the air. "I just explained it."

"Someone in your family was a brewer, Ewan," said Trev.

"Oh," Brewster murmured. After a moment, he grinned. "Well, that figures, doesn't it?"

The staccato click of boot heels coming together made everyone look up. Thomas, still standing near the window, had snapped crisply to attention, eyes front.

"Thomas," said Francis Sherman, "for the last time, please stop doing that. We're not in the Army anymore. You can drop the formalities."

"Yes, sir," said Thomas. He fell into parade rest.

"That includes calling me 'sir,'" Sherman added.

Thomas glanced at the ex-general. "Respectfully, sir, 'sir' is not an honorific exclusive to the armed forces. If I am a civilian, then I may choose to address you in any way I please. I may also choose to stand up straight when you walk into a room."

Sherman sighed and rubbed at his temples.

"He's got you there, Frank," said Denton, grinning.

"I was hoping for an easy day," said Sherman. "Looks like I'm not going to get it. Well, at least it's bright and sunny out. Weather doesn't get much prettier."

"So we're a go on the scavenging run?" asked Thomas.

"We are," confirmed Sherman. The group in the room checked the weapons strapped to their waists. Sherman wound his way between the tables to the map board, and snapped the top from a blue felt-tip marker. "I don't want to head too deep into town if we can avoid it. I've been looking at one of our street maps, and if we cut west here," Sherman explained, illustrating the route by dotting a line down a one-way street, "then we can stay on the edge of town and come out here, directly across from a little strip mall and a set of town houses. We'll try for the mall first."

"What sort of businesses were there?" asked Trev.

"We haven't actually been there yet, so we haven't had eyes on it. I only know it's there because of an ad in my map for a pizzeria."

"So we could get out there and find nothing useful at all," guessed Brewster. "Aside from rotted fuckin' pepperoni."

"Maybe, but we'd still have the homes to fall back on," said Sherman. "And like I said, going this way keeps us on the edge of town."

"Always a bonus, sir," said Krueger, yawning.

Thomas noticed the soldier's drowsy-eyed expression. "Don't fall asleep on us," he warned. "If anything goes bad, you're our backup."

"I'm good for another twelve hours," said Krueger, sitting up straighter. "Just give me my rifle and a rooftop."

"You've got both," said Sherman, with a nod. "Denton, you were up all night, too, so you're off the hook. And Juni, I want you to stay and—"

"Oh, that's bullshit," she interrupted, crossing her arms.

"Hear me out," started Sherman, but Juni wasn't having it.

"I know, I know, you have a really good reason all thought out for me. But the truth is, you just haven't gotten to see me fight those things yet and you don't think I can handle myself," said Juni, her face flushing. "You saw Trev fight, so you're okay with him going along. Hell, he wades into those things with that baton like a farmer cuts into a wheat field with a scythe. And *that's* irresponsible as hell!"

Trev shot Juni a hurt look for a moment, then heaved a shrug. She was correct, after all.

"You're right," said Sherman.

Juni, about to launch into another point, stalled out at Sherman's admission. "What?"

"You're right," Sherman repeated. He spoke calmly and plainly. "I haven't seen you fight. So why would I bring you along?"

"I, well—" stuttered Juni. She collected herself. "You'd bring me along so I could prove myself."

"It may surprise you to know that I do not take your pride into account when I come up with these little outings of ours," said Sherman. "I am not throwing an unknown into the equation just so you can feel approved of. At the same time, no one is disparaging your abilities, except in your imagination. The truth is, if I really thought you couldn't handle yourself, I wouldn't give you the keys to the building's front door." Sherman dangled a key ring from his index finger. Juni eyed it silently. "Now, as I was going to say before you made my day even *more* difficult, I want you to lock up behind us, keep an eye out, and open them for us when we return. I know I usually give these to Denton or Brewster, but as it happens, today one of them is half-asleep and the other is going out. So you're our gatekeeper."

Thomas watched the mix of emotions on the girl's face. It was clear to him Juni was only half-placated. Usually Sherman sent her to the roof. The previous run, she was door guard. This was her, keeping a promotion, even a minor one. She sullenly accepted the key ring. With a glance at Thomas, she muttered, "At least it's a job I can do wearing my slippers."

Thomas remained silent.

"Thank you," said Sherman. "Brewster, you and Trev are on Anna's detail. Head back to the clinic. Did she tell you what she needed?"

Trevor spoke up before the soldier. "We've got it all here, Frank," he said, tapping the side of his head. "Pickings are getting slim, though. A lot of the chemicals she wants are expired, like the last couple of runs. And a lot of the more useful medications were looted a long time ago. She's starting to get unreasonable with us."

"I'll have a chat with her when we get back. Remember, she's running herself ragged down there in the labs. She just needs a break. She's bound to get a little grouchy until she gets one, or makes some progress she can feel proud of," Sherman said. "Everyone else, grab what you need: weapons, ammo, first aid, and empties for the haul. We're leaving in a few. And Brewster?"

Ewan stood up straight at his name. "Yo."

"No more dog food, okay?"

CHAPTER 7
THE BIG BREAKUP

Outskirts of Omaha
30 June 2007
0121 hrs_

A STAND OF TREES, growing around a natural bowl-shaped decline, flanked an abandoned highway. They grew thick and untended. Young growth bushes filled in the spaces between the trunks, creating a thick, thorny boma. From without, it appeared as nothing more than another grove of trees: dark, quiet, and barely rustling in the nighttime air. Two large olive drab vehicles sat on the side of the road, angled crazily, as if they'd crashed there, in the middle of nowhere.

Harris surveyed the activity in the camp. Half a dozen men filled the space, one silent and still, one sacked out in a sleeping bag and snoring, while two others paced restlessly, eager to reach their destination, now barely ten miles away. Two more were stationed in the darkness around the grove's perimeter, standing watch. The camp was as safe as any the group had used on their thousand-mile journey, but it was still in the open. The guards' weapons were locked and loaded.

Three of the men had come together at the center of the camp, focused on the prospect of a hot dinner.

A small campfire burned merrily, carefully surrounded by a mound of stones to stifle the light cast by the flames, and a carbon-blackened folding grill had been laid over the top of the coals. The smell of roasting meat permeated the clearing, and the venison steaks sizzled on the grill, hissing and popping as juices boiled out of the cuts and into the flames, which licked the underside of the meat.

"Careful, careful!" admonished Rico. "You'll burn them!"

"Ah, relax, Rico," said Wendell, stabbing the steaks with his Ka-Bar and flipping them. The sizzle grew in intensity as the venison's juices ran free. "I grew up cooking this stuff when Dad took me hunting. You want 'em well done."

Rico looked miffed. "Medium-rare for me, Wendell."

Wendell flipped the Ka-Bar in his hand and offered it to Rico, hilt first. "Hey, you want the job, it's all yours."

"No, no—hell no!" said Hillyard. "Last time Rico cooked it was like eating rocks."

Rico mumbled under his breath.

"Sorry, didn't catch that, bro," Hillyard said, grinning.

"I said, 'choke on a cock, Hillyard,'" Rico repeated, flicking the man off for good measure.

"Hey!" Harris said. The three sailors gathered around the fire looked up into his angular face.

"Commander," Wendell said, nodding.

"Evening, Harris. We're cooking up some chow. Hillyard bagged a buck when he did his walkaround."

"Didn't hear a shot," started Harris.

Hillyard held up a pistol-grip crossbow. "Found it in the truck. Wounded him and tracked him down. Followed the blood trail. Got just enough meat off of him for a few of these steaks. You want one, Commander?"

Harris tried to look stern. "That's not why I'm here. You three are being too loud. We can't see what's coming, now that it's night, and the carriers'll be more active. You'll have to put that fire out and keep your voices down."

"Aw, sir—" started Allen from behind him. "I been looking forward to a steak coming off sentry duty."

"Don't 'aw, sir' me," Harris said. "You screw up, it costs all of us. The fire's gotta go."

Allen sighed and went to return to his post.

"Sir, two more minutes and these babies will be done. First hot meal we'll have gotten in days. What do you say, sir? Come on—a little risk in return for a world of morale?" asked Wendell, gesturing at the grill.

"And full stomachs," added Rico.

Harris grumbled under his breath, and finally relented. "All right. But hurry it up. And douse that goddamn fire the second you're done!" He turned to have a talk with another pair of his charges, but was stopped by a query Hillyard shot at him: "Sir? What about that steak?"

Commander Harris barely turned. "I'm not proud. Save me one."

Rico and Hillyard grinned at one another. The Commander wasn't a hard-ass. He just tried to act like one.

He walked off with a ghost of a smile on his face, marching across the clearing, taking stock of their situation. His guards were positioned at either side of the clearing, covering each other with 90-degree fields of fire. They seemed frosty and attentive, having eaten first and been given a chance to nap while the rest of their compatriots set up the makeshift camp. One of them was Allen, the other Stone.

At first, the others had resisted having Stone stand over them while they slept, but as the trip wore on and hours of sleep got short, they relented. And after all, wasn't he the one that had facilitated their escape?

Harris would have pushed on to Omaha, seeing as it was only a dozen miles away, but he'd deemed it too risky. The sailors, despite the prospect of their long journey's end, secretly agreed. It was just too dangerous to travel at night. The infected were photosensitive. They'd learned that much through experience on the road. It was suicide to stay in the open at night, and Harris knew it. The stand of trees and natural basin provided as safe a camp as any. He would have preferred a nice, thick brick building with steel doors, but beggars couldn't be choosers.

Harris spotted the men he wanted to talk to by themselves, sitting at a small sleeping area near the edge of the camp, abutting a rock face that jutted from the ground. One was getting out of his bedroll, shaking it free of sticks and pebbles. The other sat cross-legged on the outcropping, oiling the action of his Winchester repeating rifle.

Hal spotted Harris approaching and stood, groaning and holding his lower back. "Hey, there, Harris. What's the word?"

Harris shrugged. "Looks like we're all getting settled in, Hal. With a little luck, we'll make it to Omaha tomorrow and catch some word on the radio from Sherman or Demilio or one of the others who went in ahead of us."

Hal Dorne nodded. He wore a sun-bleached baseball cap on his head and an oil-stained long-sleeved T-shirt, complete with cargo pants restuffed with hand tools they'd found in a half-burned True Value. "Luck is right. I wish we still had that long-range radio we took from the *Ramage*. Wouldn't be a problem raising Sherman with that."

"Yeah, well, it's in pieces back in the Rockies somewhere," said the man with the rifle. "Even you couldn't fix it."

"Don't rub it in, Stiles," said Hal.

"As it is," said Harris, ignoring them, "all we have are short-range civvie models. Maybe a mile or two range on those, tops. We'll have to keep scanning channels and broadcasting as we get deeper in the city, and hope we pass close enough to this hidden lab of Demilio's for them to pick us up and guide us in."

"If not?" asked Hal.

"We'll bunker up in a building and keep trying," stated Harris, folding his arms across his chest.

Mark Stiles grinned, dry-fired his rifle, and nodded at the smooth action. "Don't know about the rest of you, but I'm ready to go in and get this trip over with."

"Aren't we all," added Hal.

SURVIVORS

"Just don't go and get gung-ho on us, Stiles," said Harris. "Remember, we need to get you there alive."

Stiles nodded, a grimace on his face. "I kind of hate being the only nonexpendable one."

"Why?" asked Hal. "I'd think you'd enjoy having us look after your skin."

Stiles shrugged. "I guess I just don't like the idea of other people dying so I can live. I mean, that's why I joined the Army in the first place: so someone else wouldn't have to go do it instead."

From across the clearing, Wendell's voice rang out: "Steaks are ready!"

Harris spun on his heel, fixing the man with a narrow-eyed glare. "I said to keep your goddamn voice down!"

"But . . . it's *steak*."

"Well," Harris said, jerking a thumb in the direction of the small campfire, "want to get something to eat? Fresh venison steaks."

Stiles licked his lips. "I haven't had a steak—even venison—since, well, hell, I can't even remember the last time—"

A shout interrupted Stiles mid-sentence. It came from one of the guard posts on the perimeter. The voice was controlled and cool.

"Contact! Contact! Contact!" reported Stone. Harris turned to see him bring his rifle to bear. "One sprinter, inbound, two o'clock!"

"Shit," cursed Harris. The group could easily deal with a single infected, but the sharp reports of rifle fire could very well bring more running. Still, there was no choice. Either they took the carrier down, or lost a life of their own. "Take him down! Single shot! Make it count!"

A moment later the quiet glen was shattered by the sound of an M-16 round discharging. The crunch of branches and rustle of leaves sounded, and Harris could imagine the sprinter pitching face-forward in the loam.

The sentry sounded off. "Tango down, Harris!"

The ex-commander wasted no time.

"I want all of you, fall back to the main encampment! Form a defensive knot! Shoulder to shoulder!"

The single sprinter might have been the only threat, but Harris was taking no chances. Best to assume there were more coming now that the gunshot had echoed across the glen and darkened fields beyond.

"God, I wish we had IR gear," moaned Wendell, taking his place on the firing line.

"There's a lot I'd wish for," said Rico. "Doesn't make it any likelier to happen, though."

The group had picked up a couple of nonstandard arms between Lexington and where they sat. One had been given to Stiles—a five-round revolver called the Judge, loaded with .410 shotgun shells. Harris had thought it would make a perfect close-range defensive weapon for the only man immune to the Morningstar strain. He could get blood all over himself in a point-blank situation and come out un-scathed.

The other was a Ruger Mini-14, which Commander Harris had claimed for himself. He snapped it up from where it leaned against a tree trunk, checked the ammo, and joined the others on the firing line.

For a long moment, silence fell on the glen once more. The small campfire cracked and popped, and the sound of safeties being flicked off were the only noise. The sailors, Hal, and Mark Stiles looked back and forth at one another, and cast nervous glances at the pitch-blackness of the forest beyond their clearing.

The sound of snapping twigs brought weapon barrels swiveling around. The defenders saw only darkness and the outline of thorn-bushes between the thick trunks.

Then a pair of sprinters burst into the clearing, shoving their way through the bushes oblivious to the cuts they received. The pair focused on the circle of defenders immediately.

"Drop 'em!" said Harris.

Four shots rang out: one from Rico's pistol, two from Harris's semiautomatic carbine, and a fourth from Stone's M-16.

Rico's shot found its mark, striking the infected on the left just above the eye. The carrier fell backward silently, arms pinwheeling through the air, and landed in a heap in the grass.

Harris's first shot missed, and his second struck the remaining infected in the shoulder, spinning it halfway around. It came back up, a low growl in its throat that quickly became a full-fledged, guttural roar, so full of rage and determination that it drained the blood from the faces of the defenders.

Stone's shot hit the infected in its open mouth, blowing out the back of its neck and sending it down to join its comrade in the grass.

"Oh, fuck, oh, fuck," breathed Wendell. The sailor had good reason to be worried. The gunshots might bring out curious infected, but the deep-throated roar of the second sprinter was a dinner bell for any remaining infected within earshot.

"Steady, men!" said Harris. "Steady. They'll be coming, now." *So close,* he thought. *So close, and we fuck up less than a dozen miles from the finish line.* "We have to hold the bastards when they show!"

Their only warning was the sound of rapidly approaching footsteps cracking branches and crunching dried leaves underfoot.

One moment, the camp was empty save for defenders.

The next, sprinters were appearing from every direction.

"Contact rear!" came a shouted alert.

"Contact left!" came another.

"More from the front!" was Rico's report.

"Shit! Shit! They're coming from the right, too!" Hillyard shouted.

"Fire! Fire! Take them down!" Harris yelled.

Gunshots rang out in staccato bursts. Carriers dropped left and right, some taken down by chest shots, others killed permanently by well-aimed rounds to the head.

"Reloading!" came Rico's voice. He dropped a magazine free and slapped in a fresh one, and began unloading rounds on the infected.

The sprinters were gaining ground. They'd closed about half the distance from the tree line to the defensive knot in the center of the clearing. The sailors' gunshots began to ring out faster and faster, as they desperately tried to kill their opposition before it closed on them.

A sprinter launched itself from the underbrush and low-tackled Hillyard, dragging itself up the man's trousers. The sailor tried to aim his MP-5 down at the sprinter's skull, but the infected batted the barrel out of the way and sank its teeth into the sailor's neck. His scream trailed off into a gurgle.

Wendell went down next, taken by a pair of sprinters. His buddies came to his rescue, pulling the infected off the sailor and bodily throwing them away from the knot. They raised their pistols and dispatched the attackers with a flurry of shots, but the momentary breach in the line allowed more of the infected to close to melee range.

"They're everywhere! They're everywhere!" Allen shouted. Panic was beginning to creep into his voice.

Harris picked up on it. "Steady, men! Keep up the fire!"

Slowly, the sprinter attack began to slacken off. What had been dozens tearing through the underbrush slowed to half a dozen at a time, then pairs, and finally, the assault ceased entirely. The final sprinter fell, taken by a shot to the throat by Mark Stiles's Winchester.

Silence fell once more. The smell of gunpowder and the sickening scent of coppery blood overpowered the tantalizing odor of the forgotten venison steaks, now beginning to blacken and char on the grill.

"Is that it?" Rico asked, blood pumping. His eyes were wide, and he scanned the tree line for more threats.

Harris waited a moment, heard nothing, and nodded, using the lull to reload his M-14.

"Damn," Allen said. "We're down two more. If we don't get out of here soon, I don't—"

"Check these bodies!" Harris said, cutting Allen off. "Finish off any of the bastards that didn't get hit in the head. Don't want them getting back up."

The sailors spread out, abandoning their defensive knot, and flicked on flashlights, inspecting the bodies of the deceased carriers. Here and there a shot rang out as a sailor finished a sprinter.

One of the infected, leaning against a tree with a bloody smear leading down the bark to where it lay, snapped its eyes open. With a shudder and a moan, it leaned forward, and tried to lift itself to a standing position.

Hal Dorne took aim with his pistol and finished it off with a shot to the forehead. The undead slumped back against the trunk, stilled for good.

Harris took a look around the now-ruined camp, shaking his head. "All right, gents. Let's pack up. It's not safe here anymore. We'll have to move out."

"In the dark, Commander?" asked Rico. "Won't that just get us attacked again?"

"Maybe," admitted Harris, "but it's better than sitting here and hoping more aren't on their way."

✯ ✯ ✯ ✯ ✯

Perhaps it was bad timing on Harris's part, or perhaps the universe was simply betraying its twisted sense of humor, but at that moment the night breeze carried the sound of low-pitched moans to the group.

"Oh, shit," said Stiles.

"Shamblers," agreed Allen. "Lots of them."

"But from where?" asked Rico, turning in a circle.

Stiles turned, too. The moans seemed to come from everywhere.

Harris made a quick decision. "All right, men! Grab up your weapons, ammo, and food! Leave your bags and packs! We can scavenge more clothes and gear in Omaha! We've got to beat it to the trucks, *now*!"

The sailors gave him no argument. They grabbed what precious little ammunition remained, slung their weapons, and prepared to move out.

All the while, the sound of undead moans grew closer and closer. The enemy's footsteps were now audible. By the time the group was ready to bug out, the first of the shamblers had appeared on the edge of the clearing.

Rico took aim at the closest, but Harris stayed his hand. "Save your ammo, Rico. We might need it. All right, men! Due east! Stay quick, stay quiet, stay low, and watch your flanks!"

The group, minus the two unfortunates who had been lost to the sprinters, took off at a dogtrot through the woods. They ducked branches and weaved past thornbushes, doing their best to remain silent.

Stone, in the lead, took the group down a culvert than ran alongside the highway, counting on the dip to hide them from view. It would have been a good move, except one of the shamblers happened to be standing on the edge of the decline. It let loose a deep moan and tottered toward the survivors. Rico fired once, missed, and tried again, this time nailing the shambler below the chin. Bits of skull and gray matter sprayed from the back of the thing's skull, and it fell forward, rolling down the hill to come to a rest at the survivor's feet.

"Watch the blood," cautioned Harris, pointing at the shambler. "Walk around it."

"Sir," said Allen, his face gray as a granite headstone, "I think we have bigger problems." The sailor pointed to the edge of the highway above, where half a dozen more shamblers had appeared. Joining them was a lone sprinter, snarling and twitching, staring with bloody eyes at its prey. It let loose another roar before it charged.

Harris's M-14 bucked once, putting a crater in the sprinter's chest. It hit face-first and slid, unmoving, down the hill into the culvert.

The crowd of shamblers was right behind it, making their way down the steep decline toward the soldiers, the hill giving them a bit of added speed. Gunshots lit the night and muzzle flashes created a strobe effect in the darkness. Harris glanced behind and saw that the shamblers they'd left behind in the camp were catching up. They were flanked.

A shambler tripped on its way down the hill, causing Stone's pistol shot to miss high. The shambler rolled head over heels and came to a stop at the man's feet. It immediately grabbed out at the man's legs, yanking him to the ground. It sank its teeth into his boot. Stone's face didn't change, and his only reaction was to kick at the shambler with his other foot. When that didn't work, he sat up and pressed his pistol against the shambler's head and fired, blowing the back of its skull off.

One by one, the sailors began to report their dwindling ammunition. Their voices took on an edge of panic. Stiles felt fear begin to blossom in his own chest.

Immune or not their teeth will still kill me dead.

☆ ☆ ☆ ☆ ☆

Allen, still on point, tried to lead the men onward. "Come on!" he shouted. "There's a storm drain ahead—runs under the highway! We can funnel them in one or two at a time! We could stand a chance there! It's just over here—!"

Allen turned to point and found himself standing face-to-face with a shambler that had come around the wide trunk of an ancient oak. It was missing one eye and a chunk of its throat had been torn out. Allen, gagging against the stench, raised his pistol, but the infected leaned forward and tackled the sailor, bringing him to the ground.

"Help! Help me!" Allen cried. His pistol had been dropped in the tussle, and he was now grappling with the infected, trying to keep its head and fingernails away from his flesh.

Harris ran with Stone, trying to pull the infected off the desperate man. Harris yelled orders, tried to rally his men into another defensive knot, but their frazzled nerves were getting the better of them. The darkness, the omnidirectional attack, the dwindling ammunition—all conspired against them. The situation was grave, and all the men knew it.

Hal Dorne fired another shot at one of the shamblers, caught it high in the chest, and knocked it to the ground. It would be back up in moments, but at least it would slow the decaying infected down a bit. He took stock of their situation, and found it approaching hopeless.

The sailors were outnumbered. Shamblers lined the highway's edge above, and more came at them out of the pitch-black woods. The sailors' ammunition was running low. A pitched fight would see them all dead.

Think, Hal. Think. What do you do?

The answer hit him immediately.

Stiles. Get Stiles out of here.

The retired tank mechanic cast about for the young soldier. He spotted him kneeling in the grass, levering a round into his Winchester. His well-aimed shot dropped another shambler. Hal made a beeline for the resourceful young man and grabbed him by the shoulder.

Stiles shrugged off Hal's grasp and fired again.

"Stiles!" shouted Hal. "We have to go! Now!"

Stiles spared an angry glare in Hal's direction. "These guys are getting slaughtered!"

"Come on, Mark! We have to get you out of here! You're the key! We can't let you die here!"

Hal grabbed at Stiles's clothing again, trying to pull him back and away from the engagement. Stiles pushed back hard, knocking Hal on his rear.

"Fuck off, Hal!" shouted Stiles.

Hal's patience had worn thin. He pulled himself to his feet, wound up, and roundhouse-punched Stiles in the jaw, sending the soldier sprawling. Hal was on him before Stiles could recover, grabbing him by the lapels of his shirt. "Listen up, Stiles! You're our one hope for a vaccine! All of these men tonight will have died for nothing if you check out here! Get your shit together, son! We need you alive!"

The blow seemed to restore Stiles's senses. He looked around the culvert, swallowed hard, and nodded. "All right, Hal. Fine. Have it your way. Let's go."

"About goddamned time!" was Hal's shouted reply.

The pair picked themselves up, grabbed their weapons, and climbed the opposite side of the culvert.

Hal spared one final glance over his shoulder at the firefight in the ditch. The bodies of shamblers lined the ditch, surrounded by the bloodied and fresh corpses of sprinters. At the far end, Commander Harris and Stone had pulled the infected off Allen and were backing up, still firing nonstop, at the approaching horde of shamblers. They were making for the storm drain. Rico was nowhere to be seen.

Hal saw Stiles gritting his teeth, probably feeling like a traitor. Stiles turned his back on the scene and took off after Hal, who had turned to forge a trail through the tall grasses and young trees that led east, toward Omaha.

Mark Stiles moved slower.

"What is it?" Hal asked.

"My leg is burning."

The original bite, the one he'd received in Hyattsburg, hadn't infected him, but it also refused to heal properly. It was closed up and showed no signs of putrefaction, but it still pained him. Hal waved him on, and Stiles limped as fast as he could after him, swishing the tall grasses out of his way as he went.

Behind him, the sounds of gunfire began to fade. By the time Hal and Stiles had made it across a wide field and into another narrow stand of trees, the sound was little more than echoes in the distance. Hal felt sick to his stomach. He'd grown to be friends with many of the sailors, and to lose them this close to their destination struck him as cruelly unfair.

Looking everywhere but at Stiles, Hal pushed his way through the tightly knit branches of a young pine grove, emerging in a tiny, ten-foot-by-ten-foot clearing. It wasn't much better than their original camp spot, but the trees here were much closer together, forming a curtain no eyes could penetrate. If they stayed quiet, they would be safe until the sun rose and the infected retreated to their shady hideaways.

"This will do," whispered Hal, kneeling in the center of the clearing. "We're another half mile closer to Omaha."

Stiles said nothing. The gunshots in the distance had dropped off into silence.

"I managed to save my pack," Hal went on, unslinging the rough leather knapsack from his shoulders. "We have a little food, some medical supplies, and one of the short-range radios."

"We just lost a bunch of good men," whispered Stiles, his face a mask. "We were so close."

"Don't," replied Hal. "If we get a vaccine out of your blood, all of it will have been worth it."

"Yeah," said Stiles. "I keep hearing that."

"You don't believe it?" asked Hal.

Stiles shrugged.

"Get some faith or get used to it," said Hal, pointing a finger at Stiles. "You're humanity's greatest asset right now, my friend. We gotta keep you safe."

"Safe," mused Stiles.

Hal scoffed. "There are safe places. Little place in the islands in the South Pacific. Had myself a nice little shack there. Plenty of beer. Beautiful native girls. You know—perfect tans. Water's just as blue as the Caribbean. Paradise. That's why I retired there." Hal chuckled. "Fucked that one up pretty good, didn't I?"

Stiles kept his mouth shut.

Hal continued. "Yes, sir, right now I should be hitting golf balls in my backyard, sipping a beer and listening to Skynyrd. But here I am instead—dodging infected, back in the good old U.S. of A. Hell of a retirement. Take my advice, Mark."

"What's that?" asked Stiles.

"Don't bother investing in a retirement fund. Spend it all now, while you're young enough to enjoy it."

"Never did start one."

"One what?" asked Hal.

"A retirement fund," said Stiles. "Guess I never thought that far ahead."

"I knew I liked you for a reason."

✯ ✯ ✯ ✯

Time passed in silence. Overhead, the waxing moon was disappearing behind the treetops. Stiles checked his watch, remembered he'd traded it a while back for a few painkillers from the sailors' medic to help him with his leg, and gave Hal's foot a tap. "Got the time?"

Hal pulled back his sleeve and checked his watch. "It's two-thirty. About four hours to sunup. We should get some rest."

Stiles laughed. "Yeah, like I could sleep after everything that's just happened."

Hal shrugged, tucked his knapsack behind his head to serve as a pillow, and leaned back against it, crossing his ankles. "You've got first watch, then. Wake me in two hours." The older man pulled the brim of his baseball hat down over his eyes, and within a few minutes was breathing deeply and regularly, out like a light.

Stiles watched Hal sleep for a moment and marveled at the man's ability to drift off after such a frantic firefight, especially one in which many friends had been lost. He reminded himself that Hal Dorne was more than a civilian. He'd seen combat—real live combat—before, and had probably learned to catch a few winks whenever the opportunity presented itself. Stiles was too high-strung to consider sleep. His guts were twisted up at the thought of his sailor friends lying dead in a ditch half a mile away.

He wondered how Harris and the others had fared in the storm drain. Though he hated to think it, Stiles realized that, most likely, they had run themselves out of ammunition and been overwhelmed. He shook the thought from his head. No use focusing on it now.

Stiles spent his guard shift slowly patrolling the tiny glen, using his ears more than his eyes. Nothing disturbed the silence of the night, however. Near the end of his shift, birds in the trees began to wake, and their chirping calls heralded the coming dawn.

When the time came, he shook Hal awake. The older man awoke with a start and murmured, "Whuzzat?" before coming fully to his senses. He rubbed at his eyes. "Oh, right. My turn. Anything happen while I was out?"

Stiles shook his head. "Quiet as a grave."

Hal frowned at the soldier.

"Okay," Stiles conceded with a small grin, "poor choice of words. You want the Winchester while you're up?"

"Sure," said Hal, accepting the antique rifle. He turned it over in his hands. "God, this is a nice piece. Where'd you say you got it, again?"

"Basement of a sporting goods store in Hyattsburg. Consolation prize for getting my ass bitten on the way out," Stiles said, gesturing at his leg.

"Hell of a prize," said Hal, checking the chamber. The weapon was loaded. "All right. Catch some sack time."

"I'm still not sure I can sleep," said Stiles.

"Try," said Hal. "And if you can't, at least get some rest. You'll need it. You'll be no good at all if you're just wandering around in a daze all day."

Stiles took the older man's advice, taking his place on the ground next to the knapsack. He closed his eyes and tried to clear his mind of the death and violence he'd seen over the course of the night. Perhaps he was more tired than he thought, or maybe he'd finally grown more used to the killing than he'd care to admit, but within minutes, Stiles's chest rose and fell slowly as he drifted off into sleep.

★ ★ ★ ★ ★

Hal shouldered the Winchester and took up his rounds.

The dark sky began to lighten slowly. First came a graying of the sky to the east, followed by the first rays of sunlight peeking over the horizon. The sun finally broke through, shining brightly. It looked to be a beautiful day, with barely a cloud in the sky.

When Hal's two hours were up, he shook Stiles awake, who opened his eyes and groaned.

"Did I fall asleep?" asked the soldier.

Hal grinned and nodded. "Slept like a rock. Told you that you needed the rest."

"Guess you were right." Stiles stood and stretched with a sigh, spinning his shoulders back and forth to pop his vertebrae.

Hal looked disgusted. "I don't know how you can stand to do that."

"Feels great," said Stiles. "Wakes me up." He leaned down to touch his toes. "Gotta keep yourself stretched out. Don't want to pull a muscle at the wrong moment."

"Hell," said Hal, "I'm too old and definitely too retired for calisthenics. Don't let me stop you, though."

Stiles stretched his arms out. "So what's the plan, Hal?"

"Well," said Hal Dorne, unslinging the Winchester and leaning against it, "I figure we head on east into Omaha and try to find this lab we're after."

Stiles frowned. "What about the sailors? There might be survivors."

Hal didn't say anything for a moment.

"We made it," Stiles pointed out. "Maybe some others did."

"If any escaped, they know where to head. Maybe they'll find their way to the lab, too," reasoned the retired mechanic. "Some of them have radios. It's the best we can hope for."

"We could search for them, now that it's daylight," Stiles suggested, but Hal was already waving his hands in a "no-way" gesture.

"Even if they are alive," Hal said, "they'll be spread out all over. And remember, our number-one priority is getting you to this laboratory safe, healthy, and in one piece."

"Speaking of healthy," said Stiles, "I'm half-starved."

Hal nodded at his leather knapsack. "Couple tins of potted meat in there. It ain't great chow, but it'll fill you up."

"I'm not complaining," said Stiles, digging through the pack until he uncovered a couple of cans of the processed meat. He tossed one to Hal, who caught it one-handed.

★ ★ ★ ★ ★

The pair sat in silence as the sun peeked higher above the horizon, eating their cold breakfast and pondering the day ahead of them. They'd have to ford city streets, a haven for the infected. The sunlight would help keep them safe, but one errant noise or wrong turn could cost them everything. Stiles felt an equal amount of trepidation and excitement at the thought.

He was on the last bite of his bland meal when the shuffling of footsteps outside the clearing brought both men to full attention.

Hal tossed the Winchester to Stiles and drew his own pistol.

The pair backed up away from the source of the footsteps, keeping careful aim at the spot where their visitor would appear through the pine branches.

A bead of sweat worked its way down Stiles's forehead. Even in the sunlight, a gunshot would bring more infected running.

Pine branches swayed. Hal drew back the hammer on his pistol and took careful aim, and Stiles's finger tightened on the trigger.

A face appeared in the breach. It was no infected. It was Rico.

"Rico!" said Stiles, elated. He lowered his rifle and ran across the clearing to the sailor. "We thought you were all dead!"

Rico, pale and shaking, took a moment before answering. When he did, his voice quavered. "I thought we were all dead, too, man. Thought that was it."

Hal holstered his weapon. "Are you injured?"

Rico nodded. "Cut my leg on a rock when I fell." Hal began to dig through his knapsack for his sparse medical kit as Rico went on. "Those bastards were right behind me. I thought I'd left them all behind, but a sprinter caught on to me and tried to run me down. I thought he had me when I fell, but I got him with this."

He held up a bloodstained pistol.

"Point-blank. Popped his head like a watermelon. Got any water? I'm thirsty. I'm so goddamned thirsty. Felt like I ran all night. Need to cool down." Rico shook his head to clear it, and wiped sweat from his forehead.

Hal tossed the medical kit to Stiles and kept digging.

"Sit down, bud," said Stiles, gesturing to the soft grass of the clearing. Rico slumped down with a heavy sigh, leaning his back against the trunk of a pine. Stiles wound a bandage around Rico's leg wound, a straight, narrow gash that had bled profusely but seemed to be healing nicely. "Canteen, Hal," he said.

Rico kept talking as Stiles worked.

"I saw Harris, Stone, and Allen make it to the storm drain. There was a lot of blood. I tried to get to them, but there were too many between me and them. I ran. God, I hated it, but I ran. I don't think anyone else made it out."

"I know how you feel," Stiles said, casting a glance at Hal, who wasn't paying any attention to the exchange.

"Can I get that drink?" asked Rico, taking rasping breaths. "My throat's on fire. And I'm so goddamned tired. I could sleep for a week."

"Hal," Stiles said. "Canteen?"

Hal Dorne tossed the plastic canteen to Stiles, who unscrewed the top. "Look at the bright side, Rico," Stiles said. "At least the three of us made it out. That's a lot better than none of us. Here, pal. Water. Drink up."

Stiles raised the canteen to Rico's mouth and poured in some of the water. It filled the sailor's mouth and dribbled down his chin. He didn't swallow. His eyes had closed. Stiles looked aggrieved, believing the soldier to be dead. He checked the man's throat and found a steady pulse, and felt himself calm down.

"He's in shock, I think," Stiles said. He flashed back to Hyattsburg, when he'd been treated by a pretty young medic before his suicidal run through downtown. "I wish Rebecca was here. She'd know what to do. She saved me back in Oregon. I owe her one."

Hal, meanwhile, had frozen up. He didn't seem to hear Stiles's words. He was focused on Rico, who, though unconscious, still drew in raspy breaths. Sweat poured down his forehead. Hal's hand slowly went for his pistol.

Stiles caught the movement. "What are you doing, Hal?"

"Get away from Rico," came Hal's calm reply.

When Stiles didn't immediately reply, Hal repeated himself sharply. "I said get away! Now!"

"Why?" asked Stiles. "He's just unconscious—"

Stiles looked back at the sailor. Rico's eyes had snapped back open. They were bloodshot, feral. An involuntary shudder shook the sailor's body. A moment later, Rico's bloody eyes fixed Stiles with a rage-filled glare.

"Oh, *shit,*" Stiles managed.

Rico was on him in an instant.

Cursing, Hal let his pistol drop and cast about for a new weapon.

Stiles grappled with the infected Rico. He grabbed the ex-sailor's arms, pushing him away, but Rico leaned in close and closed his jaws around Stiles's right forearm. The soldier gritted his teeth and bit back a scream as blood soaked through his sleeve.

A solid thwack sounded, and Rico's bloodshot eyes rolled back in his head. He slumped, unconscious, on Stiles's chest.

"Fuck," cried Stiles. "Get him off! Get him off!"

Hal kicked out at Rico's infected body, and Stiles scrabbled backward on all fours, putting distance between him and the sailor. Hal held a length of pine branch in his hand, and stood over the unconscious sprinter. He brought the makeshift club down on Rico's head once, twice, three times. The fourth blow came with the sickening crack of Rico's skull splitting open.

Hal dropped the bloodied, infected club on Rico's body and slumped next to Stiles in the grass.

Stiles stared, unblinking, at Rico's corpse.

"He was fine," said Stiles. "He was fine. He wasn't bitten—what the hell happened to him, Hal?"

"I don't know," admitted the mechanic. "Maybe he got infected blood in that leg wound. Maybe that point-blank pistol shot sprayed him with the virus. We'll never know, I suppose."

Stiles clenched his fists so hard his knuckles turned white. He buried his face in his hands.

"Rico. Not Rico. No. He was one of the guys who pulled me out of the comic shop in Hyattsburg. He wanted to skipper a sword boat when he got out. Oh, God. Another one gone," he lamented. "When's it going to end?"

"What, the killing, or the infection?" Hal asked, leaning back. Rico's corpse lay facedown across the glen from the pair of survivors.

"Both," said Stiles, voice muffled behind his clenched fists.

"Well, if we get that vaccine out of you, we can stop the infection," Hal said.

"And the rest?"

Hal didn't answer at first. He stood, shouldered his knapsack, and retrieved his pistol from the grass. "We've been killing each other ever since there were human beings, Stiles. That one isn't ever going to end."

Stiles said nothing, just looked up at Hal.

"Come on," said Hal, offering the soldier a hand up. "We have miles to go before we hit Omaha."

"Yeah," muttered Stiles, staring at Rico's corpse. He accepted Hal's hand and stood, leaning on his rifle. "Miles to go."

CHAPTER 8
ABRAHAM BURNING

Abraham, KS
30 June 2007
0020 hrs_

SIX DOZEN FEET RUSTLED in wet grass and soil, the noise covered by the patter of a falling rain.

Quietly, like heavily armed ghosts, the teams of four made their way closer and closer to the sleeping town of Abraham. Working quickly at each entry route, the point men clipped through wire-link fences and pulled new gates open wide to let their comrades through. As Fire Team Alpha passed through with Fire Teams Delta and Foxtrot, the point handed off his bolt cutters and shouldered his M-249 Squad Automatic Weapon, looking for his assigned high ground. He could barely make out the tower in the weather, but the maps had been excellent.

A wave farewell to the fire teams, and the man trotted off to his post. Another easy paycheck, it looked like.

☆ ☆ ☆ ☆ ☆

Sheriff Keaton stood by the window of the darkened station and watched the rain come down. He sipped from an old coffee mug that he absolutely refused to let anyone wash.

"If you're the type that washes your mug," he'd often say, "then you don't know how to drink coffee."

The office was in a state of mild disarray, the way a place will look when it's well lived in and the person that inhabits it knows where every scrap of paper goes and where it came from. It was softly lit by a single candle, the Sheriff and townspeople having gone to great lengths to make themselves harder targets than before. The several brushes with Lutz and his raiders had awakened them to the fact that even in this world where the dead walked, the greatest threat still came from fellow man.

In this environment, the unmoving Sheriff looked like a fixture with his mug, an odd bit of statuary that might have been donated by a rustic philanthropist.

Wes came in from the wet and shook off his poncho. "Cats and dogs, Sheriff."

Keaton looked back at Wes, breaking the illusion, then into the sky. "This?"

"Well, not *yet*. But just you watch. It's coming." He hung his poncho over the bucket by the door and sniffed the air. "Jesus, man. How old is that coffee?"

Keaton took a gulp and smiled. "Old enough to stand on its own, I guess. Be learning to walk soon."

Both men laughed.

"That stuff's gonna kill you—"

Wes's words were cut off by the chatter of automatic weapons fire.

"The hell? Wes, grab a rifle."

The Sheriff doused the candle and strapped his gun belt on. Ever since Lutz escaped, he'd gone wearing two Berettas around his waist and kept a rack of shotguns and AK-47s at the back of the office. The better to hoist Herman upon his own petard.

If you're back and looking for a fight, Lutz, you'll by-God get one.

Wes came back with both assault rifles and flashlights.

"Put those away, man. The flashlights. You want to get us both killed?"

"Um. Right," Wes said, pocketing one of the Mini-Mags and leaving the other on the Sheriff's desk. "You see anything?"

Keaton shook his head. "I can't see anything with the rain. Come on; we're going to have to go out in it. How did they get past the guards?"

The Sheriff opened the station door and the spit dried out of his mouth; he saw a group of four men arranged in front, one holding an M-4 rifle with what looked like a long stick coming off the front of it.

"Oh, shit!"

He slammed the door and dove away from it, driving Wes back into the station. There was a single rifle shot, and the station door exploded inward, scattering fragments all about the Sheriff and his man.

"Go, go," he said, scrambling to his feet. "Out the back. Sound the alarm on the way."

Wes went first, the Sheriff tearing after to the rear of the station and hitting a big red mushroom-shaped button on the wall as he flew past it. Another thing they'd installed since the most recent clash with the raiders, it set off a siren mounted to the top of the police station, as well as its twin, mounted atop the chapel, almost on the other side of town.

$$\star \quad \star \quad \star \quad \star$$

As if in response to the rising wail of the sirens, the rain increased its assault, thunder cracking overhead and drowning out the sounds of battle that had erupted across the town. In ones and twos, the townspeople were emerging from their homes, armed and angry, firing shot after shot at the insurgents in black, driving them back the way they'd came. The townsfolk were emboldened by the true numbers of the invaders they faced; the initial gunshots were widespread, giving the impression of a large attacking force, but with the civilian counterattack, the groups of four were found to be very few, indeed.

With rising gusto, the people of Abraham fired at their attackers until, almost as if it had been synchronized, to a man the force turned and beat a hasty retreat. With a cheer, the people gave leisurely chase, more concerned with patching the holes in their fences than with meting out any kind of justice.

The cheers and jeers continued until the first house exploded.

★ ★ ★ ★ ★

"What the hell is all this?" Wes asked as he and the Sheriff ran from the station. "Who were those guys? How did they—"

"Wes!" Keaton barked, his eyes on the fireball somehow rising up in the now-torrential downpour. "Keep moving. Look up, look for shiny things."

Wes's footsteps halted as he tried to process this order. "Look up?"

The Sheriff, who was doing just that, tackled Wes and drove him down as rounds chopped the wet grass to the side of them, thudding into the dirt at around eight hundred rounds a minute. Keaton looked up, seeing the muzzle flash as the gun spat bullets through the air.

"Look *up,*" he said, pointing. He rolled to a long-parked car and hoped that whatever the gunner was using wouldn't punch through an engine block. Wes was right behind him, gripping his AK-47 and looking lost.

"Did you see him?" Keaton asked. Wes nodded quickly, his wits seeming to return. "Okay. When I count to three, I want you to get your ass up here and get his attention with that." He pointed at the Russian-made firearm. "Don't get killed, but I need you to throw a lot of rounds at him. All right?"

Wes nodded again, his eyes closed as he leaned against the car. The Sheriff duck-walked to the other end of the car and hoped that this would work. He knew the AK-47 wasn't made for long-distance sniping; it was made to put a lot of bullets in a given area and to do it quickly, whether the gun was covered in mud, sand, or tar, or was fresh out of the box.

"All right, Wes . . . now!"

Wes turned and rested against the hood of the car, shooting bursts at the tower the gunman was firing from. As he did this, Keaton crept over the lip of the trunk and sighted in. He saw the long barrel swivel back and shouted for Wes to get down.

As long as I don't move, I'll be all right.

The iron sights of the AK-47 rested on the dark area the muzzle flash was coming from. After a moment, there was a gleam as the barrel moved again.

"One more, Wes . . . now!"

The deputy swung over the hood and fired again. Keaton kept his eyes on the gunner . . . there! The man fired back at Wes, and Keaton had him. He let loose a single round and watched as the spurt of flame from the automatic weapon described an arc up and away from the front of the car they hid behind. He whooped and yelled to Wes.

"We got him! Did you see that? We—"

The Sheriff stopped as he looked over at his partner, his friend.

Bleeding.

"Ah, Wes."

Keaton dropped and crawled to his deputy and rolled him up. It wasn't a bullet that had got him; Wes's face and neck were covered in blood pouring from a ragged wound that started under his jaw and wrapped around the right side of his face to dart up between the unfocused eyes. A shard of metal, the same shade brown as the car they'd taken shelter behind, protruded from the deputy's face, its broken end sticking out, wicked edges shining in the wan light of the burning buildings.

The rain pelting his face, Keaton reached down and took the flashlight from Wes's pocket. "I'll be back with this," he said. "I promise."

★ ★ ★ ★ ★

The perceived route of the intruders turned into a massacre as the people of Abraham chased the figures in black, only to find they'd been led into fiery traps. As each contingent of townsfolk reached the point of no return, the houses on all sides of them exploded, detonated remotely by Agent Sawyer at the control panel. He was taking reports from the teams in the field and humming as he snapped switches that turned other human beings into broken sacks of meat.

Beside him, Lutz and his small crew watched through binoculars as miniature rag dolls were thrown wide by the sudden blasts. The retreating teams made radio contact as they cleared the perimeter.

"And the Sheriff?" Sawyer asked.

Lutz didn't hear the response, but he knew it wasn't a good one from the way Sawyer slammed his hand down next to the control panel.

"Are you fucking kidding me? He's a hick sheriff, with maybe a deputy at his side. One, two men. You couldn't bag him?"

A pause.

"Out the back, right. And then what?"

Another pause.

"He *what*? How? With an AK-47?"

Sawyer whistled.

"All right. Hold on a minute."

Sawyer flipped up the covers on all the munitions and swept his hands across the board. The night rocked with the mass of explosions from the center of Abraham all the way to the edges, houses and commercial buildings going up in balls of fire that would eventually be beaten down by the unrelenting rain.

"Okay. Everyone back in. Shoot everyone but the Sheriff. And the doctor, he might have something from Demilio. But everyone else is a target, copy?"

Sawyer yanked the headset from his ear. "Lutz! You and your boys might have something to do anyway. Grab some gear and get in a Hummer."

He stalked away, clearly in a foul mood but excited by the prospect of the chase. Ritter looked at Blue and twirled his forefinger by his temple.

Lutz nodded. "Yeah. He's crazy. So crazy, we better do what he says. Grab some gear, then."

The raiders armed themselves from the cache of weapons left behind by the assault teams; Lutz got an M-4 with an attached grenade launcher, Ritter and Patton came away with two Browning Hi-Powers each and Blue and Jenkins armed up with SPAS-12 shotguns.

With a wicked smile, Lutz recognized his knife in the tire well of a truck, sitting balanced on the rubber. He grabbed it and stuck it in his waistband, then turned to the raiders.

"All right," he said. "See if we can't bag us a sheriff."

★ ★ ★ ★ ★

Ritter and Blue looked at the contingent of soldiers that were packing the equipment for moving out, then at each other. Something passed between them; Patton noticed it, Lutz had not. He was so full of himself at that moment, Patton knew his eyes were full of Sheriff Keaton's big death scene and nothing else.

Patton, who knew the men better than either of the Lutz brothers ever had, knew that, whatever the outcome of the day, they'd be walking away from Abraham with two fewer raiders than when they started.

Hmm. Maybe four less, if Coke didn't catch up to Charlie. I wonder how that went?

★ ★ ★ ★ ★

"Open the door!" Coke yelled. "Open the fucking door, Charlie!"

He ran at the head of a disorganized pyramid of sprinters, all with their arms out, reaching for his back and howling as they ran. It had been this way for the past mile, and the rain wasn't helping any. Coke had taken one misstep and almost lost everything when a sprinter grabbed the trucker cap off his head, and with it the light that was clipped to the bill. Even with all the time he'd spent on the treadmill, Coke knew that if he didn't get into the truck, that was it for him.

Dimly, he could see Charlie in the driver's seat, his chin tucked down on his chest and fast asleep.

Not slowing his stride any, Coke bent down and picked up a stone as he ran, scooping and throwing in one motion. The small rock bounced off the side of the truck, startling Charlie awake.

"Open! The! Door!"

Charlie's eyes went wide as he saw what was coming his way. He unlocked and opened his door, moving over as Coke's hurtling form shot into the truck at high speed. The door slammed behind him, and so did the forms of three sprinters, moving too fast to check their speed as they collided with the metal of the truck and each other.

"Did I miss it?" Charlie asked, wiping the sleep from his eyes.

"Shut up," Coke breathed at him, trying to catch his breath. "Water."

"Yeah, yeah. Here," Charlie said, holding out a bottle. Coke snatched it from his hand and tore the top off, upending the plastic container over his face and drinking deep.

"Whoo!" he yelled as the empty bottle hit the inside of the windshield. "I am *never* doing that again."

"Do what? Did I miss something?"

Coke thumped Charlie in the arm. "Fuck yeah, you did. You missed getting goddamn killed."

"But what about—"

Charlie's question was cut off by the first explosion from Abraham. The pair of raiders were entranced by the billowing fireball, and then it was joined by another . . . and another . . . and another.

"Jesus, God," Charlie said. "Sawyer is not fucking around with these people."

Coke looked over and punched Charlie again. "And you, you son of a bitch!" He punched him again. "I ran all this way, in the *dark,* being chased by those dead fuckers, so I could stop you, and you were *asleep!*"

Charlie rubbed his arm and shoulder where the punches were landing. "Th-those aren't the dead ones. They move too—"

"Ah," Coke said, waving him off. "You know what I mean. Goddamn. There's my hat."

He pointed out the window to one of the shamblers massed against the truck among the sprinters; the fiend in red that had grabbed his cap. The infected waved its arms up and down as it tried to get through its companions to the truck, the little flashlight cutting swaths through the darkness of the rainy night.

"Anyway. Lutz says to hang back. Says he'll try to signal us when the convoy moves out, so we can follow behind, and we'll try our surprise another day. It's not like they care, anyway," he said, hooking his thumb back to the full garbage bed, where a mix of sprinters and shamblers bumped around against each other.

Charlie put a pair of binoculars up to his face and clicked his tongue ring against his teeth. He let out a quiet whistle. "Take a look at that. Gunfire around the flames."

"Yep," Coke nodded. "You should see the hardware they got in that camp. You think we had some nice stuff? Pfft." He looked back out the window at the throng of carriers clawing at the steel door. His eyes were drawn back to his hat and flashlight.

"Pop the top, Charlie. I'm going to get my hat."

✯ ✯ ✯ ✯ ✯

Sheriff Keaton lay in the dirt uncomfortably close to a fire. He'd seen the thing they fired at his front door before, when he was at a law-enforcement seminar in Kansas City. It was called a SIMON breach grenade, and he'd wanted one.

Funny to want something so bad and finally get it, he thought. Didn't want it that way, though.

He counted himself lucky that the insurgent forces had used the SIMON instead of just slapping a plastic explosive on the door. The breach grenade was designed to destroy just the door, with minimal collateral damage to whatever was on the other side.

Collateral damage.

Wes.

With a sigh, Keaton moved closer to the fire, in case they were using heat detection, and took stock of his situation. A sharp pain caught his arm and he moved away just a little. *Easy, pard; catching yourself on fire might be the only way to make this night worse.*

Whoever these people were, they'd wanted him alive. The gunner in the tower couldn't have known who he was shooting at, not in the rain and at that distance. But the others, the ones that stormed the station . . . other than the SIMON, they hadn't fired a shot at him or Wes.

Wes, lying in the gutter with his face torn in two . . .

He shook his head. No time for that now. Right now, he needed to survive. He needed to avenge.

Voices. At least a pair of men coming toward him. He looked up and saw a ditch that ran from the wreckage of the building that was merrily burning at his back. He closed his eyes and held his breath, then rolled into it.

Immediately, he regretted it. He'd been hiding out behind the remains of Eileen's pub, and now he was in the shit trench they'd dug out back after the pipes clogged, up to his eyeballs in shit and piss and puke and whatever else made it out the back of this place.

Two men in black gear walked past the fire, looking through the flames into the pub. "I don't know why Sawyer wants this fucking guy, anyway," one of them was saying. "He's just a fucking hick sheriff, right?"

The other, this one with a mustache, snorted. "Maybe. But he's the one that's been the thorn in Lutz's side for months now. Agent Sawyer has plans for him. Keep an eye out, all right? I got to take a bad piss."

The doubter shrugged and turned away. "What I don't understand is, why even have a camp out here? This place is nowhere, man."

Mustache unzipped the bottom of his coveralls. "You still don't get it. This place was thriving. I know it doesn't look like it now, but I've seen the reports. They had crops and shit, safe and sound in their little town. This was supposed to be the beginning of the new breadbasket for the RSA.

"Now, it's just a practice run for Omaha."

When the man was done talking, Keaton exploded up and grabbed the front of his coveralls, pulling him into the trench, the downpour covering whatever sounds they made.

"Good for us," the other man said, looking around the other burning buildings. "How come Lutz fucked it up so bad?"

Mustache's answer, if the other man could have heard it, was a shit-filled gurgle as Keaton held him under, one hand pressing hard on Mustache's windpipe while the other felt his gear for a knife.

He found one.

Flicking it open to reveal a wickedly sharp edge, he smiled and drove it down into the man's side, the only spot his thin body armor didn't protect. Keaton knew that Kevlar wouldn't stop a knife, but he didn't want to dull it too much. After all, he'd need it again.

"I said, how did Lutz fuck it— Hey!"

Keaton looked up and saw the other man staring at him, eyes wide and disbelieving. Raising his offal-covered AK-47, the Sheriff pulled the trigger and blew the man back into the burning remains of Eileen's pub.

When the man finally lay still in the flames, Keaton looked at the Russian-made gun and grimaced.

"I'd kiss you, but not right now. I'm sure you understand."

Taking in what he'd overheard, the Sheriff made up his mind to head back to the station. If this Sawyer wanted him taken alive, then they wouldn't have blown the office, or at least not yet. And since they already chased him out of there, would they expect him back? He hoped not.

He looked down at himself. The shit-bath he'd just taken would camouflage him pretty well . . . he just hoped the stink wouldn't give him away.

AK-47 and knife at the ready, Keaton stalked back to the station.

✮ ✮ ✮ ✮ ✮

In the field, Agent Sawyer was a different man than he was at the command tent. Before, he'd been a strutting cock, chest puffed out, in command, barking orders and always ready with a threat. In the field, a change came over him that, frankly, scared the dog shit out of Lutz. The agility that was apparent in his effortless way of doing things came to the forefront as he led a fire team and Herman's raiders through the breach in the fence; the man went forward the way a jungle cat does, sinuous movements and fearsome grace. Even the seasoned troops that followed behind and ranged out in the town already didn't move that way.

The raiders clumped close together, arms held low. A letup in the rain made it easier for Lutz to see the disaster that Abraham had become. Former buildings now resembled hot configurations of tongue depressor and matchstick houses after a pyro kid was done playing with them. Remains of the townsfolk were strewn everywhere, some bodies whole, but most not. As the crew made their way deeper into Abraham, they passed through the worst of the trap, treading on arms and torsos of all shapes and sizes. At one point, Ritter stepped on crumbling ashes of a doll and he went gray as it croaked out its last "mama."

Sawyer came to a full stop and turned back to the fire team leader. "Check your radio with me."

"Yes, sir," the soldier said into his lapel mic, and Sawyer shook his head.

"Loud and clear. Damn. Fire Team Alpha isn't responding to my hails. Take your men and rendezvous with Fire Team Bravo at the clinic. Keep your ears on. Lutz, you and your men are with me."

Blue and Jenkins looked at each other with identical questioning expressions, and Lutz knew he also looked confused. Patton just checked his gun and nodded.

"I like that," Sawyer said. "This one understands just following fucking orders. Now come on."

"I don't get it," Lutz said to Ritter as they trudged through the burning aftermath of Abraham. The rain and fires were at constant odds, alternatively chilling and heating the group as they walked through a precursor to Hell.

"He doesn't trust us," Patton said from behind them. "So he keeps us with him. The plan was to go to the clinic first, but now the fire team doesn't answer, so he's going to check it out."

"And we're his backup?" Blue asked.

Patton snorted. "The day *we're* his backup, check your ass for monkeys flying out of it. He's babysitting us."

"Yeah, but—"

Jenkins's retort was cut off by Sawyer, who was stopped again in the street, his hand up in a fist. Three of the four-man fire team lay in the street, unmoving, their arms spread out in empty-handed death.

Their weapons were missing.

"Son of a bitch," Blue said.

The radios were gone, too.

With his bullpup FN P90 aimed at the yawning black doorway at the front of the station, Sawyer soft-footed over to the dead men. He swore as he scanned their name tags; the team leader was unaccounted for. He turned back to the raiders and saw only three standing there.

At his look, Herman turned around and saw Ritter and Blue missing. "What the fuck?"

"They were right behind me," Jenkins said, turning in place and trying to take in all of Abraham that he could at one time. The edge of panic crept into his voice. "They were right goddamn here!"

"Hey. Hey!" Patton said, grabbing Jenkins by the face. "Calm down. Keep it quiet. Whatever happened to them, you want it to happen to you?"

Jenkins shook his head.

"Keep it down, then." Then turning to Sawyer, he nodded.

Agent Sawyer jerked his head toward the station and went forward, his blunt submachine gun at the ready. Lutz, Patton, and Jenkins followed behind, creeping into the dark station.

The small lobby of the station was empty of everything but the plastic seats that had been there since the building was put into service. The partition glass along the front counter was gone, only the frame remaining. The way to the small squad room beyond was open, though the floor was littered with plastic cups and bits of the front door that the fire team had blown in on their approach.

No matter how carefully Sawyer moved through the room, every sliding step disturbed a bit of debris. Herman followed behind, his gun at port and trigger finger itchy. As Sawyer stepped into the squad room, a shape hurtled out of the ceiling and swung at him. He dove and rolled away, passing smoothly between desks as Jenkins screamed and fired slug after slug from his SPAS-12 shotgun as fast as he could pull the trigger.

Old and cold blood splattered from the body as it swung through its arc and Jenkins screamed himself hoarse. With every impact, the body spun crazily and altered its course, but still Jenkins tracked it, firing until the semiautomatic shotgun clicked empty.

"God*damn,* what the fuck is wrong with you?" Lutz yelled at Jenkins, who spun and pointed the empty shotgun at Herman's face.

Click.

For one stunned second, Lutz stood there gaping at the set of Jenkins's wide eyes. The second passed, and he reversed his M-4 rifle and hit Jenkins in the face, dropping the man to his knees.

✯ ✯ ✯ ✯ ✯

Sawyer, ignoring the raiders and their drama, instead scanned the office with his SureFire flashlight for any other booby traps. Not seeing anything, he finally shined the light on the swinging and turning figure. Grimacing, Sawyer barely recognized the pulped and destroyed face of Fire Team Alpha's team leader. Of course, without his body armor, the shotgun slugs had ripped him up. Bits of him were hanging on by tendrils of stringy flesh and gristle.

"Fuck," Sawyer whispered. The game of fox and hound had changed, and the agent was starting to realize that maybe Sheriff Keaton wasn't just some bumpkin from hickville.

✯ ✯ ✯ ✯ ✯

"Jesus, Coke," Charlie said as the other man popped the modified top to the dump truck cab. "It's just a hat, man. You telling me that you're gonna go back out there, with *them,* for a hat?"

Coke looked down at Charlie. "Yep. Got that cap from my boy before all this shit went down. Everybody else we come across, they've all got pictures or letters or something from before. Me? All I got is that cap, and I aim to fucking keep it."

With that, he sprung up and levered himself out of the cab. "Pass me up the baseball bat, huh?"

"Before you go and get your ass killed, how about filling me in? What are we doing next?"

"Bat."

Keeping his mouth shut, Charlie passed the bat up and watched.

✯ ✯ ✯ ✯

Coke paced the top of the dump truck, shifting his grip on the bat and glaring down at the seething mass of undead creatures. That was his hat. That was the last vestige of the old world, of his old life, and he was going to by-God get it back. Perhaps he wasn't the best man ever, or even the best man he could be, but he'd loved his boy more than anything or anybody else and that hat was all he had left of him.

The flat nose of the dump truck gave him some pause . . . if he leapt down and started swinging, the only way he'd get back up is if Charlie opened the door again. The raiders had modified all the big vehicles they used for moving around the infected so that an enterprising (or lucky) carrier couldn't lift the latch and get the door open. So, it was either the door (from the inside) or the hatch up top.

Let's see . . . ladder up the back. Yeah.

"Come get it, you dead shits!"

He leapt off the passenger side of the front and banged the grill covering with the bat, making sure all the shamblers saw where he was. One or two got too close before the rest had homed in, and Coke reversed his grip on the bat and hit them with backhanded blows to the temples. The first one went down in the path of the others, and Coke saw what he needed to do.

Backing up, he kept just out of range, swinging the bat now and again at hands and knees, herding the shamblers behind him in a shaggy ring around the dump truck. He darted in, swinging the bat and knocking shamblers back as he needed, until the one with the hat was at the back of the pack.

"I'm coming, Charlie! Get the engine started."

With a hard swing, Coke knocked a linebacker-sized zombie into the dead shithead behind him and sprinted around the truck. He came up on the back of the line in no time, snatching the ball cap out of the carrier's hand . . . or he tried to. The thing's grip was monstrous.

"Fuck!" Coke screamed. The mass of carriers in front of the one he had turned at his exclamation.

He lifted the cap and hand as high as they would go, and turned, launching a powerful side kick into the carrier's underarm. With a wet, squelching pop, the thing's arm wrenched out of socket. Coke swung the bat one-handed into the dead man's face, then repeated his kick. This time the arm came completely off the dead man, and Coke reversed himself, running for the back of the truck.

One dead man stood between him and the ladder, and Coke flipped the bat at him, the aluminum bludgeon spinning end over end until it smashed into the shambler's face, knocking it back a step. Coke leapt, planting one foot on the thing's hip and using it as a springboard. He made the ladder and climbed, his left hand full of ladder rung, his right full of arm. As he clambered up the back of the truck, he felt himself jerked to a stop. Looking back, he saw the tallest of the bunch, an undead Wilt the Stilt, grabbing his boot and pulling, jaws open wide and slavering.

Coke dropped the arm to the top of the dump truck and gripped the edge with both hands. He drew his other foot back and grit his teeth, then drove it into the top of the trapped foot, breaking the zombie's fingers, and maybe his own instep. He got up, pulling himself upright, and tore the ball cap out of the dead fingertips.

He limped to the front of the truck and dropped into the cab.

"Okay," he said. "About what comes next."

✫ ✫ ✫ ✫ ✫

Sheriff Keaton combat-crawled into the woods on the outskirts of Abraham, dragging a weapons-laden canvas behind him. The new body armor (courtesy of the government goon that he left hanging as a present) didn't fit quite right yet, but there wasn't much he would be able to do about it until he found some shelter.

The mud slicked everything over, both helping and hindering him; his progress was slow because hand and footholds were tenuous things, but progress was fast enough because the heavy canvas sled didn't catch on much with the thick coating of mud on the bottom of it. He just hoped that the slackening rain held on for long enough to obliterate (or at least blur) the track he was leaving behind him.

Whoever they were, the insurgents were dispersing and drifting out of the ruins of Abraham in teams of four. Keaton thought for a minute about following them back to their camp and using some of the weapons he'd rescued from the police station, but he knew this wasn't just about Abraham. The soldier he'd drowned in shit had said Omaha. Whoever these people were, whoever they worked for, they were headed to Omaha, Nebraska, and they had bad things in mind for the people they found there.

Casting a last glance at the pyre of his home, Keaton lay in wait for the troops to completely disperse. He had to get to Jose the mechanic's place, grab an ATV.

Maybe he would beat them there.

Some time later, Keaton awoke to silence. He hadn't intended to sleep, but it was that kind of day, the one that just wears on you, beats you down until you feel every ounce of atmosphere weighing on your back. Wes was gone. Hell, the whole *town* was gone. What had they done to—

His thought was interrupted by a footstep. A stealthy footstep, but there was nothing the walker could do about the squelch from his or her boot coming up out of the mud.

Maybe that's what woke me?

The Sheriff lay completely still on his stomach, wondering if his arms had fallen asleep and if that's the way he would go out. That would be a fine ending to his quest to avenge his town: caught napping with a numb gun hand.

A snapping branch caught his ear and he darted his eyes to the left.

There he was . . . Keaton could see government-issue combat boots strapped up over the legs of a set of black coveralls like the ones the men from the night before were wearing.

"Checkpoint Mike, all clear," a man said, and that was followed by a short burst of radio static. He continued through the woods around the perimeter of the town. In retrospect, Keaton decided, the attackers had been lucky for the torrential downpour the night before . . . if these woods had caught fire, none of them would have made it out alive. Or maybe it had been planned that way.

The man's careful progress continued past Keaton's hiding space, and as he passed, the Sheriff (*ex-sheriff,* he thought) rose slowly to his feet, hand brushing the big knife on his belt. He drew a large, staghorn-handled bowie knife, one of the things from the station, from a leather sheath and followed the soldier.

He moved quietly, watching his feet and keeping clear of mud patches, staying behind the soldier for about a quarter of a mile.

"Checkpoint November, all clear," the man said into his radio. The burst of static was drowned out by Keaton's sudden lunge through the brush and a pair of strangled cries as he buried the knife completely into the man's back and twisted as hard as he could. With a cry of shock, the man half-turned to the Sheriff, but a knee in his kidney stopped him. With an instant fury that he didn't even know he had, Keaton unleashed a storm of elbows and punches to the already dying soldier. The bigger man sagged, his life leaking around the hilt of the bowie knife, and Keaton hit him repeatedly.

Soon, the woods were still again. The Sheriff knelt by the perimeter guard, a high, keening sound coming from his throat at the loss of everything *again*. His breath came in ragged gulps and his chest heaved. Eventually, he stood and planted his foot on the dead soldier's spine, bent down, and yanked the knife out of the man's back. With a sneer, he drove it down again, neatly bisecting the dead man's neck, severing the brain from the body.

Find the other one.

Get to Omaha.

CHAPTER 9
ONE-STOP SHOPPING

Omaha, NE
30 June 2007
0923 hrs_

A DULL BOOM ECHOED across the asphalt parking lot as Brewster's crowbar slipped free from the door frame with a resounding clank. It clattered to the ground.

"Shit," Brewster murmured.

The pair froze in place, glancing nervously over their shoulders.

Long moments passed, and nothing came tearing out of the shadowed alleys or scattered doorways at the building they occupied. The street remained clear and quiet.

"Okay," said Trev, careful to not let his annoyance at Brewster's mistake show, "let's try that one more time, minus the noise."

"It slipped out!" protested Brewster. "Piece of shit crowbar."

"Don't blame the tools, Ewan."

"Hey, brother—only three people call me Ewan: my mother, my father, and people who outrank me."

"Yeah, yeah. Just get that bar wedged back in there."

The pair of scavengers were trying to force a door that led to the back room of a long-abandoned pharmacy at the clinic they'd been raiding for medical supplies. They had already emptied the more accessible outer areas of the clinic—the administrative offices and the handful of operating rooms and curtained checkup stalls. The waiting room was a mess. Water damage discolored the carpets and the fluorescents had been dark for months. They'd lit the hallway with a pair of LED lanterns.

Brewster wedged the crowbar in the door frame once more and, with the help of Trevor, gave it a mighty tug. This time, the frame popped free, and the door swung outward, revealing a narrow room flanked on either side by stainless steel modular shelving, each shelf covered in plain white bottles of medication.

Brewster, haphazard as ever, began scooping bottles into his pack without reading the labels.

"Hey, hey!" admonished Trevor. "Read the labels, Brewster. Look at this shit!"

Trevor began to paw through Brewster's knapsack. He held up a bottle in front of the soldier's eyes.

"What the hell are we going to use this for?" Trev asked. "Since when is erectile dysfunction high on our list of medical priorities?"

Brewster, indignant, spread his arms wide and spoke up in his own defense. "How the hell am I supposed to know what's good and what's useless? I'm not a goddamned pharmacist and we don't have a list."

"Here," said Trevor, plucking a bottle from a shelf. "Good. Amoxicillin. And here—Vicodin. Painkillers, antibiotics—*these* are our priorities. How many times . . ."

Brewster looked undecided.

Trevor acquiesced. "All right, all right. Tell you what. You start searching those drawers for bandages, instruments, syringes—that sort of thing. Leave the chemicals to me."

It didn't take long for the pair to fill their packs. Most of the medications were swiftly approaching their expiration dates, but Trevor wasn't one to look a gift horse in the mouth. He grabbed everything that could be useful, hoping they wouldn't have to make yet another run. This was the farthest out they'd ever been.

Pack bulging, and making mental notes of the remaining supplies in the nearly picked-clean storage room, Trevor made his way back to the front of the clinic, Brewster in tow.

"All right, buddy," said Brewster. "Another mission accomplished. Back to base?"

"Back to base," agreed Trevor.

He pulled open the clinic doors and they began the slow retreat to the Fac, sticking once more to the center of the streets.

"This is the kind of mission I like," rambled Brewster. "No real surprises. Just a milk run."

"Kind of have the feeling we're being watched, though," Trevor said, glancing around.

"Hell, I've had that feeling ever since we got here. Probably a carrier staring at us from some alleyway right now. But, um . . . check it out."

Brewster reached down to a cargo pocket on the side of his pants and retrieved a collapsible baton.

"See? Maybe I am learning something from you. Let 'em watch."

★ ★ ★ ★ ★

As it turned out, the pair of survivors were indeed being watched.

Crouched in a stand of bushes, Private Mark Stiles held a pair of binoculars to his face. All he could make out were the backs of the retreating figures, laden with bulging backpacks.

"Who is that?" whispered Hal.

"I can't tell. Might be friendlies. Might not."

Stiles grimaced. His eyes went back and forth between the wounded man behind them and the swiftly retreating figures in the distance.

"Come on," prodded Hal. "Make the call."

Stiles growled in frustration and racked a round into his Winchester. "Okay. I'm going to call out. You be ready to shoot if they turn on us, though."

"Yeah, yeah. I'm ready," said Hal.

Stiles stood, revealing himself, and raised his weapon above his head.

"Hey!" he called out, as loud as he dared. "Hey! Over here!"

The response from the retreating pair of survivors was immediate. One of them dropped flat on the pavement. The other ducked behind a stoop. Both had their weapons aimed in his general direction.

"Hold your fire! We're not infected, and we don't want any trouble!" Stiles went on.

There was a long moment of silence.

The man who had hit the dirt slowly pulled himself to his feet, a look of disbelief on his face. Even across the considerable distance, Stiles could hear the man's incredulous reply. "Stiles?"

Stiles recognized the voice. "Brewster! Ewan Brewster! Holy hell, is it good to see you!"

Each man let out a whoop of joy and ran toward the other, ending up in a bear hug, both speaking at once.

"I thought you were dead back in Hyattsburg!" said Brewster.

"I never thought your ass would make it this far!" said Stiles.

"But—whoa," said Brewster, suddenly breaking free from Stiles's embrace and taking a long step backward. "You were bitten, man. No offense, but keep back from me."

"Relax," laughed Stiles. "I've been bitten twice. Didn't take; Hal here says I'm immune."

"Immune?" asked Brewster's companion. Stiles saw that the man had shaggy hair and four-day beard stubble. He wore loose-fitting, comfortable clothes, and had an ASP on one hip and a Beretta in his hand. "But no one's immune. Morningstar's got a hundred-percent mortality rate."

"Well . . . ninety-nine," Stiles said.

"It's true," coughed Hal. "We found him in Hyattsburg. Hadn't turned. Figured your doc would want to take a look at him."

"Damn straight, she will!" said Brewster. "She's been bitching and whining about never making any progress—kept saying 'If only I had someone with antibodies.' I'm guessing that's you, right?"

"I suppose so. You have a base, then?"

"Yeah," said Brewster. "All right, come on! We'll give you a hand! Let's get back to the Fac! Anna will know what to do."

"Anna?" asked Stiles. "What happened to Rebecca? Is she . . . ?"

"Oh, no, she's fine. Except for being a royal pain, she's fine."

Stiles breathed a sigh of relief that didn't go unnoticed by the others in the group.

"Let's get a move on," prodded Trevor. "The faster we make it back to the Fac, the faster the Doc can get started."

★ ★ ★ ★ ★

The sun had reached its zenith. Barely any clouds were in the sky, bathing the outskirts of Omaha with bright sunlight, both a blessing and a curse. The bright sun kept the survivors hot, sticky, and uncomfortable . . . but safe from the infected, who were cloistered indoors, and away from the group.

General Francis Sherman surveyed the strip mall with narrowed eyes. The darkened storefronts gave him pause. They made for beautiful hideout spots for infected during the blazing summer sun. Still, they needed food and supplies, and risks would have to be taken.

Sherman turned to the tall, wide-shouldered black man next to him. Mbutu Ngasy, as if feeling Sherman's scrutiny, inclined his head in Sherman's direction, a quizzical expression on his face.

"Frank?" asked Mbutu. He seemed more and more comfortable using the General's first name over the previous months. "What is wrong?"

"I have a vibe. Place feels off. What are you getting?"

Mbutu nodded. "It's too quiet." Mbutu Ngasy had an uncanny ability to spot an ambush before it was sprung. Rebecca Hall, when she had first met Ngasy, called it his "sixth sense." Sherman had little use for paranormal buzzwords. Ngasy said he merely paid more attention to what was going on than others.

The general sighed. Even with the previous run, they only had enough food for another few days, tops, and then they would be down to Vienna sausages and crackers. Again.

"Okay, gentlemen. Do we try it?" Sherman asked.

"Just give the order, sir," growled Thomas, unstrapping his Beretta from its holster.

"I don't give orders anymore, Thomas," sighed Sherman. "I'm asking your honest opinion."

Ahead of them, the strip mall beckoned, darkened storefronts and all.

"Well, sir, if you want my opinion, I say go. This place is as good or bad as any other. And we don't have much choice. We can die by the infected or we can starve to death. Personally, quick infection seems the lesser of the two evils."

Mbutu slowly nodded. "I would prefer not to, but what Thomas says is correct. We need supplies. We will die without them. We must try."

"Then let's get to it," Sherman said. He unbuckled his holster and unslung one of the MP-5 submachine guns confiscated upon their appropriation of the Fac, checked the chamber, and flipped the selector to semiautomatic. "All right, let's do this smooth and by the numbers— we'll start with the far left storefront. It has a nice open field, and we should be able to see anything coming from a long way off. Thomas, you're point. I'm your back. Mbutu, stand right here in the doorway and give us a heads-up if we have any company."

"Sir," was Thomas's grumbled reply.

Mbutu nodded silently and unholstered the Beretta at his side, scanning the parking lot for contacts.

Turning from him, Sherman and Thomas pushed open the doors to the first store.

At first, a groan of disappointment nearly passed Sherman's lips. The nearest displays were of little more than pale mannequins wearing moth-eaten dresses and ratty straw hats. Nothing but a clothing store.

Thomas and Sherman, silent as the grave, flashed hand signals to one another.

Thomas/flank left/advance to cover/hold, came Sherman's rapid-fire hand signals. *Sherman/flank right/advance to cover/hold,* came the second set of instructions. Thomas nodded.

The pair split up immediately, making their separate ways slowly down darkened aisles, checking the floors and corners for smears of dried blood or—worse—a still-crawling undead carrier lurking around the metal shelving units.

After several silent minutes, where the loudest noise in the shop was that of the soft click of boot heels on the linoleum, Sherman relaxed.

The store was empty, and had not one single piece of useful gear to show for it.

Defeated, they moved on to the second store.

Mbutu was waiting for them outside.

"No one in sight, Frank," reported Ngasy.

"No one in the store," returned Thomas. "Nothing useful, either."

"Well, let's not dawdle. Daylight won't last forever, and we won't want to be stuck out here when night falls. Let's try the next one," Sherman said, gesturing at the nearest door.

The sign above it read "The Dollar Stretcher." Sherman figured it was a good omen. Most of these kinds of stores had a mishmash of goods—everything from cheap furniture to cleaning supplies to food aisles.

"This one looks more promising," agreed Thomas. "Same deal, sir?"

Sherman nodded. "Mbutu, watch the road. Don't let us get trapped inside."

"I won't."

Once more, Thomas and Sherman shouldered their way into the darkened store.

Almost immediately the food aisle stuck out. It looked to Sherman as if most of the end racks had been picked clean by panicked refugees in the early hours of the pandemic. They'd taken whatever was at hand—potato chips, pastries, loaves of bread.

Sherman grinned as he scuffed his way along the food aisle. Most of the canned goods were fine. Some were scattered along the floor, and Sherman slid them aside as he made his way along, scooping the remaining cans from the shelves into his empty knapsack. He could hear Thomas in the next aisle over, stuffing his own bag with essentials.

Then a third sound—a low scraping—drew Sherman's attention. His head snapped to the right, searching for the source of the noise.

It wasn't hard to locate. A stocky shambler, pulling himself around the edge of the shelf at Sherman's feet, appeared. Thick, dark blood crusted its face, cloaking the features it had worn in life. Its plastic name tag, hanging loose from a ripped button-up shirt, was the source of the scraping noise. It dragged along the tiled floor as the shambler crawled forward.

Sherman backpedaled, but the shambler, moving more quickly than Sherman had given it credit for, shot out an arm and grabbed for the General's ankle. Sherman stumbled, and the shambler brought him crashing to the ground.

"Thomas!" was all Sherman could muster.

The command sergeant major appeared a moment later behind the grounded undead and planted his boot firmly on the ex-man's neck. A quick stomp and snap later, and the corpse fell still.

Sherman shuddered and shook his boot free from the cold grip of the infected.

"I owe you one," breathed Sherman.

Thomas shrugged. "I owe you more, sir."

Mbutu Ngasy had poked his head into the store. "Is everything all right?"

"We're fine! We're fine!" barked Sherman. He pointed over Mbutu's shoulder. "Keep your eyes on the street! Thomas, how's your bag?"

"Nearly full, sir. Can't say it's great eats, but it'll keep us going."

"That's good enough for me, Thomas. Let's just hope the other foraging parties had similar luck."

Thomas looked undecided for a moment. "Should we try one or two more of these stores while we're here?"

Sherman considered the idea a moment, then shook his head. "No, we have enough now to last us the rest of the week, maybe longer. And that was a close call," Sherman said, eyeing the corpse on the aisle floor. "Let's not push our luck."

"Back to the Fac, sir?"

Sherman nodded. "On the double. And take the western route—let's skirt town as much as possible. We'll mark this place on the map when we get there."

The trio set off in the direction of home.

✯ ✯ ✯ ✯ ✯

Gravel crunched underfoot as Mbutu Ngasy, Francis Sherman, and Command Sergeant Major Thomas walked apart from one another down the sloping gravel drive that led behind prefabricated steel storage sheds. Thomas glanced about, eyes flitting here and there, never off his guard.

The gravel gave way to packed earth, kicked up in small clouds with each boot step.

They had made it halfway when Thomas froze, staring off into the underbrush that flanked the dirt alleyway.

Sherman knew better than to speak up, and instead slowly flicked the safety on his weapon over from safe to semi, and took careful aim at the disturbance in the bushes.

"Who goes?" Thomas ventured after a long, tense moment.

The reply from the brush was loud and almost disappointed: "Two thousand goddamned miles from anywhere with a titty bar, and the first asshole I run into is you!"

It took the command sergeant major a moment to place the voice.

"You from the *Ramage*?" was Thomas's reply.

Allen appeared out of the tree line, a pistol in his hands and a grin on his face. "Still alive and drinking, when I can find something to."

"How the hell did you get out here?"

"That's a long, long story. But we don't have time for it. Harris is hurt."

"How's that?"

"Come on out here, Commander," said Allen. "Doubt our friends will want to shoot you."

Branches rustled, and out from the undergrowth stepped Harris, clutching his belly.

Sherman's jaw dropped. Even Thomas seemed stunned.

Mbutu, on the other hand, peeled his lips back into an ivory grin. "It's you. And you're alive."

"Barely. I don't know where the thing came from, but it got me and it's all I can do to keep my insides inside."

Thomas eyed the bloody bandage on Harris's stomach. "Looks like it. We better get a move on."

Harris flinched. "Throbs like hell. No painkillers out here. Makes me wish for a morphine shot." Something flickered in his face. "How is Rebecca? Is she—I mean—she wasn't one of the ones who didn't . . . ?"

"No, no. Becky's fine. She's a little edgy these days. She feels bad, I think," Sherman explained with a sigh. "Between killing Decker and seeing all this, I don't blame her."

Harris nodded. "I understand. We had another man with us, but we lost him along the way. Tall, built just like Thomas here, wearing khaki. He's scouting. Don't shoot him, all right?"

The Fac
30 June 2007
1534 hrs_

Sherman, Mbutu, Thomas, and the other scavengers arrived at the Fac's main entrance, packs filled with assorted supplies, only to find that Junko Koji was taking her new duties very seriously.

Thomas was the first to approach, pack bulging, and he knocked heavily on the door.

A long moment of silence passed.

From within, Juni's lilting voice drifted out in a singsong manner. "That wasn't the code!"

"Oh, for fuck's sake, Juni, it's us. Open the damn door."

"No."

"Juni, this is General Sherman," the de facto leader said from behind Thomas. "It's me. Open the door."

Her muffled voice came through again. "Oh, sure, you put me on door detail but then you won't even give me the password. No, sirs. I'll just sit here until you give it to me. Serves you right!"

"Juni!" he shouted. "Open the door. Get downstairs and get Anna! Find Rebecca! We've got wounded!"

A stunned second passed, and then came the sounds of Juni unlocking and dragging the door wide. "I'm on it," she said, taking off at a dead sprint down the corridors of the Fac, yelling for the young medic and Army doctor.

"Cheeky," grumbled Thomas.

"With pink bunny slippers," Sherman reminded Thomas with a frown. "She wishes you'd take her more seriously. Maybe you'll find she'd reciprocate."

Thomas grumbled and headed off deeper into the Fac, a shrug his only response.

"Let's bring those men in," said Sherman. "Get Harris to the Doc. Trevor and Brewster should be back soon."

Sherman and Mbutu gave the heavy doors a shove, and Allen and Stone came into the Fac supporting Commander Harris, whose face had gone white from blood loss. He barely seemed able to support himself. After, Mbutu pushed on the doors and had nearly closed them when a hand shot out, grasping the edge of the door frame.

"Wait!" came Brewster's voice.

Sherman and Mbutu froze as Brewster's head poked in the doorway.

He grinned—not one of his impish, happy-go-lucky grins, Sherman noted, but rather an honest-to-goodness smile of joy.

"We found something, General. Something great. Something that—well, you'll just have to see for yourselves. Mark! Hal! Get in here!"

Sherman's mind was swimming. Mark? Hal? Those were two names he hadn't heard in months. But if Harris was there—

—and then there they were.

Private Mark Stiles and Hal Dorne, U.S. Army, retired, appeared in the doorway.

"Good Lord have mercy," breathed Sherman. "I can't believe it."

"I couldn't either, Frank," said Trev. "Not after what they told us."

"But—" Sherman was at a loss for words. "But you were bitten, Stiles! We all saw it! You were infected!"

"Still am," Stiles said, shrugging.

Sherman recovered from his shock at the sight of the soldier he had given up for dead months before and turned back to the wounded man. The group laid Commander Harris on one of the couches in the reception area, keeping pressure on his stomach wound.

"Don't worry," said Stiles. "We'll see you through this."

Harris's only reply was a shuddering groan.

A few moments later, Rebecca Hall burst through the doors into the reception room, bearing a shoulder bag stuffed with medical supplies. She took one look at Harris's stomach wound and gritted her teeth. "We'll have to move you down to BL1. All of our best gear is there. Looks clean enough—but you've probably got a perforated intestine. If we don't stitch it up, the wound'll go septic and you'll die of infection."

Harris swallowed and managed to nod.

Sherman stood off to the side, watching the young medic at work. He caught Stiles doing the same. She applied a fresh pressure bandage to Harris's wound and called out for assistance. Mbutu, Thomas, and Stiles stepped forward, each lifting Harris onto their shoulders. They wound their way through the Fac and down the stairs that led to the laboratories.

☆ ☆ ☆ ☆ ☆

The group shoved the door to BL1 open, startling Gregory Mason, who had been lounging in his bed reading a paperback novel.

"What?" he wondered at the sudden commotion. "What's going on?"

"New roommate for you," said Rebecca. "Hope you don't mind."

"Not at all. Anything I can do to help?"

"No! Just stay right there!" snapped Rebecca. "The last thing we need is for you to open your wounds again."

Mason held up his hands in mock surrender and leaned back on his pillow. "Whatever you say, Doc."

"Anna!" called Rebecca. Harris's wound was beyond her ability to heal. "Anna! Where are you?"

✮ ✮ ✮ ✮ ✮

Juni had been busy, pounding on the BL4's hatch and furiously punching buttons on the keypad, trying to get the attention of the Doctor within. Finally, she appeared, disheveled, and with dark circles under her eyes.

"What is it?" Anna asked. "Are we under attack?"

"No!" said Juni. "We found more survivors! One of them is wounded! I think they took him to BL1."

"Oh, damn," muttered Anna, grabbing a white lab coat from a peg on the wall and throwing it around her shoulders. "Grab my tray of surgical gear and prep it."

Anna sprinted down the hallway, skidding to a stop when she reached the BL1 doorway. Inside, she found a small cluster of people gathered around a man lying half-dead on a gurney. Juni pushed past her to a tray of sterile instruments. Anna took one look at Harris's pale face and knew immediately what her first course of action had to be.

"Quick!" Anna said, grabbing Harris by the shoulders. "What's your blood type?"

Harris responded in a weak voice. "A-positive."

"Who's A-positive?" Anna asked, casting about the room.

Thomas raised his hand. "I'm A-positive."

"So am I," Stone said.

"Grab a seat. We need your blood," Anna said, not looking twice at the other new arrivals. "Rebecca, start drawing blood. We need to replace what this man has lost, as fast as possible. Then we'll go in and see if we can patch up the internal damage."

Harris looked as though he was fading out quickly. He blinked a lot, as if his vision was growing dim.

"Don't worry, pal. They fixed me up," Mason said. "They'll fix you up, too."

☆ ☆ ☆ ☆ ☆

It had taken some doing, but Commander Harris was stable. The blood transfusion and the quick work of Anna Demilio had taken him out of immediate peril. He was still in bad shape, but hopes were high that the man would pull through.

While Jack the Welder and Junko Koji sorted canned goods in the makeshift kitchen and break room, Hal Dorne was being peppered with questions about his cross-country trip. He seemed happy enough to answer, and went on at great length about the trials and tribulations he'd been forced to go through when he would just as soon have spent the rest of his life swilling home-brewed spirits on his private island retreat. Allen sat off to the side, "just glad to be indoors again, with no guns pointed at me." Stone nodded at this.

Mark Stiles, on the other hand, found his mind wandering, and couldn't focus on the conversations. Soon he found himself walking through the whitewashed halls of the Fac searching for someone in particular.

He found her grumbling to herself, brushing a lock of dirty-blond hair out of her eyes. Stiles turned the corner and watched Rebecca Hall hunched over a rolling metal tray overflowing with gauze pads and first-aid gear, here and there an orange prescription bottle. Rebecca was trying to sort the mess Trev and Brewster had left in their wake. From the snorts of frustration she uttered, Stiles guessed the job was getting the better of her.

"Anything I can help with?" asked the soldier, approaching the young medic.

For a moment, Rebecca's unreadable expression broke to one of momentary surprise.

"Stiles?" she asked. She had thought Stiles had been gone for months, lost in the survivors' action in Hyattsburg. Preoccupied with Harris, the young woman hadn't even noticed him as she'd struggled to save the commander's life. The last time she had seen him she'd given him a shot of morphine to dull the pain from a carrier bite he had suffered. "But you—you're dead!"

Stiles smiled and waved at her. "I get that a lot. I'm starting to feel like Snake Plissken. It's good to see you, too, Becky."

Rebecca pulled herself together, wiping the surprise from her face and replacing it with a neutral expression. "Well, I'm glad you made it. Welcome to the Fac."

"Thanks," said Stiles. He repeated his earlier query. "Looks like they've been keeping you busy. Anything I can help you out with?"

Rebecca didn't look up, her tone cold. "No. I don't need any help."

"I don't mind. Besides, I owe you," said Stiles.

Rebecca didn't reply.

"You helped me back in Hyattsburg," Stiles explained. "I couldn't have made that run if you hadn't been there to fix me up. I'd like to return the favor, if I can."

"You don't owe me anything," said Rebecca. Her eyes never left the mess of gear on the tray before her. "Look, excuse me. I have to get these down to BL4."

The young woman pushed the trolley ahead of her, leaving Stiles alone in the hall, a disappointed look on his face.

"Okay," managed Stiles, as Rebecca disappeared around a corner. He raised his voice. "Hey—this conversation isn't over!"

★ ★ ★ ★

Down the hall, Rebecca cast a glance over her shoulder, half-expecting to see Stiles watching her go, but the soldier had already turned around, hands in his pockets, trudging away toward the front of the building.

Rebecca sighed, then shook her head. She had a delivery to make.

The journey down to BL4 wasn't very long, but it felt that way to her. Her gaze ran over the white walls, as it did every time she made the trip, and she was simultaneously comforted and intimidated by the blank slate the walls represented. The only sounds in the hallway were her muffled footsteps, the squeaking of the cart, and her breathing.

Her mouth felt dry, and she realized she'd been panting again. BL4 worried her. It wasn't enough that there were millions of corpses topside, was it? No, they had to have the bug in here, with them.

She passed through the security point and stepped into the prep room, pushing the cart ahead of her. Down here, away from the eyes of others, sometimes she liked to just shout and get it out of her system.

Rebecca wasn't the only occupant of the room, however. Across the small space, resting on a bench, sat Dr. Anna Demilio, tugging off stubborn woolen socks as she prepared to enter BL4. Her figure struck Rebecca as odd for a moment, and then she placed the irregularity—Dr. Demilio was humming to herself, a wisp of a smile on her lips.

"You've heard about Stiles?" Rebecca asked.

Anna nodded and smiled.

"He's been bitten twice and hasn't turned."

Anna's smile widened. "Frank filled me in after we patched up Harris. Do you have any idea how important this is?" Anna's voice was becoming animated. "It's a quantum leap forward. I was expecting years of work. With a little luck, I can have it down to months, or even weeks! We can *stop* this thing!"

Rebecca agreed wholeheartedly. "What do we do?" she asked.

"Well, I'll need to get a mess of Morningstar samples set up for us to use in the tests, first. Don't worry about that—I can handle it. You can take care of the other samples I'll need."

"Just tell me what you need me to do."

Anna considered it a moment, then shrugged. "You know how to use a needle, right?"

Rebecca smirked. "You know I do, Doc."

"Then go get me some blood samples from Stiles. But be careful," warned Anna. "Even if he's immune, he could still be contagious."

"I just ran into him upstairs."

"Then you should know where to find him," said Anna. She made a shooing motion with her hands. "Go on, now. This is important. The faster we get this done, the faster we can move forward."

"Okay! Okay! I'm doing it! Where do you want the cart?" Rebecca asked, as an afterthought.

"Oh, just leave it here. I'll bring it into the lab when I'm ready." Dr. Demilio had slipped into a Chemturion suit and was busily duct-taping the seals around her wrists and ankles.

"If you need me," said Rebecca, retreating toward the exit, "I'll be stabbing Stiles."

"Be gentle."

✮ ✮ ✮ ✮

Rebecca wheeled a tray into the BL1 laboratory, now home to two patients. Gregory Mason still had his head buried in his paperback, and Commander Harris was sleeping. Mark Stiles was there, looking in on Harris.

The two occupants of the room seemed to pay them little mind. Rebecca Hall was busy focusing on preparing to draw blood from Mark Stiles, and Mark Stiles was busy focusing on Rebecca.

"You know," said Stiles, leaning against an examination table as Rebecca, dressed in a thin white lab technician's coat, inspected a hypodermic needle, "after that shambler got me in Hyattsburg I could barely walk—"

"I need some of your blood," Rebecca said.

"What?"

"I need. Some. Of your. Blood. For the Doc."

Rolling his eyes, Stiles folded back his sleeve. "The bite. It's like a burn, you know? A never-ending throbbing? I could barely stay on my feet. And then you showed up with that morphine, and suddenly I could run again."

"And then you drew off the infected and saved the rest of our lives. I'd say that makes us pretty even," murmured Rebecca, flicking the needle with her index finger.

"If it wasn't for you I couldn't have done any of that."

Rebecca shook her head. "I've done just as much bad as I have good since this whole thing started. Just—please—drop it with the score-keeping. We're all damned for what we've had to do."

Stiles, preoccupied, didn't notice the needle descending toward his arm.

"Ow!" he cried, jumping a bit in his seat.

"Oh, don't be a *girl*," drawled Rebecca. "There. Let this pump out, and we'll be all finished. This blood sample should give Anna something to work on for a while. Who knows? Maybe the secret to the vaccine is right here in this vial."

"With a little luck," said Stiles.

He took the hint, sitting quietly while the tube filled.

"Okay," she said. "That's enough for now."

"Beautiful," Stiles said, unrolling his sleeve. "Do you think we could—"

"I'm going to get this to Anna. Everyone else is either lounging around or out in the courtyard. Maybe you should join them." Rebecca, sample in hand, made a beeline for the door.

"Wait!" protested Stiles. Rebecca Hall stopped slowly, and cast a glance over her shoulder.

It took a moment for the right words to come to Stiles. "Look, uh, I know you think we're square, but you gave me a fighting chance. You saved my life, right? If I couldn't run, I wouldn't have gotten away with just the one bite. Look—I don't care if you want to push me away or brush me off or whatever it is you're trying to do, but I just want you to know one thing—one of these days, I'm going to repay the favor. Really."

Rebecca seemed to consider this for a long moment. Finally, she gave a curt nod. "Thanks, Mark."

With that, she disappeared through BL1's swinging doors.

Stiles sat a moment in the examination room, alone, his face a mask. After a moment, he broke into a wistful smile.

"Hey, she called me Mark."

Across the room, Agent Gregory Mason dropped the novel he'd been reading to his chest and turned his head to look at the soldier, smirking. "I'd call that a good start."

CHAPTER 10
THE FAC

Omaha, NE
30 June 2007
1815 hrs_

WELL BEFORE NIGHTFALL, THE various groups had reassembled at the front of the Fac.

Brewster was the first to approach the bulging packs, and leaned heavily on the door.

A long moment of silence passed.

From the couch, Juni's lilting voice drifted to his ears in a singsong manner. "That wasn't what you were supposed to bring back."

Brewster looked up at her, the happy smile still on his face, but now a little tired. "Better than dog food, isn't it?"

"You got me there, GI."

Brewster's eyes adjusted to the low light, and he took in Juni, an impish look on her delicate features.

"You're such a smart-ass. We're not GIs anymore. Does stubbornness run in your family, or something?"

"Does it run in yours?"

Brewster looked uneasy for a moment, but quickly scoffed. "No."

"Bet it does."

"Doesn't."

"Does too."

"All right, all right, all right. Kids," muttered Sherman, rubbing at his temples as he walked up. "Let's see what we've got."

The survivors in the Fac were less interested in the freshly foraged supplies the two groups had brought back than they were in the new faces.

While Jack the Welder and Junko Koji sorted canned goods in the makeshift kitchen-slash-break room with Stiles and Juni, Allen found himself peppered with questions about his cross-country trip. He was happy to answer.

★ ★ ★ ★ ★

Jack the Welder was giving Hal Dorne a tour of the grounds. So far, the retired Army tank mechanic had spotted several projects that needed tending to, from loose gaps in the perimeter to easy ways to bolster their defenses.

"I originally joined the Army to pay the bills," Hal explained, "but I like building things from scratch for the hell of it. I'd've done it for free if it came to that. Now, for example, about a block away, I see a radio tower." Hal pointed off in the distance, where a solitary metal structure stood. "We could use that. The whole way here, I was broadcasting a signal; who we were, where we were going. Never heard anything back."

"Well, sure, if you could get it running. We couldn't. And we tried. And even if you did get it to work," Jack asked, "who are you going to talk to?"

Hal shrugged. "You never know. Could be a town in range with a working receiver. Or maybe one of our surviving sailors. Shortwave will go goddamn everywhere with an antenna and radio station power source."

"Knock yourself out."

Hal grinned at Jack. "I believe I will."

The door to the Fac swung open and Francis Sherman scuffed dirt as he made his way across the courtyard to where the two men stood. "I take it Jack's giving you the grand tour?"

Hal chuckled. "It ain't the Plaza, Frank, but she'll do in a pinch. I was just talking about trying to get that radio tower up and running again."

"It's shot," said Sherman with a shake of his head. "We already tried."

"That's what Jack told me. Let me try my hand at it. I think I can coax a little power out of her."

"If anyone can," said Sherman, "it would be you. But that's not what I wanted to talk to you about."

"Oh, right," said Hal, throwing his arms in the air. "You're a general. Looking to get in a debriefing, aren't you?"

Sherman grinned. "You've got me."

"You brass are all predictable. All right, so—got an office to talk in?"

"Actually," said Sherman, tilting his head back toward the sun, "I figured we'd walk the perimeter and chat. Jack, you're welcome to join us, if you wish."

Jack waved them off. "I promised Mitsui I'd help him get dinner ready."

"Is it your shift?"

"No, but it never hurts to be nice, right?" chuckled Jack, making his way toward the Fac's back door.

"Hey! Wait a second!" Hal called out.

Jack stopped and turned.

"Never caught your last name, Jack!" said Hal.

Jack turned slowly, and grinned. "I'm just a welder, Hal. Just a welder."

A moment later, the contractor vanished into the Fac, the heavy door swinging shut behind him. Sherman laughed, and Hal shot him a curious glance.

"What's so funny?"

"He hasn't told anyone his last name. There's an unofficial pool going. Some of us think he's on the lam—or was, before the law went out the window with everything else—and some others think it must be a terrible name, for him to keep it secret."

"I guess it's his business," shrugged Hal.

"Well," said Sherman, "shall we walk?"

"Sure," said Hal, following alongside Frank. "Hey, I've been meaning to ask, you guys got anything for a fellow to drink around here? I'm sure Allen would love a snort, too."

Sherman made a so-so motion with his hand. "Trevor knows how to rig up a still. He's got it up on the roof. Can't say I can stomach the stuff myself, but for a vet like you, it'd probably go down smooth enough."

"Remind me to badger him for a cup, later."

"It's a multipurpose brew," Sherman said. "You can drink it. You can also use it to strip rust off a bumper."

Hal laughed. "That's what I like to hear. Finest kind."

The pair was walking along the edge of the chain-link fence that kept the Fac's backyard safe from intruding infected. Sherman stopped at each post to check that the mesh was securely bolted, and hadn't worked its way loose over the weeks.

"So, tell me about your little cross-country trek," Sherman said as he gave one of the posts an experimental kick. It held firm. "Somehow you made it from the islands all the way to the mainland. What happened? You get tired of retirement?"

"Don't get me started on that," Hal said, scowling. "They kicked me out when I spoke up for the sailors."

"The sailors from the *Ramage*?"

"Of course. What, do you think any other ship would just come stumbling into that little atoll in the middle of nowhere? You'd have to get a local topo map to even see it. As far as the world is concerned, my island doesn't exist. Or, my ex-island, anyway."

"So they came back. Captain Franklin and his crew, I mean."

Hal nodded. "They had nowhere else to go. I wanted them to come live on the island, but the LIPs weren't too hot on the idea." Hal slipped back into Army lingo for native individuals—Local Indigenous Personnel. "They have their own idea of quarantine, you know. And it's a pretty good one. Just cut off everything, and hope the plague misses you. It works, too. Never saw a single infected while I was there. My neighbors didn't want the sailors around. Thought they'd bring Morningstar in with them, even though I told them the ship was clean."

"And so one thing led to another . . ." began Sherman.

". . . and suddenly I find myself being driven out of town with pitchforks and torches. Figuratively speaking. It was more like spears and bows." Hal appeared thoughtful for a moment. "And one 1911. Still not sure where that guy got a hold of a .45." He shrugged. "*C'est la vie*. Right?"

"I'm sorry. About your retirement, I mean. I know it meant a lot to you, living out there."

Hal shrugged. "I got over it. Mostly. What's that they used to say in the Army, about getting used to new circumstances?"

"'Adapt and overcome,'" said Sherman, by rote. "Many of us live by it. Ask Thomas, if you're really curious. He follows doctrine like an evangelist follows the Holy Bible."

Hal nodded. "That's it."

"Then what happened?"

The pair had worked their way halfway across the fenced-in yard and stood under the shadow of a rusting grain lift. The lift was one of Krueger's favorite places. He would climb the ladder on the side with his rifle over his shoulder and a book taken from one of the many abandoned stores and relax atop the structure, ready to give covering fire in any direction. The sharpshooter would even sleep up there from time to time, weather permitting.

Hal continued his story. "Well, the crew was getting restless. A lot of infighting. They couldn't last much longer cooped up. Franklin brought us back to the coast and told us all to abandon ship."

"Franklin didn't survive the trip here, then?" asked Sherman, a pained expression on his face.

Hal rushed to reassure him. "Oh, no. As far as I know, he's still sitting comfortably on the *Ramage*. She's anchored right off the coast of Washington. There's still one or two missiles on that destroyer. Maybe he didn't want to leave them unattended."

"Or maybe he just wanted to stay with his ship."

Hal shrugged. "Maybe that. The quintessential captain: staying with his ship until the very end."

A shrill whistle cut through the air. Sherman and Hal's heads shot up. Denton, having taken over as roof guard while Mitsui and Jack prepared chow, was leaning over the edge, pointing excitedly into the distance behind the pair of old veterans. His voice rang out over the courtyard, tense and animated.

"Here they come!" Denton warned. "Two of them! Shamblers! Coming up as fast as they can manage! Should I sound the alarm?" Denton was referring to the building's fire alarms. They'd deactivated the water from the sprinklers, but the sirens and lights worked fine. The little setup let everyone in the building know when trouble was afoot, and would summon every survivor to their battle stations.

"No, hold the alarm," said Sherman, waving Denton off. "We can handle two shamblers ourselves. Well, Hal," Sherman muttered, "welcome to your first defensive action at the Fac."

Hal reached for his sidearm, but felt Sherman's hand clasp over his before he could pull the weapon free from its holster.

"No," Sherman said. "We don't shoot unless we need to. We've got a different way to deal with the shamblers. See those tamp bars leaning up against the Fac, there?"

Hal looked. Among the overgrown grass lining the brick building was a pair of tamping bars. Normally, they were simple digging tools, but thanks to a grinder the survivors had found in the abandoned industrial complex behind the Fac, they'd narrowed down the wedge ends of the tools to sharp points. The bars were heavy and unwieldy, but, then, they weren't forged for pitched battles. Despite this, the survivors had found a creative use for the six-foot lengths of steel.

"Yeah, I see them," said Hal.

"Grab one," Sherman said, striding off in the direction of the tools.

Above, Denton watched their progress and called down from the rooftop: "Need any help?"

"No," said Sherman, "we'll take these two. Who's on shit detail?"

Sherman rarely swore, but he'd adopted the lingo of his men—"shit detail" was what the survivors had taken to calling corpse disposal.

"Uh, Brewster is, I think," said Denton, after a moment's thought. He was distracted by the approaching shamblers.

"Who else?"

Denton shrugged. "Just Brewster."

"Wonder what he did to deserve that?" murmured Sherman, raising his eyebrows. He pushed one of the modified tamp bars in Hal's direction. He raised his voice to shout up at Denton. "Grab Krueger! Have him give Brewster a hand once we finish these two off. Make sure they burn the bodies down to ash. Tell him to be more thorough this time. Last time he left half a shambler in the trench!"

"Will do, Frank."

"The spare diesel cans are in the back of the utility truck," Sherman added. "Tell him to be generous. The last thing we need is for all of us to get sick from one of those bodies lying out in the sun too long."

The shamblers, meanwhile, had crossed most of the distance to the fence. Spying live prey, they had picked up their pace, managing a quick walk. They were nearly on the perimeter. Hal felt a shudder run down his spine at their moans.

"All right," said Sherman, grunting slightly as he hefted the tamp bar on his shoulder. "It's as easy as this. Watch and learn."

The first shambler, missing a cheek and three of the fingers on its right hand, stumbled up against the fence, pressing its face against the links.

"And, thus," said Sherman, thrusting the bar forward in a smooth motion. The pointed end of the bar speared the shambler through an eye socket. Sherman twisted the bar in his hands and yanked it free. The shambler stood frozen in place a moment, and slowly crumpled to the ground, motionless. "Next one's yours."

Hal grinned. "Hey, pretty clever. Much better than shooting at them on the run." His spear thrust caught the second shambler above the bridge of its nose, caving it in. The force Hal put behind the blow wasn't quite enough to punch through to its brain, however, and the shambler loomed up again. A second thrust penetrated with a sickening noise, and the undead attacker went down, crumpling to lie next to its companion in the grass outside the fence.

"Damn. Two tries," muttered Hal. "Guess retirement's no good for my muscles, eh?"

"You'll get better," Sherman said.

The pair regarded the corpses on the ground a moment longer. Sherman shook his head and grasped Hal's shoulder, leading him away from the scene. Brewster and Krueger would be along to dispose of the infected corpses soon enough.

"So, where were we?" he asked. "You were telling me about landfall."

Hal rubbed at the back of his neck. "Landfall. So it was myself, Commander Harris, and about twenty sailors who set out from the *Ramage*. Our thought was to follow the track you'd left us—straight inland, making a beeline for Omaha."

"Makes sense."

"That's what we figured, too. We thought we might even catch up with you along the way. We lost a couple of good men in the woods before we hit the first town," Hal sighed. "It's hard to see where those running bastards are coming from when you can't see more than ten feet in front of your face. Finally, we found some civilization."

"Don't tell me," Sherman interrupted. "Hyattsburg."

"Yeah, that's the place," said Hal.

"We nearly got wiped out in there," Sherman said, going back over the events of months long past in his head. "If it wasn't for Mbutu's driving and Stiles's running we could have all been carrier chow."

"It was pretty quiet when we went through, Frank. Except for one thing."

"Stiles."

"You got it. He was hiding out in a store. Thought we were infected. Shot at us a couple of times before we realized he was one of us. A few of us shot back."

Sherman whistled. "You want to talk about luck—that's luck. Imagine accidentally shooting the one guy we know of who's immune to the Morningstar strain."

"We'd have felt pretty foolish."

"Anyway," Sherman said, replacing the bloodied tamp bar, gore side planted firmly in the earth, against the Fac's outer wall.

"Anyway, what?"

"Anyway, what happened after Hyattsburg?"

"Smooth sailing, General," Hal said. "We made it from Oregon all the way through the Rocky Mountains without so much as a skirmish. Thought things were settling down. We walked a lot, but here and there we found a vehicle or two that could get us a few miles down the road before giving out. We made good time. We even stopped in Abraham."

Something about Hal's tone bothered Sherman. "I take it that the smooth sailing didn't last?"

Hal nodded. "Just happened, three, four days ago. There was a dozen of us left then, most of the way here. Lost three on a bridge, then a couple of civilians where we picked up Stone and a couple of vehicles."

Sherman stayed silent during Hal's retelling of what happened at the military history museum, his face set hard when he heard of Ron and Katie's deaths.

"And last night, we were nine, maybe ten miles from here. Harris thought it would be a good idea to hole up for the night and wait until the sun was out again before we risked the city. You know how those infected bastards like the shade. We were in a pretty good spot. Trees all around. Thought they would block us from prying eyes, you know? We even got a little fire going to get some hot food in us. That might have been our mistake."

Sherman listened intently.

"For the first couple of hours, everything was calm. We had guards watching out for us, of course. I don't know what happened. Everything was fine, and then . . . chaos. They were in us, among us. Sprinters at first, but then shamblers, too, drawn in by the gunshots and screams. They came in from every direction, right out of the trees. It was chaos. Panic. At first we tried to drive them off, but one by one we broke and ran. It felt hopeless to stay."

"Are you four the only survivors?" asked Sherman.

"I don't know," Hal admitted. "We all went off in different directions. I saw one guy—couldn't tell who it was, in the darkness—throw down his gun so he could get away faster. Like I said, it was pure panic. Maybe some of them made it. Maybe none of them. I just don't know."

Sherman kept his face a carefully controlled mask, but felt his shoulders sag. The sailors from the naval destroyer had fought their way across half a continent to deliver Stiles to Omaha, only to be butchered in the final hours of their journey. Frank remembered many of their faces from the time he had spent on the *Ramage,* and their bravery when confronted with an infection on board. They were good men, and they would be missed.

The practical side of Sherman's mind reminded him also that the reinforcements would have been a welcome addition to the Fac's defenses. All of the survivors were weakened by the loss.

"This Stone fellow. Is he a good hand?"

Hal nodded. "Oh, yeah. It took us a little while to get used to the idea of having him with us, but he's a good man to have at your back. He doesn't complain and he'll shoot the ass off a gnat with that M-16."

The pair of old soldiers paced slowly across the Fac's yard, moving far enough from the freshly dispatched shamblers to avoid their stomach-churning stench. They stopped near a steel carport that abutted the Fac's rear wall. Hal leaned his back against one of the vehicles, a large utility truck painted in flat woodland camouflage, a mottled mix of dark green, brown, and black. He looked past Sherman, through the fence and out at the city beyond.

Hal sighed. "Hell, Stiles and I got lucky twice in the past day: first when we got away from that ambush, and again when we ran into you. We might have spent a week searching this place, otherwise. So if there are any survivors left out there, I doubt they'll be looking. Most of us had radios, but they were short-range jobs, one, maybe two miles, tops."

"We have the same problem." Sherman clenched his jaw. "We could try radioing every quarter hour or so, but it's a big city. They could walk right past us, just out of range, and never know how close they were."

Hal grinned. He pointed across the Fac's yard, outside the fence, to the squat metal dispatcher hut that sat in the corner of the industrial yard. Its rusted antenna perched atop. "All the more reason to get that radio tower up and running again. Just needs some juice, and a little tender, loving care."

"I'm afraid juice is something we're in short supply of here. All those solar panels on the roof of the Fac barely power Anna's BL4 lab and our infirmary. We're on strict power rationing."

Hal nodded as Sherman spoke. "I'll see what I can do about that. You know, electrifying this fence you have wouldn't be a bad idea, either."

"Are you hearing me, Dorne?" asked Sherman, glancing sideways at the retired tank mechanic. "We just don't have the power."

"I'm hurt, Frank. I thought you knew me," Hal said, frowning. "You know, I once built a boat out of a golf cart, a ceiling fan, one thousand six hundred empty plastic bottles, and a lawn mower engine. Trust me, Frank, I can make this place tick again."

Sherman laughed out loud at Hal, but admitted that the retired tank mechanic had a way with machinery. "All right, Hal. What did you have in mind?"

Hal looked Sherman straight in the eye. "Well, are there any parking garages around here?"

The Fac's back door clanged open, revealing a short man with a runner's build, short, straight black hair, and a smear of flour on his cheek. It was Mitsui, the Japanese contractor, gesturing at the pair in the courtyard. His English was almost nonexistent after Hyattsburg. Each of the survivors in their turn had tried to pry the reason why from the contractor, and they all had failed.

"Dinner ready!"

"Oh, yeah," said Hal, rubbing at his stomach. "Haven't eaten since last night."

"Don't get your hopes up. We've been getting used to canned food. Nothing gourmet," warned Sherman.

"At this point, I'd eat a rat. You know, my grandfather said that during dub-dub-one they'd barbecue rats in the trenches and—"

"Oh, God, stop it, Hal," said Sherman with a groan. "I barely have an appetite as it is."

Hal looked hurt. "I was going to say they ended up better than the food the Army mess served. But all right. I'll shut my trap."

★ ★ ★ ★ ★

Boisterous laughter drifted down the Spartan halls of the Fac as Hal and Sherman made their way to the break room, now serving double duty as kitchen and mess hall. Apparently, the meal was well under way.

The pair turned the corner into the squarish room with its round folding tables and single, boarded-up window. Glances in their direction meant the occupants noticed the new arrivals. Only one diner reacted differently. Command Sergeant Major Thomas shot to his feet, shouting, "Group, atten-HUT!"

With a chorus of grumbles, the diners turned back to their meals, indifferent to the command. Thomas's eyes drifted from person to person, daggers in his stare.

"All right," said Sherman. "Let's make this official. Thomas, I hereby order you to disregard all military decorum. We are civilians."

Thomas, grumbling a few choice words of his own, settled back down to his plate. "Yes, sir." A moment later a thought struck him. "But I'll still stand up when you walk into a room, sir."

Sherman fought back a grin and pretended to ignore the remark.

He and Hal grabbed paper plates from a countertop and helped themselves to the meal Mitsui and Jack had cooked up. It wasn't anything special. Pasta, with something red that passed for sauce, sans meat, and a spoonful of creamed corn. A Styrofoam cup of plain water completed the meal.

"God," said Denton, tossing down his fork. "I know we're not supposed to say anything if the food is bad, because none of us was a chef before the shit hit the fan and it's bad for morale and all, but I have to say: I've had better Italian food in fucking Texas. Jack. Mitsui. Damn you both for this travesty."

"This isn't Italian," said Juni, a greenish pallor on her face. "This is American egg noodles with ketchup. It's horrible."

"Don't knock it. It has the calories. Eat up, people," Sherman said, digging in with gusto. "Never say no to a hot meal. Take it from a guy who spent two months eating raw C-rats."

"You ate sea rats?" Juni made a face. "God, gross."

"C-rats," Sherman repeated, frowning. "C-rations. Canned food."

"Oh."

To Hal, it was obvious which survivors had once been military and those who had never been in the service. The ex-Army men and sailors dug in with gusto, powering through their nearly flavorless helpings. The civilians—Denton and Juni among them—picked at their food, wary.

"I don't think I can eat this stuff much longer," Juni said. "God, I want . . . you know what I want? I just want some plain steamed rice in a bowl. That's all. Nothing much. And my grandmother's tempura, but not the way my grandmother made it—the way my *mother* made it. And—"

"Yeah, and I'd like a twenty-ounce New York strip steak. Doesn't mean we're gonna get it," Denton said.

"You want to know the trick?" said Krueger around a mouthful of pasta. His plate was nearly empty.

"Trick?" asked Juni, arching an eyebrow.

"Don't use your tongue. Just chew off to the side and then swallow. That way, you don't have to taste it."

"It's true," added Brewster. He was scraping the last bits of pasta from his otherwise clean plate. "Works the same way with MREs."

"That's where we got our practice in," added Krueger, with a grin. "Don't want to taste the cat food? Don't taste the cat food. Simple as that."

"Ugh, now you're eating cat food?" Juni's voice took on a quiver.

Brewster and Krueger burst out laughing. Even Sherman had a smile on his lips.

"Not cat food. But you crack open one of those MREs, guess what you smell?" Krueger asked.

"Cat food," answered Brewster, picking up for Krueger. "It smells just like cat food."

"Better than the four fingers of death," Krueger said, referring to the MREs that came packed with four finger-sized frankfurters. He forked another helping of pasta into his mouth, chewed, swallowed, and continued. "Damn near inedible."

Brewster pushed his plate away, sated, and took a long, slow look around the room. "Looks like we're missing a few people. Where's Stiles, Anna, Mason, and Becky?"

"Stiles was by earlier. He's taking food down to the labs for Anna and Becky. Mason's resting in his room, keeping an eye on Harris."

"How're they doing?" asked Krueger.

"Coming along," said Sherman. "Mason still seems a little off his feet. Don't blame him. A pair of bullets will do that."

"Oh, I wasn't knocking him, just—"

"Figure another week or two and he'll be good as new," Sherman went on, ignoring Brewster's interjection. "He'll be fine. I'm more worried about Anna and her research. Stiles's blood is a 'quantum leap' forward for her. I'm hoping for good news, and soon."

"All of us are," said Denton, upending a salt shaker on his plate. "Can you even imagine? A *vaccine*? We could save what's left of the human *race*."

Struck by a thought, Sherman changed the topic. "Out of curiosity, who's up on guard duty tonight?"

Thomas's gruff voice answered. "That'd be me and you, sir."

"That's 'you and I,'" corrected Juni, around a mouthful of pseudo-pasta. Thomas ignored her.

Sherman shrugged. "Thought it was getting close to my turn."

Denton wiped his mouth and raised his hand. "Point of order, Frank."

"What is it?"

"We've got enough food from this run and the one a couple of days ago to last us about a week. Maybe—while it's quiet out there—we should try for another run, see if we can scavenge up a surplus."

Sherman considered the thought for a moment, and finally decided Denton was right. "Good call."

"Get while the getting's good," Denton said. "You didn't fully clear out that store you hit, right? What was it?"

"The Dollar Stretcher."

"Let's hit it again, and scratch a few other addresses off our list while we're at it," said Denton.

"Good thinking," Sherman said. "I suppose you never know when some infected will decide to change venues."

Denton nodded. "They do seem to move around a lot at night. Could end up anywhere by the time the sun comes back up."

"Right now, it's a ghost town," Thomas said. "We've cleared out most or all of the infected within a four-block radius, but we're still playing Russian roulette every time we go out there."

Sherman nodded. "That's a risk. But then, everything we do outside the Fac is risky. Denton, it's a good idea. We'll run with it. Get two runs out of the way so we won't have to worry about it for a while."

"It's your show, Frank."

Sherman frowned. "It's *our* show. We're all in this together."

"Figure of speech, Frank."

"Well, that'll do it for me," said Sherman, tossing down his plastic fork. "I'm full."

"Anything on the docket for entertainment tonight?" asked Denton.

"It's Juni's turn," Frank said, pointing at her.

The slight Japanese girl brightened at the mention of her name. "Shadow puppets! I've been working on it all week!"

The rationed electricity didn't allow the survivors the luxury of television, and so they had made do with improvisational presentations, taking turns, much as they did for guard shifts.

"Should I get set up?" asked Juni.

"Sure," said Denton. "At this point a mime show would entertain me."

"Hey, are you knocking my puppets?" Juni said, faux-hurt filling her voice.

"Not at all," said Denton, holding up his hands in surrender. "I'm just saying any entertainment is good entertainment these days."

QM3 Allen eyed Private Brewster. "Is there any liquor around here? I need to get blind drunk for shadow puppets."

Brewer looked back. "Race you," he whispered.

"Well," Hal said, "as promising as shadow puppets sounds, I think I might spend the night at the dispatcher station. I've got flashlights and batteries; all I need are some tools."

Mitsui the contractor stood at this and hurried out of the room.

"I might go with you," Stone said. "Helping the elderly might ease my way into Heaven."

Hal's eyes narrowed at Stone. "When did you develop a sense of humor?"

Stone shrugged as Mitsui came back into the room with a Fluke multimeter and a small, red, hard plastic case. He presented them to Hal with a quick bow.

Hal, taken aback a bit, returned the bow and took the tools. Inside the red case was a set of screwdrivers in different sizes and heads, as well as a small ratchet set.

"Thank you," he said to the Japanese contractor.

"We'd better go," Stone said, rising. "Before the sun goes down. You ready?"

With a nod, Hal stood also and winked at Thomas.

"Hold on, old-timer," the grizzled sergeant said. "Best take a walkie-talkie with you. Never know."

✯ ✯ ✯ ✯ ✯

The BL4 laboratory was sealed to all but Anna and Rebecca, but Mark Stiles didn't mind waiting outside the heavy steel door for the pair to exit. It took longer than he'd thought, and by the time the pair had called it quits for the night he'd been leaning against a steel guardrail for the better part of an hour, a covered tray in front of him.

Anna and Becky seemed surprised to see him.

"Stiles!" said Anna, with a smile. "Come to check up on our progress?"

Stiles shook his head. "I came to bring you dinner." He gestured at the cart. "Pasta, I think. And something that I think is supposed to be some kind of red sauce. It's almost ketchup. Almost. Not too bad, though."

"That's nice of you," said Anna, uncovering the food. She grimaced at the sight of it. "Or maybe you're trying to kill us."

"Hey," shrugged Stiles. "I didn't cook it. I'm just the delivery boy."

"Thanks," was Rebecca's simple reply. She grabbed a plate from the tray and walked off toward the stairwell that led to the Fac's upper floors.

Stiles stared after her. Anna caught the look.

"Well?" she asked.

"Well, what?"

"Well, follow her! She needs company. I'm the only person she talks to, and I'm pretty boring."

Stiles hastened to reassure the Doctor. "Aw, Doc, I'm sure you're not as boring—"

"Ribonucleic acids have been the keystones to deciphering the pathological structure of filoviridae in every known strain—"

Stiles waved his arms, unable to control his laughing. "Okay, okay, I get it! Enjoy the dinner."

Anna smiled at him. "I will. Now, hurry up. Becky eats on the roof, where she can be alone."

Stiles favored the Doctor with a smile of his own, nodded his good-bye, and took off at a dogtrot in the direction Rebecca Hall had taken.

Anna stood alone in the doorway to biosafety level four laboratory, the tray of pasta at her waist. She stared after the soldier and medic, a wistful look creasing her forty-one-year-old features. "Oh, young love." She turned her attention to the food, and poked at it with an experimental finger. It wiggled like Jell-O at her touch. "And old food. Eck. I'd rather eat Marburg samples."

Doctor Anna Demilio left the tray where it lay, spun on her heels, and reentered BL4 to pull another shift, her only company for the evening microscopes and test tubes.

✳ ✳ ✳ ✳ ✳

Rebecca had just settled down on the edge of the Fac's roof, her legs dangling over the edge, when Stiles appeared.

"Ugh," muttered Rebecca upon sighting him. She picked at her pasta. "What part of 'leave me alone' don't you understand?"

"Oh, I understood it," Stiles said, plunking himself down next to the young medic with the dirty-blond hair. "I just don't care."

"So you're not an idiot . . ." said Rebecca.

"Nope."

". . . you're just an asshole."

Stiles stuttered over that one a moment, and let it go.

"Hey, your reasoning, not mine," said Rebecca, twirling pasta on her plastic fork.

"That . . . wasn't really the reaction I was going for," admitted Stiles. He shrugged. "Look. Let's start over. Pretend we've just met. I'm Mark Stiles. Private. U.S. Army. You are?" Stiles extended his hand.

"Not interested."

Stiles looked disappointed. He held his hand out a moment longer, but when it became apparent Rebecca had no interest in taking it, he dropped it to his lap and sighed.

For a long moment, silence reigned on the rooftop. Rebecca managed a few bites of her pasta, then gave up and set the plate on the edge of the roof next to her. The pair stared off at the ruined cityscape as night fell. In days gone past, it would have been alight, with activity in every building, headlights on every boulevard. The sounds of HVAC systems and traffic would have wafted over them, drowning out the noises of the night. Now all was silent, save for the chirping of crickets and the buzz-saw rhythm of cicadas. The high-rise buildings in the distance were dark and abandoned.

Stiles, suddenly feeling nostalgic, began to speak.

"I saw an IED go off in Iraq once. First tour," he said. He didn't bother looking over at Rebecca, instead focusing on the darkened buildings in front of him. "It's not really like they say in the news. On TV, you only ever see the aftermath, after everything's been cleaned up. In real life, it happens out of nowhere. One second, everything's fine. The next . . . you don't even know what hit you. It's like—for a second—the world stops. They tell you what it's like, but it's nothing like being there, seeing what . . . seeing what these things do. But I—I saw a . . . it's just that . . . a few seconds before it went off, I saw a wire. Just a little thing—like a cable cord, you know, that they run into houses?"

Rebecca had stopped staring off at the skyline of Omaha, and was watching Stiles out of the corners of her eyes, a blank expression on her face.

"This guy, Sergeant Wellton—funny guy, I could tell you some stories—anyway, he's walking ahead of us, and he's watching the buildings on either side of the street. And in front of him's this dark spot. Disturbed earth, I mean. Where someone had been digging. And I saw it, and the wire, and . . . I don't know, I just . . . froze. I didn't say a thing. I don't know why. Maybe I thought that if I was wrong I'd get chewed out, or . . . maybe . . . I don't know. Wellton—no, wait, his name was Anthony. Anthony Wellton. He was from Pittsburgh. And he stepped right on it."

Rebecca's face remained expressionless.

"When I came back to my senses I was lying on the ground a few feet away. Couldn't hear a thing. Just a high-pitched whine, you know? Nothing else. There was smoke everywhere. Dust. I couldn't breathe. Then I remembered Anthony. I had a couple of pieces of metal in my arm, felt the blood and all, but I crawled over to him anyway. I found his leg, started to pull myself up to see if he was all right, but . . . ."

Stiles trailed off. His eyes were moist.

"That was all there was. Just his leg. They said"—he paused a moment to gulp for breath—"they said they found some of him across the road. And they found the rest in a ditch a few feet away. A ditch!" Stiles's voice became filled with anger. "A fucking ditch! He deserved better! He had a daughter! A two-year-old. Oh, Christ, I could've saved him! I saw the wire! I saw it *coming*! If I'd said something, I could have saved—I could have *saved* him! Oh, God, I could've saved him." His voice trailed off.

The pair sat silently for a long moment more, the silhouetted cityscape their only distraction from the words of each other. Finally, Rebecca spoke.

"You think you killed him," she whispered.

Stiles didn't answer.

"You think you killed him. And that's why you tried to kill yourself to save the rest of us in Hyattsburg," Rebecca went on.

"You know what I did that night? After Wellton died, I mean?" Stiles finally asked.

"What?"

"I sat in my barracks. Took out my pistol and held it up against my head. I figured it was my fault that girl was going to grow up without a father. I wanted to punish myself. Make things right," Stiles said. "Then something happened."

"What?" Rebecca asked, her attention now fully focused on the soldier.

"There were some guys playing poker at the other end of the building. I could hear them talking. One of them lost big. He just said, 'Well, shit happens.' I know, corny, right? And it didn't make me feel any better about Wellton, but it did make me think. Sometimes, things just go wrong. I might have been right about that wire, but what if it had been someone else in my spot? They might not have even seen it. So now I don't think about suicide. We're all going to die some time. One of these days, shit'll happen to every one of us. It wasn't my turn that day. Even in Hyattsburg, when I thought I was going to turn into one of those things, I couldn't pull the trigger. I kept thinking, if I'm going to die, I'm going to die, and there's nothing I can do about it. And now I'm waiting for it to be my turn for the shit to happen to me, just like everyone else."

Rebecca sat silently a moment, thinking it over.

"Sometimes things just go wrong," repeated Stiles, eyeing Rebecca expectantly.

"Sometimes they do." Rebecca's answer was little more than a whisper. Her arms were folded in her lap, and her eyes stared off at nothing.

For a moment, there was silence on the rooftop of the Fac. Then a voice broke the stillness.

"You know," drifted a gruff voice from across the rooftop, "we can hear you over here."

"Oh, leave them alone, Thomas."

"Yes, sir."

☆ ☆ ☆ ☆ ☆

"Looks like they're settling in for the night, sir," said a man in a black balaclava, squatted on a rooftop half a block from the Fac, lowering infrared goggles from his face. One red light on his radio transmitter blinked and stuttered. "A pair of them just left, too. Heading south."

Sawyer's voice answered over the radio. *Let them rest.*

"Sir?" asked the man, rolling his eyes, glad that the NSA agent wasn't there to see him do it. "Why don't we just take them? We have position. We have the advantage in firepower. We could storm that place. Why not now?"

"Because," grunted Sawyer, the grin evident in his voice, "I'm not there yet. And we're bringing some extra party favors. Besides," he continued, annoyance creeping into his tone, "don't you think they'd be expecting an attack at night? They've got sentries, they're watching."

Confused, but too intimidated to press Sawyer further, the man turned back to his goggles and resumed his watch, chalking up Sawyer's answers as one of life's little mysteries.

☆ ☆ ☆ ☆ ☆

Nighttime at the Fac was quiet. Since all the electricity was being channeled to the labs below, the rooms were dark, save for the flickering light of candles and oil lamps scavenged from the surrounding buildings.

When Sherman wasn't on the roof pulling a guard shift, the sound of music would drift through the hallways. Sherman was fond of classical music, saying it helped him fall asleep, and had brought in an ancient, wind-up phonograph and had accumulated a small collection of records. Tonight, with Sherman topside, the halls were silent save for a few murmured conversations in the various rooms.

Rebecca Hall retired to her dorm, closing the door behind her. She twisted the lock on the handle and leaned against the cold steel of the door, arms folded across her chest, a sigh escaping her lips. She thought for a moment about the story Stiles had told her on the rooftop, and that thought led her to their newfound hope for the vaccine, and that thought, in turn, started her thinking about Stiles himself.

She shook her head before the thought could establish itself, and cast about her small room for something, anything, to distract herself with.

It was unsafe to become attached to anyone, she knew, moving from the door to the corner of the narrow cot she slept on. She sat down and planted her elbows on her knees, head resting on the palms of her hands. They all died in the end. Best to just stay alone and alive and soldier on until, as Stiles had put it, it was her turn to go. For shit to happen.

Her eyes scanned the room around her. She'd never been one for housekeeping before Morningstar, but ever since, she couldn't stomach disorder. What little she had was arranged neatly, almost obsessively. An unused table lamp sat just so on the edge of a filing cabinet that served as her dresser. Next to it was her pistol belt, canteen and ammunition pouches clipped inches apart on it. The pistol and holster themselves were missing. She felt the solid weight of the weapon digging into her side. Ever since the *Ramage*—ever since Decker—she'd never left the weapon more than a few feet away.

Other survivors in the group had scavenged creature comforts on their forays into Omaha—posters and pictures and paintings, mostly, to liven up the dull block walls of the Fac. Sherman had his phonograph. Denton's room was full of camera gear that he sorted through and cleaned during his downtime. Jack had brought in an acetylene torch and was fond of throwing together small metal sculptures. Brewster had found a portable CD player and speakers, but after one night of Metallica blaring through the Fac, the other survivors forced him to get a pair of headphones to go with it. Rebecca's room, on the other hand, remained nearly as bare as when she'd first claimed it. The only addition she'd made was a calendar, each day that passed without her death marked off with a solid red X.

Rebecca heard muted laughter from down the hall. It sounded like the sailor, Allen. He'd finally started to warm up to the soldiers, and last time she saw him, he was arm-wrestling for a bottle of liquor with Brewster. The other survivors were taking their time before turning in, telling jokes and sharing stories. She'd never felt any reason to join in. Once upon a time, she would have, but no longer. It was easier to watch a stranger die than a friend, or a lover.

The thought made her gut churn, and she felt her breath catch in her throat. She held a hand over her mouth and clenched her eyes shut, stifling the sob she knew was coming. When the feeling had passed, she relaxed, and lay back on her cot, wrapping her arms around herself and drawing her knees up close, staring off into nothing. The moon was out, and it bathed the room in a dull blue glow. A single tear fell from her eye, rolled down her face and soaked into the pillow beneath her head. She paid it no mind. She merely lay still, and tried not to think about anything at all.

★ ★ ★ ★ ★

A pair of gunshots rang out. Rebecca found herself running toward the source of the noise, apprehension etched on her face.

The gray steel corridors of the ship were narrow, but well lit. The hum of the engines was ever present, but even that couldn't drown out the sound of gunfire. Rebecca turned a corner and saw General Sherman and a group of soldiers standing in front of a sealed door. They were arguing.

"Sir? They might still be infected!" one of the soldiers was protesting.

Sherman disagreed. "Open the door. They're clean. They've been in there long enough."

"Yes, sir."

Rebecca found herself running toward them. "No! Don't open the door! Please, don't open the door!"

The soldiers ignored her. The man Sherman had been arguing with reached for the latch.

Rebecca felt frantic. "No. No! Don't open it! Please, don't open it!" She grabbed at Sherman's shoulders, shook him, pleaded with him. He merely watched the guard at work, ignoring her. "Please!" It was as if she didn't even exist.

The door swung open.

Ewan Brewster appeared, sweat-stained and anxious, but otherwise unhurt.

"Finally! After a week in there, getting some fresh air's a nice change of pace!"

"No, no, no!" Rebecca yelled, close to tears. "Close the door! *Please* close the door!"

No one responded to her pleas. No one looked over at her. She may as well have been a phantom.

Rebecca looked down at her hands, and saw that she had her pistol grasped firmly in her left. Her right was balled up in a white-knuckled fist.

"Please," she whispered. A part of her knew what was coming next. "Please, close the door."

"*Get down!*" came a cry from one of the soldiers in the corridor. He fumbled with his sidearm.

"*No,*" Rebecca whispered.

Behind Brewster, a figure rose up, eyes bloodshot, a feral growl emanating from its throat.

Rebecca, lips trembling, felt the pistol in her hand come up until the sights danced before her eyes.

The bloody-eyed figure grabbed Brewster's shoulders, but instead of attacking, it looked up, and fixed Rebecca with a grim stare.

It was Mark Stiles.

"No," repeated Rebecca. "No, not again."

SURVIVORS

Stiles opened his mouth and leaned forward to tear into Brewster.

The pistol in Rebecca's hand bucked. The casing *tinked* off the steel bulkheads, rolled to a stop against her foot. Stiles's head snapped back, and he fell, laying in a twisted heap on the floor, a hole drilled neatly in his forehead.

With a cry, Rebecca turned and heaved the pistol away with all her might, but it wouldn't leave her hands. She couldn't let it go. It stuck to her palms as if coated in glue. Frantic, she beat the weapon against the nearest bulkhead. Try as she might, she couldn't let go of the pistol. She looked down at it, and was horrified to see that a trickle of blood, instead of tendrils of smoke, was dripping from the barrel.

She let fly a scream of grief and terror that echoed throughout the bowels of the ship and beyond.

☆ ☆ ☆ ☆ ☆

Rebecca's eyes flicked open.

Across from her sat the tan filing cabinet with its perfectly positioned but nonfunctional lamp perched atop it, and next to it, her pistol belt. The calendar hung on the wall, just as she had left it.

She used to bolt awake after her nightmares, but over the months she had become so accustomed to them that she no longer shot upright, clutching at anything and feeling short of breath. She still felt the cold sweat that soaked the sheets of the cot, and the frantic beating of her own heart, however. Hardly a night had gone by since her journey on the USS *Ramage* without at least one nightmare plaguing her sleep.

Rebecca felt her teeth chattering, and she willed them to stop. When that failed, she clenched her jaw tightly shut and pulled the thin sheet of the cot up to her chin. She hadn't even remembered falling asleep.

She hoped she hadn't called out in her sleep. She'd done it before, and had been awakened by concerned group members when they were on the road and all slept in the same room. Here, at the Fac, no one would come running. They were all used to it, and some were far enough away down the hall that they might not have heard her at all.

A soft knocking at her door drew her attention. Her eyes flicked in the direction of the noise, but otherwise, she remained perfectly still, curled up on the cot.

"Wha—" she started to say, but found her voice was still quavering from the shock of the nightmare. She took a breath and swallowed to calm herself, and tried again. "What is it?"

The voice outside answered immediately. "It's, uh, me. Mark. I heard you screaming. Are you all right?"

He sounded genuinely concerned. Rebecca closed her eyes and sighed. Of course. Stiles wouldn't have known about her nightmares.

"I—I'm fine," Rebecca said, without opening her eyes. She remembered who it was she had just shot in the dream, and clenched her jaw once more. "I . . . saw a mouse. That's all."

"Oh," Stiles said. "Okay. Just wanted to make sure you were all right. Uh, good night."

Rebecca lay still until she heard Stiles's footsteps fade, and the muffled click as his own door swung shut. There was no way she was going to fall asleep again. She could feel it. The nightmare had been different from the others, and it stuck with her, wiring her awake. She sat upright, letting the covers fall away. She hadn't even bothered to undress before retiring, so she simply rose and walked across the room to the only other piece of furniture it had: a simple wooden desk and swiveling office chair. On the desk, neatly arranged in a row, were medical volumes Anna had given to Rebecca to better learn the nuances of assisting a researcher in BL4.

Rebecca pulled open a desk drawer, withdrew a candle and a book of matches, and lit the former, bathing the desk in a dull glow. She pulled out the third volume, bookmark protruding from the middle, and began to read, trying to lose herself in the text.

CHAPTER 11
CALM BEFORE

Omaha, NE
1 July 2007
0834 hrs_

BELOW, IN THE BL4 laboratory, Anna Demilio was beginning to feel exhaustion setting in. Lack of food and sleep conspired against her. She sat in her blue Chemturion suit on a stool in the lab, staring at the small cage containing the inoculated lab rat. The hiss of air entering her suit from a hanging valve threatened to lull her into a doze. She had always been a sucker for white noise, and the escaping air drowned out lesser sounds.

Slowly, her head slipped forward, hands sliding from her lap to her knees. Only when she had nearly slipped free from the stool did she reawaken with a start, straightening herself out and looking around as if to catch anyone who might have seen her nod off.

"God, what time is it?" Anna muttered behind the thick faceplate of her suit. She couldn't wear a watch into BL4—and even if she could, she wouldn't be able to see it through the suit's protective sleeves. But such was her level of exhaustion that she looked anyway before catching herself and rolling her eyes. She shifted her position to catch a glimpse of the clock hung on the wall, just above the lab's exit doors, and sighed. "Morning again."

Anna swiveled on her stool to face the lab rat's cage once more.

"Well, little buddy, it's been almost a day since you were given some Stiles blood. Time for another sample."

Anna reached into the cage and plucked out the rat. It squirmed in her hand, but she kept a tight hold on it as she fetched a hypodermic with her free limb. A moment later, she had drawn the blood sample and replaced the rodent in its cage.

Blood sample in hand, Anna unhooked her air hose and walked briskly across the lab to a station where a bank of microscopes awaited. Once there, she hooked herself up to a new air nozzle and breathed a sigh of relief as cool air rushed through her Chemturion suit once more.

She spent the next few minutes preparing to view the rat's blood sample, slipping the sample under the telescopic eye of the microscope. She pressed her eye in as close as the suit would allow, squinting to see better. A long moment passed. Anna's mouth fell open slowly.

Anna shot to her feet, knocking the stool behind her to the ground. She turned and ran for the exit, but forgot about the air hose attached to her suit, yanking herself backward. She cursed, her hands trembling in excitement as she ripped the nozzle free and bolted for the decon room. Inside, the spray of disinfectant that washed over her seemed to take hours.

This is big. This is very big.

Finally, the decon showers shut off to a trickle, and the light beside the second exit door blinked over from red to green. Anna shoved it open with her shoulder, tearing the duct tape from the joints of her suit as she went. For a moment, she considered changing back into her regular clothes. She decided against it, pausing only to yank the helmet from her head and toss it on a bench as she passed by on her way out.

The final door to BL4 was opened by access code, both for those entering and exiting. Anna, in her excitement, punched in the wrong code twice before she hit the correct sequence and the heavy steel dead bolts in the door swung back.

Anna tore down the ramp that led to BL4 and through the swinging double doors. She ran past the other biolabs, which the survivors had taken to using for storage and, in the case of BL1, their infirmary. Her feet slapped the floor and echoed in the empty hallway.

As Anna passed BL1, Mason leaned up on his elbow from his bed to see what the commotion was.

"Anna?" he called out. "What's the matter?" Then, noting her odd attire, he added, "Anna, are you all right?"

Anna Demilio didn't answer. She ran right on past the open door-way, and out of sight. She heard Mason say, "Well, good morning to you, too, Doc," before the heavy click of the stairwell door swinging shut cut him off.

Anna took the steps up to the Fac's main floor three at a time, grasping at the handrail as she went. She burst into the hallway, looked left and right, and spotted Francis Sherman just emerging from his room, preparing for the day's outing.

"Frank!" she yelled.

Sherman turned, a surprised look on his face, his hands still working on the last button of his shirt. "Good morning, Anna. What's the—"

"It worked!"

Sherman narrowed his eyes and fixed Anna with a stare. "What worked?"

"It worked! Stiles's blood worked! I injected a rat yesterday and infected it with Morningstar and today I took a blood sample and the immune response is—"

Sherman cut her off. "Whoa! Whoa. Slow down and try again. What happened, now?"

Anna took a deep breath to steady herself. "The experimental vaccine. The one I cultured from Stiles's blood sample. It worked, Frank. It *worked*. The infected rat isn't showing a single symptom. The Morningstar in its bloodstream is still there, but it hasn't infected any of the rat's blood cells. They're fighting off the virus!"

Sherman's face broke into a grin. "You mean we have the vaccine?"

Anna sucked in a breath and glanced at the ground. "Sort of."

Frank frowned at her. "I had a feeling there would be a catch."

"I still need to test it on a human subject," Anna hastened to explain. "I mean, there's still a ton of observation to be done with the rats, too. Rats and people are two different systems, even though they're pretty close, which is why we use the rats in the first place, but I don't know where we can find a human test subject—"

"Just ask for a volunteer," Sherman suggested. "I'm sure any number of us would be willing."

Anna shook her head. "You don't understand, Frank. If something goes wrong in the human test—if the vaccine doesn't take—the volunteer, well . . ."

Frank finished for her. "The volunteer would become one of them."

Anna nodded, and quietly mouthed, "Yes."

A third voice, confident and calm, broke in on the conversation.

"I know where you can get your volunteers."

Anna and Sherman turned. Standing in the doorway to his room was Trevor Westscott, chewing on the end of an unlit cigarette. He had one hand resting in his pocket. The other twirled a pack of paper matches deftly between fingers.

"Who?" asked Anna.

Trev jerked a thumb over his shoulder down the corridor. "Use the prisoners. Maybe Brewster was right after all. Maybe there was a good reason to keep them alive."

Anna looked undecided for a moment, but finally shook her head. "I can't do that."

"You can't?" protested Trev, narrowing his eyes. "Did you forget these are the guys that held guns to your head? The same guys that killed Matt? The same ones that would've killed us all, if we'd given them the chance? Use 'em, I say."

"I can't," repeated Anna. "It'd be . . . unethical. I'd feel like . . . like Dr. Wirths in Auschwitz. No, I need a volunteer."

Trevor sighed and folded his arms across his chest. "It'd be much easier to just stick those two assholes, and to hell with their feelings."

Anna shook her head.

Sherman decided to change the subject. "If you get a human volunteer, how long until you can have the vaccine up and running?"

"Well, if the vaccine works on a human body, then it's already complete. We'd just need to start producing it."

"And what do you need to do that?" Sherman asked.

"I just need to culture some more antibodies from Stiles's blood sample and distribute them into individual doses. I need some incubators and eggs. Chickens? Frank, look, I can't tell you how excited I am right now. These things can take years—decades—to develop. This vaccine is like magic. One day we don't have it—the next day, we've got an immune lab rat. This is like winning the lottery."

Sherman's curiosity was piqued. He called over his shoulder. "Thomas!"

The grizzled NCO poked his head out of a doorway, looking left and right until he spotted Sherman. "Sir?"

"Tell Denton to take over the run today. He's in charge. You and I are going down to the labs. Anna's on to something and I want us both there. Oh, and grab Stiles, just in case. Might need more of his blood. And get Rebecca!" Sherman added. "Maybe she can help."

Trevor, meanwhile, had turned back to his room, yanking equipment from a battered wooden chest at the foot of his makeshift cot. He muttered to himself.

✫ ✫ ✫ ✫ ✫

The group that assembled in the Fac's entry hall was slimmer than usual.

Brewster, shouldering an empty knapsack, grimaced at the head count. "We're missing some people," he muttered.

"Yeah," added Denton. "Where's Frank? And Thomas? I thought we were all going out on this run. Risking all our asses at once, as it always is, eh?"

"Me, too," muttered Brewster, checking the barrels of his shotgun to make certain they were loaded. He snapped the break-action closed with a metallic click, satisfied. "I suppose rank has its privileges."

The twin doors leading deeper into the Fac swung open, pushed apart by Command Sergeant Major Thomas. His expression was blank.

"Change of plans," he said in his trademark growl. "Sherman is indisposed, and won't be joining us today. Stiles!"

Mark Stiles, busily sorting through a box of assorted equipment liberated from the surrounding buildings, stopped and looked up. "Sergeant Major?"

"Drop what you're doing and hoof it downstairs to the BL wing. Sherman and Demilio want you there, ASAP. Where's Hall?" asked Thomas, hands on his hips, eyes scanning the room.

"Here," came Rebecca's soft voice from the corner. She was curled up in a chair, her face buried in a six-month-old magazine. She'd read it enough times that she could nearly recite the articles verbatim, but she read on, anyway.

"That goes for you, too. BL4. Sherman and Demilio will be waiting on both of you. Come on, come on, we don't have all day!" Thomas ordered, gesturing toward the doors.

Rebecca tossed the magazine on an end table and stood lazily, stretching, a yawn escaping her lips. "All right, all right. I'm going."

Stiles held the swinging doors open for the young medic. She passed through without a word of thanks. Casting a bemused glance over his shoulder at the other survivors, Stiles followed Rebecca, letting the door swing shut behind him. The pair walked off down the hallway together, heading for the stairs that led to the biosafety laboratories below.

"Guess you're in charge, then, eh, Thomas?" asked Denton with a grin. "Seeing as Sherman's unavailable."

"No," drawled Thomas, crossing his arms across his chest. "They want me down there, too. You're in charge."

The Canadian seemed taken aback. "Wait—what, me? I'm a photographer! I can't lead worth hell. Pick Brewster or something."

Brewster quickly shook his head. "Oh, no. No, no, no. That never works out well. Once, in Basic, they made me squad leader. Lasted a whole day. No."

"What happened?" asked Jack, a grin on his lips.

Brewster opened his mouth to reply, thought better of it, and shook his head. "You wouldn't believe me if I told you. But they took me out as squad leader that same night. Let's just leave it at that, okay?"

Jack shrugged.

"At least I finally get to go see some action," said Junko Koji, shouldering a knapsack of her own and strapping a pistol belt around her slim waist. "It's about time I got to go out."

Thomas frowned. "Sorry, Juni. We still need someone to watch the front doors."

Juni froze, and fixed Thomas with a look that might have melted a lesser man into a steaming puddle. Her voice was acid. "Frank said every available hand. I'm an available hand. I'm going."

"No, you're not," said Thomas. "Orders."

"I'm not in your goddamned Army!" shouted Juni. "Your orders don't mean shit to me!"

The rest of the occupants of the room had fallen silent, and were watching the back-and-forth intently, as might a group of tennis spectators.

"And if you go," said Thomas, calmly, "who'll let us back in when we return?"

"Get someone else to do it. The new guy isn't going, what's his name, Allen. Let him handle the doors. Why is it always me?"

"You're the youngest. You're the least experienced. I could go on," said Thomas.

Juni threw up her arms in exasperation. "This is bullshit. That's b-u-l-l-s-h-i-t, bullshit. I can handle myself out there!"

"Nobody's doubting you, Juni."

"Sure seems that way." The slight Japanese girl sulked down into a cushioned chair and folded her arms across her chest. "Fine. But don't expect to get in without using the right password, this time."

"Okay," said Denton, drawing in a breath, the weight of command settling squarely on his shoulders. "Gear up. Empty packs, and weapons and ammo. First aid kits?"

"Got mine," said Brewster.

"In a cargo pocket," chimed Jack.

"Okay!" Mitsui threw a thumbs-up.

"All right, gents and ladies, let's get to it," said Denton. "Remember, we're just making a circuit around the outer block, then heading straight back in. Get anything you can—especially food."

"We know, man, we know," said Brewster, buckling a vest across his chest. He tucked a Beretta into the cross-draw holster on the breast of the garment, nodded, and looked back at Denton. "We'll all make it back."

Denton nodded in agreement. "Especially if we all watch our backs. Keep an eye on any shadowy spots. You know how those infected bastards like to lurk in there."

Nods all around.

"Okay. Any final questions?"

No hands were raised.

"Let's get to it, gang."

A moment later, sunlight streamed into the Fac's reception room. The foraging party moved out.

★ ★ ★ ★ ★

"Sawyer, Delaney. Lots of activity out front of the target's entrance. Looks like a whole group of them exiting the building, over."

Sawyer was on the outskirts of Omaha, urinating against a rusting pickup truck. He cursed, shook, and zippered the front of his black BDU trousers. It took him a moment to answer, but eventually he clicked the handset of his radio.

"How many, over?"

"Uh, hard to get a count, sir. They're all bunched up," was Delaney's reply. "I want to say all of them. Let me see. Looks like half a dozen, sir, over."

"Their direction, over?"

"Uh, they're splitting up, sir. Half heading north, the other half east. Looks like they're out scavenging for more supplies, sir. Over."

Jackals that they are, Sawyer thought to himself. Picking at leftovers.

"Shall we engage, sir? Sadler has a sight picture on one of them right now. We could—"

SURVIVORS

"Negative, negative," came Sawyer's response. His first serious read had been Sun Tzu's *The Art of War.* Divide and conquer, the old master had advised. Sawyer had taken the words to heart. "Hold fire. We've got them where we want them, now. There should only be a few people left in that building. One of them will be Anna Demilio. We should know their door code by now. Get the men ready. We're about to move into town. Sawyer, out."

"Yes, sir!" came the enthusiastic reply. "Mustering the men. Out."

☆ ☆ ☆ ☆ ☆

Denton had split the foraging group into two. With him, he had Mbutu and Trevor. The other group consisted of Brewster, Jack, and Mitsui. The plan was to swing around in a pincer, searching building after building, then meet up finally at an intersection two miles from the Fac.

Denton found the streets eerie, even in broad daylight. He felt like ghosts of the past were all around him. Sale signs still hung in dirt-streaked windows, and cars still lined the sidewalks, parking meters all in the red. It always felt to him as though time had stopped one day, that human beings had simply vanished, and left behind these eclectic tombstones to mark their passing.

"It is a nice day," said Mbutu, breaking the silence. Denton liked Mbutu's way of talking. It sounded proper, perfect. He enunciated each syllable, each letter. It had a calming effect on the photojournalist. "In Kenya, a nice day meant it was hot, but not so hot you couldn't go outside. Here, a hot day is like early spring in Mombasa. Cooling to the skin. Refreshing."

"I'm glad you like it," said Trev, wiping sweat from his forehead as he trudged along the asphalt. "To me, this is what a taste of hell must be like. Too goddamn hot."

Ahead of the trio was a line of town houses, each one identical to its neighbor. Denton eyed them, and decided it was as good a place as any to start.

"All right," he said. "We'll go in one by one, starting with the one on the far left, there, with the red mailbox. Work our way down, and meet up with the other group."

Mbutu and Trev nodded.

"Remember," cautioned Denton, "these infected can be tricky. Watch your corners. Check the floors for crawlers. Don't open any locked doors without backup."

"We know the drill, Denton," said Trev, unstrapping his pistol. He preferred to use his snap-out baton to mete out justice on the infected he encountered, but indoors, the pistol was the better choice.

The trio approached the first door.

"Okay, gents, here we go," said Denton. He leaned back and gave a mighty kick aimed at the door frame. It shuddered, but held. Chagrined, he turned to his comrades. "Little help?"

With all three working together, the door burst free from its hinges in short order, revealing a narrow, white-painted hall with thin carpeting.

Denton dropped his voice to a whisper. "Mbutu, cover the stairs. Trev, come with me. Let's clear the first floor."

Trev nodded and followed a few steps behind Denton. Behind them, Mbutu Ngasy settled in at the foot of the stairs, his weapon aimed at the landing above.

Denton and Trev stalked through the first floor of the town house, weapons at the ready. They walked silently, heel to toe, glancing around corners and eyeing the floor for disabled shamblers. They saw none. The place appeared pristine. No blood marred the tile or carpet, no streaks of gore marked the walls.

"Place seems clean," whispered Denton.

"Don't drop your guard," returned Trevor. "These things have a way of catching you with your pants down."

"Amen, brother."

A quick search of the ground floor revealed little. The pantries in the kitchen held scant goods. The biggest find was a can of creamed corn, which Denton reluctantly stuffed in his knapsack.

The pair returned to the entry hall, where Mbutu Ngasy was still on watch, rifle pointed upstairs. He hadn't moved.

"Any activity?" Denton asked.

"No," said Mbutu, narrowing his eyes at the stairwell. "But I keep hearing something up there."

Weapons snapped up.

"What was it?" asked Denton.

"I do not know," admitted Mbutu. "A creaking noise. Not footsteps."

"All right," said Denton. "Let's check it out. Slowly, now. Careful, people. Careful."

The trio began the ascent. The town houses were fairly new, and the stairs were silent underfoot. At the top of the stairs, a hall ran in both directions. This close, all three survivors could hear the noise Mbutu had mentioned. It repeated itself at intervals, a steady creak.

"What is that?" muttered Trev.

"Shh!" admonished Denton. "Could be a carrier."

The three zeroed in on the noise. It seemed to be coming from one of the bedrooms.

Denton pointed at Mbutu, then gestured across the doorway. Mbutu nodded, changed positions, and took aim at the door. Trevor took up a spot directly in front of the portal, while Denton, kneeling, reached out a hand to grasp the doorknob.

The creaking noise had grown louder. They were right on top of it.

"Open it!" said Trev, leveling the barrel of his pistol at the doorway.

Denton twisted the knob and shoved the door inward.

Revealed was an average suburban bedroom. It wouldn't have appeared out of place in a home fashion catalog, complete with pure white down comforters and lacey curtains overhanging the windows.

The only difference in the otherwise picturesque room was the body that hung from the ceiling fan in the middle of it, swaying slightly from side to side, the thick rope tied around the victim's neck creaking with each movement. A toppled chair lay on the floor beneath the corpse.

Mbutu averted his eyes.

The flesh on the body was brown, desiccated. It had been hanging for weeks, maybe months. The eyes were sunken pits, and the lips had pulled back into a macabre grimace, exposing teeth. Despite the decay, it was obvious that the body had once been a woman.

"We should cut her down," intoned Denton, pulling a folding knife from his belt and moving toward the body.

"Wait," said Mbutu, his eyes narrowing. He held out a hand to steady Denton. "She is not right."

"What do you—"

A moment later, the woman's arms shot out, grasping for Denton. He stumbled backward, caught by Trevor before he could fall. A low growl escaped the woman's lips.

"Jesus," whispered Denton. "She hung herself before she turned. But it got her anyway. Son of a bitch."

Trevor stepped forward, his ASP snapping out in one smooth motion. "I'll take care of it."

Denton averted his eyes. Mbutu looked on. Trevor wound up and swung the baton at the hanging woman's skull. It sunk in with a sickening crack, and the body fell limp, unmoving, swaying gently from the rope wrapped tightly around its neck.

"Rest in peace," said Mbutu.

"Demons don't rest in peace," said Trev, wiping his baton on the white bedsheets, leaving behind streaks of reddish brown. "They burn."

Mbutu remained silent. The three men stood a moment in the room where the woman hung, their heads bowed. It was yet another reminder of the hell that surrounded them. None wanted to dwell upon it.

A longer moment passed before Denton snapped out of it, turning to face his comrades. "Well, that's it for this place. Let's move on to the next town house. Maybe we'll find something better there."

"We can only hope," whispered Mbutu.

1 July 2007
1009 hrs_

The sun rose once again into a cloudless sky, portending another beautiful day. Krueger came strolling along, weapon in tow, on his way to climb the grain lift to watch over the scavengers on their way in and out. He saw Hal wander outside to inspect the radio antenna he'd spent the night working on.

He stood, motionless, for several minutes, hands planted on his hips. His only movement came from his eyes, scanning the structure up and down through narrowed slits.

Krueger noted Hal's automaton-like behavior and deviated his course, walking over to stand next to the older man. He watched him intensely a moment, then followed Hal's gaze; he was scrutinizing the steel tower.

When he could stand it no longer, the sharpshooter spoke. "Anything I can help you with, sir?" Krueger asked with raised eyebrows.

Hal didn't answer for a moment, then dropped his arms and turned to face the soldier.

"She's doable," was Hal Dorne's conclusion upon inspecting the rusting radio tower. "Just needs a little more TLC."

"You're gonna end up with a bunch of one-way conversations, even if you do get it working," said Krueger, slinging his rifle over his shoulder.

Hal shrugged. "It'll keep me busy."

"You could always volunteer to help reinforce the perimeter," suggested Krueger. "We all take turns filling sandbags and digging a trench outside the—"

Hal laughed him off. "I put in more than twenty years so I could avoid having to shovel dirt into sandbags. No, I think I'll tinker with this baby a while longer, see what else I can get her to do. I've got some tools. Been broadcasting all night, really. It's just, there's no way to know how far out we're getting."

Krueger grinned. "Good luck. You need any help, you know where I'll be."

"Right above me. Don't drop anything on me, kid. I may be retired, but I don't have health insurance."

Grinning, Krueger began the long ascent to the top of the grain elevator, where a small rounded platform allowed him to sit comfortably with a perfect view of the surrounding area. Krueger was a born sharpshooter. He claimed to have never picked up a firearm before joining the military, but found his calling on the range. He took excellent care of the scoped .30-06 he'd acquired in Hyattsburg, and maintained the boast that he only kept track of his misses. He only had to remember the number four. He knew the survivors always felt an added degree of comfort when he climbed the tower.

Allen was the second guard on duty, taking his place on the roof of the Fac. Night watches both took the roof, but in the daylight, they split up, with the better rifleman on higher ground.

★ ★ ★ ★ ★

Downstairs, in the biosafety level four laboratory, Dr. Anna Demilio carefully pushed the tip of a delicate hypodermic into a vial of dark blue liquid. She'd been successful in preparing Stiles's blood sample, and was ready to try out the prototype vaccine. The hiss of air in her suit distracted her, but she pushed the annoyance to the back of her mind.

In front of her was a clear plastic cage, and scurrying about within were half a dozen white lab rats.

When Anna had first begun in medicine, she'd felt terrible about injecting the innocent rodents with deadly diseases and experimental cures. Now she was just numb to it. They had their part to play. Reaching into the cage, she plucked free one of the squealing rodents and jabbed the hypodermic into the creature. It squealed again, and then fell silent as Anna retracted the needle. She placed the rodent back in the cage, then turned.

For the benefit of the tape recording her research, she spoke out loud. "Injection of prototype vaccine at eleven hundred hours."

Behind her, resting on a countertop, were vials similar to those containing the dark blue fluid. The only difference was that this batch was dyed a brilliant red. These were samples of the Morningstar strain, cultured in the very lab in which she stood.

Anna peeled back the plastic wrapping from a second hypodermic and inserted it into one of the tubes. She drew back on the plunger, filling it with a small amount of the deadly living liquid.

She turned back to the rat cage. The rodent she had injected previously had taken to its exercise wheel. No matter. She was after a different rat, one that had yet to be injected with anything. Her hand shot out, but her target was too quick, scurrying out of the way. Anna managed to corner the rodent and picked it up, jabbing it with the needle and pressing the plunger.

Anna glanced at the clock as she replaced the rodent in its cage, and spoke again. "Injection of Morningstar strain at eleven-oh-three hours. Maximum exposure. Estimate one hour until symptoms manifest."

It actually took far less than an hour for the rodent to turn on its fellows. The first to be attacked happened to be nearest, lapping at a water dispenser. The infected rat and its victim rolled over and over, until finally the infected rodent broke free, leaving behind a gasping, bloodied rat in its wake. Anna frowned. The wounded creature would fall victim to the same viral curse shortly.

Again and again the infected rat attacked its former comrades in captivity. One by one, they fell. Finally, only the inoculated rat remained.

Anna leaned forward in her seat. It was the moment of truth. The inoculated rat would certainly be bitten, but would it turn? That was the question.

The pair faced off in a corner of the cage. The infected rat didn't hesitate. It charged straight at the inoculated rodent. Another flurry of fighting ensued, and with much the same aftermath: the bitten, bleeding inoculated rat lay wounded and winded, while the infected rodent staggered off in search of fresh prey.

Quickly, Anna reached into the cage and plucked out the inoculated rat, placing it in a separate observation cage. She would have to wait and see if it began to exhibit symptoms of Morningstar. If it didn't . . . well, only time would give her that answer.

Anna picked up the cage containing the infected rats, walked over to a drawer in the wall marked INCINERATOR, and dumped it in, letting the heavy steel door swing shut behind her. Then she returned to her seat in front of the inoculated rat, folded her gloved hands across her lap, and waited.

★ ★ ★ ★ ★

Behind the Fac, across from each other in the grassy yard, sat Mark Stiles and Rebecca Hall. Rebecca had her hands clasped around her knees, drawn up tight against her chest, and Stiles lounged on his side, picking at blades of grass.

"Okay," he said, picking his words. "What's the best place you've ever been?"

"The best place?" repeated Rebecca, a thoughtful look crossing her face. "Honestly? Home. There are things about home I never really noticed until after I left. The way it smells. The routines. The sticky back door. My mother kept a little garden in the backyard. Every summer she'd make strawberry jam. I'd help her can it. We're far enough away from everyone else that in the winter, when it snows, you can forget you're even on earth. Everything's perfectly still. Perfectly quiet. Yeah. Home's the best place I've ever been."

Stiles nodded. "Sounds really nice."

"It's probably burned down by now," said Rebecca, her eyes downcast. "I don't even know if my mother's still alive."

"Hey!" said Stiles. "That's not how we play the game! Only happy memories, right?"

Rebecca took a moment to answer. "Right. Sorry."

Stiles looked at the young woman a moment longer. When she didn't reply, he spoke out: "It's your turn to ask."

"Right," Rebecca said. She sat silent for a while, then looked up. "What was your best moment?"

"What do you mean?" asked Stiles. "You mean, in my whole life?"

Becky nodded.

"That's easy," grinned Stiles. "Running that diversion in Hyatts-burg. I mean, I was sure I was dead, but what a death! Saving lives by giving my own . . . I don't know if that kind of opportunity will ever come around again. Most of us don't even get it once. And half the ones who do just stand there and let it pass them by. It sounds twisted, right? But we're surrounded by senseless death, everywhere. My death was going to mean something. So, yeah. That was my best moment."

"It's a good best moment," said Rebecca. A smile tugged at the corner of her lips. "We might not have made it out, otherwise."

"And I couldn't have made the run without you," added Stiles, placing his hand on Rebecca's arm.

Rebecca abruptly recoiled, drawing her legs back farther and tightening her grip around her knees. "That was just my job. I already told you, you don't owe me anything."

Before Stiles could muster a reply, Rebecca had picked herself up off the ground and dusted off the back of her pants.

"I'm sorry—really—but I should go see what Anna's doing downstairs."

Stiles sat in the grass a long minute after Rebecca had departed, staring at the ground.

After a while, the sound of rustling metal drew the soldier's attention, and he looked up and across the fenced-in section of the Fac's backyard. Just beyond the fence, partially obscured by the chain links, he spied Hal Dorne, busily picking through a toolbox. Next to the retired mechanic was the rusted-out radio shack. The older man really was making a go of it.

Stiles picked himself up from off the ground with a sigh and walked over to the fence. He hooked his fingers through the links and squinted at Hal.

Hal cast a glance over his shoulder, spotting his visitor. "Hiya, Stiles. Figured on making myself useful. It's not in bad shape, you know," he added, glancing once more at the soldier. "Just needed some rewiring, mainly."

"One good windstorm will knock that sucker over," Stiles said, eyeing the rusted metal supports.

"Oh, she'll hold," said Hal, patting the pockmarked struts. "She's held this long, hasn't she?"

"Why don't you just build us one of those rail guns you're always talking about?" Stiles asked, heaving a curious shrug. "You're always on and on about them."

"Why? Because I already built the damn thing," muttered Hal, yanking a wire stripper from his toolbox. "Where's the fun in building something twice? You already know what it takes to make it work. That, mister, is what took all the fun out of being a tank mechanic. Always the same goddamn problems every time. It got boring. Imagine twenty years of fixing the same shit, over and over again! No, sir. Not for me."

"All I'm saying is we could use a quiet gun around here. Be great for keeping the perimeter clear. Wouldn't attract any noise."

Hal stopped in place. He dropped the wire strippers and the claw hammer he'd added to his hands on the ground next to the toolbox. He stalked over to the fence until he was a scant three feet from Stiles and fixed him with a narrow-eyed stare.

"Tell you what, pal-o-mine, you got three options right now."

"Yeah?" asked Stiles, a grin on his face. He knew Hal well enough to know that the annoyed attitude was a facade.

"One: you can go find me some car batteries. New ones! Not some half-assed, drained, used POSes. I suppose I could rig up something useful with them—something better than a one-shot magnet gun."

"Okay." Stiles shrugged. "And option two?"

"You go out and get this town's power plant back on line so I can plug into a wall outlet somewhere. You do that, and I'll feel generous enough to work on a new rail gun for you."

Stiles shrugged. "Okay, I get your point. There's not enough powder in the barrel."

Hal shrugged. "That's a fine way of putting it, yeah. So I'm rebuilding a dispatch station instead." With that, the older man turned away and crouched down next to his tool bag.

"Wait a second," said Stiles, holding up his finger. "What's the third option?"

Hal half-turned to fix Stiles with a stare. "That's you, going to get me a length of copper wiring from that industrial shed over there, so I can get this stupid thing really ticking again."

Stiles looked over his shoulder. He spotted the storage shed in the distance. "What? Really?"

"Yes, really!" shooed Hal. "I'm retired. I don't have time to bullshit. Come on, come on, this thing isn't going to upgrade itself!"

Mark Stiles, unsure as to how he'd become pressed into duty as a wire-fetcher, strode off across the fenced-in courtyard, his thoughts more on a withdrawn young medic than the rusting dispatch station or its eccentric benefactor.

With a wandering mind, he passed under the grain lift and headed for the metal shed Hal had pointed out.

★ ★ ★ ★

Above Stiles, Krueger perched on the round metal platform that sat alongside the top of the grain elevator. He'd placed rusted-out, empty metal drums along the outer edges of the space, rendering him nearly invisible from the ground.

Usually Krueger spent his downtime reading, or dozing with his rifle across his chest.

Not today. Today, Krueger was on the hunt.

"That's right, bitches," Krueger whispered, eyes fixed on his scope. "Sergeant Carlos Hathcock is taking aim at the enemy. It's a long way off. Winds are off the chart. There's no way anyone could make this shot. No one . . . but me."

Krueger mouthed the word "Blam!" and jerked his rifle back in a passable imitation of recoil.

Half a mile away, the wooden clothesline he had been aiming at stood resolute, unaware of its brief role as target.

Krueger threw up his arms. "He's done it! Hathcock takes down Ho Chi Minh with a single bullet! The Vietnam War is over!"

"Ahem."

The sudden interruption brought Krueger to an immediate halt. He dropped his arms, a guilty grin crossing his face.

Juni stared at him from the top rung of the ladder. "I won't ask."

"Hey, come on, Carlos Hathcock happens to be one of the best snipers who ever lived, okay?" Krueger said, then sulkily added, "Besides, can't a guy have a little fun now and then?"

"Here's lunch, *Vasili*," said Juni, tossing a plastic-wrapped sandwich to Krueger. The sharpshooter caught it easily, then eyed the contents.

"Do I want to know what's in it?"

"Fried Spam."

"I just decided I don't want to know what's in it," Krueger said with a grimace. He tucked the sandwich away for later.

"Sorry. Maybe next time it'll be roast beef," said Juni, with a smile.

"Sure, and maybe it'll be ant loaf."

Juni began the slow climb down the grain elevator, and when her feet touched dirt, she headed for the Fac's rear entrance. It was just past noon, and it was her turn on kitchen duty. The pickings might be slim, but she didn't want to disappoint.

✮ ✮ ✮ ✮ ✮

"Excellent," Sawyer said into his radio. "You just make sure you hold off until you get the word. I don't want anything ruining my surprise party for these bastards."

Sawyer, putting the radio away with a wide grin, turned to see his second in command arrive. "Huck," he said, motioning the lieutenant over. "Talk to me about our preparations."

Lieutenant Finnegan didn't quite roll his eyes, but it took every inch of military bearing he possessed.

"The advance units are all in place, sir. Our men are seeding themselves into Omaha and should be in their assigned spots by sixteen hundred. Minimal contact with infected, as was expected. I haven't gotten a report from the team you sent to Offutt AFB—"

"I have," Sawyer said. "They have accomplished their objective and are on hot standby. Then we get Mason and Sherman and whoever the fuck else is in there and punch their tickets. The men are clear on this point, correct? Everyone in that facility, with the sole exception of Dr. Anna Demilio, is to be exterminated on contact."

"Yes, sir," Lieutenant Finnegan said. "Will that be all?"

"No," Sawyer said. "Find Lutz and his band of idiots. Make sure they're not in position to fuck any of this up."

✮ ✮ ✮ ✮ ✮

He was dying, he knew that much for sure. He had to be. Why else would his life be flashing before his eyes?

It was his first day on the USS *Ramage*. This was a day that he was sure he'd remember for a long, long time. He walked up the long gangplank, keeping one hand on the handrail, feeling the ropes holding the ship's banner tied to it. USS RAMAGE (DDG-61) it said. *Par excellence*. When he got to the top, he said, "Request permission to come aboard. Commander John Harris, reporting for duty."

The young quarterdeck watch nearly twisted himself in half, trying to decide what to do next. He knew that they were expecting a new executive officer, and that the new XO's name would be Harris, so he was torn between giving a quick salute and greeting to the Commander or piping him aboard over the 1MC, the general announcing system.

Luckily for him, the Officer of the Deck came to his rescue and sent one of the messengers to alert the CO that his new second in command was reporting. Then he stepped forward and greeted Harris. It was Rico, alive and well.

This is how I know I'm dying, Harris thought. Rico wasn't the OOD. He was never the OOD.

"The captain is on board and waiting for you, sir. I assume you're familiar with the *Arleigh Burke* class destroyer?"

"I am. Does that mean I don't get the pre-report tour?"

"Sir, no, sir. We have everything ready for you, Commander."

John Harris smiled then, ready to get to work. He'd put a lot of time in on other ships, and this was his next-to-last trip before a command of his own. Had it all been worth it? He'd asked himself that question many times over his long career. Time missed with family and loved ones, events that he would never get another chance at, days spent hunched over a manual, back when he was a junior officer, or overseeing a gang of blueshirts performing repairs in the engine room. So much time spent on these islands of steel.

Instead of following Rico into the ship; he walked to the handrail and looked out to the sea. It was true, what they said: once you got it in your blood, it would always be a part of you. The siren song of the open ocean, calling you back.

He turned and looked back over the deck and saw himself ready to leave. With something of a start, he realized that was the day they'd abandoned ship.

I don't get any of the good memories in between, then?

"Secure that weapon," he said. "Double-knot those boots, son, what do you want to do, have them come off in the mud?" He raised his hands and his voice, as if beseeching the Almighty. "Oh, Jesus, give me strength, sailor! You wear the damn webgear like *this*."

From the corner of his eye he spotted Hal, snickering at the sailors. Harris snorted at Hal's expression. *He probably thinks he's got that smirk concealed.* He continued up and down the line, dressing down whoever needed it.

The greatest journey of his life was about to begin.

CHAPTER 12
THE STORM

Omaha, NE
1 July 2007
1734 hrs_

BY THE TIME JUNI rang the dinner bell, the sun had settled behind a group of clouds, blunting its glare.

The survivors filed in, some from the yard, others from their rooms, and took up their places in the break room. All were present save Anna, still working in the lab below, and Krueger, who had elected to remain behind and keep a watch while the others ate. With the sandwich to tide him over, he was perfectly willing to settle for leftovers. Hal and Stone were still at the dispatch shack, plugging away.

"What's on the menu tonight, beautiful?" Brewster said with a grin as he filed into the break room. "No, wait, let me guess. It's either Spam or more pasta."

Juni planted a hand on her hip and fixed Brewster with a disapproving stare. "That's just about all we have, Brewster." Her attitude brightened. "But I think you'll like what I've done with the stuff."

Juni presented the ragtag group with a steaming bowl of noodles, mixed with bits of green and red.

"What is this?" sniffed Brewster.

Juni looked hurt. "Vegetable pasta. We had some cans sitting around, so I added them in. There's corn, and potatoes, and peas. Eat it. It's good. I already tried it."

Brewster eyed the dish a moment, shrugged, and helped himself to a serving. "Dinner might be monotonous around here, but at least there *is* a dinner."

"That's the attitude we're looking for," Sherman said in approval, grinning.

"I don't know," said Jack the Welder, forking up mouthfuls of the dish. "I kind of like it. Nice work, Juni. You can be the cook every night, in my book."

Pleased, Juni managed a half bow. "Thank you. At least *someone* appreciates it." She smacked the back of Brewster's head as she passed, causing him to choke on a mouthful of vegetables.

"Ow," he managed after swallowing, rubbing at his head.

"Maybe this will make you feel better," she said, coming back with a handful of dark croutons. He eyed them for a moment as she dumped them onto his plate.

"Wow, Juni," he said, momentarily touched. "Thanks, really. I didn't—"

"Shh," she said, looking at him sweetly. "Just eat."

With a wide smile, Brewster dug into his plate. He scooped some pasta into his mouth and worked at it, the beatific expression on his face slowly changing to confusion.

"These are kind of crunchy. They kind of . . ."

"Make you want to sit up and beg?" she asked, and Thomas, who could no longer hold it, let go with a belly laugh that none of the group had ever heard from him.

"Fucking dog food," Brewster said, and Thomas laughed even harder. Sherman was so surprised, even he stopped eating. He, Denton, Jack, and Trev all stared at Thomas.

"What?" he asked, the laughing finally tapering off. "I don't get to laugh, ever?"

Denton shook his head. "Never thought I'd see the day."

Mbutu Ngasy smiled widely and dug into his dinner. "Good omen to start a meal with happiness."

"Happiness and dog food," Brewster moaned, which started Thomas off again.

"Jesus Christ, it really is the end of the world," Denton said.

While the survivors were all grouped together, Sherman took the opportunity to remind them of their upcoming foray into Omaha. "Remember, folks, get to bed early tonight. We'll be heading out once the sun is fully up so we'll have plenty of daylight to work with."

"We remember, Frank," said Denton. "The supply run to end all supply runs."

"At least for a while," added Jack.

"Until we eat it all," agreed Brewster.

"In any case," Sherman went on, oblivious to the banter, "make sure you're ready to go before oh-nine. The earlier we get started, the longer we have to search."

"Your wish is my order, oh three-starred one," said Brewster, which would normally earn him an irate look from Thomas. That day, however, the sergeant major just smiled.

"Woof," he said.

✮ ✮ ✮ ✮

Deep in the Fac, Anna was laughing.

All by herself in the BL4 lab, and encumbered in her Chemturion suit, she did a rough approximation of a happy dance. The rat bitten that morning was wounded pretty badly, but . . . no signs of turning.

"Come here, you little survivor, you," she cooed as she tried to grab hold of the little rat. A blood sample would tell her for sure what she dared to hope.

Finally grabbing on to the squirming rodent, she stuck it with a hypodermic and sucked some of its blood into the clear chamber. Her next thought was to dump the rat into the incinerator with the rest of its brothers, but something stayed her hand.

At first, she thought maybe it was errant sentimentality. Should the rat survive Morningstar only to be consumed by fire? She shook her head. Maybe she was just tired. She shook her head again.

"I'm always tired. What is it?"

Like a bizarre statue, she stood there with a full syringe in one hand and a squealing lab rat in the other, lost in thought. Her eyes closed and opened, alternately scanning the room and looking over the body of the rat, all its wounds . . .

"The wounds!" she practically screamed. "The fucking wounds! Why won't Stiles's leg bite heal up? What about the arm?" She eyed the rat carefully. "Why am I asking you, you might be wondering? Well, I'll tell you, Ralph," she said, leaning her hip against a stainless steel counter. "If I can heal you, I can heal him. If I can heal him . . . well, shit. I can heal anyone. Back you go."

She put Ralph the Rodent back into his cage and closed it, turning to take a closer look at the blood in her hands.

One hour and a triple-check later, Dr. Demilio came out of the BL4 labs at a run once again. "Frank!" she shouted. "Come look at this!"

She burst into the improvised Situation Room, where Sherman and Thomas were going over the map of the local area with Denton.

"Frank!" she said. "Come on. Grab Stiles and Becky. You too, Thomas. You need to see *this*."

★ ★ ★ ★ ★

Mbutu and Brewster were taking their turn on the Fac's roof, pulling guard duty. Unaware of the ecstatic discovery about to be shared below them, the pair had settled in for a long night's shift.

"I hate night shifts," lamented Brewster. "Nothing ever happens."

"I prefer them," said Mbutu. "Nothing ever happens."

"Krueger snagged a shambler yesterday. How much you want to bet we don't see a single one?"

Mbutu chuckled, but didn't reply.

A distant pop drew the attention of the rooftop guards, and they both peered over the edge to locate the source of the noise. They could hear a fizzling overhead, and a moment later, a bright orange flare lit up the twilight, suspended by a parachute. It lit up the entire block.

"What the fuck?" wondered Brewster. "Where'd that come from?"

A moment later, a second flare popped in midair, joining the first in lazy flight.

★ ★ ★ ★ ★

At that moment, something came over the radio in response to Hal Dorne's frequent queries. He and Stone sat straight up in the radio shack and eyed the speakers, then looked at each other.

"What do we do?" Stone asked.

"Shit if I know! You go tell someone, and I'll keep trying to raise them," Hal said, smacking the radio apparatus with one hand and gripping the mic with the other.

"Right," Stone said, running from the shack.

As he got outside, he saw the flares, as well as the silhouettes of Brewster and Mbutu on the roof. "Hey! Hey . . . uh, Brewster!"

"Huh? Oh, hey, Stone!"

"Yes, Stone! Hal says he caught something on the radio."

Pointing at the lazily descending flares, Brewster said, "Do you think that's them?"

"Could be. Should we go out and see?"

Brewster shook his head. "I can't make that call, man."

Stone put his hands up. "Well, who can, then?"

★ ★ ★ ★ ★

"I'm sorry about all the rigmarole," apologized Dr. Anna Demilio. "But you have to wear the suits into BL4 or you'll be exposed to . . . well, I'm not even sure you want to know what else is in here besides Morningstar."

Sherman, tugging one of the blue Chemturion suits on in BL4's staging area, nodded in agreement. "I wouldn't mind staying in the dark."

Thomas, meanwhile, seemed frustrated with his own suit, grumbling as he pulled it on. "I never signed up to be no goddamn astronaut."

"You get used to them," said Anna, rolling duct tape around the joints of her gloves. "After a while, you don't even realize you're wearing them."

"I don't know," said Stiles, flexing his arms to get a feel for the Chemturion. "Kind of makes me feel like a space marine."

"That's not far from the truth," said Anna, checking her seals. "You're all about to enter a completely contained environment. We keep it under negative air pressure, so if there are any leaks, air flows in, not out. It's totally sealed off from the outside world. Once you're inside, you have to hook up to air hoses pumping clean atmo from outside the lab. You can't breathe the air in there. It's contaminated. It's the closest thing to being in space you'll ever get to experience, short of an actual shuttle ride."

Rebecca, also present, worked her way into her suit without a word of complaint. She'd been through the procedure a dozen times working with Anna, and knew precisely what to expect.

"All right," said Anna, satisfied that her group had suited up safely and securely. "Next we go through decon."

Sherman grunted. "I thought this was decon."

Anna chuckled. "Oh, no, sir, we don't take any chances when it comes to these bugs. BL4 agents, I mean. There's a whole mess of security to pass through before we're in the lab."

Sherman shrugged. "Lead on. I'm in over my head here."

Thomas grunted in agreement.

"It's not so bad," said Stiles. "Seems pretty fun. And good company, too." He glanced at Rebecca, but she stared straight ahead, ignoring the soldier.

"Decon shower," said Anna, pulling open a door and gesturing into the compartment within. "Everyone inside."

SURVIVORS

The party made their way into the decon chamber. Anna pulled the door shut behind them, and a bright green light on the wall clicked over to a dim red, bathing the room in a dull glow.

For a moment, nothing happened. The occupants stood silently, waiting.

Stiles found his voice first. "Is something supposed to—"

Jets of disinfectant sprayed out from nozzles on the wall, drenching the occupants in moments.

"Oh," added Stiles, wiping disinfectant from the faceplate of his suit. "Never mind."

After a brace of minutes, the showers shut off, leaving the occupants of the narrow room soaked and dripping disinfectant onto the grated floor. Stiles felt thankful for the suit. Inside, he remained dry as a bone.

"What next?" asked Sherman.

"Next? Just open the door. We're clear to enter," said Anna, gesturing at the heavy metal door at the far end of the decon chamber. The red light on the wall had changed back over to bright green.

Sherman pushed open the heavy portal.

Tiled floors and walls gave the impression of impeccable hygiene, and every instrument on each of the numerous counters was placed just so, inches apart from one another. Everything was neatly ordered.

"Welcome back to BL4," said Anna, her voice muffled behind the faceplate of her suit. She walked over to a coiled nozzle hanging from the ceiling and plugged it into the back of her suit. The hiss of oxygen was audible even to her guests, and her suit swelled up. She raised her voice to be heard above the rush of air. "Find yourselves a hose and hook up."

✱ ✱ ✱ ✱ ✱

"Sherman!" Brewster bellowed as he came into the Fac. "Or Thomas! Fuck . . . Denton!"

He ran farther into the Fac, yelling for Sherman and Thomas. Passing the break room, he almost collided with Denton.

"What's up, man? Infected?"

Brewster grabbed Denton's shoulders. "No. Living!"

"What?"

Breathlessly, Brewster related to Denton the radio contact that came with the flares.

". . . so I came in here to find Sherman. If there are more survivors out there, answering the call, they might have wounded. Or, you know, the sun's going down. They'll probably end up with carriers on their asses."

Denton nodded. "Well, bad news. Sherman and Thomas are both down in BL4 with the Doc, looking into her breakthrough. Who knows how long they'll be down, and Anna and Becky are the only two who really know all the ins and outs of getting in there."

Brewster eyed him. "So, it's up to you, then."

"What?" Denton exploded. "What the hell are you—"

"Come on, Denton. Sherman put you in charge of the next big scavenging run tomorrow. As far as I'm concerned, that makes you third in command. So make the call."

"Make what call?" Jack the Welder asked.

"Survivors," Brewster said. "Hal raised some on the radio, and—"

"Survivors?" Jack nearly yelled, bringing Juni and Mitsui running. Allen came not long after, rubbing sleep from his eyes.

"All right, all right," Denton said, holding his head. He blew out a big breath. "Fuck it. Suit up, everyone. Except Juni."

"Oh, *chinga tu madre,*" she yelled, and flounced off to her customary spot on the couch in the entry foyer.

★ ★ ★ ★ ★

When the rest of Anna's guests had attached themselves to nozzles of their own, she directed them to a small, clear plastic cage on one of the countertops. Within scurried about a banged-up rat, lapping at its water dispenser and pushing wood shavings into a corner, busily building a den.

"This is it?" asked Sherman, leaning forward to stare at the rat through the thick plastic of his suit's faceplate. "A rat?"

"Frank," said Anna, "I infected this rat with the Morningstar strain yesterday. With that much time elapsed, the thing should have gone wild by now. But look at it. It's fine. Not a single symptom. It's not even running a fever."

Frank peered in closer. "How's this different than the other one?"

"That rat was infected a day ago, by bites," insisted Anna. "And it's not showing any signs of the virus. Not one sign. Its blood samples are clear, like the other one. I had to make sure I tried both methods of transmission. The only problem that remains, as far as I can tell . . ."

Stiles grunted. "Healing the bites. Right?" He whistled appreciatively.

"You did it, Anna," whispered Rebecca. "You did it!"

"I had a little help," Anna said, casting glances at Rebecca and Stiles. "But yes—this is the good news I had to share with you all. Stiles's blood kept our furry little friend here alive. We're close. We're very close. We just have to tweak it a little bit, and make sure it'll work on humans as well as my rats."

"How long?" asked Sherman.

Anna shrugged, the shoulders of her suit ballooning up with the motion. "With some more of Stiles's blood, and Rebecca's help, I could have us a working test sample in a couple of days, if everything goes right."

Thomas grunted. "That's a big if."

Anna grinned at the sergeant major. "We've been lucky recently, Thomas. Just pray it holds a while longer.

"Do you need anything that's not already on Denton's list for tomorrow?"

Anna twisted her lips behind her faceplate. "Probably plenty. The normal way to grow a vaccine is to mix a virus with another virus and let them grow together in a hybrid, which takes weeks. However"—she shot another smile at Stiles—"we don't need to do that. The next thing is to measure the spread of the virus with reagents, which I've already started. The WHO expects this part to take three months if they're going to give it their blessing."

"The WHO is dead," Thomas said, his gruff voice only slightly muffled by the face shield. "Can we skip that step?"

Anna looked at her apparatus. "I think so. Morningstar grows so fast, and Stiles's blood works on it so well. That's the big bottleneck, you know, when it comes to mass production of vaccines. But like you said, the WHO is dead.

"If we had hens and eggs, we could have a big fucking batch of antigen in two weeks," she continued. "But we don't. The alternative . . . well, the alternative will only work with whoever's got the same blood type as Stiles, I think. He's our multiple-use and walking, talking incubator."

"You're going to put my blood into someone else?" Stiles asked, looking a little pale.

"Well, it's you or our other guest, the only other person in the Fac that has Morningstar in his veins. And I don't think anyone's going to want a vaccine from that batch. You guys remember Dr. Mayer?"

✫ ✫ ✫ ✫ ✫

"All right, people, listen up," Denton said. "Trev, Mbutu, and Allen come with me. Brewster, you've got Mitsui and Jack."

"What about Stone and Hal?" Allen asked.

"They've grafted themselves to that dispatch station. And besides, if Hal gets something clear, he can give us a location. As for us, we should split up, go in parallel lines down the streets to about where the flares came from. Between us, we should find whoever it was and guide them back to the Fac. Any questions? Then, uh, check your radios and good hunting!"

Brewster, Mitsui, and Jack headed perpendicular to the course Denton's group had taken. Brewster couldn't wait for the excursion to bear fruit. For one thing, the threat of death hung over his head every time he left the Fac behind. So, he reasoned, if there were more people at the Fac, the deeper the talent pool for scavenging runs. For another, and he realized that this was more important, he kept imagining trucks bulging with survivors, they way they'd shagged ass out of Hyattsburg—enough to make the difference between the small camp they had now and a real, live settlement.

SURVIVORS

He didn't normally think this way, but the weeks and weeks of unchanging company were starting to really chafe him. And he felt himself growing slightly away from his fellow ex-soldiers, which is why he'd started to feel more and more connected to Trev. And Allen, too. The arrival of just a few new people (even if one of them was badly wounded) had been enough to raise his spirits. Not to mention Stiles and his surprising resistance to Morningstar. Brewster had begun to feel the stirrings of hope, something he'd given up on some time ago.

The small group was headed for a line of squat brick structures. Brewster guessed they were apartments, and the thought eased the stress building in his mind. Apartments were easy to clear. Infected could only come from a few directions, and being surrounded was, at best, a remote possibility.

"All right," said Brewster, shotgun at the ready. "Let's take this first place. Stay alert! Sons of bitches could be anywhere."

✮ ✮ ✮ ✮ ✮

Two blocks away, Delaney lowered his binoculars, reached for his radio, and remembered that Sawyer was now sitting only a few feet away, leaning up against a stack of unused wooden crates. "That's it, sir," said Delaney. "Their search parties have gone into the surrounding streets. They're out of sight."

Sawyer stood, stretching his back with a sigh.

"That's our cue, soldier. Order the go."

"Yes, sir."

Delaney reached up a hand to switch on his transmitter. "Entry teams, go."

✮ ✮ ✮ ✮ ✮

In the street below, alleyways came alive. Men in urban camouflage appeared from behind Dumpsters and trash cans, hidden from view until their sudden movement revealed them. They held rifles at the ready, advancing slowly on the main entrance to the Fac. They took their time, scanning the rooftops for guards.

Across the Fac's courtyard, Krueger sat, staring out into the distance, watching for shamblers. The intruders, behind him, escaped his notice.

The men stacked up on either side of the Fac's main entryway, rifles tucked tightly against their shoulders, barrels aimed at the doorway.

A voice crackled over the radio. It was Sawyer. "Remember. Hit it with morse. Two Victors. Repeat, two Victors. Out."

The lead man leaned forward, extending a fist to the doorway.

He pounded out the quick code. Dot-dot-dot-dash. Dot-dot-dot-dash.

A feminine voice echoed from within. "It's about time you got that right!"

Heavy knocks sounded as the bars were removed from the door frame. It cracked open. Revealed was Junko Koji, an amused grin on her face.

"I was starting to think you'd never remember—"

Her grin faded as she took stock of the men confronting her.

Juni turned, a scream of warning on her lips.

A pair of gunshots rang out.

Blood blossomed on Juni's chest. Her scream caught in her throat, and she stumbled forward, a look of shock on her face. Junko Koji collapsed on the floor, unmoving. Her eyes, still wide open, slowly unfocused, and she settled into stillness. Blood pooled from beneath her chest, slowly spreading across the carpeted floor.

"Tango down," reported the lead soldier. "Moving in."

The masked man shot hand signals at his comrades, directing them to either flank of the room, his eyes on the swinging double doors that led deeper into the complex.

"Keep a move on," warned the shooter. He stepped over the body of Junko Koji as he spoke. "We want to be in and out before the rest of them get back. Priority one is Dr. Anna Demilio, so watch your targets. Don't shoot her."

"Roger, lead," came the chorus of replies.

SURVIVORS

✵ ✵ ✵ ✵ ✵

Below, Agent Gregory Mason heard the shots.

Despite the pain in his chest, he picked himself up and reached for the drawer in the nightstand next to his hospital bed, withdrawing a Beretta pistol. He checked the chamber and magazine. Satisfied, he tucked it into the waistband of his pants. He considered getting up and checking out the noise, but the pain in his chest, less bearable today than on others, convinced him to stay put. If there was trouble, it would find its way downstairs.

After all, Mason reasoned, that was where Anna would be found. He looked over at the very still form of Commander Harris and wished the man was awake and similarly armed.

✵ ✵ ✵ ✵ ✵

Outside the Fac, Hal Dorne and Stone also heard the pair of shots ring out. Hal stopped his broadcast from the radio tower and cast a worried glance over his shoulder, wondering where the rounds had come from.

"Probably one of the search parties," he reasoned. "Found a stray carrier too close to the Fac, yeah?" His gut, perhaps remembering the lesson of the tamping bars, disagreed. Something felt wrong.

He continued his efforts on the radio.

✵ ✵ ✵ ✵ ✵

Inside the Fac, the intruders moved quickly, securing room after room, moving efficiently down the halls, checking their corners and watching one another's backs. Behind them, the entryway doors swung open, and in strode Sawyer, pistol strapped to his waist. He didn't bother drawing it. He had confidence in his men. He surveyed the scene, cast a quick glimpse at Juni's unmoving form on the floor, and stepped over her, following in the direction of his men.

He caught up with them in the main hall beyond the reception room.

"Any contacts?" he asked.

"No one since the door guard," answered the lead infiltrator.

"'Guard,' right," Sawyer snorted. "They'll be downstairs, in the labs. Let's go."

★ ★ ★ ★ ★

The search parties, distant though they were, had also heard the shots.

"What was that?" asked Jack, staring back in the direction of the Fac.

"Sounded like gunshots," said Brewster. "Maybe Stone shot a shambler?"

"I don't know," said Jack. "Got a bad feeling."

"Yeah," admitted Brewster. "Me, too. You know what, scrap the run. If there are people out there, and if they send up another flare, we'll head back out. But first, let's get back to the Fac and see what's brewing."

The trio abandoned the building and started off at a dogtrot toward the Fac.

★ ★ ★ ★ ★

Three blocks over and one down, Denton's group had also noticed the shots. He turned to Mbutu Ngasy. "What do you think?"

The big Kenyan nodded at the radio on Denton's belt. "I think perhaps you should use your radio and ask."

"What? Oh, yeah." He pulled the radio from his belt. "Maybe—"

He was interrupted by Brewster's voice over the radio. *"Krueger! Krueger! You there, over?"*

★ ★ ★ ★ ★

They made it less than half a block before a round ricocheted off the pavement at Brewster's feet.

"Sniper!" cried Brewster. He dove for the nearest cover, the rusted-out hulk of a car parked along a curb. Mitsui and Jack followed suit, with Jack coming to rest behind a concrete stoop with Mitsui right behind him.

"Where the hell is that coming from?" yelled Brewster as a second round pinged off the hood of his cover. He grabbed for his radio. "Krueger! Krueger! You there, over?"

It took a moment for the sharpshooter to reply.

"I'm here. What the hell is going on? I think I'm hearing shots!"

"You *are* hearing shots, you dumb shit! We're pinned down in front of the Fac! Someone's got us locked down, tight! Can you spot him, over?"

"Where are you taking fire from, over?" came Krueger's reply.

"Straight ahead of us! From a building, on the corner!" Brewster ducked as a third round punched through the roof of the car he'd ducked behind. "And *hurry,* will you?"

A long moment of silence passed. Another round pinged off the pavement inches from Brewster's feet. He tucked his legs in closer. "Come on, Krueger, come on! We're sitting ducks out here."

"I see him," Krueger's voice crackled over the radio. "He's in a third-story attic, just across the Fac. One second, over."

Another round slammed into Brewster's cover, making him wince.

"Well, don't take all day!" Brewster shouted back.

A moment later, a rifle crack echoed across the blocks, and then all fell silent.

"Nailed him," came Krueger's reply. A moment later, his voice came through the radio again. "But don't look now. Seems like the shots have drawn some company, over."

Brewster glanced around. Sure enough, a trickle of shamblers had begun to work their way into the streets, half of them making a beeline for the Fac.

"Ah, shit," he said.

The other half were headed his way.

✷ ✷ ✷ ✷ ✷

Mason shook his head clear. Even that movement pained him and he cursed inwardly. He eyed the double doors to his room and that made him curse even more. If he was right about the identity of whoever had fired the shots, he knew that the next step after sweeping the ground floor was to split the teams and clear the upper floors, then the lower floors. And the uninvited guests knew the layout of the Fac, of course . . . so they'd be quick about it. There was probably a team on the way down to BL4 already, and they'd clear the lower floors along the way.

Which meant his room.

Gritting his teeth and holding his chest, Mason eased himself off his bed. He moved slowly, easing his foot lower and lower until it touched linoleum. His toe slipped as he put his weight down and he bit back a scream. Sweat sprang from his forehead and his shirt started to dampen. Slowly he turned his body, inch by inch, until he could put more of his foot on the floor.

Once it was flat, he took a deep breath and used that support to ease his other foot down. That went more quickly, but the effort had already taken a toll on the ex-agent. With a grunt of exerted will, he forced himself upright, balancing himself with his fingers on the corner of the bed.

With a herculean push, he commenced a shuffle-footed stagger to the double doors. He felt more than heard the doorway at the stairwell open, the subtle change in air pressure telling him everything he needed to know. He took two more shambling steps toward the door, the irony of his gait not lost on him.

A sudden light-headedness overtook him, and the room swam for a moment in his gaze. Grinding his teeth together, he forced himself forward another stutter step, determined to reach the door before, before . . .

Sawyer.

It had to be Agent Sawyer. Had to be. They knew about the facility, they knew about Doc Demilio's plans to get there, and they knew that they'd made it, since Derrick never returned with her. Sawyer would never let it go, and to make sure it went right, he'd come himself.

Another shuffle and Mason made it to the doors. With a sneer, he set the dead bolt, knowing the little thing wouldn't stop an inspired intruder. A quick glance around the room showed him that the only thing that he might use to bar the door was the Commander's IV drip stand.

Back on the other side of the room.

He let his head hang and almost laughed. "You're slipping, old man," he whispered.

The latch on the door wiggled for a moment. If Mason wasn't standing right there by the door, he might have missed it. The movement didn't repeat itself, and he took it to mean that they continued down the hallway to check the rest of the rooms before returning to this one. That gave him less than two minutes to find a better way to lock this door, he thought.

Sweating profusely at the strain, he turned and resolved to make it to the IV stand and back in that time.

The door shuddered under a blow and then flew open, striking him in the back and sending the wounded man to the floor.

With a scream, he turned himself over, yanking the pistol from his belt. Unceremoniously, it was kicked from his hand, and he looked up into the barrel of a SIG P226.

"Hello, Mason," Sawyer said. "Wow," he continued from behind his gun. "You look like shit. I'm trying to be real about things here. Facing you like this kind of takes some of the wind out of my sails. I just want you to know that."

Mason grit his teeth and tried not to scream as he sat up. "Get fucked, Sawyer. You always were an asshole."

"I was, I was," Sawyer said with a self-deprecating nod of the head. "On the other hand—" He fired a shot into Mason's left leg. "I don't have a limp."

Biting back the scream that was building in his chest, Mason refused to give in.

"Ooh, tough. Listen, I don't have time to do you like you did Waters. You remember Desmond Waters? You left him on the side of the road like so much meat. So." He fired another shot, this one into Mason's right leg. Then another, hitting him high on the left side of his chest.

"I'll be back for the rest after we have the Doctor. Rest up, Greg. I promise I won't kill you until we're on the way out." Sawyer's face split in a wide grin. "Wouldn't want you to die without knowing your complete failure."

✯ ✯ ✯ ✯ ✯

Coke and Charlie sat in the cab of the dump truck and debated what they should do next.

The pair had followed Sawyer's column of vehicles all the way from Abraham to Omaha, hanging back far enough that they wouldn't be noticed. Now that the sun was setting, they knew something was going to happen, and soon, but they didn't know what.

"I say, we take the truck in and dump the load. Then we get the hell out of Dodge until the smoke settles," Coke said. He cleaned the bill of his hat again as he spoke. Ever since he went out among the dead to get it back, he'd constantly wiped it clean, as if he could still smell the stench of the infected in the fabric.

"I dunno," Charlie said. "I mean, Herman's in there with them, right? We don't wanna get him, do we?"

Coke folded his arms. "Been thinking about that. You know what our lives have been ever since we signed up with that motherfucker?"

Charlie shook his head.

"Shit, Charlie. Our lives have been shit. If any of us had any fucking brains, we'd have ditched his ass after those Army dudes blew our base."

Charlie sat behind the wheel, silent. Coke sat and waited.

"Well," Charlie finally said, "if we're going to take off, I guess there's no need to keep a whole buncha dead fucks in the back, right? Why not just dump them here?"

Coke smiled. "Because I don't like Sawyer, either. Head into town, and let's get this shit over with."

✯ ✯ ✯ ✯ ✯

At the same time, in the Fac, Patton watched Lutz pace back and forth in the entry area. He could tell that the man was agitated, and Jenkins wasn't much better. He kept looking at the corpse of the Asian girl draped over the couch and wincing. Lutz noticed this and it was on.

"What the fuck is your deal, man?" Herman asked. "Don't tell me you feel sorry for this skank."

Jenkins shook his head. "That's not it. I . . . man, when we were running girls through our place, it didn't bother me none. I don't give a shit, you know that. But this one." He shook his head some more. "Man, those fuckers that blew up our place, they're coming back here. They know her! Don't you think they're going to be pissed?"

Lutz threw back his head and laughed.

"Pissed? They're gonna be fucking *dead,* Jenkins. You saw what this crew can do back in Abraham. Those Army boys won't know what hit 'em. Hey!" Lutz shouted to the soldiers down the hallway. "Either of you know which way the pisser is?"

As he stalked off to find a place to go, Patton sidled up next to Jenkins and nudged him.

"I think you're right. We need to find a way out of here."

★ ★ ★ ★ ★

Denton picked up all the chatter between Krueger and Brewster.

"Holy shit," he said. "Are we under attack?"

Allen checked his MP-5. "I knew I should have called in sick."

"Brewster, what's your situation. Uh, over?"

Ewan Brewster's strained voice came back over the radio quickly. "What do you think it is? We're running from some shamblers, and there's someone out there that was shooting at us. Over!"

"Denton, take cover." Krueger's voice came next. "Keep still when you find some. With the sun going down, the carriers are up and about. Over."

"And the shooters? Over."

Mbutu, Allen, Trev, and Denton stood staring at the radio for about a minute. It was a very long minute.

"Negative. No more contact, but keep your heads low. Let me know when you've found something. Over."

"Will do. Out."

Clipping the radio to his belt, Denton turned to his small group. "All right. I think we should hit one of these apartment buildings. Uh, that one, over there," he said, pointing across the street. "Krueger and I cleared it two weeks ago. Come on."

As the group jogged across the street, all of their heads were on swivels, looking around the rooftops for signs of a shooter. As they neared the entrance to the building, Mbutu Ngasy slowed to a walk, then held up his hand.

"I believe we should attempt to meet with Brewster. If they are set upon by the infected . . ."

"Demons," Trev whispered, and Allen looked at him sideways.

"It's just the three of them, right," Denton said. "Damn it. It had to be today, when I was in charge." He sat on the curb and held his head in his hands for a moment, tapping his pistol against his ear. "Fuck it. Let's go and find them."

He unclipped his radio and said into it, "Brewster, copy?"

The sound of gunshots came to them from blocks away. *"Argh! What the fuck do you want? Over!"*

"What's your cross street? We're coming to you. Over."

"Negative," Krueger broke in. "Negative. Hostiles approaching on your six, Brewster."

"The plan was three blocks over, right?" Allen said. "That puts them that way. Let's just go."

Denton looked to where Allen pointed in the dying light of the day and saw a shambler stumbling down the street away from them.

"Yeah," he said. "That's us. Let's go."

✯ ✯ ✯ ✯ ✯

Four blocks away, Brewster was spinning on his heels and looking behind the group, trying to see what the fuck Krueger was talking about. "Where?" he shouted, snapping his shotgun up. Mitsui backed into him.

"Oh, come on!" Brewster yelled.

"The carriers," Jack the Welder said, his voice carefully controlled. "They're still coming."

"Take them out," Brewster said. "You and Mitsui. I'll deal with whatever else's coming up."

Quickly, Brewster ran laterally and dove behind a car as Jack and Mitsui opened fire on the slowly advancing gang of infected. He lay on the asphalt and looked under the cars; he saw boots. Not shuffling, not tottering, but standing very still.

"Gotcha."

Two, four, six, eight, ten feet. Five people.

Come on, Brewster thought. *You can take on five guys, right? You were going to be an Army Ranger, for chrissakes. Pick up your balls and go, already!*

With a scream, Brewster got up and ran down the sidewalk to the spot where the owners of the feet were and began firing. The scream and his sudden appearance took the men by surprise, and two of them were mowed down before any of them got to move. The other three recovered quickly and moved into the street, away from Brewster.

Firing rapidly, they drove him back. He dove to the concrete behind a car and fired under it, the scattering buckshot hitting at least one of them. At that point, the top of the first man's head disappeared, as if a small mine had been set off in his brain.

"I love you, Krueger," Brewster yelled.

✹ ✹ ✹ ✹ ✹

Jack the Welder and Mitsui opened fire on the last remaining man and he jerked with the impact of multiple shots before falling dead to the street.

Brewster stood and marched over to the one he'd hit in the foot, who was writhing in pain on the street. He jacked a spent shell out of his shotgun and put the end of the hot barrel against the man's cheek.

"How many more?"

The man, even in his pain, was defiant. "Fuck you, jackal. Die screaming."

"You first," Brewster said, and pulled the trigger.

"Jesus Christ," Jack said, and Mitsui nodded his head fast. "Now we've got to fight the living and the dead? This is getting ridi—"

A clawing hand grabbed his shoulder and pulled him back. Brewster and Mitsui turned to see most of a corpse hanging off Jack's arm, clambering up his side to get to the exposed flesh of his neck.

"Get it off! Get it off!"

Brewster dropped his shotgun and drew a pistol. "Quit moving," he said in a calm he did not feel.

"*You* stand still!" Jack yelled, turning in place and hammering at the carrier. "Get! It! Off!"

A black streak flew at Jack from the side street and collided neatly with the infected's forehead. Jarred, it let go of the welder and fell back to the asphalt. Mitsui stepped forward and stomped on the thing's back, holding it down, and shot it, black bile and brains splattering the street.

Calmly, as if he were walking in on a picnic, Trev came into view and went for his ASP. He picked it up and tossed a salute to Jack, who returned it with a great big smile.

"Gang's all here," Brewster said, picking up his shotgun. "I thought you were headed for cover, Denton?"

"Right. And Jack here was headed for chow town. So what's there to complain about?"

Holding up his hands in a placating gesture, Brewster shook his head. "Nothing, not a thing." He picked up his radio. "How about you, Annie Oakley? See anything else? Over."

"Don't call me that. All clear. Over."

Mbutu Ngasy looked about the intersection. "We should return to the Fac," he said, a queer set to his lips. "This is wrong." The big

Mombasan turned in place, scanning the streets. "There are more headed this way."

"Well, after all that racket, what did you expect?" Allen asked. "We need to hightail it." .

Denton nodded. "We do. All right. Brewster, Trev, you take the rear. Mbutu, I want you and your sixth sense up in front. Allen, Jack, Mitsui, and me in the middle. Let's go!"

They started off, and Trev spared a backward glance at the dead men in the street. "Should have left one of them," he said. "Mason would have been able to make him talk, find out just what the hell this is."

✯ ✯ ✯ ✯ ✯

"What the hell is this?" Sawyer asked. He and six of his men stood outside the thick double doors that led to BL2. Before even coming here, Sawyer had been given the six-digit code to open the door, but it just wasn't working.

"What the *hell* is *this*?" he repeated, growing more and more agitated. "Why isn't the code working?"

His men just looked at him, blank.

"Fuck. Fuck, fuck, fuck. We need to get topside where I can use the satlink. Fuck!"

Turning on his heel, the agent went back the way he'd come, his men following behind. "Hold on," he said, turning. "Two of you stay behind. Anyone comes out of that door that isn't Dr. Demilio, you kill them."

He continued on. He turned back.

"First, you extract the new code from them. Then you kill them. Am I clear?"

"Crystal, sir," said one of the soldiers, who then shot Sawyer the finger when he turned away. "Jag off."

"Pick it up. You four get topside. Get on the horn, get me someone that can crack that code," Sawyer said. "Pull in everyone that's on the perimeter. If any of those shitheads out there make it back here, we want them to come in without any worries. Maybe one of them knows the code." He started away at a jog toward the infirmary.

When he got there, Mason was more or less where he'd left him.

"Bad news, Mason," Sawyer said as he walked into the room. He crouched where the ex-NSA agent had fallen and ran his index finger through some of the man's blood. "I can't get into the other biosafety labs. So that means I have some spare time on my hands while we cook up something that will get us through."

Mason, his back against the wall and his hands palm-up in his lap, just grunted, his eyes rolling to where Sawyer crouched.

"I was thinking, maybe one of your new friends out there knows the code? Has to be one of them. I mean, the first safety checkpoint was disabled. Hmm. I just hope we haven't killed him. Or her." Sawyer stuck his tongue out at Mason. "Oh, I hope it's a her. The boys are getting restless. Probably shouldn't have let them shoot the skinny slant at the door, huh?"

A twitch began in Mason's cheek as he stared daggers at Sawyer. "You. Special place. In. Hell."

Sawyer's eyebrows went up. "For me? No, no. You have a frozen lake in your future, Mason, down in the Ninth Circle. That's where the traitors end up. When you took off with the Doctor and her cure, you—"

"No. Cure."

"There is a cure!" Sawyer raged. "There is a cure, and she's going to give it to us," he said, more in control of himself. "And I don't give a damn about you, or this sorry bunch of losers you've aligned yourself with."

Mason started a grunting, growling sound. After a moment, Sawyer realized it was laughter.

"No. Cure. No. Cu—"

Sawyer's face a snarl, he dashed across the room and gripped Mason's neck with both hands. He bashed the injured man's head against the wall once, twice, three times before he caught control again.

"Idiot," Mason whispered, and a gunshot went off.

Sawyer looked down to see a smoking pistol, *his* smoking pistol, in Mason's right hand, and he felt the ache begin.

Mason laughed again.

★ ★ ★ ★

The group was only three blocks from the Fac when it happened. Mbutu led the group at a fast lope, Allen and Denton on his heels, Jack and Mitsui behind them, with Trev and Brewster bringing up the rear, as Denton had outlined.

"Almost there," Denton said, trying to urge the tall African to greater speed.

"It will be there no matter how quickly we go, my friend," Mbutu said. "Haste makes waste, in the words of one of your great American . . . do you hear that?"

He stopped running and held up his hand, signaling for silence. The group stopped and looked around. Allen cocked his head to the side.

"Sounds like . . . what, a truck backing up? Beep, beep."

Beep, beep, beep.

There was the unmistakable sound of hydraulics lifting a truck bed, and then the sound of things hitting the pavement.

"It's this way," Trev said. "Me and Brewster will check it out. That all right with you?"

Denton stuck out his chin. "Be careful," he said.

Trev started up a side street at a brisk jog, Brewster two steps behind and shaking his head. "I know that I say this all the time, but I have a feeling about this. Why you and me? We're the ones that are always—"

The howl of a sprinter filled the twilight air.

"Demons!" Trev snapped, picking up his pace.

"Are you fucking kidding me? Trev. Trev!"

Seeing that the other man wasn't slowing, Brewster ran faster to catch his partner. "Trev, hold on a goddamn minute, will you?"

Around the corner ahead of them stumbled a shambler. Upon seeing the running men, it let out a low moan that grew in intensity.

Seconds later, it was joined by three sprinters, then three more. They screeched at the sight of Trev and Brewster and started running, arms outstretched in front of them and jaws snapping.

"Holy fuck!"

Trev knew that six sprinters were too many for him, even in all his righteous fury. But with Brewster at his side . . . he turned to say as much to Ewan Brewster, but the man wasn't there.

He was five feet away and backpedaling. "Come on, Trev! What the fuck?"

His face a thundercloud, Trev turned to run and got three steps before his foot sank into a large crack in the street. He went down cursing and landed badly, cracking his jaw against the asphalt. Blood spurted from his mouth along with a small part of his tongue. Knowing the dead were moments behind him, he dragged himself up and started to run, but at his first step, his body betrayed him.

He went down again, pain shooting up his leg from a badly twisted ankle and knee.

"Brewster," he said, and the sprinters pounced.

Screaming, Brewster drew his pistol and put a shot in each of the ragged figures that were grabbing at Trev. Those two went down as a third launched itself, a feverish and dying panther on the hunt. It landed on Trev as the man was trying to disentangle himself from the fresh corpses, and the carrier sank its teeth into the back of his neck.

"Trev!"

Dropping his pistol, Brewster grabbed his own ASP from his belt and snapped it out, running forward. With a leap and a yell, he swung the baton in a low arc, taking the infected in the side of the head, caving in the orbital bone and jarring the slavering lips from Trev's flesh.

He kicked the carrier back and laid into it, beating it around the head and shoulders with the baton.

"Others," Trev said, and Brewster turned with his shotgun, pumping out shells as fast as he could. Blood sprayed from new wounds as he sent shot after shot down the street into the carriers. He walked over and, almost as an afterthought, put a shot into the head of the shambler that had spotted them first.

"I got 'em, man," he said. "We've got to get you—"

He was interrupted by a gunshot.

Brewster turned back and saw Trev lying still in the street, the back of his head gone and the pistol still in his mouth.

"Yeah," Brewster said, suddenly more tired than he'd been in a long, long while. "That's about right." He stared at Trev's body for a moment, then ambled forward. Bending down, he picked the ASP out of the dead man's pocket and looked at it. He collapsed his own baton and walked over to where he'd dropped the pistol and picked it up, too.

"Of course. I'm the fuckup, right Trev? And you're the avenging hand of God. But you're the one lying dead in the street. How is that fair?"

He looked up into the sky.

"How is that fucking fair?"

★ ★ ★ ★ ★

Sawyer was dragging himself away from the chortling, dying ex-agent. He had to move himself with only one hand, as the other hand was occupied, applying direct pressure to his middle. He'd been wearing his body armor, but by luck or on purpose, Mason had shot him in the pelvis, on the right side.

At first he'd tried to stand and get away, but he couldn't take the weight anymore.

Trailing blood behind him, he cursed a blue streak as he dragged himself toward the stairs.

"Radio!" he yelled. "Goddamn *radio*!"

A pair of soldiers came down the stairs at his cry. "What was that, sir? It sounded like you said—"

"Radio, motherfucker!" Sawyer screamed, and upon seeing him, they ran forward.

One of the men took his walkie-talkie off his belt and Sawyer lunged up and snatched it out of his hand. "Finnegan! Finn, this is Sawyer. Argh, Finn!"

"Go ahead, lead."

"Send a medic down. Radio the team at Offutt, tell them to get ready to come in hot."

"Sir, the targets haven't yet—"

"I don't give a *fuck,* Finn! No more cat and fucking mouse games. Safeties off. Tell your men. Turn it up, Finn. And where's my goddamn medic?"

"Yes, sir. Over and out."

Sawyer threw down the radio and turned back to the room he'd crawled out of. "You hear that, Mason? Your friends are dead, they just don't know it yet. You, too. We're out of here, and then we're going to pull this place down around your ears!"

As he yelled, one of the soldiers walked over to the room, weapon at the ready.

"I said, do you hear me, Mason?"

The soldier looked back.

"I think he's dead, sir."

Sawyer spit. "Wonderful. Where's the goddamn *medic?*"

★ ★ ★ ★ ★

Patton leaned over to Jenkins as the pair of soldiers they were supposed to stay with jogged off at a radio summons from Sawyer.

"Now would be a good time to hoof it," he said.

Jenkins's head came up and haunted eyes found Patton's. "What about Lutz?"

Patton winked. "If Lutz is too busy taking a shit to save his own skin, then I say we leave him to it. Come on."

The men stood and opened the metal-covered double doors at the entrance of the Fac. Patton stuck his head out and looked around. "It looks clear," he said. "We'll snag one of their jeeps, see how many miles we can put between us and this place before the fireworks really get started. If we're lucky, whatever goes down here will draw every deadass in town and we can scrounge up a safe place to spend the night."

Jenkins, smiling for the first time in what felt like days, followed

Patton's lead through the yard in front of the Fac. "Goddamn, it feels good just to be out of there. It feels like I can breathe, you know what I mean?"

"Oh, I know," Patton said.

☆ ☆ ☆ ☆

Across the yard, Stone stepped out of the radio shack for a breath of fresh air and saw the ex-raiders leaving the Fac. He didn't recognize them, and even though he wasn't clear on what everyone's name was, he knew their faces . . . these men did not belong. So how did they get in? He crouched low and stuck his head back into the shack.

"Hal," he said. "Two unknowns exiting the Fac. Might be more inside. Better radio the search teams and let them know."

Hal Dorne dropped the resistor he was chewing on and swiveled to grab for a handheld. "What are you going to do?"

Stone's face set itself. "I'm going to introduce myself."

☆ ☆ ☆ ☆

Patton and Jenkins were two feet from the gate to the Fac yard when the yelling started behind them. Lutz came out of the front doors at a quick jog.

"Just where in the fuck do you two think you're going?"

"Oh, fuck, oh, Jesus," Jenkins said, eyes widening.

"We're out of here, Herman," Patton said. "You think you know what's coming, but I think you're wrong. You're also an asshole, and we are not sticking around."

"I say you're getting your asses back in there, and—"

A man materialized up out of the dirt, holding an M-16 on them. "I don't believe we've met," he said. "So, seeing as we're strangers, how about we get off on the right foot and you put your guns down?"

Jenkins began to sob. "I knew it. I *knew* it. Ain't nothin' ever good of following Herman goddamn Lutz." He dropped his gun and put his hands on top of his head.

Patton eyed the man with the M-16. After a moment, he put his hands out, but he didn't drop his gun.

"Listen," he said. "We don't have anything to do with what's going on here, okay? We were coerced—"

"And armed," the man said. His eyes twitched narrow for a second. "Where's the girl that was on the door?"

A sob hitched in Jenkins's throat and Patton wilted just a little, and that was all the answer Stone needed. He raised his rifle and put a three-round burst into Patton's chest. As he turned to Jenkins, that man collapsed, screaming how it wasn't his fault. Lutz just stood there, dumbfounded.

Stone jammed the barrel against the man's head, and Jenkins found himself retching at the scent of cordite.

"You two come with me," Stone said, "and you might get to keep your skins."

★ ★ ★ ★ ★

". . . and Stone went off to investigate, over," Hal said.

"This is bad," Denton said. "That means they're inside the Fac."

He'd called a halt after Brewster came back without Trev and they took cover in the shadow of an empty shop. The radio call came shortly after.

"Well, that's perfect," Brewster said. "The sun is going down, we got drawn out like perfect suckers, and now we're locked out of our own fucking stronghold." He put his hands over his eyes. "I just want this day to end. Please, God," he said, and looked up into the darkening sky, "give me somebody to shoot."

A moment passed. Two.

"Fine," Brewster said. "I just thought I'd ask."

The sound of running footsteps came to them. Denton looked out and saw two men in urban camouflage carrying a body board between them, and they were hotfooting it toward the Fac.

"I believe in the power of prayer," he said.

"Fuck, yeah," Brewster said, and he took off running after the men.

They were double-timing it, but Brewster caught up quickly and snapped out his ASP. With a deft movement, he swung it out and took the rear man's left knee out. He fell and clutched his leg, dropping his end of the body board and forcing the man in front to stumble and fall, as well.

Not waiting for either of them to get their bearings, Brewster shot the front man from a foot away with the shotgun, then turned back and cracked the rear man across the face with the butt of it.

He fell back, the fight gone out of him with his front teeth. Brewster dipped and grabbed the camouflaged man and dragged him into the shadows where the rest of his group waited.

While everyone watched, Brewster collapsed his baton and forced it sideways across the man's upper lip. He pressed down hard and the man jerked, screaming. A quick glance at his uniform shirt gave Brewster his name.

"All right, Kent. This is how we're going to play the game. I'm going to ask you questions, and you're going to give me answers. Otherwise . . ." He chopped the side of the baton, which was still against Kent's upper lip, and the man let out another strangled yell.

Mbutu stepped forward. "Ewan, we cannot—"

"You shut the fuck up and keep back," Brewster snapped. His eyes were red-rimmed and crazy. "Those first shots we heard? Who do you think that was for, man? The only one left topside was Juni!"

"Holy shit," Jack whispered, and Mitsui sagged against the wall.

"That's right," Brewster said. "So no more Fun-and-Games Brewster."

Turning back to the man on the ground, he smiled. His face felt to him like a rictus, a death mask that might never come off.

"What the fuck is going on?"

Stone's three-round burst came to them from up the street.

★ ★ ★ ★

Inside the Fac, Sherman, Stiles, and the others were taking off their Chemturion suits. The Doctor was still in the lab, as she had other tests to run and a plan to lay out. The last thing she'd said to Sherman as they left was "We don't need volunteers for human trials just yet, but see if we can find out some blood types all the same."

The words and responsibilities echoed in Frank Sherman's head as he stripped out of the containment suit. He ignored the excited chatter from around him, focusing on the serum instead.

Thomas, who had been in a good mood all evening, was smiling. He even managed a chuckle now and again, which was for him the equivalent of bouncing off the walls without a shirt and screaming.

"I can't believe she did it," Stiles was saying as they headed out into the hallway. "It's like something in a dream, you know? After all this time—"

"Wait," Rebecca said.

"Huh? Wait, what?"

She drew closer to the safety checkpoint at the other end of the hallway. Stiffening, she turned back. "The coded entryway, it's blinking red."

Thomas's head twitched just a hair.

"So what does that mean?" Stiles asked.

The sergeant major spoke. "It means someone's been trying to get in."

Rebecca nodded her head. "Yeah. And they didn't know the code, or . . ."

"Or they'd be in," Thomas finished for her. "What do you think, sir? Sherman?"

Sherman caught up to the group and took in the worried looks on their faces. "What?"

"There's been an infiltration attempt, sir," Thomas said, instantly snapping out of his earlier mood. "We don't know who, but if it's the NSA people that Mason warned us about, it could be trouble."

"Or it could be Brewster on another bender, trying to show BL4 off for Allen," Sherman said. "Still, if it was insurgents, and they made it past everyone upstairs, we'd be better served to operate as if it is the NSA. Ideas, Thomas?"

Thomas cocked his head toward the BL2 lab. "In there, sir. That's where I keep Plan B."

He turned that way and the small group followed.

"When Mitsui killed the first checkpoint box and changed the codes for the others, I had him open up this lab for me," Thomas said as he worked the door controls. "I know that everyone gets tired of the old sergeant major and his paranoia, so I didn't say anything about this, but . . ."

The door opened on a miniature survivalist hidey-hole. Along one wall were several stacked footlockers, the one on the end and topmost open to reveal water purification tablets and distilling equipment. The footlocker next to it was lined with road flares and tools. On the opposite side of the room, sitting on nails that had been driven into the wall, were several spots for firearms. Two Kalashnikovs were on either end, facing in and bracketing a mishmash of automatic pistols and revolvers of several different makes.

Sherman turned to Thomas, a look of surprise on his face.

"Before you ask, scavenging runs," Thomas said. "Every place we went into almost, there was a handgun somewhere on the premises. There are more out there, too. Odd calibers that I didn't think I'd find ammo for. But the stuff that was common, I brought back."

He walked to the wall and pulled down a pair of Browning Hi-Power 9mm pistols. Handing one to Sherman, Thomas gave him a small smile.

"Thirteen in the clip, one in the chamber. Locked and loaded, sir."

Sherman looked at the pistol. "Don't call me that. I'm retired, remember?"

"And I'm going to keep calling you sir, sir."

Thomas also took from the wall one AK-74 and a spare banana clip.

"Hey," Stiles said. "You got something for me?"

★ ★ ★ ★ ★

Stone sat with Hal and kept his M-16 on Lutz and Jenkins.

"Lutz," Hal said. "Now, why does that name sound familiar?"

Herman Lutz stuck his chin out. "Lots of my kinfolk around these parts." He shrugged his shoulders, trying to get more comfortable.

Stone had tied his and Jenkins's hands behind them with many turns of copper wire, from wrist to above the elbow. "This sure is a good cinch you got on me, boy."

Stone spit between Lutz's feet. "Lots of practice with the crew I used to run with."

"Yeah?" Herman asked. "What happened to them?"

With a shadow of a grin, Stone nodded his head out to the street. "This group you done went and pissed off? They killed them. Shot a bunch of them up and let a whole mess of deadasses into their compound."

Jenkins swallowed audibly.

"Don't you say a fuckin' word," Lutz spat at him. "You hear me? They don't know nothin'."

Hal shook his head. "You shot the right one, Stone," he said. "That one's gonna tell us everything, but only because the stupid one told us there's stuff to tell us. Amazing who makes it through the end of the world."

Standing with a hard set to his face, Stone grunted. "You said it. Come with me, Blubber Boy. We're going to have a question-and-answer session."

With a sob, Jenkins got to his feet and followed Stone deeper into the radio shack.

Hal turned back to the radio. "Denton, come in, over."

★ ★ ★ ★

Blocks away, Denton raised the handheld to his face. "This is Denton, over."

"We got somebody. Stone is asking him questions. Any luck on your end? Over."

"Pity that fucker," Allen said.

"Brewster is ah, questioning a medic. It doesn't look good, Hal. Over."

Krueger's voice broke in. "Well, don't keep me in suspense, you fuckers. Over."

"Right, sorry. Sawyer is in the Fac, along with anywhere from eight to twenty-four men. The medic isn't sure about troop deployment. Over."

"Maybe he's lying. Over," said Krueger.

Denton paled a little, thinking about Brewster's deftness with the baton. "No, he's telling the truth. Trust me." He patted his pockets and cursed. "No fucking cigarettes. Anyway," he keyed the radio again. "There's a detachment coming from Offutt AFB, but the medic didn't know what they were bringing. Over."

There was a moment of silence, and they all heard it at once. A low thrumming, a quick pulse of chopping air.

"I bet I can guess," Krueger said. "Out."

$$\star \quad \star \quad \star \quad \star \quad \star$$

Camouflaged bodies moved closer to the Fac. The units moved well, acting as teams, tested in the field and unified. Twelve men moved in concert, headed for the area the medics were last seen jogging through in response to a call from their leader.

A moment of respite while they paused behind cover.

"What do you think got 'em?" asked one grunt, the name Summers stitched over his pocket. His squad leader (Winter, proving that the armed forces still had a sense of humor) turned back and grimaced.

"Better hope it was shamblers. Or something."

The third man, Reed, pursed his lips and blew. "What? You afraid of these guys playing army?"

Winter stared at Reed until the cocky look left his face.

"Not afraid, but if what half of RumInt says is true, these boys are part of a group that fought all the way from Suez to here. You think about that, if you're equipped for it."

The fourth squaddie, Page, nodded. "I heard that. And they got an ex-NSA guy with them, too. Bad dude; he cut up one of Sawyer's men pretty bad a couple months back."

"Right," Summers said. "Hoping for shamblers, roger, wilco."

"Whatever," Reed said. He double-checked his weapon again, though.

The squad moved out, its movements mirrored by two others, separated by a block in either direction.

Winter held up a fist and the squad stopped. He pointed at a Dumpster blocking most of an alleyway entrance and signaled for his men to approach with caution.

They moved in, quietly. Directing each other with subtle motions that an outsider might miss, they arranged themselves around the entrance to the alley.

His back to the Dumpster, Winter held up four fingers. One at a time, he started bring them down.

Three.

Two.

One.

His head lurched as his throat spurted blood from both sides at once, the splat against the green metal of the Dumpster followed immediately by a flat *crack* of a rifle report.

Brewster and Jack popped up from the Dumpster as if they were on springs, guns out and firing. The squad went down with hardly a defensive move.

"Thanks for that, Krueger," Brewster said into his radio. "Hard to believe that went down so easy. Over."

The monster roar of an SAW interrupted Krueger's reply, and Jack the Welder went down, his torso a mess of red jelly and white bone flecks. Brewster dove into the Dumpster with him, yelling.

"Oh, shit, oh, shit, oh, shit," he breathed. "Come on, already!"

Jack, realizing how bad his wounds were, began a soft and breathy laugh.

"What?" Brewster said. "What's fucking funny about this?"

Jack spat, trying to clear the blood from his mouth so he could talk. "If you get out of here, Brewster, you tell 'em; my name is Welder."

The situation momentarily forgotten, Brewster blinked. "What?"

"I'm not Jack the Welder. 'S my name. My ex told me . . . it'd help me out. Save on business card costs." He laughed, blood gurgling up through a wound in his neck and from his lips. Abruptly, the laughter stopped.

So did Jack.

Brewster looked at him for a moment longer. "I'll be damned," he said.

* * * * *

On the other end of the alley, Denton and Allen were running at a crouch toward the Dumpster. "Brewster, what the fuck was that? Over."

"Keep back," Brewster said. "That, photog, was a Squad Automatic Weapon, and they nailed Jack pretty good. They might think I'm dead, so stay back. They come to investigate, our eye in the sky will let us know. Krueger? Over."

"Loud and clear," Krueger said. "Keep an eye on your six, Denton. There might be another squad coming from that way. Over."

* * * * *

In the Dumpster, Brewster lay on the waste and watched the blood leak out of Jack Welder. Once the heart stopped, the blood slowed way down. Brewster shifted some, scooting his hips away from Jack's body, his eyes never leaving Jack's face.

While Krueger was watching for movement out there, Brewster was waiting for movement in here. He gripped his automatic and breathed.

"Why don't I have a knife? Even Denton carries a knife. So why don't I?" He sighed. "Mental note: get a knife."

Jack's head moved.

* * * * *

Behind Denton and Allen, something else moved. Another squad of four were gathered in the shadows.

"Tangos downrange," said one of them, a redhead named Mac-Cleary. He sat out in front of the group, his M4A1 rifle aimed in the survivors' general direction. He drummed his fingers on the M203 grenade launcher mounted under the barrel. "Take 'em out?"

Reynolds, the team leader, held up a hand in response. "Not with that. Not until we know where the rest of them are. You saw what happened to Blue Squad."

Mac, shifting in his uniform, was clearly unhappy with this decision.

"I say we take 'em out, bro. Then we find the rest of them and wipe 'em up."

Reynolds blew a breath out his nose. "Stand down, MacCleary. Birds are inbound. We should just mark their location and stand back."

Mac slumped over his rifle. "Fuckin' airdales get all the fun."

True to his word, the sounds of the chopper got louder and louder. Reynolds turned to Kelley, frowning at the man's three-day growth of beard. "I thought I told you to shave that."

Kelley sneered. Dee, the fourth man, copied him.

"Whatever. Get on the horn, give the chopper pilot what he needs to know."

☆ ☆ ☆ ☆ ☆

A single *pop* came from the interior of the Dumpster and the survivors frowned.

"Christ in Heaven," Denton said in a whisper. "Jack must have turned."

"I hate this waiting," Allen said. "I mean, why can't we go back—"

He was cut off by the roar of a helicopter as it sped by overhead.

"Fuckin' gunship," Allen said, shifting his grip on the MP-5 he still carried. "Did you see that? Where in the hell did they get—"

The helicopter zipped by again.

"This block isn't that interesting," Allen said. "I know, I've seen interesting architecture. This"—he shook his head—"ain't it."

Denton held out his hand. His keen photographer's eye had noticed something on the second chopper flyby.

"That wasn't the same helicopter."

"What?" Allen asked, and the helicopter came into view four blocks away, turning and racing over the rooftops.

"Ah, shit," Allen said, and the forward gun roared to life. Allen and Denton scrambled for cover, but the choppers were Apaches, and the three hundred rounds per minute of high-explosive, dual-purpose shells were making short work of all surrounding masonry and structures. Denton fell as a fragment of shrapnel zipped across the back of his knee without slowing down. He screamed for a couple of seconds, until the track of devastation laid down by the chopper's gun silenced him.

The helicopter was past and gone. Before it could come around for another strafing run, Allen bolted down the alley, back the way he'd come.

As he ran by, Reynolds again restrained Mac from firing.

"Look where he's going. He'll lead us right to the rest of them," he said, chiding Mac, a pastime he was rapidly becoming tired of.

✮ ✮ ✮ ✮ ✮

The double doors to BL2 and BL3 opened slowly and Thomas came out at a fast duckwalk. Seeing the hallway clear, he waved Sherman and Stiles through. Then he stopped Rebecca.

"You, go back to the Doc," he said. "Let her know what's happening."

He turned away and hurried with Sherman and a loaded-down Stiles along the corridor toward the bypassed safety checkpoint. Rebecca eyed the load that Stiles carried and made a decision.

"In case you need to come back," she whispered to him, propping open the double door with a clipboard from the wall outside BL3.

"Tell me where you got these from, again?" Stiles whispered to Thomas as they approached the first checkpoint. The sergeant major shot Stiles a glance that shut him up.

Something occurred to Thomas, then, and he stopped his forward advance. Instead, he turned to the recovery room, where Mason and Harris were bunked.

With a quick movement, he opened the door and covered the room. Less than a second passed, and he was on his way back to the checkpoint. Thomas answered the question in Sherman's eyes by drawing a line across his throat.

At the door, Sherman waved Thomas on, looking more tired than he had in quite a long time. Part of him was glad that the men weren't there to see him this way; he felt every one of his years on his back, on his neck, weighing him down and making him drag.

Thomas motioned for Stiles to wait, and he passed through the checkpoint silently, an armed phantom. Several long moments passed before Thomas returned, waving the general and private through.

"Armed men in the front. A lot of them. We should go around."

"To where?" Stiles asked.

"The back," Sherman answered. "The truck still there?"

A gleam came into Thomas's eye. "You bet it is, sir."

Sherman nodded. "Let's go, then."

Thomas took point and Stiles followed, leaving Sherman to watch the rear. They reached the back of the Fac in a short time, and parked there was the truck they'd gotten from Jose the mechanic in Abraham. The SAW-249 was still mounted to the top of the truck, and Stiles whistled when he saw it.

Sherman put his finger up.

"Anyone else hear a helicopter?"

☆ ☆ ☆ ☆ ☆

As quickly and silently as he could, Stone made his way to the front doors of the Fac, M-16 in hand and a pipe wrench in the carpenter loop on his pants. The doors weren't as impregnable as they looked, Hal had told him, and if he undid the three center bolts on each door, the crossbar inside would drop.

"Well," Hal had waffled. "It *should* drop."

That would make quite a clatter, Stone knew, so after that he could be in the spotlight and under fire. But, according to what Jenkins had said, the men inside were scattered through the first level with a minimal guard near the front.

If he got through all right, it would be room-to-room fighting. The mercenary side of Stone told him that this would be an ideal time to beat feet, just like Jenkins and the man he'd shot . . . the rest of Stone, however, was against that notion.

No, he thought. I traded up when I left Lexington. I traded up in quality, and I'm going to live to the ideal.

Looking around, Stone took the wrench to the door and began working the bolts loose.

✯ ✯ ✯ ✯ ✯

Inside the Fac, in a darkened room across from Mason's, Sawyer and one of his men watched as Thomas, Sherman, and Stiles exited the hallway. As the protected double door was propped open, an evil grin crossed Sawyer's face, momentarily replacing the pain.

He tapped the soldier on the knee—his name was Stephens—and pointed. "We go through there."

✯ ✯ ✯ ✯ ✯

In the street, Allen ran. Brewster snagged his collar as he ran by the basement walk-down and yanked his drinking buddy back.

"Gunship," Allen wheezed.

"Yeah, I heard," Brewster said. "Denton?"

Allen shook his head.

Brewster looked around, taking in the expectant faces of Mbutu and Mitsui, then Allen. They were all looking at him.

"What the fuck are you looking at?"

"Brewster," Mbutu Ngasy said, "you are all that's left of the military command. I understand why you turned to Denton when the decision had to be made to search or not, but your crutch is gone, now."

"My crutch is dead," Brewster said, looking into the darkened sky. "These streets are going to be crawling with infected. Apaches. Snipers. And who knows how many men are inside the Fac." He sat on the stone steps and rubbed his mouth. "What a fucking day for a field promotion."

The helicopters made another pass over the street. As the sound of the rotors faded, another sound took over.

"Hey, Brewster was right," Allen said. "Crawling with infected."

Unlimbering a mirror from his pack, Brewster held it up over the end of the steps. Twenty or more carriers were stumbling and shuffling down the streets, converging on their alleyway. A minute passed.

"All right," he said. "They're just milling around right now, but sooner or later they're going to come this way. There are too many for them not to. We need to find a way inside . . ."

"Right this way," Allen said. Brewster turned to see Mitsui holding a door open and waving them all in.

"What?"

Allen shrugged. "Right, ask me like I speak fucking Japanese. Get inside, will you?"

The group of four hustled in, Allen closing the door behind them.

A flashlight cut a swath through the darkness, checking the four corners of the basement apartment they were in. Brewster fumbled in his pack.

"What now?" Allen asked.

Brewster gave him a grimace. "I feel like Chuck Heston. Hold on."

From his pack, Brewster pulled out a hand-drawn map and unfolded it. He laid it out on the back of a couch and smoothed it with his hand. "Okay, okay, we are . . . *here*. Right. Okay. I think we're good. Krueger cleared this building last month."

"You think it's still clear?" Allen asked.

Mitsui sniffed.

"You think shamblers can pick locks?" Brewster shot back.

Allen put up his hands and walked to the street-level window.

"Sure are a lot of them. I bet they don't have a permit . . . whoops."

Three heads turned to Allen.

"What does this mean, when you say 'whoops'?" Mbutu Ngasy asked.

Allen dropped the small drape and turned, putting his back against the wall.

"Douse the flash," he said, his eyes wide. "Or, don't. I don't know, which will bring more attention? There are people out there."

Brewster killed the flashlight and walked to the window. "Yeah, two dozen or more. Except they're all dead already."

"No, I mean people. I think we found the other squad."

Brewster peeked out. He strained his eyes until he saw movement. "There they are. Quiet bunch. The carriers aren't even looking at them."

"That is a nice trick," Mbutu said.

With a tilt of his head, Brewster said, "Yep. Let's ruin it. Get ready to run."

"Run where?" Allen asked, his pitch raising several notes.

Brewster shrugged. "Don't know yet. Whichever way these guys run? Wait until the deadasses take off after them, then go the other direction."

Allen stared at Brewster. "That's your plan?"

One corner of Brewster's mouth quirked up. "Yeah."

He held the flashlight out until it was more or less where he'd seen movement in the dark, then turned it on and waved it back and forth quickly, making a strobe of the area.

One or two of the dead turned to look, but they kept on.

"Brilliant," Allen said.

"Just wait for it. Okay. Mitsui, take my shotgun and put a round in the middle."

Quickly, the contractor took Brewster's long gun and racked it once. He waited until Brewster had a finger in his ear, then pulled the trigger, blowing the window and curtain out into the street.

"Duck!"

Return fire came almost immediately, and the group could hear Brewster laughing over the ruckus.

And then they could hear the moans over *that*.

Up on his feet, Brewster ran to the door, cracking it open. "They went thataway," he said, pointing to the right. "So we go thataway. Come on. Back to the Fac."

CHAPTER 13
METTLE

Omaha, NE
1 July 2007
2034 hrs_

DOWN IN BL4, REBECCA was helping Doc Demilio out of her
Chemturion suit.

"They went off and I haven't heard anything since, but I don't want
to just sit down here and wait."

Anna nodded. "I know what you mean. We should go up and see
what else Thomas has in his armory." She put down the Chemturion
suit and worked her way into a set of coveralls. "I won't be able to
work, knowing that there's something going on, anyway. Come on. We
should grab a radio, too, so at least we can listen in."

Opening the security checkpoint for BL4, Doc Demilio found herself looking at the wrong end of an M4A1 rifle, held by a stranger in
urban camouflage.

"Hello, Doctor," said a voice from slightly lower, and Anna looked
down to see Agent Sawyer slumped down against the wall, holding a

blood-soaked bandage against his hip. "This has been some time coming, I think. But I'm so glad to see you again."

The Doctor put her hands up. Rebecca, unseen behind her, drifted backward into the dress-out area, looking around for a place to hide among the racks of suits and trolleys, the latter still piled high with medical supplies from the previous couple of scavenging runs.

"Sawyer," Anna said. "You don't look so hot."

The agent barked out a laugh. "Well, you should see the other guy. Come on, help me up. Just don't try anything stupid, or my man here will ventilate a nonessential part of you."

Gingerly, Anna Demilio walked over to the downed agent and stooped to help him up. He was heavy, but he helped with his good leg enough for her to do it. He began shuffling her toward the door she'd just stepped through.

"All right. Now, we grab your cure and head for the hills. We have a ride to catch back to Mount Weather."

The Doctor stopped the slow shuffle and looked at Sawyer with incredulity.

"The . . . the *cure*? You came here and did . . . well, whatever it was you did for the cure? Jesus Christ, you're a monster. A deluded monster."

Sawyer's face lost some of its good cheer. "Fuck you, Doc. That cure is the result of research conducted under the authority of and bankrolled by your government, and you will—"

He was cut off by the sudden peal of laughter from the Doctor's mouth.

"I can't believe you people. Before yesterday, *there was no cure*. And the only reason we might have one today is all blind fucking luck." She laughed more, harder, and Sawyer's face reddened.

His man, on the other hand, paled a bit.

"What are you talking about?" he yelled, pressing in on the Doctor with his rifle raised. "Intel was that you'd developed a cure and ran with it. That's what . . ." The rifle swayed a bit to a point between the Doctor's face and Sawyer's. "That's what *he* said."

SURVIVORS

✯ ✯ ✯ ✯ ✯

Krueger was having his own bad day.

After taking out the last of the guerrillas that were plaguing Brewster and Company, a shot *panged* off the side of the handrail at the top of his watchtower. He rolled back smoothly, putting the thick metal walkway and empty drums between him and the countersniper.

This, he thought, this is what it's all about.

From his pocket, Krueger took a small green memo book and flipped to a blank page. Withdrawing a Skilcraft pen from a pocket on his sleeve, he turned to where the round had struck.

For a moment, he just looked, then started sketching. As he was drawing, a second round popped through an empty drum and careened off the wall of the tower above his head.

"Thank you," he said, finishing one sketch and starting on another. He lifted up to eye the hole in the drum . . . and the entrance hole.

"Thank you very much."

Relying on his memory, he went through possible nests in the area surrounding the Fac that would provide a clear shot to his spot on the grain silo. There weren't many. As he looked out, he crossed two off his mental list right off the bat; he could see them from where he was lying. Given the angle of the hole, those were off the list.

He began scooting his way down the walkway, dragging himself around the side of the tower to the ladder on the other side. The helicopters had, by this time, started their strafing runs, but as long as he was pinned down, there was nothing Krueger could do for his teammates.

Finally making it to where he thought he'd be safe from the countersniper, Krueger got to his feet and ran to the next ladder.

✯ ✯ ✯ ✯ ✯

"Checkpoint four. All clear," said the man with the radio. The next thing to pass through his throat was four inches of steel.

Stone eased through the unlocked and unguarded BL1 doorway,

M-16 at the ready. He'd avoided most of the men stationed on the ground level of the Fac; not out of fear, but because he knew he would be no help to the Doctor if he was dead. And this direction was the way he'd need to go, according to Hal. There were three men who had died on his blade, and he kept one ear out for their discovery.

He kicked a spent shell as he passed the room where they'd searched earlier, where the prisoners were, and they started with a horrible racket.

"We're in here!" one of them yelled, pounding on the door with the flat of his hand. "Hey! Hey! We're with you guys! We came with Derrick! Let us out!"

Stone put his back to the door and looked up and down the corridor. He kicked back once, and the pounding stopped immediately.

"Just keep it down for now," he said. "There are more of these bastards skulking around. I'll be back to let you out after I clear this level."

"Fuckin' ay," the other one said. "RSA forever, brother."

Stone blew a breath out his nose. "Yeah, that."

He continued down the hallway, stopping once at the recovery room, grimacing at the mess in there.

"Damn," he whispered. He kept a close eye on the still forms of both men as he stooped to grab the firearms on the floor in there, a Beretta and a SIG P226. Slinging his M-16 over his shoulder, he continued down the hall with an automatic in each hand.

At the double door at the end of the hallway, Stone stopped, seeing drops of blood on the normally clean floor. They didn't surprise him, considering the amount of blood coming out of Mason's room, but he did wonder who the blood belonged to. He followed the trail back to a side room, where he found towels ripped to strips and sodden with the red stuff.

"Not one of ours, then," he said, deducing that whoever was bleeding that much had been through a grinder with Mason.

Checking the safeties on the automatics, he eased open the double door past BL2 and BL3 and slid through it.

SURVIVORS

✮ ✮ ✮ ✮ ✮

As he climbed, Krueger thought back to the days before Morningstar and shook his head. He would never admit this to any of the others, but he was kind of grateful for the virus, or whatever it was.

No, that wasn't quite right.

He didn't like the disease, or what it had done to his friends and the people he'd served with. What it had most likely done to any and all of his family here in the States.

But he was glad for the change. He never really felt at home unless he was holding a rifle. The only way he felt he could really connect with people was when they were swanning around in his crosshairs. If he'd said anything like that before Morningstar, they'd have him in a psych eval before he could say "Section Eight." But these days?

He was an asset.

He got to the absolute top of the grain silo and combat-crawled to a box he'd secured up there some weeks earlier, when the threat of Sawyer and the RSA seemed imminent. Before weeks passed and no one showed and everyone got complacent.

In those days, he'd risked his hide to bolt this box to the top of the tower, just in case he needed some extra shelter.

Just like Thomas with his armory in BL2, Krueger was prepared.

Having made up his mind as to which of the buildings was the other sniper's nest, he got comfortable and sighted in after consulting his memo book for the range.

"Here we go," he sang lightly. Slowly, carefully, Krueger moved his reticule from one structure on the rooftop to the next, keeping his eyes and mind open for a collection of shapes that might be a man.

A third shot rang off the side of the tower, impatience taking the countersniper's edge.

"Yeah-huh," Krueger said, seeing the slight movement in the dark that he knew was the sniper, working the bolt on his rifle.

"Gotcha."

✮ ✮ ✮ ✮ ✮

Brewster's mouth moved in silent pantomime in Lieutenant Finnegan's binoculars. He recognized "Run, goddammit, run!" Behind the last four were some more of his own men, and behind *them,* more of the walking dead.

He spoke to his radioman. "Tell Blue squad . . . is that Blue or Red? Fuck it. All three teams, order them off. I'm calling the choppers on the tangos." He cleared his throat. "Then call the choppers on the infected."

The radioman turned and relayed the information to both parties, then turned to look through his own binocs.

"I don't think they're going to make it, sir."

Finn looked at the magnified view as a sprinter came out of a side street and tackled the rearmost of his men. "Run faster, you assholes!"

Another sprinter came from behind the shambler horde and took yet another RSA soldier.

"No time," Finn breathed. "Tell those chopper pilots to get off their asses and run some goddamn interference!"

Frowning, the radioman relayed the further order, wondering what the hell the lieutenant was thinking. He knew that the Apaches were loaded with high-explosive rounds and nothing else. Picking off carriers while his men ran down the street wasn't going to be pretty.

✮ ✮ ✮ ✮ ✮

The truck started easy enough, and as they came around the front of the Fac, Thomas, Sherman, and Stiles saw the chopper start its strafing run.

"See?" Thomas asked, pointing. "And nobody wanted to go to see what the National Guard had. Good thing I went anyway. Stiles, take the wheel. I'll hump these over."

Grabbing the cases from Stiles, Thomas jogged to the middle of the yard and set them down. With an efficiency born from experience, the sergeant major had the first Stinger weapon-round case open and ready to go.

Stiles, watching this and shifting his glance from Thomas to the Apaches and back again, told Sherman, "Maybe you better take the wheel, sir, and let me man the gun."

Sherman looked out at Thomas, already in motion: the BCU was in place, and the weight of the Stinger sat on Thomas's right shoulder, with his right hand on the pistol grip. He unfolded the antenna and raised the sight assembly, plugging in the IFF unit and directly ignoring it.

Sherman looked at the helicopter, knowing the pilot would be alerted by his radar warning receiver as soon as Thomas started to lock on to him. "Maybe you better," he said, opening his car door.

As Stiles and Sherman exited the truck, they heard the characteristic windup of the Stinger. Five seconds passed as Stiles got into the back of the truck, and that was plenty of time for the sergeant major to do his job. Neither Stiles nor Sherman could hear the tone change from where they were, but as Sherman slammed the truck door, Thomas fired.

Holding his breath, Thomas threw down the spent system and started cracking open the second weapon-round case before the missile had even found its target.

And find the target it did; on a jet of fire and rage it sped skyward, tracking the chopper's last-minute evasion attempt and meeting it with a yellow and red blast, creating a temporary sun in the night sky.

The second chopper turned from its strafing run and approached the Fac.

"Thomas, move your ass!" Sherman yelled. Then to Stiles, "Get shooting, man!"

Thomas was mostly deaf from the weapon launch and did not hear the ex-general, but knew he had to be quick. Stiles was already there. He swiveled the SAW-249 around and was spitting lead at the second chopper in an instant.

That instant came too late. Before the first chopper's fiery remains were settled on the street, the second chopper pilot had loosed a complement of seven Hydra-70 rockets on Thomas's position.

☆ ☆ ☆ ☆ ☆

The cheer wrenched from the survivors at the first chopper's demise died in their throats as the second chopper fired its rockets. The Hydra pod spat seven glowing rods of death toward the Fac, and not even the approaching shamblers from behind stopped the survivors from ceasing their run. Brewster fell to his knees as he recognized the target.

"Oh, fuck no."

Earth and fire geysered from the Fac yard where the ordnance struck home, obliterating any trace of the sergeant major. The truck, now driven by Sherman, started back around the side of the Fac, while Stiles on top kept up his fire from the SAW.

The chopper pilot, an experienced one, slid his attack copter around the stream of fire and repositioned to better return some of that aggression. Bullets heated the air between the chopper's portion of sky and the Fac yard.

☆ ☆ ☆ ☆ ☆

"Sir, there's something else," the radioman said. "Look here; there's something on another radio frequency—"

Finn turned back and raised his binoculars. "Tell the pilot to stop fucking around and take that shithead out. Then turn his guns on the shack. Son of a bitch, I thought that radio equipment didn't work?"

☆ ☆ ☆ ☆ ☆

The pilot and gunner worked in tandem to finally strike the truck, taking out the engine and front end. As it rolled, Stiles was thrown wide, coming up painfully against the side of the Fac and waiting for the next volley to finish things.

It did not.

Instead, the chopper turned and loosed more rockets at the small radio dispatcher shack, exploding it and everything inside.

"Good work," Finn said with a smile. "Send in the APC and extract the agent and our goddamn cure."

Keeping his eyes screwed shut, Krueger put his head down as the first chopper exploded. It was bright enough that, even with his eyes closed and his head down, his night vision was messed up.

"Ah, shit, shit."

He blinked rapidly, trying to clear the blobs from his sight, and could hear the chatter of the SAW as it fired on the second chopper.

Turning on the tower top, he looked up in time to see the first rocket volley.

Balanced precariously at the tower top, he thought he'd have a better shot if he was back down on the walkway, but with the constant back-and-forth of machine gun fire, he knew that by the time he got down, it would be too late for whoever was on the receiving end down there.

Added to that, the helo pilot was a good one. The helicopter jerked around in the sky, making full use of all three dimensions. Krueger grinned . . . most gunners he knew (*had known*, he thought) had difficulty adjusting for the fact that helicopters could backpedal if they needed to.

A thought struck Krueger and he dug around in his shirt pocket.

"Come on, I know you're in there. Fuck yeah."

Working the bolt on his rifle, he withdrew the round from there and put in its place the cartridge from his pocket, one with a green tip and gray ring. He set himself and tracked the chopper's erratic movements and wondered, idly, if he'd be able to hit the pilot.

"Bet your ass," he said, and pulled the trigger as the second rocket volley sped away from the helicopter.

And it *dipped*.

Krueger's shot streaked through the night, a bright white line between him and the chopper that went high, higher than he thought, even buffeted by the rotor wash as it would be, and missed the cockpit, instead hitting rotor housing above and behind the pilot. A small explosion went off there, rocking the helicopter.

And Krueger, stunned for a moment that he had missed, froze in place until the chopper began to swing around to his position. More HEDP rounds from the M-230 chain gun ate their way up the side of the tower as he scrambled for the back and hoped that whatever was inside was enough to stop the molten-metal armor-piercing rounds.

The gunner, tired of this game already, let loose one more rocket, and the top of the tower blew apart in an ever-expanding rain of metal and fire.

✮ ✮ ✮ ✮ ✮

Underneath, the survivors had regained the small lead on the carriers and did not stop for this fourth explosion. They ran for the Fac, intent on jumping onto the fence and taking their chances with the razor wire there, if only to get away from the screaming, shambling horde behind them, which was growing by the second.

A backward glance by Allen showed him that the sprinters were being held back and frustrated by the sheer numbers of shamblers, but he knew that wouldn't last forever.

The throaty roar of a large engine caught their attention, and from a main road directly ahead of them rolled an M2 Bradley Fighting Vehicle. Its hatches were closed and, as it hit the straightaway on the way to the Fac, it accelerated to top speed, leaving the survivors coughing on diesel fumes.

They raced after it as the APC rolled through the fence around the compound and continued on toward the front doors.

✮ ✮ ✮ ✮ ✮

Stiles popped his head around the side of the building and saw the M2 coming on. He turned back to the overturned truck. Thomas had left his AK-74 in there, he knew . . . getting to his feet, he lurched toward the truck, stumbling badly as his aching body rebelled against the movements he was forcing it through.

Ducking down, he crawled into the wreck, looking for the rifle. A cough caught his attention, and he looked up to see the bloodied face of Frank Sherman staring at him.

"Finally come for me, have you?"

Stiles opened his mouth, but nothing came out, confused as he was.

"That's all right, you don't have to say anything," Sherman said, coughing again. "Been expecting you. I know you've had a lot on your hands, with Morningstar and all. I understand. I wondered how some of us made it so long. After all, the death rate is the same for us as for anybody . . . one person, one death, sooner or later. Guess you came later."

Shaking his head, finally understanding, Stiles put out a hand. "I'm not death, sir. I'm Stiles."

"If you say so, son. If you say so."

Sherman closed his eyes.

Knowing the men in the Bradley were only moments away from storming the Fac, Stiles dug for and found the AK-74. As he dragged himself out of the wreck, he saw Brewster, Mbutu, Allen, and Mitsui running up.

And he heard another truck.

✯ ✯ ✯ ✯

The survivors stopped and stared as the camouflaged five-ton wrecker sped down the street toward the Fac, red canisters duct-taped all over the front and hood of the vehicle. Making a last course correction, the driver popped open the door and dove away, rolling on the asphalt to a stop against the still-standing portion of the fence. The wrecker was a juggernaut, tearing through a different stand of fencing as it barreled on to the rear of the Bradley.

The helicopter pilot, coming around for a pass, saw the truck and his gunner opened fire. The HEDP rounds chewed through the chassis of the truck, but it was already too late . . . physics had taken over, and the wrecker slammed full force into the back of the M2. A brilliant fireball erupted from the front of the wrecker, engulfing it and the back of the APC in flames.

Standing from his stopping place along the fence, Sheriff Keaton picked up his own AK-47 and commenced firing at the helicopter.

Laughing, Brewster did the same with his shotgun, as did Mbutu Ngasy and Mitsui, all unloading at the chopper. Allen started to do the same with his MP-5, but noted the closeness of the oncoming carriers.

He turned and fired one round at a time, trying to take out the front line of infected.

Stiles added his firepower to Allen's efforts, seeing the carriers as as big a threat as the helicopter.

And in a moment, that worry was over.

From the sky streaked a white-hot finger, touching the side of the Apache and turning it into a blossom of fire and shrapnel, and a different Apache helicopter sped past, spitting rounds into the approaching crowd of shamblers and sprinters.

"Holy shit, we have a cavalry," Brewster said.

✭ ✭ ✭ ✭ ✭

Two blocks away, Finn put down his binoculars. "Pack your shit," he said. "We're pulling out."

✭ ✭ ✭ ✭ ✭

At the BL4 entry foyer, Stephens had his rifle tilted more toward Sawyer than Dr. Demilio.

"I can't believe you, soldier," Agent Sawyer said. "We're probably ten feet from bringing the cure to the Reunited States, and you're buying her line of shit."

Stephens's lip twitched. "Been fed a lot of shit in my time in the Army, sir. Hers doesn't taste as bad as the rest."

"There is a soldier, his name is Stiles," Anna said, talking quickly. "He was bitten in Hyattsburg, way back in January. He was bitten again two, three days ago and didn't turn. He—"

Sawyer cut her off. "Enough with the fairy tale, Doctor! Just tell my man where the stuff is, and we'll all be on our way."

"It's true," said a voice from the doors.

Everyone turned and saw Rebecca standing in the BL4 entranceway.

"I saw it. He was bitten in the leg, and I gave him a shot of morphine so he could run. He drew off—" She broke into a sob. "He ran and got the carriers to follow him so we could escape. I thought I'd killed another one."

Sawyer's lip lifted in a sneer. "This is all very touching, but—"

"There's more," said a voice from behind them. The soldier, Sawyer, and the Doc all turned to find Stone behind them, an automatic pistol in each hand.

Stephens brought up his rifle to cover Stone, who ignored it.

"I was with Stiles's group when we were attacked by infected just outside Omaha. I wasn't with him when it happened, but I know he received another bite that day. I've *seen* it. The man is immune."

Little by little, the end of the rifle dropped.

"Oh, for Christ's sake," Sawyer said, and snaked out his hand to retrieve the Beretta 92 off Stephens's belt. He jammed it up under Dr. Demilio's jaw. "You, girl. Get the serum or cure or whatever the fuck it is, bring it to me. Anyone moves to stop me, and I spread the good doctor's gray matter all over this room."

Rebecca didn't move.

"Better go," Stone said.

"It'll take a couple of minutes. I have to get into the suit, and—"

"Just fucking *do it*!" Sawyer yelled. His breath came in fast gulps and a sheen of sweat had erupted on his forehead.

"You don't look so hot, mister," Stone said. "Mister, ah . . ."

"Sawyer," he said. "Agent Sawyer. Don't say they didn't tell you about me."

Stone shrugged. "I keep to myself."

Tense minutes passed while Rebecca was gone. Sawyer's face became more and more haggard as the strain of standing with a weapon on the Doctor got to him. A touch of a tremor started in his gun hand, and he clamped his jaw down and fought it.

Rebecca came out of the lab, a sealed vial case in her hand. "This is what we have," she said. "It's all we have."

Sawyer cocked his head. "Grab it, Doctor," he said. Once she had it in her hand, he turned her. "All right. I'm out of here. Stephens, you can come or stay, I don't give a shit anymore. If you come, I'll probably have you court-martialed. Anyone tries to stop me"—he jammed the gun under Anna's jawline even harder—"you know what happens."

Stone moved out of the man's way, keeping him covered with both guns. Sawyer laughed as he backed down the hallway. "This is what it's like to be a winner," he said as they moved. "No one can stop you. No one can even slow you down. The only person that came close was Mason, and all he did before he died was hurt me some."

Stone, Stephens, and Rebecca followed up the hallway.

"And it's all worth it. I get back to Mount Weather, the Chairman can kiss my ass. I have the cure, and I have the doctor that made it happen. And who else is there to stop me? Who?"

Stone stopped walking, and put a hand out to stop Rebecca, too.

"No one can stop me."

Stone smiled. "Mason can still stop you."

"What?"

From the doorway to his room, the creature that was NSA Agent Gregory Mason lurched out and grabbed ahold of Sawyer. With a yell, Dr. Demilio dove away, hot blood following her as Mason tore into Sawyer's neck with his teeth. Screaming, Sawyer turned, firing his weapon and trying to get free. It wasn't until they were on the floor and Mason was gnawing on Sawyer's neck that he was able to put one in the carrier's head.

Sawyer lay there, gurgling and dying. Stone approached, no emotion showing on his face.

"Not a winner," he said, and shot Sawyer in the head.

EPILOGUE

Omaha, NE
1 July 2007
2334 hrs_

THE INITIAL CELEBRATIONS OUTSIDE the Fac were held off while Mbutu Ngasy, Allen, Mitsui, and Brewster struggled to stand the fence back up and Keaton and Stiles worked to extract Sherman from the wreckage of the truck.

"Gonna need something to hold it up," Allen said. Mbutu looked thoughtful.

"I believe there is a van," he said.

"There is a van, but there's no gas," Brewster said. "You gonna wish it over here, big guy?"

A bright smile slashed across Mbutu's face. "If you can hold back the cursed, I can bring it. But I will need the help of the Sheriff."

Grunting, Brewster turned his back on the fence, holding it that way. "Well, there he is. Go ask him."

Mbutu got the help of Keaton and Stone, the latter having exited the Fac with an M4A1 rifle in his arms and an M-16 over his back. Dr. Demilio and Rebecca were right behind him, each armed with a pistol.

Once the van was in place, the group stood in the yard, trading hugs and yells, and sometimes falling silent at the mention of fallen comrades.

Brewster turned back to the ruined tower. "We should see if Krueger made it," he said.

Allen put a hand on his shoulder. "Come on, man. The place is crawling with carriers. And I think we're about to have company, anyway." Looking up, Allen pointed to a chopper approaching. "You think it's the same guys that blew that other chopper away?"

"No, that's not them. That was an Apache, like the one that went down. This is a Little Bird." Brewster set his mouth in a hard line. "But they'd better be *with* them."

The helicopter set down carefully in the area to the side of the Fac, the last clear spot that the pilot could put it down. Brewster, Keaton, Stiles, Stone, and Allen approached from the side with weapons ready. The door opened and a black man in combat uniform stepped out. Blacked-out insignia sat on his collar points, an oak leaf.

Brewster stepped forward.

"Who goes there?"

★ ★ ★ ★ ★

The man from the chopper was Colonel Forrest, from NORAD command, Cheyenne Mountain, and he came just in time.

"We were already on our way to Offutt AFB to disarm some of the ordnance there when we picked up some radio chatter, mostly from an operator named Hal and the Sheriff there," he said, pointing at Keaton. The colonel was a compact man, short but not stubby, and his dark brown hair was cut in a regulation high-and-tight. No stubble showed on his brown face. "A response was sent out, but we never received a comeback, so here we are. You can thank Hal for his detailed description of Sawyer's attack, also. There's a detachment back at the Air Force base to round up whoever comes running back with their tails tucked in."

"So, you're here to save us from the bad men?" Brewster asked, eyes slits in his face.

A small movement happened on the colonel's face, barely recognizable as a smile.

"As it happens, no. We heard all of Sawyer's radio chatter, too, and he said something about a cure."

Dr. Demilio blew out a breath and put her head on the table. "Not this again."

"I'll take it from here," Stiles said, standing. "If there's a cure, it's in me. Check it out." He rolled up his sleeve and pant leg, showing the colonel both bites. "Immunity."

"I'll be damned," Forrest whispered. "You have been touched by God."

"And the devil," Brewster said. "Twice."

"Here's the long and short of it, Colonel," Anna said. "We haven't done human trials yet. We're maybe weeks away from that. Especially here, where we're out of touch and supplies are dwindling."

The colonel stood, putting his cap on. "I'll see what I can do."

He walked away, and Allen sat up. "Isn't anyone going to stop him?"

Brewster put out a hand. "From what? We tried to stop Sawyer, and look what it cost us. Thomas. Krueger. Denton. Jack. Juni. Trev. Mason. *All* your guys except you and Stone." He shrugged. "This is where I say no more."

He got up and went to his room, locking himself in.

The rest of the night passed, everyone telling their part of the story, including Keaton (who refused to answer to "Sheriff" now), who told of the end of Abraham.

Omaha, NE
2 July 2007
0737 hrs_

The next morning, there was a knock on the Fac door, in the correct code. Mitsui ran to open it, and there stood Krueger, a bent and twisted piece of metal as a crutch and a smile on his face.

"They ruined my tower," he said, and Mitsui had to catch him as he fell.

"Hey!" the contractor yelled. "Krueger!"

The ensuing mania was reminiscent of the day before, and Krueger was unconscious for it all. The only two missing were Brewster and Dr. Demilio, who were drinking coffee in the rec room.

"You find yourself a match, yet?" Brewster asked.

Anna shook her head. "No. Stiles is an AB negative. That's pretty rare. Less than three percent—"

"I'm an AB negative," Brewster said, upending his cup and finishing it. "Give me the shot."

The Doctor put down her cup. "Are you kidding? Because I'm in no mood for that kind of shit, Brewster."

He made a face. "No, this time I'm serious. All the serious people are gone. Denton and Thomas were the serious people. So was Trev. So, I'm serious. Give me the shot. My time here is done, anyway."

"What do you mean?"

He stood up. "Come on, Doc. I had a thing with Juni, and she's dead. Came all the way from goddamn Suez with Thomas and Denton and Jack, and they're dead. All I see now are faces that I know will go the same way, and you know what? I can't take that shit anymore. So hit me up with the shot. I have a lot of miles to cover before sundown."

Seeing that Brewster was serious, she got up and left to go to BL4.

✯ ✯ ✯ ✯ ✯

After Rebecca was done ministering to Krueger and Sherman for the morning, she came back to check on Mark Stiles.

"Hey," she said.

He looked up and saw it was her. "Hey, back," he said.

"You okay?"

Stiles sighed. "I don't know. Just sitting here and waiting for that Army guy to come back, I get a feeling in my gut. Good or bad, I can't tell yet, but there's something about to happen."

She nodded, sitting next to him. "Me, too." Reaching out, she took his hand in hers. "I guess we can only wait and see."

Mark Stiles, frozen, didn't say anything . . . he just relished the feel of her hand.

"Yeah," he said. "We'll see."

Later in the morning, Colonel Forrest reappeared in the same helicopter.

"Not an attack chopper," Allen said to himself on the roof. "Good sign." He radioed down to let everyone know the man had returned.

A short while later, they were gathered around a table in the Fac.

"The government," Colonel Forrest started, and was cut off by the Doctor.

"Which one?" she asked.

The almost-smile flittered across the colonel's dark face. "The remnants of the United States Government, Doctor. We're still around, and we're still here to help. I've been empowered to tell you that a team of virologists will be on their way to study, ah, your specimen"—he nodded in apology to Stiles—"since this is the best place for it. You, if you choose, will be the head of the team. Work is already under way to reinforce the Offutt AFB for materials and personnel."

Dr. Demilio just stared. "That's it? No demands?"

The colonel shook his head. "None. That all of you here have made it for this long is nothing short of amazing. The president has great respect for that. And you."

The Doctor smiled. "Tell him I said yes."

Omaha, NE
4 July 2007
0922 hrs_

After Colonel Forrest departed once more, the entire group gathered around the entrance to the Fac, saying their good-byes.

"Gonna miss you," Rebecca said, hugging Brewster's neck and patting his back.

"Yeah," Krueger said from the couch. "Skip out before the real work begins." Then he smiled, and Brewster smiled, and they shared a hug, as well.

"And you're still feeling okay," Dr. Demilio said, looking into Brewster's eyes.

"I'm fine, Doc," he said. "I just want to get on the road. Allen's still topside, isn't he?"

Stiles nodded.

"Tell him to tie one on for me. I might be done drinking for a while." He turned to the door, patting his belt to make sure both ASPs were there. "Oh, shit! I almost forgot," he said, turning back. "Jack wanted me to tell you about his last name. It was Welder."

Walking out of the Fac, Brewster strode past the scorched earth where Thomas had made his last stand. He stopped and knelt there. He looked down at the ground, then up into the sky. A quiet minute passed.

"Hey, Sarge," Brewster said. "I guess I'm still a fuckup, but I'm trying now. Wanna get past it. I just wanted to let you know, all right? I think all my time with Trev really straightened me out. If you saw that coming, then kudos to you, Sarge. So, I think I'm going to wander for a bit. If I find other survivors, I'll let them know the good news. And I'll make sure all of them know the names of the people who made it possible.

"Kick ass on the other side, brother. It's Independence Day."

He stood and walked out the gate.

Permuted Press

delivers the absolute best in **apocalyptic** fiction,
from **zombies** to **vampires** to **werewolves**
to **asteroids** to **nuclear bombs** to
the very **elements** themselves.

Why are so many readers turning to
Permuted Press?

Because we strive to make every book
we publish feel like an **event**, not
just pages thrown between a cover.

(And most importantly, we provide some
of the most fantastic, well written, horrifying
scenarios this side of an actual apocalypse.)

Check out our full catalog online at:
www.permutedpress.com

And log on to our message board
to chat with our authors:
www.permutedpress.com/forum

We'd love to hear from you!

The formula has been changed...
Shifted... Altered... *Twisted.*™